'What do you know of our land?' the major asked. 'You come in your aeroplanes to admire the ruins where in one day the Indians sacrificed ten thousand people. Priests gouged their hearts out with a stone knife.' The major grabbed Miguelito by the hair, aping the act. The theatre completed, he shoved the young man away so that he fell to the ground facing his elder brother – his half-brother.

'Mulatto,' the major said, as contemptuous of African genes as he was of Indians. 'We Spanish know who we are, Bergman. We possess a sense of history. We have learnt that the army alone stands against chaos.

'Look,' he commanded and spread his arms to encompass the buildings he had destroyed. 'I acted here so that the army, my people, are assured that I will avenge one death with the slaughter of an entire town.'

The major rocked forward in his chair and carefully refilled their glasses with Chivas.

He sipped and patted his narrow moustache dry on his handkerchief.

'Excellent, Bergman. I congratulate you on your taste.'

Simon Gandolfi, second son of Duke Gandolfi, was a resident in Cuba until the completion of *Aftermath*, and his sons attended primary school within the Cuban state system. He has an intimate knowledge of and love for the people and ecology of the Caribbean, and is a keen sailor and fly fisherman.

Also by Simon Gandolfi

Golden Girl
Golden Web
Golden Vengeance
White Sands

Aftermath

Simon Gandolfi

ORION

An Orion paperback
First published in Great Britain by Orion in 2000
This paperback edition published in 2001 by
Orion Books Ltd,
Orion House, 5 Upper St Martin's Lane,
London WC2H 9EA

A CIP catalogue record for this book
is available from the British Library.

ISBN 0 75283 753 2

Typeset by Deltatype Ltd, Birkenhead, Merseyside
Printed and bound in Great Britain by
Clays Ltd, St Ives plc

Those to whom this book is dedicated must remain nameless – such is the modern history of both Cuba and Guatemala.

Foreword

My two sons were five and eight years old when we moved to Cuba from the Dominican Republic in 1994. We lived in Havana for four years. We rented a bungalow in the suburbs and Joshua and Jed attended the state primary school. For holidays and half-terms we built what Jed refers to as our double-decker, a small house of lapstrake and thatch in the sierra in the province of Pinar del Rio. In this children's paradise, the boys bathed and fished in the river, climbed the hills, rode horses, and were taught ecology by the *campesinos*.

We have memories of love and friendship, of the warmth, innate kindness, humour and generosity that is Cuba; and of course *salsa*, Beethoven, *bolero*, and perhaps the greatest corps de ballet in the Americas. And, for myself, the occasional very small *mojito* . . .

And we have memories of the fearful, of those who suddenly dropped from view and whose names disappeared from conversation. And we recall the hardship suffered by our friends, their frustration, their sense of being imprisoned.

Such memories seldom agree with the reports we read in newspapers and watch on TV. In *Aftermath*, I have attempted to portray Cuba through Cuban eyes.

For our family experiences visit our web site at, www.SimonGandolfi.net

Optimismo es la lógica de los estúpidos
(G E – 1997)

Washington Post

The CIA and US military-trained-and-equipped anti-Communist military forces are widely believed to have killed more than 100,000 peasants during a decade-long anti-insurgency, according to US intelligence, military and diplomatic officials.

(R. Jeffrey Smith & Danna Priest)

Independent

President Bill Clinton yesterday stopped CIA funding of a Guatemala intelligence unit suspected of human rights abuses. But that move alone will not stop the spreading scandal here over US links with Guatemala's repressive military and police, alleged to have killed or tortured almost two dozen American citizens over the last two decades.

Long overshadowed by the wars in Nicaragua and El Salvador, Guatemala is emerging as another shabby showcase of clandestine US involvement with some of the most brutal regimes in the hemisphere – conducted either in the ignorance of elected policy-makers or with their deliberate connivance.

(Rupert Cornwell in Washington)

Time Magazine

The CIA has always considered Guatemala its private playpen. It was in Guatemala that the agency learned to overthrow Latin governments, engineering the 1954 coup that toppled leftist President Arbenz Gusman. Administrations have come and gone. So has the Cold War. But the freewheeling tradecraft the agency practised has hardly changed.

Now the cowboys have been swept up in an investigation of CIA complicity in two Guatemala murders (one of a US citizen, Michael Devine).

The White House is investigating whether the CIA in 1990 secretly increased aid to the Guatemalan military to make up for the Bush Administration cut-off of overt military assistance as a protest over the Devine murder.

(Douglas Waller & Elaine Shannon in Washington and Trish O'Kane in Guatemala City)

The Tablet

The School of the Americas (SOA) in Georgia is known to its critics as the School of Assassins. In its fifty-year history, the school has trained over 60,000 troops from Latin America, and consistently the countries with the worst human rights records have sent the most soldiers to it.

Alumni include General Banzer, dictator of Bolivia from 1971–78; General Noriega, the Panamanian dictator; and Colonel Roberto d'Aubuisson, the death squad leader in El Salvador who ordered the assassination of Archbishop Oscar Romero. Other alumni include three of the soldiers who raped and murdered four United States nuns, nineteen soldiers who took part in the murder of six Jesuits in 1989, and ten of the twelve officers involved in the massacre of 900 peasants in the village of El Mozote in El Salvador.

It is hard to think of a coup or human rights outrage which has occurred in Central or South America in the past forty years in which SOA alumni were not involved.

(Gerard W. Hughes)

One

1

Fabio

Terror was their sole tactic, so they were terrorists. No philosophical argument or claims that they were freedom fighters could alter that fact. They wore jungle greens and US special forces rubber boots. They were armed with Kalashnikovs and automatics and carried Semtex and detonators. Eight were Indian, three mestizos, two Hispanics.

Fabio, elder of the Hispanics, was their leader. Thirty-eight years old, he was a small man, skeletal with recurrent malaria and dysentery. Fatigue and apprehension had scoured ravines in his face and left bruised moons beneath his eyes. While a law student at Guatemala City's American University, he had campaigned for Indian civil rights and been targeted by the government's death squads. Cuba was his only refuge. There he was recruited by Castro's military intelligence, the DOE, and trained at the Punto Cero guerrilla warfare school in the Sierra de los Organos. After graduating, he was infiltrated back into Guatemala where he was now a legend.

A farm truck had dropped off Fabio and his men at the track on the far side of the volcano. For fourteen hours they clambered up through thick jungle to the volcano's shoulder, then down the far side. Cloud leaked grey tendrils through the tree tops; rain beat incessantly on the leaf canopy. At nightfall they reached the road leading from the gringo's finca to the army camp. The finca was their target, the finca and the detachment of Guatemala's élite counterinsurgency force stationed at the camp. Ten miles separated the targets.

The first night they set mines above the road, then retreated into the jungle, sleeping till midday. Now the finca lay below them. Tea grew on the higher slopes with coffee lower down. They would attack at midnight. Later they would be hunted, so they curled in the shelter of the jungle edge, one on guard while the others rested.

Midnight and the men slipped between the dripping tea bushes. The rain, pattering on the trees, cloaked their footsteps and dimmed the arc lights set high above the link fence protecting the tea and coffee factories. More arcs lit the manager's bungalow; still more lit the approach to the gringo's house built on a low knoll carpeted with lawns; his swimming pool was on a lower terrace.

The Indian workers lived half a mile away in thatch huts hidden from the gringo's house by a fold in the ground. All this land had been Indian before a past president of Guatemala, a general, had declared it property of the state and sold it to the North Americans.

One of the men mimicked the call of the pygmy owl, twice, three times. Fabio waited anxiously for their Indian infiltrator to answer – though fighting for the Indians, Fabio had little faith in their reliability. He had been preparing this attack for three months. The date was important: In memory of San Cristóbal de los Baños.

The call came and they moved down through the coffee bushes to the belt of cleared land surrounding the perimeter fence. Armed guards with leashed Dobermans patrolled the fence.

Again the men waited. Fabio lay on his belly, a Russian twelve-shot 9mm automatic with integral silencer held two-fisted. Amongst other tools in his backpack were a wire cutter and a retailer's tool for securing garments with small plastic ties.

Thirty metres of open ground separated him from the

blockhouse to the left of the chain-link gates. Radio connected the blockhouse to the guard barracks, to the office and to the manager's bungalow. Heavy wire protected the slit window overlooking the road. The window facing the gates was glazed with bulletproof glass.

The pain between his legs was a familiar prelude to action as were the cramp in his belly and the sour taste in the back of his throat. Rain, dribbling down inside his jacket, collected cold and clammy in his armpits. Ticks and leeches had squirmed in under his collar. The whine of mosquitoes was incessant. Suddenly a pig screamed under a knife to windward of the factory compound, the stench of hot blood designed to distract the Dobermans.

Fabio eeled out across the mud. A guard cursed at a Doberman leaping against its leash. A bell shrilled in the blockhouse and Fabio froze as a shadow blanked the slit window. He imagined the manager demanding what was happening – the guard answering that Indians were slaughtering a pig up in the coffee. At this time of night? The manager would order the men from the barracks to check the perimeter fence. Fabio wanted them at the perimeter.

He reached the blockhouse, rested his pistol against the concrete and pulled the cutters from his pack. The jaws shut loud as thunder as he clipped the wire up the side of the gate. This was how he had planned it: the pig, this small square of the gate hidden in deep shadow from the blockhouse yet apparently secure to the patrols, the snap of the cutters muffled from the blockhouse by bulletproof glass.

He peeled back the square, wriggled through and refastened the chain with plastic ties. Shouts came from the barracks and engines started. Spotlights swept circles as the drivers spun their vehicles towards the fence. Fabio longed to sprint the fifty metres to the office building – let the bullets cut him down. As he crawled, he took shelter in a vision of his body laid out on a wet army poncho, death so tempting. He couldn't do it. Not yet. But the time must come, as perhaps it had for

5

Che Guevara, those few moments of pain welcomed as the entrance to final peace.

An open jeep raced towards him. He felt the lick of its headlights on his feet as he rolled into the shelter of a Mazda pick-up parked to the left of the steps leading to the office block. The jeep, slewing round the corner, spattered the pick-up with mud – four guards, army helmets glistening in the rain. Fabio mounted the steps in a crouch and slid a steel pick into the lock. Sweat stung in his eyes and he rubbed them on the back of his arm. He could feel the guards behind him. He wanted to face them. Face them. The lock gave, a soft click.

Fabio dragged off his boots and wet socks so as not to leave tracks. The lights outside showed a small lobby. A corridor led off the lobby, four doors on one side, five on the other; the fifth opened to a cupboard for the cleaning staff. Fabio hooded his small torch between his fingers, hid boots and socks under a wet cloth, found a bucket. He flinched as the tap hissed. Water slammed into the bucket and he raced barefoot to the entrance door, eased it open, and sluiced the steps free of his scent.

He had to keep going – first replace the bucket, then immobilise the satellite telephone in the accountant's office. He was blind for a moment as headlights splashed the window. Training held him rock still. The lights swung on and he grabbed the telephone.

Torch between his teeth, he sat cross-legged under the desk and unscrewed the telephone's base plate. Fresh headlights spun round the walls. This time brakes squealed. Steel tipped heels snapped on the steps, heavy footsteps pounded up the corridor – two men.

Fabio eased the telephone back onto the desktop. Pistol ready, he crouched in the shadows of the desk's leg well, one more rat caught in a trap, a sneak thief, no final opportunity to fake glory.

The door crashed open, boots on the wood floor, click of the light switch. A transformer hummed overhead followed by the rapid blinking of the phosphorescent tube on the ceiling. Out in the corridor a second man snarled an expletive, 'Shit rain, shit Indians, we're on guard in an hour.'

The man at the door grunted agreement. The light snapped off. The door slammed.

Fabio wanted to curl up, cradle himself. Shit Indians, he echoed as he listened to the men retreat through the lobby. He knew that bad timing had made him a legend when in fact he was more the victim of a student's need to appear interesting. Nowadays it would be ecology. When he was at university it was civil rights. Son of a bank president, he had thought himself safe. The only Indians he knew were servants out at the family's summer house on Lake Atitlán. Though he fought for their rights, he hated them. Dumb, slow, placid as cows, never afraid.

Grabbing the telephone, he prised a wire free. Out in the corridor the polished wood floor was slippery with mud from the guards' boots and he lost his footing, falling hard on his left shoulder. He lay there a moment, heart thudding against his ribs. Scrabbling down the passage on his knees, he found the door to the manager's office, picked the lock and immobilised the communications radio. Now the satellite telephone in the gringo's library and the radio in the manager's bungalow were the only links to the army camp.

Retrieving his footwear, he stood at the end of the corridor and looked out through the barred window in the back door. Two huge mango trees and a massive ceiba hid the gringo's house. A jeep swept the perimeter with spotlights. The driver turned up between the tea sheds and parked outside the guard barracks. Fabio counted four jeeps. The fifth must be on the far side of the compound.

First he set a Semtex charge with a seventy-minute fuse in the cleaning cupboard. Then he picked the lock on the back door and slid on his belly across the mud to the nearest drying shed. Though in deep shadow, he crawled the length of the building. Arc lights projected high on each corner of the barracks, the jeeps parked in a neat row to the left. The headlights of the fifth jeep bucked as the driver hit a drainage ditch. The jeep circled the coffee factory. The driver drove slowly, the guard standing in the back searching with a spotlight mounted on the roll bar. The guard was very thorough – probably one of three ex-special services instructors recruited as shift commanders. Thirty-six security men protected the finca, all ex-army.

The driver parked and the men clambered down, stretching the stiffness out of their shoulders as they shoved in through the swing doors. Fabio imagined them peeling off their wet clothes in the kitchen. The men would be irritable at having their sleep disturbed. A few of those due on guard in eighty minutes might stretch out on their bunks. Most would gather in the kitchen, drink, perhaps play cards, curse.

Fabio slithered out from the shelter of the shed into the brightness of the arc lights. Rain had left a sheen of water across the red clay, the ground slippery and, on his belly, easy to negotiate. He reached the corner of the barracks and set his first charge. He set four more down the rear of the barracks, and two low on the kitchen wall. The charges were set to blow ten minutes before the change of guard. The men would be in their underclothes, grumbling, sipping coffee. He retreated to the shed and gathered himself.

Eighty metres of open ground separated the shed from the gringo's garden. Rain beat on the back of his neck as he crawled to the wall. Two Dobermans ran loose in the garden. The dogs were more dangerous than those patrolling the perimeter – attack dogs, schooled by a self-styled colonel in one of the right-wing militia in the Midwest of the United States. The gringo had bought them because they were trained to be silent and wouldn't disturb his sleep. Only the dog handler dared enter the gardens when the dogs were loose.

Fabio followed the garden wall until he was directly below the front of the house, then squatted for a moment steadying his breath. Leaping, he caught the lip of the wall, scrabbled up and lay flat along the capping stones.

Tiger lilies formed a crescent halfway up a lawn that sloped to the foot of the pool terrace. Fabio drew his pistol. Dropping to the ground, he sat with his legs tucked up, back against the wall.

He whistled.

One dog loped round the pool, hesitated.

Fabio whistled again.

The dog sprang from the pool terrace and charged straight through the lilies. Fabio dropped it with his first shot. He had clear visibility for forty feet. He couldn't see the second dog. He whistled a third time, eyes switching left and right. Fear almost conquered him as an owl burst out of a clump of bougainvillaea. He caught a slight stir in the lilies. He wasn't sure of it. He fought to keep his heart and his breathing calm. He tried a further whistle but his mouth was dry.

A black shadow raced suddenly fast and low along the foot of the wall. Fabio swung to face it. His shoulder, hard against the wall, tipped him off balance and his first shot ricocheted off the stonework. The Doberman was in the air, black in the arc lights. Fabio fired twice and tumbled sideways as the Doberman hit him. Its teeth bit into his left shoulder. He felt the blood run as he tumbled out from the wall dragging the dog. He clubbed it in the eyes twice with his pistol butt and rolled again so that the dog was under him, his right forearm rammed across its throat. He thrust down hard as the dog jerked and thrashed. Something burst inside the animal. One final spasm and it was dead, more fuel for the legend – the Fabio legend.

Fabio raced to the deep veranda shading the front of the house. An expert from the United States had installed the alarm system. Fabio had studied the waybill copied by a sympathiser at airport customs. The gringo had chosen durability rather than sophistication. Front and rear doors operated pressure switches and wires covered the windows. Open either door and the system allowed ninety seconds to reach the master switch in a steel cabinet.

Fabio ran round the back of the house to the garden shed. The lock was easy. He found the aluminium ladder the gardener used for picking mangoes. Climbing onto the roof, he hauled the ladder up and laid it flat on the tiles. He struggled out of his jacket and packed it between two rungs to deaden the sound as he fired twice straight down. Removing the shattered tile, he snipped through the wooden slats with wire cutters and cut the joists with a carbon wire file. He kicked the ceiling in and wriggled through, hanging one handed from the joist as he flashed his torch. A wall rose to his left, a dressing table directly below and a padded stool. He had hoped for a bed. He swung out and dropped. His foot struck the edge of the stool and he tumbled sideways onto a rug.

He found his way through to the rear lobby and the steel cabinet containing the alarm controls. Fabio timed himself and had the cabinet open in four minutes and thirty-eight seconds.

There were three guest bedrooms with bathrooms attached, the gringo's own bedroom with dressing room and bathroom, a library, dining room, and a vast living room opening to the front terrace. Twenty-seven Indian primitives hung on the back wall of the living room. Art and culture reviews had run articles lauding the collection. Fabio had planned fifteen minutes to clear the pictures. Word that he had saved them would spread amongst the Indians – evidence of his respect for their culture.

He carried the canvases out to the protection of the mango trees where he stood the frames upright on folded blankets, covering them with a sheet and more blankets. He set charges fused for eleven minutes, one at each corner of the house and two against the centre wall. Finally he unplugged the gringo's satellite telephone in the library and stuffed it into his backpack. The batteries were fully charged.

Back on his belly he crawled down the left verge of the drive towards the manager's bungalow. The rain had slackened and the familiar stench of an Indian village drifted up the slope to mix with the cloying fragrance of the jasmine and camellias in the gringo's garden, the scent of tea leaves and coffee beans on the revolving beds in the drying sheds and the thick perfume of the wet jungle.

With two minutes to go he was still fifty metres from the bungalow. Fear could have drawn his men back into the jungle. Fabio had lost many over the past two years, killed or surrendered to the government's promises of amnesty. Now the newly elected president had declared a unilateral ceasefire in the clandestine war; Fabio's men saw no gain in this attack. The invulnerability of the helicopters terrified them, the helicopters' ability to hunt the *guerrilleros* through the jungle, cannon stripping the trees, napalm. Fabio had assured his men that cloud and rain would keep the aircraft grounded.

Fifty seconds. Fabio's hand trembled as he knelt at the front door of the manager's bungalow. The lock gave and he slipped inside. His torch flicked over a combined dining and living room. Thirty seconds. Two bedrooms. The first was empty. The charges on the barracks blew as Fabio opened the second door. The scream from the naked Indian girl took Fabio by surprise. She was young, fifteen at most, her breasts small and glistening with sweat as she lay in bed.

The manager cursed as he grabbed for the alarm that activated the radio to the army camp. Five 9mm bullets slammed him sideways across the girl. Her screams were drowned by the charges in the blockhouse and the office block and the gringo's house.

Her dead body discovered in his bed would prove the manager's abuse of power.

Fabio raised his pistol.

Fear paralysed her.

There had been years when Fabio could have argued his cause to himself. Now it was hit and run, the reasons lost in the fear that accompanied him, the knowledge that he had no alternative, no retreat. The Cuban had made that clear – the old one, the one they called 'The Spider'.

'Get out,' Fabio said to the girl.

She slid from beneath the manager and stood beside the bed incapable of covering herself. Blood streaked her belly.

Fabio dragged the sheet off the bed. 'Wipe yourself.'

The girl reached for the dress draped over a chair beside the

bed. The manager's blood had fountained over it. Fabio
dragged off his muddy jacket with the bullet holes and tossed
it to her. Her face remained expressionless as she slipped her
arms into the sleeves. She sidled past him and he felt her flinch
as their bodies brushed.

Fabio shot the radio and changed magazines. The girl was at
the door out onto the terrace. He saw the glint of a steel helmet
and was already running as he shrieked at her to get down. He
saw the muzzle flashes and felt the bullets smash into her as he
hit her with his left shoulder. Flat on top of her, he snapped
three shots into the muzzle flashes, swung left and hit a second
guard in the chest. It was all automatic now, no time for fear as
he raced for the ruined barracks while his own men poured fire
from the jungle into the guards and the guard dogs at the
perimeter fence.

All but one corner of the barracks had collapsed. A single
light still blazed from the corner. Fabio watched the few
survivors crawl clear. One man made an effort to defend
himself. Fabio dived skidding across the clay and shot him
twice. The remainder formed a sad, stunned little group, half-
dressed, their underclothes soaked by the rain.

The fire fight down at the fence was finished. The youngest
of Fabio's Indians had been shot in the belly. The Indian lay
on his back, his best friend kneeling beside him. They couldn't
take him with them. The soldiers would torture and shoot
him. His friend held his hands while Fabio shot him in the
temple.

Fabio walked back to the manager's bungalow. The girl lay
where he had thrown her, face in the mud. He turned her over.
She looked so young, no more than a child. He kissed her on
the forehead and carried her to the bungalow where he laid
her on the bed in the spare room. Fetching a towel from the
bathroom, he wiped her face. He wanted it known that he had
tried to save her. One of the guards he had shot was alive. He
ordered two of the prisoners to carry the man into the
bungalow and dispatched one of his own men with a jeep to

fetch the finca's nurse. The care he demanded for the wounded man gave the prisoners hope.

Fabio left them under guard and led the rest of his men down to the village. The Indians stood numb and dumb outside their huts in the rain, men, women, children, small of stature, broad faced, almond eyes dark as ink. *Los humildes* they called themselves – the humble. In the early days Fabio would have made a speech: Indian land rights, gringo exploitation, revolution. He had no belief left and no energy. Other leaders had already been tempted to the negotiating table, the war was lost. North American training of the special forces was too thorough, their weapons too sophisticated, mass graves in the jungle evidence of their ruthlessness. The same was true throughout Central America.

Nervous for a moment, he touched his fingers to his throat. 'Fabio,' he said.

Trapped in his own legend, he ordered the infiltrator to indicate the overseers. One Indian bolted for the jungle and Fabio broke him with a single shot midway up the spine.

They marched the overseers to the factory compound, tied one into a jeep and lined up the rest with the guards against the ruins of the office block. Fabio wanted them seen by the first soldiers to reach the finca. He pointed to two of his own men, Indians. The more dead at their hands the less chance of their believing in forgiveness. 'Shoot them.'

They blew the factory and the drying beds and the small hydroelectric plant that supplied power to the finca and to the Indian village and the clinic. Then they took the jeep and drove fast towards the army camp. The dirt road cut into the side of the mountain. Fabio braked fifty yards before a second bridge. The river banks were vertical and the road swung sharply to the left fifty yards beyond the river.

He ordered the overseer in behind the steering wheel. One of the mestizos held a jacket over the man's head and forced him forward over the wheel while Fabio shot him from behind in the right lung. The wound would have permitted the overseer to drive this far. One of the Indians slid a sharp stick into the wound and worked it round until the man died. His death had to look right.

Fabio led his men across the bridge and on round the corner for a further hundred yards. Each man picked a different route off the road and up the mountain. Fabio checked the road edge for tracks before following. He worked his way back along the mountain to a point above the bend from where he could see the road clearly in both directions. Activating the satellite telephone, he called the editor of *El Tiempo* at his home in Guatemala City. They had been fellow students at the American University, where the editor had been a social star; now he was the voice of government. He was full of sleep and irritation.

'Fabio,' Fabio said. '*In memoriam: San Cristóbal de los Baños*. We have destroyed Finca Patricia.'

He hung up and the telephone rang almost immediately.

'Fabio,' Fabio repeated quietly.

He knew that he was speaking to the army and he laughed softly. 'Come and get me, if you have the *cojones*.'

An armoured car came first followed by two armoured personnel carriers. The commander was very careful, keeping his vehicles well spaced. The armoured car nosed round the bend. The driver saw the jeep and slammed into reverse. The first APC closed up. Two men dived from the rear doors and rolled for cover below the edge of the road. One inched forward round the bend. The rear man passed him and continued half way to the bridge. The first man closed up and advanced to the river bank. Fabio watched him peer down into the river. The bridge was the only way across. The man spoke into a handheld radio. A pause, then the second soldier joined him. Their voices drifted up to the *guerrilleros*, the words indistinguishable above the tearing rush of the river. Finally one of the soldiers rose to his knees, then to his feet. He raced across the bridge and dived flat into the protection of the ditch that ran beside the jeep on the up-mountain side of the track. Again there was a pause before the soldier rolled to inspect the vehicle. The turret of the armoured car opened in response to his report and the commander slipped to the road.

Two more men jumped from the APC and covered the commander as he ran along the inside of the road and crossed the bridge. Reaching the jeep, he checked the dead man for booby traps before opening his jacket to inspect the wound.

The gringo controlled vast investments in Guatemala and the commander would be under pressure to reach the finca fast. Wasting ten minutes over a dead man would end his career. The rest of the soldiers in the first APC leapt down and formed a circle round the two vehicles. The second APC closed up. A dozen men ran forward to cover the bridge while the first four searched the structure for explosives. Next they checked the side of the mountain above the jeep for mines. Finally the commander was satisfied. He and the soldier on that side of the bridge laid the dead man on the edge of the drainage ditch before shoving the jeep clear of the road.

The commander withdrew his men round the bend in pairs, both sides of the mountain covered. He waited until all his men were back in the APCs before mounting the side of the armoured car.

'*Buenas noches, compañero,*' Fabio called down, 'Fabio'. He pressed the button. The line of Semtex charges blew and the side of the mountain split as neatly as a fresh pack of playing cards. A hundred tons of red earth buried the soldiers.

2

Bergman

Bergman had been waiting in line for the hog roast all day. The sun was very hot overhead and dust and particles of soot from the roast floated on the air. Leaving the line was forbidden.

The other people in the queue were all strangers to Bergman. The men wore grey suits and the women wore grey dresses. The suits and the dresses were cut from the same coarse material and had no shape.

The closer people came to the head of the queue, the more frequently they looked back at Bergman. Their faces were melting in the heat from the sun and from the coals. Finally they had no features left.

Bergman's turn came. He wasn't hungry. Two Guatemalan soldiers turned the double spit while a heavily built sergeant brandished a butcher's carving knife and a big fork. The meat dripped grease and was the colour of ducks hanging in the window of a Chinese restaurant. The sergeant asked Bergman which cut he preferred and jabbed the fork into the meat. The roast changed into a roasting man and the man screamed.

Bergman gagged and sat bolt upright, listening to the shrill of the telephone on his bedside table. CIA Head of Station in Guatemala, Bergman had suffered variants of the dream for ten years. Happy tenth anniversary, he thought as he switched on the light above the headboard and checked the cheap alarm clock on the bedside table. Three o'clock in the morning, so Bergman hoped someone was calling a wrong number. Instead

16

he got the duty officer at the US embassy. Fabio and his goddamn *guerrilleros* had destroyed Finca Patricia.

The duty officer said, '*In memoriam: San Cristóbal de los Baños.* That's what Fabio told the editor of *El Tiempo.*'

Bergman had been awakened by hundreds of calls during his years as head of station. Even a few months back he would have been prepared for an attack. However, Guatemala's new president had declared a unilateral ceasefire. In response, the *guerrilleros* were abandoning their jungle hideouts and surrendering their arms to UN observers. The attack on Finca Patricia was pointless – unless Fabio hoped to derail the peace process.

'Mister Vorst is flying in from New York, landing at seven fifteen,' the duty officer said.

Vorst was president of North American Food & Agriculture Corporation. A US agro-multinational, NAFAC owned 20,000 hectares of banana plantation in Guatemala, 3000 hectares of rubber trees, 6000 hectares of teak and a vast ranch in the Péten. These were commercial holdings. Finca Patricia was different. Bergman knew that Vorst had developed the finca as an ecology star to boost NAFAC's corporate image. Vorst had named the finca after his wife. Having it destroyed would irritate the hell out of Vorst. He would need someone to blame. Bergman was the likeliest target.

And Bergman was already in trouble. He enjoyed Guatemala. The climate up on the plateau was near perfect, the scenery beautiful, he liked the country people and he was good at his job. Or so he had thought. Now, however, a congressman was querying the CIA funding of Guatemalan counterinsurgency units and the press had mounted a witch-hunt with Bergman as quarry. Questions were being asked concerning a bunch of nuns who'd got themselves shot for stirring trouble amongst the Indians. A son of a bitch with an inn up in the jungle had been another troublemaker – an army intelligence unit had sawn his head off. The nuns and the innkeeper were US citizens. And now Fabio was attempting to reawaken memories of San Cristóbal de los Baños, an incident Bergman had

17

thought safely buried. Add Vorst as an enemy and Bergman's career would end.

'Shit,' Bergman said. He plucked his top-plate dentures out of the plastic tumbler of disinfectant beside the telephone and repeated himself. 'Shit.' The word sounded more forceful with his teeth in. 'What report do we have on casualties?'

Casualties were Guatemalan and outside the duty officer's brief.

Bergman called the colonel commanding the province's counterinsurgency troops. He learnt that HQ had lost contact with the first patrol sent up the dirt road to the finca. The colonel awaited a report from a second patrol.

Bergman swung his feet to the floor and combed his fingers through what remained of his hair. Life was a bitch, he thought and switched to scratching a mosquito bite.

A further ten minutes passed before the Guatemalan colonel called back to report a landslide. Bergman requested an army driver and a helicopter. Even on a clear night, flying through the mountain passes was a recipe for death.

'None of those hot-shot kids for a pilot,' Bergman warned. 'Get me someone scared and with kids and a wife he loves. We'll have space for a doctor and a couple of nurses.'

Bergman dressed and stuffed a change of clothes into a nylon holdall. Kidnapping was Guatemala's major growth industry and he checked his 9mm Beretta before unlocking the triple bolts on the rear door to his small town house, where he waited for the army driver.

They were flying from an army barracks within the city limits. A middle-aged pilot greeted Bergman with hate and a weather report that showed a cloud ceiling that could have passed for a carpet.

'Yeah, well, keep us out of the goddamn trees,' Bergman said.

A young doctor shared the rear of the helicopter with two army nurses who had passed their use-by date in the senior officers' sex stakes.

Airborne, visibility was poor to miserable; conflicting air currents played ball with the aircraft. The nurses prayed and vomited; the doctor wrapped his arms round his head; the pilot cursed Bergman. The pilot cursed in English and in Spanish and in a mixture of the two languages. He began with imagination and ended with an endless repetition of the F-word. Bergman concentrated on the cone of light flung by the helicopter.

They were in the air an hour before spotting the burning warehouses at Finca Patricia. To their left a jeep flashed lights to lead them down to the landslip burying the soldiers. Fabio had blown the bridge to stop the army fetching heavy equipment from the finca. Twenty soldiers and a further twenty civilians were digging at the wet earth with spades.

Bergman requested the pilot to fly the medical team to the finca. 'Wisdom suggests that you wait for daylight before returning to the city.'

The pilot retorted that Bergman had been suckled at the breast of a whore.

'Possibly,' Bergman said.

He grabbed a spade from one of the civilians and began shovelling soil. They hit the side of an APC soon after dawn. A further hour and they had gained access to both APCs and the armoured car. The soldiers were dead.

Bergman crossed the river via a rope bridge rigged by the military and rode in a jeep to the finca. The flames had either run out of fuel or surrendered to the rain and he inspected the wreckage with an old warehouseman who had witnessed the attack from beneath the tea factory. With the manager and foremen dead, the Indian workers were without direction. They stood in the rain in small groups, small men, faces careworn as they attempted to foretell the reaction of their gringo employer.

Bergman was determined that Vorst should see the dead and ordered the bodies placed in line against the ruined barracks.

Entering the bungalow, he found an army captain at the table taking a statement from the one surviving guard. The workers had laid out the manager's girl on the bed in the spare room. Someone had sponged away the blood and the mud and dressed her in a long-sleeved white shirt from the manager's wardrobe. The shirt stretched to below her knees and accentuated her youth and the darkness of her skin.

Bergman showered and changed his clothes while the manager's cook prepared coffee and an omelette. He wondered whether the attack could be simple spite against the largest US investor in Guatemala's agriculture. Whatever, it put paid to Fabio's joining the negotiators at the peace conference. More, the murder of the soldiers was Fabio's death warrant. Fabio had to be crazy – or have a very good reason for continuing the war.

Two company engineers flew in to assess the damage ahead of Vorst's arrival. Vorst landed in company with NAFAC's resident CEO and the colonel in command of the counterinsurgency forces.

Vorst's pilot put down in front of the manager's bungalow. The army captain ran forward and saluted. Vorst nodded and hurried across the mud to the shelter of the bungalow veranda where Bergman waited. They made an odd pair.

President of NAFAC, Vorst employed over 100,000 people worldwide. Ten times as many were dependent on his decisions. And it showed – not in arrogance or in any obvious demonstration of power – but in that ineffable quality of presence. Fifty-three years old, he looked younger in his Ralph Lauren chinos and Lacoste shirt. He was tall and slim; his eyes were clear blue; grey shaded his dark hair at the temples. His carriage was erect though relaxed. And he was neat. Very neat.

Bergman, in contrast, was aggressively untidy. Short, broad shouldered and twenty pounds overweight, he wore jeans that refused to zip the top two inches, a dark red T-shirt faded grey at the armpits, a Texas A&M cap and a blue denim jacket draped over his shoulders.

Rain dripped from the eaves and dimmed Bergman's view of the mountainside. He thought of the *guerrilleros* clambering up through the jungle, wet, close to exhaustion. And Fabio? Was he simply elated that his attack threatened the peace? No, it didn't make sense. There had to be more.

Vorst appeared impassive as he viewed the destruction, yet he had flown from New York. Looking down, he noticed a red stain on his loafer that was a darker red than the mud.

Bergman pointed back along the path to a sticky mess leaking tendrils into the puddles. 'Where the kid died, the one your manager was balling.'

The resident CEO had gone into conference in the living room with the two engineers. Meanwhile the captain gave an analysis of the attack to the colonel. Bergman borrowed waterproof ponchos from a couple of soldiers for Vorst and himself. The Indian workers watched as he led Vorst over to inspect the dead.

'A year's wages in compensation and a full pension to the families,' Vorst decided. He wrote a reminder with a gold pencil in a leather-bound pocket diary.

The two North Americans picked their way through the ruined buildings and up the knoll. Vorst's house had imploded, tiles capping the mound of rubble. Vorst selected a clay fragment from one of the roof tiles. Turning it over between lean executive fingers, he scratched at a small patch of moss. 'Wanton destruction,' he said and slipped the shard into his jacket pocket. 'I had the house built to show my commitment to what we've been trying to do.'

Bergman was unsure whether Vorst's commitment was to the propaganda value of the finca or to the investment NAFAC had made on behalf of the local Indians: school, health centre, electricity from the finca's hydroelectric plant.

'Fabio stacked the art over there,' he said, stabbing a finger at a heap of wet sheets and blankets under the mango trees. 'Fabio's got balls and he's hot as shit on PR. Trying to save your manager's woman earns him points in the villages. Same with the art.'

Vorst wasn't interested. Perhaps the paintings had been his interior decorator's idea, part of the image – Bergman was almost deliberately bad at image.

Vorst nodded at the colonel and captain who were examining the remains of the blockhouse. 'We still financing them?'

'It's not official,' Bergman said.

'How much?'

'Couple of million.'

Military assistance had exceeded $7,000,000 annually under the Bush Administration – aid that had made Bergman a major influence in the appointment of ministers and in the conduct of the clandestine war.

Vorst said, 'We're getting poor value for money.'

Bergman thought to mention the truce that had been forced on the *guerrilleros*. There was no point and he kept his mouth shut.

The Guatemalan colonel had finished his inspection and the two North Americans watched as he picked his way across the mud and up the drive.

'San Cristóbal de los Baños – what is it? A town?' Vorst asked the colonel.

'It was a town,' the colonel said. 'A small town. Now it is a military training area.'

'What happened that warrants this?'

The colonel looked to Bergman.

Bergman had written the reports. He said, 'A general got murdered.' It wasn't sufficient and he added, 'There were some reprisals.'

Vorst drew a line in the mud with the edge of his shoe. Perhaps it was a battle line. 'Where's NAFAC's involvement?'

'Gringos are the generic enemy,' Bergman said. 'NAFAC's the biggest gringo in Guatemala, Mister Vorst.'

'That's it?'

'That I know of,' Bergman said.

The colonel had nothing to add.

Vorst said to the colonel, 'The embassy's going to be pushing on this. We get back to the city, I'll meet with the ambassador.'

The embassy, *the* ambassador – as if the US possessed the only embassy and ambassador in Guatemala. It was a detail; however, one that Bergman knew irritated Latin Americans.

The colonel shrugged and looked up through the trees at the cloud cloaking the mountains. Skeletal and very white-skinned, he reminded Bergman of an ibis.

The colonel said, 'With this weather we'll never spot the *guerrilleros* from the air. It would be easier if we had body-heat detection.'

It was an old argument.

Bergman said to Vorst, 'Lose a helicopter and the Pentagon's scared Castro will pick up the technology from the terrorists to use against his own people.'

'Terrorists in Cuba?'

Bergman said, 'We help put people in.'

'I hadn't heard.' Vorst's disbelief was obvious. He nodded at the ruined buildings. 'Do this in Cuba and you wouldn't last a week.' Turning back to the colonel, he said, 'Fabio – how many men does he have?'

The colonel was dismissive. 'A dozen – maybe less.'

Yet thirty-six guards had been shot and twenty-four soldiers buried alive. Bergman had known many of the soldiers. Counterinsurgency troops, the CIA had stipulated their training and supplied their equipment.

'Who trained Fabio?' Vorst asked.

'He spent four years in Cuba.'

'Be specific,' Vorst said.

Bergman shrugged at the reproof. ''DOE – that's Estoban Tur.'

'Seems he's done a better job than we have.'

Bergman was tempted to tell Vorst to go screw himself.

Vorst

Vorst had known that there was nothing he could do in Guatemala; however, he had wanted to witness the wreckage before deciding on his response. He didn't think in terms of revenge. It was his power that he needed to demonstrate, not only to the terrorists and the Guatemalan government, but more immediately to his board and major shareholders. Failure and a year of negotiations would be wasted.

Vorst flew to Spain on Friday night and spent Saturday morning inspecting citrus groves south of Valencia. The citrus was owned by a Dutch Antilles holding company owned in turn by a Bermudan nominee. NAFAC was sole owner of the nominee. Vorst planned to use the holding company as a vehicle to circumvent the US economic blockade of Cuba where the Israelis had already developed a large citrus stake. Blockades were political. Vorst believed in balance sheets and control of market. The Israelis were the enemy.

The NAFAC team flew to Alicante in the late evening. Vorst and his party took cabs in from the airport to the Hotel Sidi San Juan. While his assistant registered the rooms, Vorst walked across the road and hailed a fresh taxi. The driver dropped him a half block from a Sixties apartment building that had changed its occupancy over the years from new rich flash to lower middle management with painful mortgages. An optimist had spent a lot of money opening the street level restaurant back in the Sixties. The restaurant had failed under eight owners.

There were two waiters – a young one manicuring his nails with a tooth pick and a pensioner inherited with the lease by the present owners. A mid-forties couple trying to look younger sat midway down the left. The Cuban was the only other customer. He flagged Vorst from the rear cubicle on the right. A junior finance minister in the Cuban government, Jorge Mendez was younger than the North American, late thirties, and smaller, his frame lean, face angular, hair clipped short. Green eyes gave evidence of his Galician heritage. A Zapata moustache drooped over a slightly petulant upper lip. This was their tenth meeting. They shook hands before taking seats at the table. Vorst would pay and he ordered for them: butifarra with white beans, followed by grilled sole and a green salad. They drank a *Marqués de Riscal* with the butifarra and a light Navarra with the fish. The salad was almost fresh.

Their conversation didn't lead anywhere until the waiter

24

brought coffee. Vorst suspected the delay came from Jorge Mendez's desire to save face. Intelligent and quick-witted, no doubt Mendez had been fawned over by women in his childhood. Now he found it galling that he had to refer each stage of their negotiations to cabinet; a cabinet ideologically opposed to everything Vorst represented: capitalism, multinationals, US economic domination. Castro had driven his country out of servitude onto the world stage. However, it was only theatre, the illusion transparent once the lights came on. The lights showed an economy on its deathbed. Only huge transfusions of foreign capital could revive it. Investment was dependent on a confidence that didn't exist. A derivatives manager with the Chemical Bank or UBS channelled more capital into the market in a week than the total annual inflow to Cuba. That was the reality, and that Cuba needed NAFAC more than Vorst needed Cuba. He listened carefully to the minister's account of the cabinet decision to welcome NAFAC as a joint-venture partner with initial holdings totalling four thousand hectares. The decision was of principle rather than detail. Now it was Vorst's turn.

'The board's provisional agreement is for thirty million – that's a beginning. We'll put in a further three million a year for the next five years. It's all here,' he said, and passed the documents across the table. 'Take your time. When you're ready, contact me through the usual channels.'

The Cuban had tensed. 'Provisional on what?'

'All but one point is in the documentation.' Vorst had brought photographs of the finca. He handed Mendez the Kodak envelope.

Politeness or an occasional detail gave the Cuban pause but most of the pictures he simply shuffled to the bottom of the stack as if they were holiday photos.

Finca Patricia was Vorst's creation. He said, 'It's in Guatemala. The property of your prospective joint-venture partner. The man who led the attack was trained in Cuba by your DOE.'

Vorst had rehearsed the scene in his head and was prepared

for the minister's angry protest. 'This isn't a matter of blame,' he assured the Cuban. 'I'm discussing tactics, Jorge. You and I have suffered opposition to this deal. We've needed to be persuasive. Now the groundwork's done. If I sign, you'll have other US corporations interested. They'll visit with me first. I'd like to assure them that you are a reasonable man, someone they can do business with, that you represent the new Cuba, a new direction.'

Easing himself back in his seat, he touched the tablecloth with his fingertips. 'That's what I believe, Jorge. But the DOE, its director, Estoban Tur, the man's a dinosaur. That's not a criticism of your revolution,' he continued smoothly. 'You've done great things in education and health. Now you need capital investment to pay the bills. That's something I'd like to help you with. In return, I want this one act to offer my board. I want Estoban Tur's head.'

Sheltering in anger, the Cuban cursed quietly, distaste cutting his words short. His eyes hunted the shadowed restaurant and came to rest on the couple opposite.

Vorst wouldn't let him escape. He tapped the photographs. 'Deliberate choice of target, Jorge.'

He paused to sip his wine and refilled the Cuban's glass.

'Logic says someone your end is trying to sabotage the deal. Someone who sees NAFAC as the enemy. That's the way it's been for forty years.'

The Cuban had retreated inside himself – like a kid sulking.

Vorst determined to draw him out. 'Forty-five million, Jorge. That's our proposal. And it's not some whim I need satisfying and it's not how you personally feel that counts. We're talking what's good for Cuba and that means maintaining my board's approval. Don't lose this late in the game,' he said. 'For what? You're not even doing that stuff any more – exporting revolution. It's what I said. Tur is a dinosaur. Give him up.'

The Cuban switched his eyes back to the couple opposite. For something to say, he said, 'They're both married to other people.'

'That would be my guess,' Vorst said. 'The husband charges in with a gun and we'd be on CNN as witnesses.'

Mendez smiled despite himself. 'It won't be easy.'

'We have specialist help available,' Vorst said – Bergman.

3

Bergman

In answer to Vorst's summons to a meeting at NAFAC's plantations near Lake Izabal, Bergman drove out of Guatemala City towards the Caribbean coast soon after dawn. He drove a ten-year-old Toyota jeep powered by a four-cylinder diesel engine. The Toyota had rusted at the back of a Florida car park for six months. Bergman had bought it cheap and replaced the original body with a fibreglass copy. He had padded the doors with Kevlar from old flak jackets and sandwiched Kevlar into a double floor beneath the front seats. The two front windows and the windscreen were cut from bulletproof glass; steel channel strengthened the front end of the chassis; the winch mounted on the front crash bar worked and Bergman carried a Danforth anchor in brackets on the bonnet so that he wouldn't need a tree to winch to if he got stuck in the mud.

Bergman had done much of the rebuild himself and was proud of the result. That the Toyota was slow didn't worry him. He was safe from mines and small arms fire and could ram a car or a tree clear of the road. City drivers steered clear and car thieves weren't tempted. Added to which, the Toyota was cheap on fuel and easy to maintain. Bergman ran it at a profit and he needed the extra money. He supported two daughters at college and an alimony addicted ex-wife who complained that she couldn't remarry because she was Roman Catholic. She had walked out on Bergman at the end of his third year in Guatemala and had left an army of lovers behind.

The war had got to her, so she claimed, and the insects and that the servants didn't speak English. She hadn't appreciated Bergman's reminder that, prior to his posting, the closest she had come to a servant was watching actors play the part on TV.

Bergman's wife would have preferred Paris or Rome, for the romance. Central America was more Bergman's style. There hadn't been much competition for the Guatemala job; CIA careers were made in Russia and Eastern Europe. The end of the Cold War had put many of Bergman's contemporaries out of jobs, while Bergman had retained his little empire – though for how much longer was in doubt.

He braked on the crest of the last hill before the coastal plane. Below lay Lake Izabal, shimmering like anodised aluminium in the noonday sun. Thirty-five kilometres long by fifteen wide, Izabal was the largest of Guatemala's lakes. To the right of the lake spread the deep green sweep of NAFAC's banana plantations. Bergman could see the company airstrip to the east of the administration buildings. Vorst was due mid afternoon. Bergman had no idea what Vorst wanted of him and didn't waste energy on conjecture.

He drove on down the hill and pulled into a car wash below a grove of flamboyant trees that shaded a concrete house with a kitchen on the ground floor to the rear of a palm thatch *rancho*. There were twelve tables with bench seats under the *rancho* and some string hammocks.

Bergman left the Toyota to be hosed by the Indian help and climbed the short slope. The woman owner smiled a lazy welcome from a chair by the kitchen servery hatch. Late twenties and buxom, she wore her thick black hair long and tied back with a red ribbon from a broad face shiny with sweat from the kitchen stove. She cradled a five-year-old boy on her lap while an older boy, seven years old, drew with a stick in the dust at her feet. Armed men had robbed the place a few months back – ex-soldiers or ex-*guerrilleros*, impossible to tell which. They had shot the woman's husband dead. There was nothing unusual in the incident. Armed bands were endemic to the country.

Bergman asked how she was managing and she answered with a shrug that said it all. Nothing was good, nothing was too bad. Life happened and there were no alternatives.

Bergman ruffled the elder child's hair and gave him a stick of gum before seating himself at a table facing the road. Late morning and he was the only customer. He slipped the 9mm Beretta automatic from his shoulder holster, setting it on the bench by his right thigh. A mestiza waitress took his order. The tortillas were fresh, beer came cold, the chicken was free range, rice properly cooked, the beans tender and flavoured with oregano. Most members of the embassy lived in permanent terror of hepatitis and dysentery and would have avoided the food like the plague but it suited Bergman. Replete, he belched and pushed his plate back to make room for the small cup of strong, sweet coffee. Then he ambled over to a hammock and stretched out, holding the Beretta on his belly beneath his shirt.

Six *campesinos* in an open jeep followed a tanker into the car wash. Climbing to the shade of the *rancho*, they shouted to the waitress for a bottle of rum which wasn't their first of the morning. The leader of the pack fondled the waitress while the others laughed. The owner brought a glass of cold water to Bergman.

Nodding to the new arrivals, she said, 'There is greater quietness upstairs. There is also a fan. When you are finished, you can shower.'

Bergman wasn't in need but he liked the woman and she needed the money – Bergman's sex life was mostly like that. Upstairs he watched while the woman locked the bedroom door. The Beretta didn't surprise her. He laid it on the bedside table. A gaudy colour print of the Virgin Mary hung above the bed, right hand raised in blessing. The sheets were fresh and scented with cheap soap.

The woman played with him then climbed on top. She appeared to please herself; after he was finished, rather than return directly to the *rancho*, she curled up against his belly, her head pillowed in the crook of his arm.

Her breathing was soft and cool where it stirred the hairs on his forearm. Bergman lay on his left side, the pistol within reach, and he resisted a moment as she reached for his right hand, drawing it down to cup her breast. He listened through the rowdy laughter of the *campesinos* for the scratch of grit beneath a shoe on the concrete stairs. So easy for the woman to cling to his hand for the few seconds necessary. He counted to fifty before slipping his hand free then gently stroked, with his trigger finger, the damp valley in the nape of her neck. She stirred against him, lazy in her contentment, and her breathing deepened.

A fly settled on the Beretta. Bergman watched it dab its proboscis in the thin skim of machine oil on the blued barrel. According to the armourer's report, Fabio had used a 9mm automatic at Finca Patricia – the model with integral silencer issued to their illegals by the KGB during the Cold War. Now the KGB sold them to collectors.

Despite the fan, the woman's buttocks were slippery with sweat. Bergman's thoughts drifted to Vorst cool in the comfort of the corporate jet. And Fabio hiding somewhere in the jungle.

Bergman imagined Fabio and his men slipping down through the trees towards Finca Patricia. Hoping for low cloud and rain, Fabio would have listened to the weather report. However, the date had been set by San Cristóbal de los Baños.

Bergman had visited Fabio's family home in Guatemala City a dozen times. A private road with armed guards led to the house set in a walled acre of lawn shaded by tall pines. It was a white house with white marble floors. Even the servants were white, butler in a starched white jacket, maids in white aprons. Fabio had to be out of his mind to exchange such comfort for the sweat and stink of the jungle. Bergman hated the jungle. He knew it too well: the heat and humidity so thick that breathing became an effort; tarantulas, mosquitoes, snakes – and leeches hanging from your flesh. Whichever the jungle, there were always leeches.

He listened to a truck climb round the bend below the car

wash. The *campesinos* were suddenly silent. Bergman was already reaching for the Beretta as the truck pulled in beside the *rancho*. Instinct woke the woman. She sat up and swung her feet to the floor. Nothing showed in her face. Naked, she crossed to the window.

'*Uniformes*,' she said without looking back at Bergman.

It was the word the country people used for both *guerrilleros* and army. They saw no difference between the two sides; both were equally vicious.

'The men are yours,' she added in the same flat voice that went with her lack of expression.

She stood sideways to the window so that the wall protected her from a stray shot. All part of the learning process, Bergman thought. She had a nice arse. He knew his own shape too well – overweight, hair thinning, podgy features – and would have been embarrassed to put his body in the same bed as real beauty. Embarrassed and guilty. This woman suited him as did the others he visited round the country. They were much the same type: working women, placid and undemanding – unlike his fellow countrywomen who exacted what they called relationships which turned out to be hours of pointless conversation. Bergman hated talk. Talk got people killed.

So did the army and the *guerrilleros*. And they were bad for business. The *campesinos* were already in their jeep, Bergman saw as he joined the woman.

The soldiers all came from the same square mould, hard muscled and confident. And the woman was correct, they were Bergman's men – special forces.

He said, 'They must have seen the Toyota.'

The woman nodded. The fear hadn't left her. The rules in Guatemala were simple: feed the army and the *guerrilleros* killed you. Feed the *guerrilleros* and the army killed you. It had been that way all her life and the ceasefire wouldn't change anything.

'First I must shower, then I will move them on,' Bergman said.

She fetched him the remains of a bar of Lifebuoy soap

wrapped in plastic. Bergman had brought her the soap months back.

'Forgive me,' he said.

She was pulling her dress over her head and perhaps she didn't hear. With her face covered he couldn't tell. It had started out a good day. Under the shower he began swearing to himself.

The soldiers had taken the table closest to their truck. They sat like labourers after a hard day in the fields, silent, hunch shouldered, knees spread, bottles of cold Gallo beer clutched in their hands. Rather than show their faces to Bergman, they sneaked glances at him sideways. One of them had lost skin off his knuckles.

Their commander, a major, stood at the kitchen hatch gnawing a chicken leg. In earlier days he had served as a lieutenant in the mountains around Lake Atitlán. He and Bergman had worked together and been friends of a sort. Bergman had sent the Guatemalan on courses at Fort Bragg and the School of the Americas. Bergman had pressed for his promotion to command of the counterinsurgency forces in the coastal province. Then came San Cristóbal and bitter disagreement over methods. Now the two men kept their hostility hidden and used each other.

The major nodded a greeting. He spoke in English. 'I called your office. They said you were on the road.' A second nod indicated the Toyota. 'We spotted you.' The breach of American security pleased the major. He smiled and flicked the chicken bone at a wooden post supporting the roof. The bone hit and ricocheted under the nearest hammock.

'Fort Bragg training,' Bergman said. The children and waitresses had disappeared. He reached through the hatch for a beer from the icebox and snapped the top on his teeth. It was a trick he'd been doing for years and now the teeth were capped. Careless of the foam, he tilted the bottle to his lips then wiped his mouth on the back of his hand and dried the hand on the seat of his pants.

Perhaps the major was impressed; he didn't show it. 'Dengue

fever,' he said in explanation of a straggler they had picked up from a *guerrillero* band operating north of the Rio Dulce. 'There's sixteen of them in the group. Usual arms. He says they're observing the ceasefire.' The major chuckled at his own joke and one of his soldiers laughed.

'He's in the truck. You want to talk to him, you don't have much time.'

Bergman hefted himself over the truck tailgate. The *guerrillero* was past answering questions and the soldiers hadn't bothered tying him. He sprawled in a corner of the truck like a bag of rags. The torn side of his trousers showed a white thigh mottled with insect bites, he'd lost most of his teeth and one eye had burst – probably a boot. Bergman had seen worse and not looking would have lost him face and given the major pleasure. The whiteness of the *guerrillero*'s skin marked him as a student radical. Bergman's eldest daughter was about the same age. The boy was probably beyond pain but there would be fear there deep inside. Kneeling beside him, Bergman dug for the carotid artery. It took only a few seconds. He would have done the same for a dog. Vaulting from the truck, he brushed the dirt off his knees.

The major said, 'The father's in import export, small time. Drives a six-year-old Nissan.'

A new Mercedes and the boy might have lived. The boy's death, if discovered, would be another mark against Bergman at the embassy. Nor would it help his case in Washington.

The major read his thoughts. 'We'll dump him in the lake, weight the body with a chunk of old iron. A few days and there'll be nothing left.'

Bergman said, 'Do that now. I'll pay for the beer.'

He watched the army truck reverse out of the car park and head back on the lake road. He didn't approve or disapprove of what had been done to the boy. It was how it was – Guatemala. Bergman was a foreigner. He could pay men; he could send them to the States for training; he could supply intelligence material; he could make suggestions on the ground; there had been times when he could exercise financial pressure to have a minister or a general replaced. However, he couldn't change the country's people or its history. Guatemalan whites had been grabbing land and enslaving or killing Indians for four hundred years and no president survived without support from the military.

He finished his beer and dropped the empty bottle into the bin before turning to the woman. Her fear had erected a barrier between them. Bergman was responsible for the fear and though it was only a small thing it mattered to him. He said, 'I have business down in the valley. Perhaps one hour, two. It is possible for me to spend the night afterwards, though I must leave early in the morning.'

He watched as she calculated the profit and loss account. He was a *poderoso*, one of the powerful. Half an hour in mid afternoon made her a whore. All night carried prestige; enough of his power could wash off on her so she wouldn't have to bribe the police and the health inspectors. However, the army might use her place more. She didn't want the soldiers. They never paid and the *guerrilleros* could mark her as an enemy.

Guessing part of her thoughts, Bergman said, 'The ceasefire is mostly holding.'

The mestiza waitress reappeared and Bergman watched the woman's younger boy, the five-year-old, tiptoe round the corner of the kitchen. Nervous, the child slipped on the edge of the *rancho* and slithered down the bank, grazing a knee. Trapped in her calculations, the mother was unable to move and the boy wept silently as he clambered back up the slope. Had Bergman touched the child the woman would have been insulted, so he watched, uncomfortable with the child's pain.

Reaching his mother, the boy dragged on her skirt. Pulled out of her reverie, she picked him up, wiping his nose between her fingers before scooping up the major's discarded chicken leg from under the hammock. She gave the bone to the child to suck and cradled his face against her breasts. Her children mattered most and she needed money. She could tell Bergman next time he passed about the army. He would pay the soldiers' bill and she could even pad the bill a little. Satisfied, she stroked the child's hair and nodded agreement.

'When you return, drive round the back and park in the shed. There is a track that loops back through the hills to the main road.'

Bergman knew the track. The extra exit was why he had initially chosen the place as a stopover. He said, 'I will buy a fish at Lake Izabal.'

4

Bergman

Crepe myrtle trees shaded and spattered the main road with pink blossoms for the last half mile before the big wooden sign pointing to NAFAC's plantations. Beyond the myrtles spread the vast, gently stirring banana forest with the long purple curve of the Sierra del Espíritu Santo in the distance, streaks of thick grey cloud spilling along the mountains' flanks. Bergman showed his pass to the mestizo manning the entrance gates. The dirt road from the gates was straight and freshly graded, rain channels clean on either side. The side road to the airstrip preceded the administrative compound and employee housing. A guard saluted and raised the pole barricade.

Bergman spotted the manager's Chevy Blazer in the shade of a mamey tree to the right of the lone building midway along the fringe of the tarmac, white clapboard with a bleached shingle roof extending to shade a narrow terrace. Jasmine spilled from green glazed pots each side of the steps leading to the terrace; pink bougainvillaea and orange trumpet vine climbed the corner pillars. The Texan manager sat in one of two white canvas director's chairs in the shade. The Guatemalan head of the plantation's security occupied the other.

Bergman parked beside the Blazer and nodded to the two guards dozing against the mamey tree. Predictability was the greatest danger to security. Bergman had been instrumental in designing a system of random patrols for NAFAC's plantations. Which of fifty routes and at what time a patrol set out depended on the throwing of dice in the guardhouse as did whether the guards patrolled on foot or by jeep or on horseback. Bergman took a good look round but couldn't see any other guards.

The temperature here on the coastal plain was ten degrees higher than in the capital, the humidity was thick, the breeze off the mountains too faint to stir the windsock limp against its pole. Bergman was already sweating as he reached the terrace. The manager and head of security greeted him without enthusiasm. This meeting with Vorst probably worried them. They knew Bergman had problems in Washington. Perhaps they thought he planned to retire from government and take their jobs.

There were only two chairs. Bergman squatted against the wall and laid his Beretta on the floor. He still couldn't spot any guards other than the two under the jacaranda tree. With Vorst flying in there should have been a sense of threat. 'How many men do you have on patrol?' he asked the Guatemalan.

The Texan answered for him. 'No one knows Vorst's coming.'

Bergman shrugged. 'Except us three and whoever. If the peace holds there'll be a lot of soldiers demobilised. Same with *guerrilleros*. There'll be fewer bombs but more kidnap gangs, so you want to watch yourself.'

The Guatemalan stirred and spat a thread of tobacco off his bottom lip. 'Bandits don't have the organisation to hit the big plantations.'

'Yet,' Bergman said.

A silver speck flashed against the broad stripes of dark cloud hugging the mountains. The speck grew into NAFAC's Lear 31B. Vorst's power drew the three men out of the shade to watch the jet tilt in towards the far end of the landing strip. Corporate pilots tried harder, Bergman thought as he watched the pilot touch down wing and nose wheels simultaneously, neither bounce nor harsh squeak of rubber on the asphalt. The jet ran on past them, swung and taxied back to the far end again where the pilot turned and came to a halt positioned for take off into the light breeze. Hydraulics opened the door and lowered steps to the ground. A pale-skinned mulatto ducked through the doorway. Six foot something of hard muscle, he stretched and yawned as he descended the steps. The elastic straps of a steel-spring shoulder holster cut across the white of his sport shirt.

The bodyguard acted as a sheep dog, cutting Bergman out of the threesome and up the steps. An older man, grey and neat in a dark blue cashmere suit, greeted Bergman at the door. Corporate cleanies, was Bergman's instant judgement of the two young men seated with Vorst at a narrow conference table that ran down the centre of the main cabin: talcum powder, lots of deodorant, gold watches and the latest IBM laptops. They had taken off their jackets and ties; however, their shirt cuffs remained buttoned. None of the men were fruits so the absence of women was probably Vorst avoiding the intrusion of sex in business.

Many men of Vorst's power would have remained seated. Vorst rose from the table. His smile seemed genuine. So did the teeth. He held out a hand to Bergman. 'Good of you to drive all this way.'

Bergman pictured the boy in the back of the truck and the woman's arse as she stood naked at the window, their sweat damp on her thighs. Blood and sweat didn't fit with corporate jets. It was all very clean, very neat, healthy.

'Seems you have some problems up in Washington,' Vorst said as he lowered himself into his chair. He'd made the statement in front of his people so that Bergman would know that they were aware of his vulnerability. The first card on the table, Bergman thought. And Vorst wanted something from him, something outside the normal parameters of his job.

Vorst drew the legs of his trousers up a few inches to protect the creases before folding his hands on the table. His finger-nails reflected the overhead lights. Bergman wondered whether Vorst had them polished – a visiting manicurist to the office? Once a week at most. Vorst wasn't the type to waste more time. He probably had his suits made by the half dozen to cut down on his visits to the tailor. Or did he have the tailor come to him? Bergman doubted whether that was Vorst's style: playing the billionaire, using his power. Sure, Vorst used it, but for a reason rather than as decoration.

Bergman shifted uneasily as the flashes of insight came – stills from a movie that he needed to sort. He wasn't a quick thinker. He'd got to where he was through hard work. He needed time to assess Vorst. Who Vorst was inside.

'You've been a good friend to NAFAC over the years,' Vorst was saying, and, to his young men in suits, 'We could use a little privacy.'

Microphones had destroyed the concept. Bergman grinned. Secure on his own territory, he let his eyes rove the cabin. 'Why don't we take a walk, Mister Vorst.' And to Vorst's assistants, 'Nothing personal. It's the air-conditioning. Messes my chest.'

Accustomed to the heat and humidity, Bergman had hoped for an advantage but Vorst appeared as comfortable strolling up the airstrip as he had in the plane. They kept to the middle of the strip, the mulatto bodyguard walking to their left and a little ahead while the grey older man in the good suit and tie kept to their rear. The suit was Vorst's man, Bergman realised. The mulatto was part of the corporation's key personnel insurance, obligatory whenever Vorst visited countries on the insurer's danger list. Obvious as a Judas goat, a hit squad or kidnappers would take him out first while the older man hustled Vorst to safety. Bergman was about to ask whether Vorst carried a gun but Vorst spoke first.

'What motivates you, Mister Bergman?'

Thinking of himself as the assessor, Bergman was caught off guard.

Vorst continued, 'Money, you wouldn't be in government. Status? Patriotism? Where did you start out?'

'New Mexico.'

Vorst waited for more but Bergman saw no advantage in recounting the fifty acres of dry dirt and trailer home that his mother had given up trying to keep clean. Bergman's dad had called it the ranch when sufficiently sober to pronounce the r.

'We may be able to assist each other,' Vorst said. 'First I'd like to learn a little of who you are.' He didn't offer any of himself.

Ahead, the clouds were growing out from the mountains, wisps tearing free along the front edge.

'We'll have rain in quarter of an hour,' Bergman said. Rain had been a constant of his childhood – longing for rain to damp down the grit that got into everything: food, bed, clothes, his schoolbooks.

'You're in real trouble, Mister Bergman.'

'Yeah.' Bergman kicked a pebble and watched it rattle across the smooth tar. 'I'm out of date. That's what the papers say.'

'You and the Cuban, Estoban Tur. Is that what you believe, Mister Bergman?'

Mention of the Cuban unsettled Bergman. He couldn't see the connection. 'The revolution was always shit,' he said. 'Not the need for change but the how.'

He looked out across the bananas. The grass was mown along the side of the airstrip, the road was maintained, the red earth showed clean in the thick shade between the pale greens and browns of the ranked tree trunks. Blue plastic bags protected the bunches of bananas from insects. He could see no yellow amongst the leaves, all was health, green, lush, and well maintained. Brushing their teeth was the closest the average Latin American came to any form of maintenance.

Bergman wasn't a believer in any philosophy. He used his eyes. Latin Americans had the same brains as North Americans. They moved to the US and the next generation were as competent and disciplined. In their own countries, however, they always messed up. Lack of faith in a stable political future was to blame. As a result they thought short term: minimum investment, total corruption.

'People here need technical education and health care, proper housing. That means good jobs and the only good jobs come with the big corporations. You don't pay them what you can afford, Mister Vorst, and I'd be in there organising a strike.

41

Pay them well and I defend you. That's my job and I've been doing it well for the past twelve years.'

Vorst cupped his elbow. 'So you're a believer.'

Bergman hated to be touched. 'Yeah, I'm a believer. So is Tur. We're probably not that different. It's the methodology. Land reform.' Suddenly angry, he almost spat the words. 'That's a one-acre plot so the Indians stay peasants for the goddamn left-wing intellectuals to patronise.' It was how Bergman had been reared; the farm too poor to feed a rat, they had lived on food stamps. He recalled shrinking inside himself as the welfare woman patted him on the head – stupid bitch pretending to do good while his dad drank the welfare cheque. He turned to free himself of Vorst's hand. 'What is it you want, Mister Vorst?'

'Tur.'

Bergman managed to hide his anger. No surprise in his voice, he said, 'The Cuban?'

'That's who we're discussing. Wrapped up in a neat parcel, Mister Bergman. Do that for me and I'll see you protected in Washington.'

Bergman pictured Vorst standing coldly angry amongst the ruins of his house on Finca Patricia. Revenge? Vorst wouldn't waste his energy. So it was something else. Something tied to the attack? Something affecting NAFAC. Or affecting Vorst's position in NAFAC?

He said, 'Tur doesn't travel outside Cuba. It's a rule they have. Same with their military. They get outside, Castro's scared they'll defect.'

'The situation's changing,' Vorst said.

'Castro?' Bergman didn't bother hiding his disbelief and Vorst smiled.

'The young ones. We have a friend, a minister. Come up with a plan that gets Tur to Guatemala and he'll help. I want Tur captured. I want him on the news so everyone sees his picture.'

An advertising campaign. Advertising Vorst's power. Bergman saw it clearly. Not the why but the fact. Lightning flickered across the cloud front and the breeze stirred through the canopy of banana leaves, cool and thickly scented by the rain. Bergman had planned to retire, not here on the coastal plane but up in the mountains, a few acres of lake front where he could sit out on his porch in the late afternoon and watch the rain drive in across the water. Have a woman look after him, eat his own fruit and vegetables, breed a few pigs so he could cure hams and make sausage, status of an elder states-man with visiting journalists driving out from the city to seek his opinion on the country. It was what he had worked for all his life – status and respect. Now even his pension was at risk.

Lightning flashed again and he said, 'We'd best get back to your plane, Mister Vorst.'

They walked in silence, hurrying a little under the warning pressure of the breeze, strong now, on their backs. The pilot fired the jets before they reached the plane. The grey body-guard was up the steps first, hovering in the doorway, careful eyes scanning the banana trees. Vorst touched Bergman again on the elbow. 'You haven't answered.'

Bergman shrugged and the breeze lifted the back of his shirt; his sweat chilled and he shivered. Vorst's hand unsettled him. Twenty years and he'd never freelanced. He didn't like it. He thought of the woman calculating his offer to stay the night. 'I'd need to see if it's possible,' he said. 'It's not something you can hurry, Mister Vorst. We're probably talking months.'

Turning to free himself, he ran for the Toyota. The first raindrops hit as he clambered in behind the wheel. He switched on the windscreen wipers and headed for Lake Izabal to buy a fish.

Bergman

Bergman had been upgraded from business to first class on the American Airlines flight from Guatemala City to Miami. Across the aisle, an elderly Guatemalan in a pale fawn cashmere suit sipped champagne with a companion old enough to be his daughter if he had married late. The gold links fastening the Guatemalan's cuffs would have sunk a rowing boat and his watchstrap would have kept Bergman's ex-wife in alimony for the next ten years.

Bergman hadn't committed himself to Vorst. If he handled it right, he could earn career points through delivering Estoban Tur. More importantly, he would gain Vorst's support in Washington, where he was marked within the Agency as a Cold War warrior, out of date. Even that he was overweight told against him these days. The new breed were slim on health foods and working out. And they never rocked the boat – didn't even board the boat, Bergman thought as he accepted a fresh beer from the stewardess. His own methods were very different. He worked hands on – in the special forces training camps, in the jungle, or down in the cells where the men, whom Washington pretended they didn't pay, interrogated prisoners.

He knew his strengths and accepted that the Tur operation required a subtlety foreign to his accomplishments. He would have to move carefully in Washington, restrict his contacts to men such as his own chief, survivors of the old guard. However, for the planning, he would have to go outside. The tame Brit they kept penned in the Zoo was Bergman's choice.

Funded by the CIA, the Zoo was a Federal penitentiary on a military base. The cages were comfortable bungalows facing across a nine-hole golf course with well trimmed fairways sloping to a twenty-acre lake. The men occupying the bungalows had been found guilty of crimes committed in the service of the United States of America. Newspapers were primarily responsible for hounding the men to trial. As far as the outside world was concerned they were in jail.

The Brit was a class act. He had started out as an officer in one of those Brit cavalry regiments that celebrate screw-ups – the Brit's had worn red pants for the past couple of centuries in memory of an afternoon picking cherries when they should have been in battle. From the cavalry, the Brit had transferred to Military Intelligence where he reached the upper echelons before being caught attempting a hit on his tame killer. The Brit had been trying to bury favours he'd done for his friends in Washington, and enough of those friends remained to keep the Brit protected. Like Bergman, those friends were survivors from a hands-on time in the Agency.

Bergman changed planes in Miami and overnighted at a married friend's house in Washington. The air conditioning on the black Ford he drew from the Langley car pool in the morning might have sufficed on a summer's day in northern Alaska. Roadworks delayed him half an hour and his shirt and pants were wet with sweat by the end of the drive out to the Zoo. He sat in the car with the windows up and air conditioning off for a few minutes before entering the gates.

The Brit lived in bungalow 4.

Bergman parked in the unused carport. He dragged on a blue blazer over his wet shirt, deliberately left the top shirt button undone and didn't bother straightening his tie. Checking the mirror, he thought the image was right – a crude, sweaty clown.

A Filipino steward in a starched white jacket and black trousers opened the door to him.

'Straus,' Bergman said. It was a name he'd used before and he fumbled a medium quality business card out of his breast pocket. The card introduced him as an economist advising the Latin American desk at the State Department.

The Filipino led him across an open-plan living room to a terrace that faced out over the fourth fairway of the golf course. The terrace was lightly shaded by pink bougainvillaea trained across an overhead trellis. The Brit sat at ease in a white canvas director's chair, a small cup of black coffee on the table in front of him beside the remnants of his midday meal. He was a tall, spare, square shouldered man in his late sixties with a full head of trim grey hair and a military moustache fiercely clipped. He wore one of those baggy suits of lumpy linen Brits considered smart, a double-cuff, cotton Oxford shirt and a striped tie that probably meant something to other Brits. Bergman resisted the temptation to look under the table; he

45

would have wagered a month's pay on the Brit's shoes being brown wingtips.

The Filipino announced him, 'Mister Straus, Colonel.'

The Brit didn't look at the card, merely inspected his visitor with cool amusement. 'Bergman,' he said. 'Guatemala. Sit down.'

So the Brit's memory still functioned after three years' hibernation in the Zoo. Bergman hid his satisfaction behind embarrassment at the unmasking of his deception. While the steward cleared the table, Bergman fetched a second chair from the side of the bungalow. He sat facing the Brit. A ray of sun struck his right eye. He wondered whether shifting his seat would give the Brit greater satisfaction than continuing to sit in discomfort. Either way the Brit would feel superior, which was what Bergman wanted. Bergman had never liked Brits – or Europeans in general. Superior sons of bitches, all of them. And devious. That was the main quality he required from the Brit.

He said, 'Estoban Tur.'

He was certain that the Brit knew to whom he was referring. The Brit just sat there waiting.

In other circumstances Bergman would have longed to kick the Brit in his supercilious arse. Now he was happy to play the country simpleton. He said, 'Cuban – head of their DOE. I want him. Build me a scenario that works and maybe I can get you out of here.'

The colonel took a slim gold cigarette case and a gold Ronson lighter from his pocket. He tapped the tip of an oval shaped cigarette on the case a couple of times before lighting up.

Bergman grimaced and turned his face away from the perfumed smoke.

'Abdullahs – Egyptian,' the Brit said. 'I have them sent from London. Your customs people tend to get quite excited. So what's Tur done this late in the game?'

'His people are screwing up my territory,' Bergman said.

'They've been doing that for thirty-five years.' Watching

46

Bergman through the smoke, the Brit added, 'And Latin Americans claim you've been interfering with their territory ever since they threw the Spanish out. That includes stealing New Mexico, Texas and half of California.'

That it was true didn't help. 'Drop the lecture,' Bergman said.

The Brit flicked ash from his cigarette. 'You're a new face. I don't get many visitors.'

'So, you want to work or stay here the rest of your life?' Considering the comfort enjoyed by the Brit, it wasn't much of a threat.

As if to emphasise the point, the colonel rang a small silver hand bell – one ring sufficed to bring the Filipino steward; he must have been hovering within easy earshot.

'A little more coffee please, Roberto, and I think a small whisky. Two glasses. Malt.' The Brit inspected the sky as if the weather made a difference. 'Springbank – the fifteen-year.' And to Bergman, 'Too warm a day for the twenty-five.'

Or I'm too downmarket, Bergman thought. Leaving his shirt button undone had worked – and sweating. Sweat was a great feeder of superiority.

'Tur travels?' The Brit didn't seem interested but the question led in the right direction.

'Not in five years,' Bergman said with a heavy shrug that further rucked his shirt. 'Castro's scared he'll defect. Tur's scared we'll snatch him.'

'Intelligent of him, given your intentions.'

Bergman answered the colonel's smile with one of his own, a little sheepish. 'Yeah.' He counted to ten before saying, 'We have an asset.'

The colonel allowed himself a dry chuckle. 'You've had a lot of assets. An entire brigade at the Bay of Pigs.'

'This one's different,' Bergman said.

'They're all different. You require effectiveness.'

'A *poderoso* . . . one of the new, young ones,' Bergman insisted. It was what Vorst had promised and Bergman hoped that he sounded confident.

47

The colonel smiled through the perfumed smoke. 'I suppose he strolled into your office in Guatemala City and said, "Señor Bergman, I've always been a great admirer of the United States and of you personally. I long to work for you."'

Bergman kept his cool. 'Give or take.'

The steward returned with a silver tray. Cut in the shape of a thistle, the small crystal glasses spattered sunlight.

The Brit's grey eyes were reflective as he poured carefully. 'There's a timescale?'

'Not so it matters.' Bergman considered asking for ice but decided that to do so would be overacting. He let his gaze drift over the golf course, then back to the colonel's garden.

The whisky glowed gold against the white of the Brit's moustache. 'Tur's a tough catch. Wily.'

Bergman flashed one of his tough guy grins. 'Yeah, well if you've got something better to do.'

The Brit didn't hear him. Though his eyes followed a magpie as it hopped across the fourth green, he was away in his own thoughts. Trapped by the desire to show off his intelligence, Bergman hoped.

Close to five minutes passed before the Brit turned back to face Bergman. His tone of voice had changed: quieter, heavier. 'You have confidence in this *poderoso*?'

'Some.' The time had come for truth. 'He's a minister. In Cuba you get promoted because you're loyal to Castro. Give him something personal and he'll do it. Political and I have doubts.'

The Brit nodded. 'And safe. Dictatorships don't foster risk-takers.' He was enjoying himself, no longer at Bergman's expense, but at the mental exercise. 'I'll require access.'

Slow, Bergman warned himself. He had to rein in a little before he lost control. 'Access may be tough,' he said. 'I can bring anything you want.'

The colonel gave a dry little smile. 'I don't know what I'm looking for. I'll need to browse. Hope something comes up.' Again that little smile. 'It usually does. Merely a matter of time.

A couple of days – less than a week.' He nodded to himself. 'Yes, there'll be something there. Something we can use.'

Bergman watched the Brit mime drawing slack from an imaginary trout reel. A slight flick of the wrist floated the dry fly into the shadows beneath the rose hedge. A quick strike. 'Got you,' he said.

Got you, thought Bergman.

The tip of the Brit's tongue touched the underside of his upper lip as he smiled. 'That's what we need. A fly to draw the target out of the shadows. Something special. Something very special.'

Orange gold gleamed as the Brit prodded his cigarette case across the white tablecloth into a patch of sunlight. He flicked the Ronson and watched the flame for a moment before lowering the cap.

'Get me everything available on Cuba, media as well as official. A couple of days to read it through and I'll let you know what else I want.'

Bergman nodded his agreement. Rising from the table gave him the opportunity to read the inscription in the Brit's cigarette case. *'For my best man, John Smith,'* followed by a signature, *'Paddy Mahoney'*.

A John Patrick Mahoney had made the hit at San Cristóbal de los Baños.

5

Colonel Smith

Colonel Smith had been sleeping on his back. His bedroom was sparsely furnished. A large mahogany wardrobe and a double dresser held his clothes; one chair, an upright trouser press, a monastically narrow bed with a hard mattress. The narrow bed and the cold shower with which he began each day were constants of his life, from nursery, through prep-school dormitory, Eton and Sandhurst.

Feeling for his bedroom slippers, he shuffled stiffly through to the kitchen where he set a kettle to boil on the gas stove. In the shower he scrubbed himself, using a long-handled brush on his legs and back. The solid silver razor and shaving brush had been a sixteenth birthday gift from his father. Trumpers, convenient to the colonel's old office in Curzon Street, had rebristled the brush every five years.

Wrapped in a towelling bathrobe, he returned to the kitchen. He was precise in the making of his tea, first heating the silver pot before filling it with boiling water and adding three level teaspoons of Twining's Queen Mary's Breakfast Mixture. He carried the tray through to his study and drew the curtains back on the first light seeping in out of the east. Bunkers showed as pale blobs against the overall grey of the landscape, the oaks and cottonwoods no more than a distant blur rising beyond the water.

He poured tea into his cup and sipped before drawing a fresh sheet of paper from his desk. He wrote with a silver pencil, raising the soft lead carefully: *INTENTION – rehabilitation.*

Prior to Bergman's visit, the colonel would have said that he was content where he was. Disgraced by his arrest, his old life was closed to him. Now, suddenly, there was the glimmer of hope – not because of Bergman's offer: Bergman hadn't the power – but because Tur was a major project. He could dress Tur's entrapment as an operation planned years back and for which his guilty plea to attempted murder of his agent had been a cover. It was a plot out of a Deighton or le Carré novel – the type of scenario civilians loved. The rumour mill could be manipulated in his favour:

Smith, you know. Never did believe it. Man like that. Known him for years.

The colonel imagined letters from the club secretaries: *The committee wishes to apologise. Members recognise that in requesting your resignation they acted hastily and with great injustice . . .*

He sat sipping his tea and thinking it through. Manipulation was his favoured tool – small hints eased into conversations, minute clues that little by little destroyed certainty and left the field ploughed and fertile for the planting of the colonel's chosen reality. First he had to examine every scrap of information the CIA computers held on Estoban Tur. He placed the Cuban's name lower down the page on the left-hand side, underlined it and wrote beneath:

Relationship to his superiors

Attitude of his superiors to the present political situation

Superiors' stability in the Castro pecking order

He added question marks, drawing them neatly. Then he blocked out *stability* and wrote above it, *insecurity*. The search was always for vulnerability – however slight, some weakness to work at as if he were a dentist easing the needle tip of his probe beneath a loose filling. He winced at the imagined pain and sluiced his mouth with tea.

CIA headquarters at Langley would provide the colonel's best opportunity to spread the word that he was working with the CIA. He had to outwit Bergman who would plan to keep him isolated. Bergman wouldn't be easy – behind the sweaty buffoon lay a good mind, not brilliant but experienced, solid and very careful. The evidence lay in Bergman's survival. The colonel's own career had ended through underestimating a field officer; it was a mistake he determined not to repeat.

Bergman's courier arrived soon after breakfast with the background reading on Cuba. The package contained think-tank summaries, newspaper and magazine articles, the CIA's own synopses. The collapsed economy and infrastructure were familiar. New were hints, however muffled, of antagonism between the leaders. A minority, more pragmatic, accepted the necessity for foreign investment while the doctrinaire *comandantes*, old friends of Castro, viewed even minimal foreign intrusion as a threat to their control of the island.

And there were small signals of opposition from the intellectuals – not suddenly discovered bravery but placing markers for a future they believed imminent. Lastly came reports from the streets. Castro had been endlessly lecturing Cubans that revolutionary Cuba belonged truly to its people. Increasingly the people were accepting their leader's word. On salaries ranging from four to twenty-five dollars a month, and with the state the sole employer, Cubans now stole everything from the state farms, from the dollar shops, from building sites, from hotels and restaurants, from the cigar factories, from petrol stations.

It was a picture more of anarchy than of organised opposition. Of the latter the colonel found only a few dozen human rights activists, these mostly either in jail or under house arrest. And Bergman's young *poderoso* was of no account; of this the colonel was certain. Ministers were little more than clerks employed to implement the *Comandante en Jefe's* latest whim. All true power remained with those of the old guard who retained access to Castro, survivors grown cunning on years of palace intrigue.

A sudden childhood recollection came to the colonel of wriggling ecstatically within the comfort of his bedclothes on a chill winter's night. Now it was the pleasure of feeling his old skills reawaken.

A picture came to him – a picture of the tall, determinedly erect Castro dominating the vast May Day crowd in Havana's Revolution Square. Castro, dressed in his military fatigues, relishing his image as the eternal guerrilla leader. Yes, and above all else, denying his years. That was it – the colonel's requirements were for a member of the old guard whose physical dissolution had become an unwelcome reminder to the ageing president of his own mortality. Semi-banished from the presence, a man prepared to trade in return for a route back into the magic inner circle.

First the colonel required history: Hugh Thomas' *Cuba* was best and Tad Szulc's *Fidel: A Critical Portrait*. And TV news. Calling Bergman, he requested the books and for all Cubavision's local news coverage from the past five years.

The colonel smiled as Bergman's voice cracked with disbelief.

'Five years! You plan watching TV for six months?'

The colonel said, 'Bits and pieces. I'll know where to look.'

He had spent all day at his desk; he had found his direction. Easing his chair back, he rose and stretched the stiffness from his shoulders before rewarding his efforts with a light whisky and soda. Colour had returned to the golf course with the gentle evening sunlight. Strolling out to the terrace, the colonel watched a pair of magpies peck worms from the fourth green.

Bergman delivered the books and videos the following evening. The North American had acted confident at their first two meetings. Now he was nervous and irritable, urging the colonel to hurry his research.

'There's things happening,' he told the colonel. 'I have to get back to Guatemala. Call me when you're close.'

Bergman

Bergman would have been more truthful had he told the Brit that he had to get out of Washington. Three senatorial aids faced Bergman across the table. Their faces had the harlot's look of polish and expensive hairdressers and they wore clean costly suits and clean costly shirts and safe costly ties. One of the three was black and all three were basic scum: Washington lawyers, bright as knives, but who didn't know shit and were determined not to learn anything that could damage their masters' careers. They were on the hunt for a scandal their masters could uncover – preferably a scandal that could be released to either harm the president and his administration or leave them unscathed. That way the senators could bargain for Federal support to their respective states.

Bergman was booked on the mid-afternoon flight to Guatemala City and had brought his bag and his briefcase to the committee room. The receptionist had picked him for a low-level travelling salesman and had sneered while searching for his name on her clipboard. The three senatorial aids viewed him as prey. Their questioning concerned San Cristóbal de los Baños.

Bergman said, 'I wasn't there when it happened. All I did was clear up the mess.'

'They were your goons,' one of the three said.

'Guatemalan army,' Bergman corrected.

'You trained them.'

'The US army trained them.' Bergman had made junior sergeant in the army and been employed as an admin clerk, a job that provided ample time for study. The three suits were too young to have been in the military. They must have attended school aided by their dads' finance or with scholarships, or on a mixture of the two.

The one on the left said, 'The soldiers were trained at your behest, Mister Bergman. That's what we understand. You were CIA Head of Station and pretty much ran the country.'

'That's what you read in the Washington Post,' Bergman

said. Their youth was an insult. Or perhaps they merely looked young. The black managed to look white. Even their ink pens were interchangeable.

Bergman said, 'We've got the beginnings of a peace down in Guatemala. Digging up what's in the past isn't going to do Guatemala any good.'

They weren't interested in what was good for Guatemala. What happened in Washington mattered.

'It was done with US aid,' the one on the right said. 'That makes it our business. We want to know how many died and how they were killed. We have the evidence of the Englishman, Mahoney, that they were shot one by one. Is that correct?'

Vorst was maybe the only man who could save Bergman from this. 'I've told you. I wasn't there and I didn't count,' he said.

'You controlled seven million in aid and you're telling us you didn't count?'

'A body count,' Bergman said. 'That's what you asked – how many people died. The way you ask the question doesn't change the answer. I wasn't there and I never met Mahoney and I didn't count the bodies. That's fact – if you want fact. If you prefer make-believe, make it up yourself. I don't have anything to add to what I've already said.'

The one on the right said, 'Co-operation doesn't appear to be your strong suit, Mister Bergman. Given your situation, that could be a mistake.'

Flying into San Cristóbal had been Bergman's mistake. He said, 'I can't help what you think and I can't change the truth. You want to know? A hog roast, that's what I remember. It smelt like being right up front at the Democratic Party hog roast at the State Fair. Maybe that's a detail that escaped the reports you've read and it's something you don't have to sleep with the rest of your lives.'

He pushed back from the table and stood up. 'Now, if you'll excuse me, gentlemen, I have a plane to catch. That's a seat the taxpayer paid for and it's not refundable.'

The one on the left noticed the tag on Bergman's briefcase. 'You fly first class, Mister Bergman.'

'Business,' Bergman said. 'That's what I buy, and with American Airlines, which is a US carrier. I don't request an upgrade. It happens, I don't refuse. Nor does anyone I've heard of and that probably includes the Pope and the Dalai Lama.'

Colonel Smith

The history took two and a half days' hard reading. The afternoon of the third day the colonel spent designing a spreadsheet on his IBM laptop.

A dozen boxes held the video tapes of Cuba's TV news recorded daily by the US interest section in Havana with all foreign reports edited out. The colonel moved an armchair and the big Sony TV with integral video into his study so that he could watch the screen in comfort and within easy access of the documentation. On his knee he held his laptop, the spreadsheet divided into years and months drawn off against the names of the true *poderosos*. Of the inner triumvirate only Raul Castro remained, impregnable at the ministry of defence: Che had been killed in Bolivia, Celia Sanchez dead of cancer.

Beneath Raul came Amando Hart, the recently retired Minister of Culture, and Osmani Cienfuegos, Minister of Tourism. Osmani's position stemmed from his brother, the sainted Camilo, killed at the moment of victory in a plane accident of which no trace was ever found – or murdered, as most young Cubans believed, for the threat his popularity posed Castro at the end of the revolutionary war.

The new ones, Lage as titular head of government, Raibaina at the foreign ministry, Anacon, president of the national assembly, Eusebio Leal with his empire built on the reconstruction of Old Havana, these men were of no interest to the colonel. It was the old guard he was after.

As important as Hart and Osmani were the three *comandantes* of the revolution, the equivalent of Britain's military dukes, Wellington and Marlborough: Guillermo Garcia who, with his father, had rescued Castro from the cane fields after the disastrous landing from Mexico and had led him to safety in the Sierra Maestra. Now Guillermo bred horses and hosted cockfights on one or other of the huge ranches within his fief and organised the shooting of African buffalo reared on his nature reserves.

Ramiro Valdes, once Minister of Interior, enjoyed the luxury of a walled estate fronting the Marina Hemingway, president of a joint venture partnership that monopolised the island's computer and software markets.

Last of the *comandantes* came Juan Almeida. Mulatto, he had been always more window dressing for the black population than truly powerful and had retired now to the chairmanship of a welfare committee for old combatants.

Next came the lesser known and it was amongst these that the colonel concentrated his hunt through the past eighteen months of Cubavision news. Castro was ever present. At each appearance, the colonel froze the tape and searched for his quarry, entering each sighting and the subject's proximity to the president. As the colonel became familiar with the faces of his subjects, so the speed of his search increased. Finally he went back five years and checked the first week in each of the first six months. A graph showed seven men whose visibility in conjunction with Castro had either ended or become increasingly infrequent.

The search had taken twelve days. He left a message on Bergman's answerphone, 'Pick me up day after tomorrow.'

6

Colonel Smith

In preparation for Bergman, the colonel wore out-of-date prescription spectacles in bed to read a 1930s World Library edition of *Pride and Prejudice*, finally switching the light off at four a.m. The small print made his eyes red and weepy. He swallowed three aspirins immediately after his morning shower, followed by two cups of strong arabica coffee and was sweating nicely when Bergman picked him up at eight thirty in a black Buick with tinted windows.

'You look like you're about to die,' Bergman said.

'Nonsense.'

The colonel pretended to sleep on the drive to Langley. CIA headquarters was familiar territory. Two men in blue suits, button-down shirts and expressionless ties manned the security barrier. The guards recorded the colonel's hand-palm and voice prints. Bergman guided him to his work station, directed him through the access procedures and left him to his hunt.

The colonel read the bones of his target first.

Estoban Tur Flores: born 11 December, 1948, in a country district of Camagüey Province.

The father, Diego Tur Garcia, was third generation Cuban. The original Tur had emigrated from Formentera, smallest of the Balearic Islands. In Cuba the family were *árentarios*, men who worked the cane fields to pay rent on a few acres of hillside. Estoban's family had lost their rented land twice – first when a slump in sugar prices bankrupted their landlord, the second time through illness.

The early pictures were black and white. The first showed the paternal family stiffly posed in a dirt yard outside a plank-walled peasant shack. The thatch roof drooped over a narrow veranda and there were trees in the background: a mango, avocado, guava, chirimoya, banana, coconut palms. Leaves, shrivelled by drought, suggested July or early August. Midday sun drew short, hard-edged shadows. The family were labelled. The bony paternal grandfather with Zapata moustache stood in the centre, his white Sunday *guayabera* worn outside loose cotton trousers tucked into leather boots. The grandmother was thin as a stick in a mid-calf skirt and ruffled blouse. Estoban's father was equally thin, his moustache clipped to a line that matched his lips, stubborn chin, fists clenched below unbuttoned shirt cuffs.

Pregnancy swelled Estoban's mother. A white apron accentu-ated the darkness of her skin, hair dragged back, lips puffed by African genes.

And Estoban Tur, a dusky, solemn, slightly plump child – the mother hugged him against her hip as if in protection. The caption gave his age, six years old. He wore short trousers, short sleeved white shirt, tennis shoes, no socks. He clutched a book in his right hand, indication that his parents were proud of his education – two years of country primary school had left the father barely literate and the mother learned to read only with the revolution. Both parents were active revolutionaries. The father joined Che Guevara's column in its sweep up the north coast. He remained Che's man and was killed by a stray shell while touring Angola with his idol.

A primary school photograph showed the target mid-picture, an early leader. There followed pictures of his progress within the revolution – boarder at the prestigious Lenin school outside Havana, communist youth league, volunteer in the cane harvest, six months of military service, then the Soviet Union and only one photograph in the following eight years – a flat winter landscape of snow and skeletal beech trees. The target was the smallest of four men muffled in army greatcoats, artificial fur hats and high felt boots. They carried hunting rifles and posed in front of a Russian Gaz jeep with two elk draped over the canvas top. A high fence in the background bore a prohibited area notice in Cyrillic letters. Beyond the fence two long wooden barracks leaked chimney smoke into the still air. Estoban Tur's companions were named. All were KGB instructors.

After eight years in the Soviet Union, the target reappeared in colour, a face always in the background – youth congress in Czechoslovakia, Arab solidarity in Syria, trade delegation to East Germany. From then on it was all Cuba and Latin America: a Panama hat shaded Estoban Tur's face as he slipped from a side door at the Honduran Embassy in Guatemala. He was caught half-face in a jungle clearing in El Salvador; quarter-face in a workman's café in the Argentine; no face as he pressed himself into the scrum boarding a Colombian Airlines flight out of Venezuela. In Cuba he was captured entering and leaving by Gaz jeep the Punto Cero guerrilla warfare school in the Sierra de los Organos; full-face bicycling downhill on 4th Street in Vedado, Havana; twice at school athletics meetings. His progress into matrimony and the birth of two children were recorded in a dozen shots that showed him leaving and entering a Fifties apartment block at the Habana Libre end of 17th Avenue. Lastly there were a score of pictures taken from an upstairs window in a side street off O'Reilly in the old quarter of the city. The caption gave the opposite corner block as the target's office

The target had worked with Russians, Bulgarians, East Germans, Czechs. With the end of the Cold War his old masters sold the secrets of their past careers for the magic dollar. The information was all in the CIA files, the target's every move catalogued. The thoroughness of the surveillance was impressive, each photograph cross-referenced and slotted into the target's biography. The digital pictures were surreally clear on the big screen, Daliesque. The mother's genes showed in the target's skin colour, the roundness of features: clean shaven, hair cropped, belly straining his shirt buttons. And he hadn't changed his dress in the past ten years: brown baggy suit shiny at the knees, white shirt, red tie, cheap, ugly shoes.

Returning to the first family portrait, the colonel found himself wondering whether love, loneliness or despair had conquered the racial divide prevalent in those days. The mother was younger than the father by ten years. No doctors in the countryside, the target was the only one of her children to survive infancy.

The shack had gone with the revolution. A new society was born in which loyalty to Castro earned the fighting men from the sierras a status often beyond their administrative capacity. The target's father entered Havana with the rank of captain. Eight months later he was promoted to a committee created by Che and Raul Castro to implement agrarian reform. With families divided in allegiance, divorce was commonplace. The *barbudos* were romantic figures. The target's father slipped into a relationship with a radical university student, daughter of a Camagüey rancher who had fled the island – white, of course.

Moved to the city and then abandoned, the mother ceased to exist in the files except as an address for the target prior to his marriage. Perhaps she had been the goad that had driven the target through his entrance exams and to the top of his class at the Lenin school. The Lenin school had made him. The sons and daughters of the revolution's aristocracy were his fellow students; the Soviet Union was a standard move for the chosen. First Jafkaya 9, the KGB superior school for foreigners. Tur had done well there to earn promotion to Naro-Fominsk. Four hours by train from Moscow, Naro-Fominsk was camouflaged as the school of aerial defence. In reality it was the training centre for 'illegals', those agents destined to work under deep cover rather than protected by a diplomatic title at an embassy.

Next came the testing period attached to various missions through Eastern Europe, surveillance reporting his every contact and conversation. Then Latin America, a courier for both KGB and the Cuban DOE. Out on his own for the first time, he had sufficient information to trade to the CIA and had ample opportunity to defect. This was the final examination. The pass mark was earned with absolute loyalty, unquestioning obedience and total commitment to the cause. Thirty-three years old, he was given command of the G2 Punto Cero school training illegals to thrust revolution into Latin America. Two years later he was head of G2.

Only the athletic meets were out of character. The target was open to the public – naked, the colonel thought. He shifted the mouse, drawing the pointer onto the target. He clicked until the face filled the screen, then only the eyes, dark round pools floating with love. Excitement filled the colonel as he sought for the source: Miguel Tur, the target's half-brother. The boy was fifteen or sixteen years old. Side slits in his running shorts displayed the long, slender, supremely graceful legs of a gazelle, gold and glowing in the brilliant sunlight. The boy's arms were raised in victory and a joyous smile lit his face as he sought for the target amongst the crowd.

The colonel clicked the mouse, drawing up the face, cheeks blushed from the race, mouth a little open as the boy fought for breath. The sexual act would have brought the same blush, the same parted lips delicate as butterflies. The beauty was absolute and there was more, a look of innocence and of vulnerability.

There had been only one love in the colonel's life, an obsession unspoken, unconsummated. The recipient was a fellow officer in his cavalry regiment, Paddy Mahoney. Now in this cold, sterile underground room with its steel furniture the colonel suffered suddenly the same overwhelming desire. His sight dimmed and there came a pounding roar of surf as he surrendered for a moment to his emotions.

A hint of Bergman's toothpaste, deodorant and aftershave lingered in the cool, faintly metallic-tasting air. The odour was sufficient to return the colonel to reality. It was the odour of the United States, chemical and antiseptic. He longed to sully it with a forbidden cigarette.

He studied his hands. Liver spots now mottled their backs – and Paddy Mahoney was long dead. Dead by his own hand . . .

Paddy had married a spender. The colonel had rescued Paddy from financial scandal twice in the early years of the marriage. Forced to resign his commission, Paddy had managed polo and jockey clubs, descending the social ladder, rung by painful rung, as his weakness and generosity drove him to dip into the funds he controlled. Finally and inevitably came suicide at his desk in Arabia where he directed a sheikh's racing stables.

The colonel had found vengeance in robbing the widow of her son. The boy had been christened John in honour of the colonel and Patrick for his father – John Patrick Mahoney. The colonel paid for his education at private school and recruited him into military intelligence where he showed an uncanny ability to identify with his targets. It was a quality that the colonel used but never trusted – product of the Irish in Mahoney, the colonel had always thought. The boy was a Catholic, of course, and educated at a Benedictine boarding school. Papists, communists, they were similar in their need to confess, whether at theatrical trials or in those squalid little boxes at the back of the church. The colonel had spent his life fighting them.

With the Cold War over, senators began digging for past heroes who's sacrifice would enhance political careers. They subpoenaed young Mahoney to give evidence on the wet work he had done for Langley.

The colonel had attempted to silence him in a Mexican military hospital where Mahoney was reported to be haemorrhaging internally. The colonel had substituted a blood sachet for one treated with an anti-coagulant. He had practised the switch; thirty seconds. It was all on video tape.

Colonel Smith had been extradited to the United States where his attempt was soon justified in the eyes of his North American colleagues by Mahoney's evidence to the Senate – evidence that reinforced political oversight of the CIA and ended a dozen careers. Fortunately there were survivors prepared to show gratitude for the colonel's loyalty – hence his comfortable lodgings.

The colonel found the connection between Mahoney and the target mid-afternoon on that first day of his search. The target, together with the US Drug Enforcement Administration resident in the Bahamas, had used Mahoney to trap a Cuban admiral involved in drug running.

The colonel studied the report carefully. As so often in the past, Mahoney had acted outside the parameters of his employment. Most importantly he had established a friendship with the target – though, typically, the North American writer of the report preferred the imprecise term *relationship*.

The colonel summoned Mahoney's picture to the screen. Thick curly hair worn long and a full beard disguised the features but the eyes were familiar, almost black. Colonel Smith softly drummed the steel desk top. Bridge had always been his game, and he could feel the cards now. First bait the trap with the target's half-brother. Isolate the target, shift him into the open so that he was forced to look for assistance outside his own people. Mahoney was the natural. It was all there in the report and Mahoney was in the area. Trent, he called himself now – a name the colonel had chosen – and he lived on a fifty-foot catamaran, *Golden Girl*.

Now to decide on a lever to set the operation in motion.

The colonel fed his list of seven *poderosos* into the computer banks. Three had died, two had retired after major surgery. Both the remaining two had studied law with Castro at Havana University. He picked the elder first, Ramirez. A recent photograph showed an obese man in a rumpled grey suit, pale watery eyes almost hidden in dark pouches, skimpy beard, bald dome of his head shiny with sweat. He gripped a cigar between yellow teeth. Ash spattered his lapels and there were food stains. Ugly and decaying, he fitted Colonel Smith's scenario and the colonel was tempted to dig deeper. However, he knew the dangers of committing too soon to a given course.

Abandoning Ramirez, he switched to the younger *poderoso*, Juan Bosch. Bosch had been active early in the struggle against

Batista's dictatorship. A member of the Students' Revolutionary Directorate, he was wounded in the assault on the presidential palace on March 13, 1956.

Escaping Havana, Bosch joined Castro in the comparative safety of the sierras. A late love affair with fly fishing explained his present absence from the inner circle. A French diplomat had converted him. A photograph showed the two men wading the sheltered flats east of Cayo Largo; another showed Bosch cradling a thirty pound tarpon caught in Los Jardines de la Reina.

Fit and neat, Bosch wasn't the colonel's man. Fly fishing struck him as an unlikely pursuit for a revolutionary; too much patience was required, too great a finesse – and too little blood. Spear fishing was more suitable – Castro's favourite sport. The colonel wondered what fly Bosch had used for the tarpon.

Pillowing his head on his arms, he dozed off over memories of his trout fishing days on the River Trent.

Bergman shook him awake. The colonel took his time responding. He didn't frown or grimace but simply sat very upright and very still, his breathing shallow as he distanced himself from the pain in his chest. Bergman must recognise the signs, both from the wounded and from victims of torture.

'Shit,' Bergman said, ever the poet. 'You want a doctor?'

'I hate doctors,' the colonel snapped. 'There's nothing wrong with me. Tired, that's all.' He gathered himself, irritable as he brushed away Bergman's helping hand. 'Damn it, stop fussing, man. Get me home. And stop hovering,' he added as Bergman shepherded him to the elevator.

He sat erect and wide awake on the drive back to the Zoo. He sensed Bergman sneaking glances at him in the lights of oncoming cars. A couple of times the American tried conversation. The colonel silenced him with an exasperated tap of his fingers on the dashboard.

7

Bergman

Bergman watched the Brit fumble for the light switch in his bungalow hallway. Bergman had seen sufficient suffering to gauge the Brit's pain. Presumably heart trouble – angina. Too many cigarettes. The older man had looked like death that morning, red-eyed and sweating. Finding him slumped over the work table had increased Bergman's anxiety. Saving his career to satisfy Vorst's whim wasn't worth working the Brit to his grave. Having him die at Langley would truly stir the shit.

Bergman had tried twice on the drive back from Langley to enquire after the old man's health. Now he tried again.

'I've told you. There's nothing wrong with me.' Irritable, the Brit stomped down the corridor. 'I need a bath, that's all.'

'Yeah, well, don't die on me.'

The Brit's Filipino worked only till mid-afternoon. Bergman found half a dozen lamb chops in the icebox, fresh lettuce and tomatoes. In the cupboard above the twin sinks he discovered cans of *foie gras*, black Italian truffles, a litre bottle of extra virgin olive oil from Luca. *Foie gras* was solid cholesterol – add his Egyptian cigarettes and no wonder the Brit had a heart condition. The price of the truffles would have given Bergman a heart attack. To save money, he had cooked for himself at university and in the early years of his marriage – the only budget his wife had recognised was the rental car agency. The Brit came from the same stable, Bergman thought as he checked the wine racks. Bergman had read somewhere that red wine was good for the heart. Drawing the cork on a half-bottle of 1988 Mâcon, he set it to breathe by the stove. He washed the salad, seasoned the chops with rosemary, no salt, slid them under the grill and laid the table out on the terrace.

The Brit joined him, nodding his appreciation. He remained haggard, eyes red-rimmed and bruised. He merely played with his food, cutting the lamb into neat mouthfuls which he shunted round his plate.

'We need to take a walk,' Bergman said. Walking had been his main transport through high school and at university, saving the bus fare, and he had done a lot of marching in the army. The Agency brought him his first car. Those early days, meetings had taken place in offices or at quiet restaurants on an expense account. Now the requirement was for sufficient background noise to confuse a mike or in the open and preferably at night.

The Brit led the way through the garden gate onto the fourth fairway. The scent of freshly cut grass, wet with dew, perfumed the air. The dew would mess the polish on Bergman's leather moccasins and he had packed just the one pair. He recalled the dry, gritty dust of his New Mexico childhood and walking to church carefully so as not to mess his Sunday shoes. Other kids had to be nagged by their mothers; Bergman had worked at being tidy. Same in the army. The way he dressed now was a statement of his independence and how far he had come.

'What do you have?' he asked.

Used to the Brit's silences, he didn't push and they walked another fifty yards before the Brit replied.

'I need another day but, yes, it's possible.' The Brit lit a cigarette, perhaps so that he could see Bergman's face in the flame of his gold Ronson. 'You have to give me the background – and how badly you want Tur.'

'I want him,' Bergman said.

'Badly enough?'

It was the question Bergman had been asking himself ever since Vorst's approach. Anger had been his first reaction; not because Vorst had proposed that he act against regulations.

Regulations were alibis invented to protect the men in Washington from responsibility. Bergman did what had to be done. He could sleep most nights because he believed his actions necessary. Freelancing was different. The request had emphasised his vulnerability and, more, the lack of value others placed on his integrity and on his status as Head of Station.

He had admitted to Vorst that he was a believer. He always had been. Way back in primary school he had been teased by fellow students for standing stiffly at attention in front of the flag. He had taught himself to slouch, disguise for an out-moded sentiment others laughed at – perhaps that too was an explanation for the way he dressed.

He believed that the US had a mission to bring peace and prosperity to the world, democracy and liberty. The Brits had preached peace and prosperity in their colonies while imprisoning those who demanded freedom. Worse, Castro, in the name of freedom, had turned Cuba into a concentration camp. And Tur was Castro's servant, not a builder but a sower of chaos and violence. No valid excuse could exist for the wanton destruction of Finca Patricia. NAFAC had brought health care and education to the mountain, put money in the workers' pockets – money that if saved could give the next generation a measure of independence.

Bergman heard the Brit's breathing ragged in the quiet of the night. Impatience had made him walk the older man too fast. Halting at the edge of a shallow bunker, he said, 'You should quit smoking.'

'And prolong my life sentence?' The Brit sniffed his amusement. 'You're in trouble, Bergman. Is this about your career? Or is there more to it?'

'It's an operation,' Bergman said.

'Nonattributive.' The Brit's disbelief was obvious.

'Whatever operation, it goes wrong, it's unattributable.' That much was true.

The Brit shuffled on into the bunker and stooped to feel the sand. 'Dry,' he said. 'I need to sit, Bergman.'

They sat side by side, legs drawn up, holding their knees – like kids on a beach, Bergman thought – or lovers. The Brit had never married and there were no women reported in his biography. Nor men. Bergman wondered what he did for sex. Look at pictures and play with himself? Or was he too old – not to be interested, but to do it? Maybe having a bad heart scared him.

Bergman said, 'You shouldn't be here. It may be comfortable, but it's still a jail.'

'I was locked away because I made a mistake. That doesn't make me naive.' Though the colonel jabbed his cigarette out in the sand, he spoke calmly enough. 'You began this thing freelancing, Bergman. Now that's how it stays, so your superiors can cover themselves.'

He fumbled a fresh cigarette out of his case and flicked his lighter open. The flame leant towards Bergman in the light breeze, then came the heavily scented tobacco smoke and Bergman coughed.

'If you don't like it, sit upwind,' the Brit said. 'You walk in out of the blue and offer to get me out of prison. We both know that's nonsense. Even when you weren't in trouble, you didn't have the weight. So you either think I'm so damn bored that I'll work for nothing or you have someone behind you who does have weight. Outside of Miami no one gives a damn for Cuba, so who is it? There has to be a Guatemala connection or you wouldn't be involved.'

'Maybe you are the best,' Bergman said.

'Because I can add two and two. Nonsense. And you haven't answered. Do you want Tur badly enough?'

Bergman watched the sparks trail as the Brit flicked his cigarette away. That made five since he'd got the old man home.

Bergman had few true allies left in the Agency. With a Democrat in the White House and the newspapers hunting him, even the closest of these was nervous of offering help. Bergman had been forced to pull old debts for support in persuading Clif, one of the old guard, to allow the Brit access. It wasn't something he could waste or repeat.

Answers came easier in the dark. 'Yes,' he said. 'Badly enough.'

'Then you'd better tell me what this thing's about,' the Brit said. 'That's if you want me to get it right.'

'Right,' Bergman said – but he wasn't ready, even in the dark, and with the Brit knowing he was freelancing. It would be easier for his ex-wife. She'd been brought up with confession. Screw some man she'd picked up at a singles bar Saturday night; ask forgiveness Sunday morning before church service. Like taking a weekly bath. Getting married a second time was different; she'd be living in sin – and lose her alimony. For a moment Bergman thought that there was a similarity in there somewhere, between what his ex-wife did and what he was doing now. He tried to chase the idea and found he was mistaken. What he was about to do was what his wife refused to do. He proposed living in sin.

He said, 'Terrorists hit a coffee finca belonging to NAFAC. Tur trained their leader. NAFAC's CEO wants him destroyed.'

'You see, it's not so difficult,' the Brit said, priest to confessor. He lit a sixth cigarette. 'Tell me about the CEO. What sort of man is he?'

Bergman said, 'It's not vengeance. Vorst's not the type. He's a calculator. And agriculture, he thinks long term. Proud of what he does. Expansionist.' Bergman had done his home-work. 'NAFAC's doubled its landholding under Vorst's leader-ship and is still growing. Six per cent of commercial citrus production. That's a lot of juice.' He wondered whether the Brit had smiled. 'Tur – I think it's a sort of advertising thing,' he said. 'Look what happens to people who mess with me. It's the why I don't see. So this finca was a pet project of Vorst's but it's not the first time he's had plantations hit.'

He sat up fast thinking the Brit was choking. However, it was a chuckle bubbling deep in the Brit's throat.

'What's he promised you?' the Brit asked.

'Support.'

'And you trust him?'

Bergman pictured the scene on Vorst's jet, Vorst demonstrating power by telling his men of Bergman's vulnerability. And wiping the girl's blood from his shoe back at the finca. Vorst disliked getting dirty and Bergman was dirty. 'Give or take.'

'Not good enough,' the Brit said. 'I think we can do a little better than that.' He felt for Bergman's hand. 'Come on, man, help me up. I'm ready for bed. You'd better stay the night.'

Colonel Smith

With Bergman in the spare room, Colonel Smith closed the curtains on his bedroom windows and laid a folded towel along the bottom of the door to hide the light from his bedside lamp. Plumping the pillows, he sat upright in bed, a notebook open on his knees. His relationship with Bergman had changed out on the golf course and he assessed the CIA man as he would have one of his field men back in his days as Head of Department at MI. Bergman's deliberate slovenliness of dress and abrasive speech suggested a social insecurity typical of so many North Americans. Their lack of roots was to blame – urban gypsies, forever moving house. Despite the insecurity, the colonel suspected that the inner man differed little from the visible – a tough core surrounded by too much flab. As to Bergman's mind, sound though somewhat unimaginative, and insular – another hallmark of the North American. Thus Bergman had failed to place his knowledge of Guatemala within a broader picture, historic or geographic.

The colonel had made the jump instantly, only in part because he had studied Cuba for the past two weeks. By nature of the island's proximity, North American businessmen had always considered Cuba theirs to exploit. The US economic blockade of Cuba forbade them trade or investment in the island. Other nationalities had seized their opportunity, not for immediate profit, but to establish a base from which to expand with the inevitable end to communism.

Now the US had strengthened the trade embargo with the Helms-Burton Act; an act which threatened non-US corporations with sequestration of their US assets if they invested in Cuba and which denied corporate officers entrance to the US. Helms/Burton had its logic in the narrow demands of American politics in a presidential election year – a bribe for the Florida vote. In reality the blockade served both to strengthen foreign advantage and perpetuate Castro's rule – his last excuse for the years of incompetence that had driven a once wealthy island to ruin. Though hating and fearing foreign investment, Castro had been forced by bankruptcy into permitting Canadians to exploit Cuba's nickel deposits, Mexicans to manufacture cement, Israelis to harvest citrus – NAFAC's field.

Bergman believed that Vorst wished to advertise his power – but over what and to whom? And Bergman had no answer as to why a Cuban-trained terrorist had attacked NAFAC's finca after the declaration of a ceasefire.

The colonel wrote on his notepad: *NAFAC flights to Bahamas? Air taxi or charter flights into Cuba?*

The Bahamas, with a hundred small airstrips, was the obvious place.

And, most important, the Cuban asset, the minister: was he Bergman's or Vorst's?

Satisfied, he exchanged his notebook for *Pride & Prejudice*. Fatigue and two hours reading with outdated prescription spectacles would reinforce his ability to ape the sick man.

The colonel listened for a while to Bergman preparing breakfast. Finally he eased back the bedding and confronted himself in the bathroom mirror. Face haggard, eyes red and weepy, he decided he looked satisfyingly ghastly. Again he dosed himself with three aspirins, then laid out his clothes. An ancient tweed suit with waistcoat together with a high-collared check shirt were unmistakably British; from the tie rack he selected the stripes of the Worcestershire County Cricket Club. He ran the shower as hot as he could bear and was sweating heavily when he joined Bergman out on the terrace for breakfast. He held himself deliberately upright and nodded an abrupt greeting to the North American. The dewed fairway glittered in the morning sunlight. 'Nice day,' he said.

'You should see a doctor,' Bergman told him.

'Nonsense.' Seating himself at the table, the colonel shook out a white linen table napkin and spread it across his lap. He gave Bergman a quick smile. 'Been out of harness too long, that's the trouble. Get this thing finished with and I'll rest.'

He slid his notes across the table.

'Planes I'll check with the DEA,' Bergman said. 'They track unscheduled flights in or out of the Bahamas.'

'Go carefully,' the colonel instructed.

He buttered a slice of wholemeal toast and nibbled a corner before setting it aside. Abstinence came easily to him. He mopped his face before folding his napkin. 'Let's move. It's going to be a long day.'

Colonel Smith chose a brown felt town hat by Lock of St James's Street, the crown high and old-fashioned by American tastes. A cavalry officer's grey topcoat added to his image as did the black, oiled-silk umbrella with the monogrammed gold band on the malacca handle.

Once more closeted with the computer at Langley, he summoned Bosch, the fisherman, to the screen and wrote notes for ten minutes before switching to the target, Estoban Tur. A further five minutes and he took a quick look at Ramirez, nicknamed the Spider.

Dreadful man, the colonel thought as he looked into the pale watery eyes, no charm, no charm at all. Yet his association with Castro began at law school and remained close for forty years.

Death followed him, tales of shootings while attending the University of Havana. Three years later came flight to the USA where the FBI named him as suspect in the murder of two exiled activists in opposition to Batista. He reappeared in Mexico during Castro's residence, survivor of a car wreck in which a visiting council member of the Cuban student movement died of a broken neck. Thus the pattern formed of his complicity in an early weeding of potential competitors to Castro for the post-Batista leadership.

The colonel switched to Estoban Tur, then searched haphazardly and without goal through Cuba's external security apparatus. Finally he listed junior ministers by age.

Ten minutes and the colonel returned to Ramirez, the Spider. With victory, most of Castro's early associates reappeared from the obscurity of exile to accept key government posts. Ramirez remained a man for the shadows, lying dormant for months only to surface on some committee for which he seldom possessed any obvious qualifications. There was no solid evidence that he travelled, merely reports of sightings which coincided with robbery, muggings, an apparently accidental death. Ramirez's targets (if they were his targets) were never of the first rank. Rather they were needling critics of Castro himself: an exiled poet, an essayist, two journalists, a gay activist, an ex-minister from the early days of the revolution.

If these actions were his, then Ramirez's absence from Soviet and East European records was proof that he operated alone. His growing absence from Castro's company coincided with the Cuban President's post Cold War efforts to rebuild his image on the world stage as concerned elder statesman rather than promoter of revolution, the soldier's uniform exchanged, when on official visits abroad, for a dark suit and dark tie suitable to the company of industrialists and bankers, ecologists and pacifists.

The colonel built his picture carefully, cloaking his interest by frequent switches back to Estoban Tur, to better-known members of Cuba's intelligence service, to Bosch and, with increasing frequency, to the junior ministers, narrowing his research to Vorst's fields of Foreign Investments, Agriculture and the Prime Minister's office. However, his decision taken, he focused mentally on Ramirez, marshalling the Spider's moves even while his fingers drew other faces to the screen.

Bergman

The colonel worked in an almost chemical sterility of grey walls and steel furniture. A window lit Bergman's office. The smaller of two VDUs on the desk showed the Brit. The larger VDU duplicated the Brit's hunt. The computer logged each name brought up by the Brit, frequency and length of time. Bergman had greater faith in the Brit's capacity for disguise than he did in either the computer or the specialist who would probe later for a pattern. And he had some faith in his own intuition, if not to pick a name, then at least to sense a direction to the Brit's enquiry. The old man looked like hell but he kept at his work – scheming, Bergman thought. It wasn't a word from his usual vocabulary but it fitted the Brit.

Fieldwork demanded different qualities – above all, never to be taken by surprise. Bergman's desk faced away from the door. Almost without thought, he had slipped a folded business card into the crack so that he would hear the door open. The footsteps were silent on the carpet. Then his boss, Clif, said, 'How's it look?'

'He's going for Vorst's man,' Bergman said, knowing that the Brit was merely covering his tracks.

'Don't let this thing get away from you.'

The second voice was unknown to Bergman. Turning, he recognised, from photographs, the deputy director, slim and aerobics youthful – one of the new power élite. Bergman hadn't expected to arouse the interest of anyone this senior.

The deputy director pointed to the smaller VDU. 'I want that man out of here.'

'Colonel Smith.'

'A convicted murderer.'

'Trying to cover our collective arse,' Bergman said and saw his boss flinch. Bergman didn't give a damn.

He smelt the deputy director's disdain. That Bergman had dragged his tie down rather than take it off didn't help and that he had stayed the night at the Zoo, so hadn't changed his shirt.

'Yeah,' he said. 'My mistake. That was before your time.'

The deputy director was already at the door.

Bergman's boss, Clif, shook his head. Clif had been fat once and had bought his present suit midway through the loss period. And he had the creased face of a smoker and drinker – ex, of course. Everyone was an ex. Except for Bergman. Tobacco was about the only PC crime Bergman had avoided in his twenty years with the Agency.

'There are people trying to save your arse,' Clif said. 'You want to charge the goddamn guns, do it on your own.'

'Yeah, I screwed up,' Bergman said. He yanked his tie down an extra inch and, shoulders slumped, turned back to the screen. 'How much time do I have?'

'An hour and you're out of here and you don't bring him back.'

'Right,' Bergman said. He took a sip of cold coffee before adding, 'And thanks. . . ' Clif had already left.

'Shit,' Bergman said. Pushing his chair back from the desk, he collected his folded business card from the carpet and shoved it back into the door crack. Habit, he thought – like trying to keep hold of his job while alienating the people on whom his continued employment depended.

Colonel Smith

Suspecting that he was on screen, the colonel had been hyperventilating surreptitiously for the past half hour while amusing himself in constructing a camouflage to his research into Bosch, the fisherman. The hyperventilation reddened his face and made his hands tremble; twice he had almost blacked out. As to Bosch, a pattern would appear through the colonel's camouflage. The Agency specialists would trace Bosch's friend-ship with the French diplomat who had taught him the art of fly fishing. The North Americans would suspect the fishing as a cover for some fresh French duplicity. From thence mutual loathing between French and North Americans would hold the ground. Meanwhile Ramirez would remain safely beyond American concern. It was a sweet scheme; the colonel was delighted with himself.

Bergman came for him. The hyperventilation had succeeded and the colonel had no need to act. He almost fell as he rose from his chair and had to grab Bergman's arm to steady himself.

'You look like a goddamn tomato,' Bergman said.

'Somewhat more attractive than a lettuce – that's positive thinking,' the colonel said with a tired smile for Bergman. 'Heart's a bit thumpy. I'm finished here. Get me home.'

Bergman attempted to help him up.

The colonel brushed the younger man aside. 'Not dead yet.'

However, his overcoat was beyond his strength and he permitted Bergman to feed his arms into the sleeves and fasten the buttons. Seeing himself in the mirror, he was a little shaken by his looks. Bergman was right. 'Dried tomato,' he said with another smile. 'You're going to have to help me to the car.'

A small crowd at the exit to the parking lot waited to board a coach from which passengers were alighting; clerk material – with Langley operating a twenty-four-hour day, probably a change of shift.

And all the world's a stage, the colonel thought as Bergman nosed the Ford out to pass the coach. Clutching his heart, the colonel gasped and buckled forward into Bergman's lap.

Bergman

Bergman nearly lost control of the car as the Brit collapsed. Next second the old man was flung shuddering back over the rear of his seat as if hit by an electric shock. Spittle sprayed from his lips as he fought for breath.

Bergman heard himself curse as he rammed the brake peddle. He flung the door open and dragged the Brit out by the shoulders. Mouth to mouth, he blew air into the old man while attempting to get his tie undone. No way could he feel the old man's heart through the overcoat and the tweed jacket and waistcoat. Shit, he thought. Shit! Here of all places. Goddamn Langley. Then he was actually praying. Please God, pull the old man through. Feet were all round him, the usual crowd at an accident. He lifted his head long enough to yell for someone to fetch a medic and call an ambulance: 'Rush it, for Christ's sake.' Then he was back to his kiss-of-life routine. The old man's spittle didn't help and Bergman paused long enough to wipe his own lips on the back of his sleeve. A fresh convulsion bowed the Brit's spine.

An ambulance screeched panic to Bergman's right. Tyres screeched and Bergman knelt back on his heels. Close on a hundred people had collected, the whole goddamn crowd craning to see the Brit.

Craning to see the Brit!

The Brit in his Brit overcoat and in his Brit suit, his Brit tie and his Brit shoes. His Brit hat spilled beside him. He had even managed to keep hold on his goddamn Brit umbrella.

Shit, Bergman thought in sudden understanding.

The crowd split to let the medics through with a stretcher and oxygen. They had the mask on the Brit, lifting him onto the stretcher where he was even more visible. They ran him into the ambulance, the tilt as they lifted the stretcher perfect for visibility. The medics' hands occupied, the Brit waved an arm as if entering a fresh convulsion and managed to shove the mask from his face. There he lay, head lolling over, so the crowd could catch his perfect Brit profile.

Bergman heard a woman gasp as he said, 'Screw you, you goddamn crafty, scheming son of a bitch. Hold it,' he yelled to the medics, waving his pass as he bulled his way through the onlookers. 'The old man's with me.'

8

Colonel Smith

The colonel had punished himself physically over the past few days. Now he was near to his goal and he lay flat on his back in the hospital bed, husbanding his strength. The slim young doctor over by the door looked Hispanic; he had been running tests on the colonel's heart for the past hour. The new arrival, also in a white coat, faced away from the colonel's bed. In his early fifties, his crew-cut had thinned at the crown and had faded from sun blond to near white; years on the golf course had burnt the back of his neck a permanent red. He used a lot of body language as he talked softly to his companion, courting the young doctor. The charm worked and he fed the Latin out through the door with a final knead of the shoulders. Turning to the colonel, he wore the embarrassed smile of a youth barely out of his teens.

A very North American performance, the colonel thought. 'I was wondering when you'd turn up.'

They had met first in the late Sixties. British liaison with Langley, the colonel had been searching for someone with whom he could build a long-term relationship beneficial both to his department and to his own career. Glen had been new to Washington, aid to a freshly elected president. Though young, Glen had been experienced in defending his patron's interests at state level, a talent he had brought to the capital. Colonel Smith had persuaded him of the dangers in unqualified political allegiance and had guided him sideways into the intelligence community. Under the colonel's tutelage Glen had become expert. They had been close associates almost until the colonel's downfall. They had co-authored operations and shared information with a degree of honesty at times considered unreasonable by their respective superiors. Counterterrorism was their field and they had specialised in extraction. Young Mahoney had been their executioner.

Glen had foreseen the swing in political mood that came with the end of the Cold War and had moved sideways again, first to a foreign affairs think-tank, then back into government as non-partisan adviser on terrorism to the current president. Glen's present embarrassment grew from the change in their respective fortunes; the colonel knew the embarrassment was as fake as his own heart attack.

Perhaps guessing the colonel's thoughts, the American said, 'Yeah,' and slumped down in the upright chair beside the bed. He didn't bother asking after the colonel's health. 'We need to discuss this Bergman thing of yours.'

'Political connotations?'

'You know how it is.' The puppy dog squirm and the smile were automatic.

'Then try acting like a grown man,' the colonel said.

The North American exchanged the smile for a soft chuckle. 'Times you can be a real son of a bitch.' He laid a hand on the Englishman's knee, squeezing gently. 'Give me the background – as you see it.'

In other words, without the partisan political advantages and disadvantages which were again central to the American and had always been foreign to the colonel. Right or wrong, he had always believed in what he did. As did Bergman, he thought; that much they had in common.

'Vorst has been in and out of Cuba a dozen times in the past year,' he began. Not a man to waste time, Vorst was obviously negotiating a major investment. The pragmatists in the Cuban government would be delighted – not so the old guard, the *barbudo*s. NAFAC was everything they hated.

'First we have the attack on the finca, Glen. That was post

ceasefire and led by a terrorist trained in Cuba and controlled by Cuba. Authorisation for the attack must have come from the top or very near the top.'

The North American nodded. 'That's our supposition.'

'The attack is enough to make Vorst's board very nervous,' the colonel continued. To keep his deal alive, Vorst required hard evidence of Cuban commitment. 'He expects the young minister he's been negotiating with to give him Tur.'

A very typically North American mistake, the colonel thought. Vorst believed the near collapse of the Cuban economy gave him power. Most countries, it would. Cuba was different. The *barbudo*s were in their sixties and seventies. 'They don't give a damn for the future, Glen. They care about now and holding on to power for their last few years.'

Major investment risked a shift of power and influence to the new boys – the technocrats in finance. 'Glen, the *barbudo*s won't permit it. Nor will Castro. They'll negotiate, sign letters of intent, maybe even sign an agreement – but it won't happen.'

'You're saying Vorst's been wasting his time.'

'You've read the records.'

Again the American nodded. The pretence at youth and affability had vanished. This was business. 'And you?'

The colonel smiled wearily. 'At least a hundred people saw me in the car park. Enough of them will gossip. Half a dozen will check the files for an Englishman my age. A week and the rumour will be circulating that I've been working with your people all this time. I'd like you to feed that for me, Glen.'

'If the operation works.'

'It will do more than work,' the colonel said.

'Works the way we want. Our hands stay clean. Same for the Agency,' the American said, no charm at all as he counted the points off on fingers blunt with muscle built on the golf course – in company with the president and losing or winning by exactly the right margin to please. 'Till you hear different, this is Bergman's private war. Bergman freelancing for Vorst.'

The rules of engagement rather than the agenda – and even there Glen was lying. Bergman was small fish. A senior official at the Agency had authorised the colonel's access to the computers. No doubt one more of the Cold War survivors readied for sacrifice, the colonel thought, the bitterness suddenly strong. He saw little difference between the Cuban *barbudo*s and US politicians: primary interest, power; primary preoccupation, destruction of the competition. The colonel had based his planning on the American's requirements.

He said, 'Castro is an all powerful and jealous king. I have a *barbudo* who has been losing access to the royal court. We give him a way back in: the CIA capturing Tur with Vorst pulling the strings. It's everything Castro loves. He has his excuse to stop the NAFAC investment. He can make one of his six-hour television tirades against the US and the CIA.'

'Castro would sacrifice Tur?'

Colonel Smith let his anger surface. 'Sacrifice! The whole damn island is a sacrifice. Doctors earning twenty dollars a month, labourers ten dollars. A ration card that is pure fiction because there's nothing in the shops. Christ, Glen, the last clothing ration card was issued three years ago and everyone still has the coupons. You think Castro and his friends give a damn for Tur? Tur doesn't belong. He's new generation, his mother is black.

'Add a Miami Cuban connection to the plot and Castro will invite my *barbudo* into his bed. Add something he can pin on Senator Helms or Burton and Castro will take his false teeth out and give oral sex better than your president ever has.'

Senator Helms of the Helms/Burton Act, right-wing scourge of the president, his election campaign financed by Miami Cubans. The boy smile flashed, the instant charm. 'I like it.'

'Yes,' the colonel said. 'I thought you might. Payment for feeding the rumour mill.'

Glen gave him a quick nod from the door and one more smile. No doubt he would exercise his charm on the doctor for a few minutes out in the corridor.

Bergman

No one had bothered with Bergman in the two hours he had waited in the hospital cardiac unit. Visiting the rest room for the third time, he examined his face in the mirror. A shave and fresh clothes would have helped. A lost dog, he thought Washington did it. He was out of place.

An early-thirties Latin American Valentino in a white doctor's coat pushed through the swing doors. 'Mister Bergman?'

'Right,' Bergman said.

'Hernandez. I'm sorry you were kept.' The doctor rested his shoulders against the wall. He looked as if he had had a tough day.

First-generation US, Bergman guessed; and upmarket California by his accent, followed by a good medical school – probably Harvard. Hispanics preferred Harvard. Everyone knew of it while Yale or Princeton or Stanford didn't carry so much fame south of the border.

'I've been running tests on your man,' Hernandez said. 'The exhaustion's real and his heartbeat was running high when he came in. That's steadied down and there's no clinical damage that I can find. We'll keep him in overnight and I'll run fresh tests in the morning.'

'I need to stay with him,' Bergman said.

'That's what they said.' *They* were the Agency. Someone must have reported to Bergman's boss who had someone telephone the hospital.

The Brit lay on his back with his eyes closed. His colour was less red and he seemed to be breathing normally. Cables connected him to two monitors which Hernandez checked before reading the chart hanging at the foot of the bed. The doctor hadn't been out of the room for long so not much could have changed.

Turning to Bergman, he said, 'We've given him medication to help him sleep.' He looked round the room for something else to say. 'I've asked for an easy chair. There's a cafeteria on the lower ground floor.'

'Thanks,' Bergman said.

'That's if you can leave the room. Otherwise ask the nurse.'

'I'll do that,' Bergman said.

'Right.' Hernandez gripped the door handle and he didn't look at Bergman. 'You're that Bergman?'

So it *had* been bothering him.

'I suppose,' Bergman said. He didn't think it necessarily personal that Hernandez didn't offer to shake hands. A doctor, he was probably good with patients' families – perhaps Bergman's relationship to the Brit confused him.

A porter brought the chair and Bergman sat watching the colonel sleep. The Brit had tricked Bergman in the car park by advertising himself. Even in childhood, Bergman had tried to hide who he was – the son of a trailer-home drunk.

Bergman had read novels and biographies in which the protagonists were epic in their excess and dissolution. There had been nothing epic in Bergman's father. Nor even pathos. Never violent or maudlin, he was simply sodden with alcohol, topping himself up with small sips from a plastic cup, then sleeping – by day, either on an old car seat propped out back against the wall of the trailer, or in a broken seated easy chair in front of the television; by night he transferred to the pull-down double bed which he shared, immobile, with Bergman's mother. His character was insufficient to generate affection or dislike or even sympathy. He had existed, that was all. Even his snores were minor.

Bergman remained incredulous as to the miracle of energy or even, perhaps, of love that had created him. His mother's dependence on a need to love had bewildered him. He had competed with sick cats, dogs, injured birds; mostly they died and his mother's incompetence had made Bergman weep for her. And that she envisioned nothing better – even in her imagination. She simply accepted. Humble, he thought, humble as were the Guatemalan Indians who even named themselves *Los humildes*.

A nurse put her head round the door and Bergman asked how he could order a sandwich. He had no expectations of his boss sending a relief. The Brit's visibility had endangered careers. Where possible, those involved in Bergman's operation would cut themselves loose or be rehearsing cover for their involvement.

Glen

Glen, adviser on terrorism and golf partner to the president, chose the seclusion of his Cherokee jeep for a meeting with Bergman's departmental chief. Light rain had fallen for the past hour. Yellow street lamps dropped splashes of reflection on the road. Glen played How's-old-so-and-so for a while, the emphasis on those of Clif's close associates dropped by the Agency with the end of the Cold War.

'Glad you stayed in, Clif,' he finished and made the transition.

'This Bergman thing came up. The way it came to us, it had your name on it, Clif. No panic,' Glen added smoothly. 'In fact this could be good, Clif. There's interest there. You know?' He wrapped his fingers round an imaginary golf club and smiled a little ruefully. 'Missed a real easy put on the fifteenth – fifty bucks. But, yeah, a definite interest. Maybe it needs a little pressure for approval, Clif. There's this idea that the senator's your best route – though don't go direct. You've had dealings with the Miami Cuban leadership. Maybe you should call that fat son of a bitch. Tell him you've got something that will really hurt Castro. Tell him you need a little help on the political side to get the OK. You can handle that?'

'Yes,' Clif said.

Glen couldn't sense what Clif felt and he didn't give a shit.

Bergman

Bergman slept in the easy chair in the colonel's hospital room. He woke at three in the morning, cold from the air conditioning. He fetched the Brit's overcoat from a hanger in the wardrobe and used it as a blanket. Even warm, he couldn't return to sleep.

'Bergman?'

The Brit hadn't stirred but his eyes opened, searching.

'Here,' Bergman said. Crossing to the bed, he filled a glass with water and held it while the Brit forced himself up against the pillows.

The Brit sipped and handed back the glass. 'Thank you.'

Tall, upright and always immaculately dressed, the Brit had verged on the impressive. Now sleep had creased his left cheek; the loose skin beneath his chin drooped sideways; patches of flaky scalp showed between thin dry wisps of unbrushed hair.

'Yesterday – great performance,' Bergman said.

A small dry smile appeared briefly amongst the white stubble. 'Insurance – for both of us, Bergman.'

'Yeah, pure friendship. That's what I thought.'

Bergman wondered whether they were bugged. He patted his pockets for a cheap ballpoint and passed the Brit his notebook.

Vorst, the Brit wrote: *His poderoso must tell Ramirez the Spider, you are working on a plot to kidnap Tur. That you are searching for a method of using Tur's younger brother as bait.*

The instruction seemed nonsense. The Brit looked so frail and abandoned.

'Believe me,' the Brit whispered. He wrote again, pressing the ballpoint hard on the paper: *Remember, Bergman. You picked me because I'm a crafty son of a bitch. Get the message to Ramirez and you will get your bait. Set the bait and you have Tur. He will get out of Cuba by yacht.*

'Believe me,' he repeated. 'Believe me, I feel like hell. The pain yesterday. God . . . ' Then a little smile, both mischievous and self-congratulatory. 'You saved my life, Bergman.'

Or returned the Brit to his old life? That was it, of course.

Bergman, trapped within the web of the Brit's deviousness, said, 'Screw you.'

'A splendidly adult comment,' the Brit said. He wrote again: *Stop worrying, Bergman. The doctors will find something wrong with me simply to cover themselves in case I die. Tur will probably use Roddy de Sanchez, Cuban Naval Intelligence, to arrange the pick-up. Tur may need help getting to the beach. That's your department. Work for your living.*

Bergman tore the sheet neatly from his notebook. He ripped the sheet into small pieces, rolled each fragment into a pellet and swallowed them. It was the one quality he knew he possessed, being careful.

The night nurse checked the old man at four a.m., bringing a cup of hot, clear soup for Bergman. She was back at six a.m. to bathe the Brit. Bergman visited the rest room. A blue-suit junior genius from Langley found him waiting in the corridor. The suit carried a summons for Bergman to meet his departmental chief down in the car park.

Bergman's boss beckoned him from the rear seat of an Agency Buick parked alongside a black limo with senatorial plates.

Clif wrinkled his nose as Bergman slid in beside him.

'You stink, Bergman. Everything you touch stinks.' He dug into his jacket pocket for a pack of Camels, then cursed as he remembered that he hadn't smoked in three years.

He turned the radio on, fiddling with the search button until he found a talk programme that would cover their conversation. 'I've spent the night trying to save your arse. We need outside support for this thing of yours. You've got breakfast with the senator,' he said, jabbing a thumb at the limo. 'He considers Cuba his territory. You have half an hour to persuade him, so act like the type of agent he admires. Strong, silent and way to the right of Attila the goddamn Hun.'

'Silent, Clif, it's difficult to persuade,' Bergman said. He was getting on as well as he ever would with Clif now that Clif was his boss and nervous. 'I'll be a real good boy with the senator.'

*

A pale-skinned Puerto Rican manservant let Bergman into the senator's Georgetown town house and led him down a short corridor to a breakfast room scented with fresh coffee and layers of beeswax furniture polish.

Clif hadn't prepared Bergman for the Cuban American seated beside the senator at the round breakfast table. Fifteen years younger than the senator and running to flab, the Cuban American led the most extreme of the Miami anti-Castro groups. The senator was in his seventies; thin and bald, age had melted the flesh off his skull. Both men wore blue suits with pressed creases that would have pleased a drill sergeant and crisp shirts that were so white Bergman was frightened for his eyes. They were munching health cereal and the jug of orange juice was bigger than the silver coffee pot. A platoon of pill boxes paraded in front of the senator – vitamins, heart and ginseng, Bergman guessed. Neither man rose to greet him.

The senator glared over the top of half-spectacles and pointed to the chair opposite his. The linen table mat was laid with a clean coffee cup.

The senator switched attention from his cereal to a plate of oatmeal and raisin crackers; perhaps he kept horses down in the south. He tapped a cracker on his plate and a raisin fell loose.

'Bergman,' he said as if the fallen raisin was the CIA man's fault. 'We've heard about you in committee – and I've read about you. Your departmental chief tells me you can produce Cuba's head of G2. Is that correct?'

'Yes, Senator,' Bergman said.

'What's my guarantee?'

'My record, Senator.'

'That's what we've been taking evidence on in committee.' The senator tapped the cracker again and turned it over a couple of times, studying it the while as if he didn't much like what he saw. There were fewer raisins in the cracker than liver spots on the backs of his hands. The skin bagged at his knuckles and his eyes were pale and watering at the inside corners. Bergman watched him nibble at a corner of the cracker. Perhaps his teeth hurt or didn't fit.

'Bergman,' the senator repeated with as much enthusiasm as he gave the cracker. 'You and your record have damaged the Agency and its friends.' He laid the cracker aside and turned to his companion. Bergman had watched him rant on TV. Now the senator's voice was as dry as the oatmeal and equally expressionless. 'I've told you. A majority of the committee want Bergman's head. That's fact. Vote today and he'd face a Grand Jury.'

So Bergman had the Cuban to thank for getting a hearing. The Cuban's flab shook as he spread his hands. 'What do we lose?'

Me, Bergman thought. The indignity of his position infuriated him. He felt the blood mount hot in his cheeks. Strong and silent hadn't earned him a cup of coffee let alone the fried eggs and bacon he longed for. He had slept in a chair, hadn't changed his clothes in two days and hadn't bathed since the previous morning; the elastic holding his ankle holster itched.

'With your permission, Senator,' he said and slipped the police special from the holster, laying it on the mat beside the clean coffee cup.

He ignored the Cuban.

'Eight years back I got offered promotion for what the Guatemalan counterinsurgency units have been doing. It's what we trained them for in Fort Bragg and at the jungle school in Honduras and at the School of the Americas. We trained them to fight communism, Senator. They've forced the terrorists to the negotiating table and had them sign a peace treaty which gives the guerrillas nothing. That's what I was sent down to Guatemala to organise. I did it and I'm proud that I did it. I'm proud to have served the Agency and I'm proud to have served my country. That's my record, Senator.'

Nothing had surprised the senator in years. He leant back in his chair, fingertips on the table edge. 'You believe that stuff?'

'I do, sir,' Bergman said.

'Yes, I believe you do, Bergman.' The senator returned his

attention to the Cuban American. 'Maybe you were right. Let's have it again – exactly what can Tur tell us?'

'He's been behind every terrorist group in Latin America the past ten years,' the Cuban said. In his anxiety to persuade, he leant towards the senator, cheeks pink with the hate he lived off. 'We want Tur's confession. Have it on CNN worldwide. That way, we destroy the new image Fidel is building.' Excitement shook the Cuban American's jowls and he spread his hands as if offering Tur on a silver platter – paid for with dollars he bullied out of his followers in Miami and to be delivered by Bergman. 'This is our opportunity, Senator. We destroy Fidel. All that goddamn holier-than-thou crap with the damn fool pope.'

The senator took off his glasses, folded them neatly and laid them on the table beside his pill boxes. Bergman watched the old man dab the moisture from the corner of his eyes on a white handkerchief, then turn to stare blindly out through the lone window that gave onto a small walled garden . . . a modern-day washing of his hands, Bergman thought. A peach tree grew against the south wall, its branches trained flat against the faded red brick . . . crucified.

'We don't want Tur up here and we don't want the Agency involved. That means you keep your distance, Bergman,' the senator warned. 'Your Guatemalans do this. The Cubans will accuse us of faking any speech recording so get it on video and make certain the words sync with his lips. You screw up, it's your arse,' he said, his dry voice harsh suddenly as a hack saw.

'Yes, sir,' Bergman said. He didn't give a damn for the Cuban American but the senator was government – Bergman's government. He wanted the senator to look at him. A thrush hopped across the patch of trim lawn below the peach tree. He said, 'If that's an order, Senator, I'll need to hear it from my superior.'

The senator reached for his spectacles. Bergman watched him thread the sprung gold wire back behind his ears. The pale eyes were hard behind the lenses and anger drew a white line down the narrow bridge of the senator's nose. 'Get out.'

'Yes, sir.'

Bergman slipped his pistol back into its holster and rose clumsily from the table. He imagined the impression he made as he walked to the door, cheap suit crumpled and two days of grime and sweat ringing his shirt collar. He fought with himself a moment as he opened the door to the corridor. Surrendering, he said, 'And thanks for the coffee, Senator.'

The deputy director drew a fresh sheet of paper from a drawer and slipped a black Mont Blanc pen from his inside pocket. 'This thing of yours, Bergman – it's going to work?'

Bergman had sought approval for operations from a succession of political appointee ambassadors to Guatemala. Each one of them had asked the selfsame question. Professionals knew better. He said, 'Yeah, maybe,' which was as close as he could get.

Clif nodded at him to continue.

'Well, these things aren't certain,' Bergman said. 'You set them up the best you can. Then you wait. They happen or they don't. The Brit came up with the concept and he's good – very good. We use Tur's brother as bait. That's through Vorst's man – the minister.'

The Mont Blanc nib ticked silently over the paper . . . rows of crosses, Bergman guessed, an excuse for the deputy director to avoid eye contact.

'Look,' Bergman said, 'This started out a thing Vorst wanted me to do. I wasn't comfortable. I brought it to Clif here and said I could maybe do it so it didn't look like the Agency was involved. That's how it could have stayed except the Brit had a heart attack out in the parking lot. Now we've got Miami involved and the senator, which is like broadcasting over Voice of America.

'You tell me, Do it, I do it. If I was looking to cover myself, I'd have been up here in Washington months back trying to save my butt. I want to know where you all stand, that's all. I thought I knew where I stood down in Guatemala. I don't want you defending me. That's not how it happens. But I want to be certain in my own mind.'

Tickety tickety tick went the deputy director's pen – an entire line and down onto the next. 'Of what exactly?'

'That you want this done.'

'Me?' The deputy director's smile was thinner than the nib on his Mont Blanc.

'The Agency.'

'Yes,' the deputy director said – though in agreement with the correction rather than to the Tur operation. 'This isn't personal, Bergman. None of it.'

Bergman thought of saying that having his name in the newspapers made it very goddamn personal. And having to do whatever it took to make the Tur operation work – getting his hands dirty. And knowing that he was out if it went wrong. And maybe out anyway. The deputy director was Bob to Bergman's boss. Not to Bergman; and Bergman was damned if he'd call the son of a bitch 'Sir'. Maybe breaking the man's pen would make him look up. Or grabbing him by the hair and jerking him forward across his desk – yeah, jamming the pen up his arse. That would gain some attention.

Clif must have sensed him ready to explode. He said, 'I think what Bob's saying, Bergman, is that we'd like this thing to happen.'

Tick, went the deputy director, all concentration. Tickety tick.

Bergman said, 'If it works, I want the Brit loose.' He looked across from the deputy director to Clif, waiting.

'That seems fair,' Clif said.

Bergman knew that was as much as he would get. He turned to leave. However, he couldn't leave it alone. 'You could nod,' he said to the deputy director. 'That doesn't commit you to shit.'

Bergman called Vorst from a phone booth. He had to run the gauntlet of secretaries and personal assistants. Operational, and he kept his cool. Down in Guatemala he dealt with generals who ordered death the way Vorst ordered orange juice. It was essential to shift such men out of their environment.

He said, 'We need to meet, Mister Vorst. Give me a time. I'll pick you up outside your office building.'

'Why don't you come here?' Vorst suggested. 'Eight o'clock this evening?'

'That's not a good idea, Mister Vorst. Remember, with the press, I'm flavour of the month.' Bergman waited into the silence. Five seconds at most before the answer came, devoid of question.

'Tomorrow. Five in the afternoon.'

Bergman flew the shuttle to New York early morning and spent two hours playing the subway and the big stores with multiple exits. Certain he had shed any surveillance, he spent the early afternoon in a movie house. Four thirty and he let half a dozen cabs pass before hailing a late-middle-aged black driver in a clean white shirt. He had the driver drop him on 8th Street midway between 3rd and 5th. He said, 'I want you to wait here. Thirty minutes.' He slid a hundred-dollar bill from his pocket. 'I need a receipt. Write it while you're waiting.'

The driver looked down at Bergman's shoes, then raised his inspection all the way up to Bergman's haircut. Then he grinned and said, 'For the hundred, officer, or you want me to pad it?'

'A hundred's fine,' Bergman said. 'What I'd like is for you to circle the block so you're parked facing north.'

Bergman walked down to 3rd before hailing a second cab and directing the driver to the NAFAC building. Vorst appeared on the pavement right on time.

'Drive south down Eighth Street,' Bergman told the driver. 'Between Third and Fifth.' He gave the driver twenty dollars. 'No change.' And to Vorst, 'We're going to switch cabs, Mister Vorst.'

Vorst was used to being in control and Bergman sensed his uncertainty. 'Being careful is the name of the game. That's for both of us, Mister Vorst. No offence,' he said and tapped Vorst down beneath his jacket for a wire.

'Here,' he told the driver. 'Move,' he said, and hustled Vorst across the road into the first cab. 'Central Park.'

They walked through trees to an open swathe where four kids were flying kites, two black, two white. 'I've had a boy do that for me as an aerial,' Bergman said as he led Vorst out into the centre of the grass. 'Let's sit.'

Vorst hesitated but Bergman had control now and slumped down on the grass, head propped on his left hand, his lips sheltered. He wriggled his right leg so that his pants rode up enough for Vorst to spot the bottom of his ankle holster. All part of the image, solid spy stuff – and this was where spies met in the movies: out in the open or in dimly lit underground car parks.

Vorst sat stiff as a garden statue. Bergman was enjoying himself for the first time in weeks.

He waited while a middle-aged couple passed arm in arm. Then he said, 'Freelancing is against the law, Mister Vorst. That's what you asked me to do. Make a mistake and we're both in trouble. This is the one time we meet until this thing's done, so there's things we have to get straight.'

'Things?' Self-mockery was evident in Vorst's smile and in his dry tone of voice.

A lot of class, Bergman thought. 'Yeah,' he said. 'It's a word we use, Mister Vorst.'

'And this thing is something you can do.'

Bergman chuckled. 'Given your Cuban's co-operation, yeah, that's what I'm told,' he said. 'I brought a planner in, one of the best.'

Vorst was watching one of the boys flight his kite over the trees. Perhaps he had a childhood memory that helped him relax.

Bergman said, 'Mister Vorst, we know how many times you've been in and out of Cuba in the past year and how long you stayed.'

Shutters opened on Vorst's eyes. Blue, they had been human. Now Bergman looked into a below-zero vacuum.

He said, 'This isn't a fight, Mister Vorst. I'm telling you so you know that we know and that we've studied this thing from all the angles. That includes how much real pull you have with your man. A minister, right? Finance? Foreign investment?'

The freezer hadn't warmed. No feelings to distract Vorst from absolute concentration

Bergman said, 'We don't have any faith in your man stepping out of line, Mister Vorst, taking risks. He has to believe himself safe and that means being able to argue he's acting loyal to Cuba.'

Vorst didn't even nod. Bergman felt himself trapped by Vorst sucking at him. A goddamn vampire. No blood left in the victim, spit out the envelope, dry skin in a downmarket seersucker suit. Real bad self-image, Bergman thought. He had to get back in the driving seat.

'We have a mass of information that you don't have, Mister Vorst,' he said. 'What we want is for you to tell this minister there's an okay on a CIA operation to capture Tur – that we're working on a plan to get Tur's half-brother into Guatemala as bait. He knows you want Tur so he knows you're involved. He's going to be wondering why you're telling him this. You tell him it's something you'd like to get to the right ears – earn points to foster whatever it is that you're not doing in Cuba; that you hear a man called Ramirez could use the information. Ramirez, they call him the Spider. He's one of the old guard, a real piece of work – not likely to be loved by your man.'

Vorst waited. Suck, suck, suck – like getting head, Bergman thought. That was better self-image. 'Your man is going to calculate that if anything goes wrong, Ramirez is the one to get hurt. He won't give a shit.'

'That's it?'

'That's it,' Bergman said. 'We think it will play. The logic's right. Talk with your man, then we wait. These things aren't easy, Mister Vorst. Things go right and everyone's happy. They go wrong or don't work the way we thought, at least you stay clean in Cuba and that's important to you, Mister Vorst, or you wouldn't be flying in and out.'

More ice.

Bergman stood up. His trouser cuff caught on the Police Special and he kicked his leg out.

Vorst was brushing the dust and grass off his clothes.

'I'm sorry about your suit,' Bergman said.

'It will clean.'

'Yeah, I guess.' Bergman looked down at his own hands. Blunt fingers. Nails trimmed short. Clean despite all the things he'd done. He knew that he ought to keep his mouth shut.

He said, 'Mister Vorst, what you are doing here is ordering a hit.'

He had a feeling that there was contempt down there amongst the ice.

'Do it,' Vorst said. He turned and walked away across the grass and up into the trees.

Bergman sat back down and watched the boys with their kites. Faces tilted back and open to the evening sun, their teeth shone Colgate white. In Guatemala, Indian kids had mouths full of decay. Yeah, a real stinking hit, that was what this thing was about. Vorst in his goddamn suit. Rush hour, maybe Vorst wouldn't find a cab. Maybe it would rain. Maybe Vorst would get mugged.

9

Bergman

Most countries seek embassies that will impress with their elegance and sophistication. Defence allied to a show of brute force are the prime requisites of the United States of America. The US Embassy in Guatemala City is an oblong concrete bludgeon facing Avenida de la Reforma in Zone 10. Each morning, a Guatemalan immigration officer at the airport delivered the list of the previous day's arrivals and departures to Bogonovich at DEA. Bogonovich had his secretary take a photocopy of the list to Bergman's office. The only Cuban in the past two weeks had been a junior consular official in transit from Mexico to El Salvador, almost certainly a spook. Now, this Wednesday, came notice that seventeen members of the Andaluz Ballet of Havana had flown in on the previous evening's Lacsa flight from San José, Costa Rica.

Bergman ran a stubby finger down the names. One from last came Miguel Tur Costa. Born Havana, February 10, 1970. Position: Public relations officer.

Son of a bitch! The Brit had got it right.

Bait.

For Estoban Tur.

The feel of victory came first. Bergman leant back in his executive chair, hands folded behind his head. Oh ye of little faith!

Because he hadn't believed, Bergman hadn't fully pictured

the next step. Now he had to move fast and with great care and he wanted the minimum of people involved.

Snatching Little Brother, though easy, was only a preliminary. If Tur responded, his only exit from Cuba would be by yacht. The Brit had named Roddy de Sanchez of Cuba's Naval Intelligence as Tur's probable contact man. Tur's route to Guatemala would be down the Caribbean coast of Mexico and Belize, or directly to Guatemala's own short coastline on the Gulf of Honduras.

To head the operation, Bergman had decided on the major who had brought the near-dead *guerrillero* to the car wash in the back of the truck. In command of counterinsurgency units operating on the Caribbean coast, the major fitted the job description. He didn't give a shit for the peace signed with the *guerrilleros*, nor for regulations. He had proven his ruthlessness at San Cristóbal and remained young enough to enjoy the risk. He was in the right place, he had the manpower, he was sufficiently senior in rank to give the orders while sufficiently junior to be tempted by expectations of promotion.

Bergman called the major from a phone booth out on the street, not at the barracks but at home. Rather than give his name, Bergman told the Indian maid that he was a friend of the major's down visiting from Fort Bragg.

Had Bergman been Guatemalan the maid would have protected her employer's security. That Bergman was a gringo gave her enough confidence to report that she didn't expect the major back in the capital before the weekend.

Ever conscious of his own security, Bergman changed servants and moved house every few months. This quarter a duplex in a secure compound in Zone 10 passed for home while his elderly maid came from a mountain village above Quetzaltenango; Bergman doubted whether she knew what an embassy was.

He showered, shaved and packed an overnight bag. Dressed in his best suit and tie, he drove over to the tourist office in Zone 4. The young woman at the counter was patently surprised at his interest in Spanish ballet – perhaps he was wearing the wrong suit – however, yes, the Andaluz Ballet of Havana would perform in Guatemala's ancient capital, Antigua, on the two nights of the following weekend. Performances were scheduled for eight in the evening in the ruins of the hermitage of La Santa Cruz.

Too easily remembered, Bergman's Toyota was an unwise choice for the drive down to the major's province and Bergman left it to have a new exhaust fitted at a back street garage. He chose a small Guatemalan rental agency rather than one of the multinationals and picked a Mitsubishi Lancer with dark windows. Bergman paid cash, knowing that the transaction would never be recorded. Half an hour's tracking and backtracking through city traffic convinced him that nobody was on his tail. Only then did he head east along calle Marti and out onto the carretera Atlantico.

The highway twisted down 1500 metres in altitude through dry rugged mountains. Sections of the highway were being widened from two lane to three and Bergman was content to dawdle behind the resulting lines of heavy trucks bound for Puerto Barrios, Guatemala's sole commercial port on the Caribbean coast. Bergman had left the capital at 16:30. The 135 kilometres to the halfway point at Rio Hondo took him two hours and ten minutes.

Bergman turned south at Río Hondo towards the three-way border with Honduras and El Salvador. A further thirty-five kilometres brought him to Chiquimula, a typical dirt-street market town, the houses built low so they wouldn't have far to fall in the next earthquake. The banks remained open late for the convenience of cross border traffic. Wanting to be remembered here, Bergman cashed a cheque at the Banco de Café and ate dinner on the streetfront terrace at the Restaurant Las Vegas. The border with Honduras had closed at six p.m. and he had no apparent reason to hurry.

Halting at a Texaco service station on the outskirts of Chiquimula, he had the oil, water and tire pressures checked and the petrol tank topped up. He drove on a further two kilometres, made a U-turn and headed straight back to Río

Hondo where he turned east again down the carretera Atlantico towards the coast.

Bergman drove fast now. An hour brought him to the woman's car wash. The interior of the *rancho* was visible from the road. Bergman had worried that the major's soldiers might use the car wash as a regular haunt; he was relieved to see that there were no military amongst the custom.

Another ten minutes brought him to the main entrance to NAFAC's plantations; a further fifteen minutes and he turned left off the carretera Atlantico towards the Petén, largest and least developed of Guatemala's provinces. A further thirty kilometres and he was in sight of the Río Dulce.

The Río Dulce and Lake Izabal isolate the Petén from the rest of the country. Lake Izabal stretches west-south-west for some thirty-five kilometres and averages fifteen kilometres north to south.

Flowing out of Lake Izabal at Fronteras, the Río Dulce soon widens into a further lake known as El Golfete some fifteen kilometres long by four wide. Below El Golfete the river has cut a narrow canyon through the foothills of the montañas del Mico to the small port of Lívingston on the Gulf of Honduras.

No roads follow the Río Dulce and no coastal roads run out of Lívingston. The high concrete bridge spanning the river at Fronteras offers the sole road access into the Petén and so on to Belize and through to the Yucatán Province of Mexico.

Kidnapping is Guatemala's major growth industry. Speed of escape and multiple exits are the prerequisite of a successful snatch. Thus the paucity of road approaches to the lake and river offer safety and have made the area a prime holiday resort for Guatemala's rich.

The Río Dulce also offers yachts one of the most protected and most beautiful anchorages in the Caribbean. Affordable satellite navigation has brought the voyage south from the US within the capacity of North American retirees, most of them tempted south more by the low cost of living than by the great natural beauty of the area, and in excess of two hundred yachts anchor out in the various creeks or swing to moorings or dock at the half-dozen small marinas.

Little intermingling occurs between the North American yachties and the Guatemalan rich. Few of the North Americans speak Spanish and anyway resent Latinos with greater wealth. The rich Guatemalans are fluent in English. However, they find the North Americans uncouth and resent the need to speak a foreign language in their own country – outside of business hours. Local transport is by launch, skiff, dinghy or traditional dug-out.

Pulling off the road, Bergman changed his city clothes for faded chinos and a dark blue sports shirt. In Fronteras a gringo in a car is more memorable than a gringo on foot and Bergman took a side turn down to the right before the bridge toll post, parking the Mistsubishi in deep shadow under the first span. Crossing the 300-metre bridge on foot, he kept his pace to a confident amble suitable to a yachtsman ashore. An over-loaded Mac truck with badly calibrated fuel injectors coughed and snarled up to the apex of the bridge. The stink was worse than the Brit's cigarettes.

Three-quarters tin-shack shanty town and one quarter downmarket cement-brick dump, Fronteras is primarily an outsize truck-stop on the frontier of the Petén. The beat of merengue, North American pop and Mexican wail welcomed Bergman. He liked dumps. This one had more atmosphere in the first block than all the truck stops in the US put together.

There should have been sentries in the concrete guardpost at the town end of the bridge; peace declared, they were watching a late-night Brazilian soap on TV at the first bar on main street. This was the only street heading north. Spurs led down a short distance east to the river and west to the Spanish fort and Lake Izabal. One o'clock on a Saturday morning and trucks were parked nose to tail up both sides of the street and the small stores, bars, restaurants and discos remained open. If any of the major's men were off duty, Bergman expected to find them in the whorehouse.

The two-level concrete building was set back from the street.

Grills protected the terraces on ground and first floor. A skinny Indian armed with a pistol-grip shotgun lounged at the foot of the stairs. A bar and pool table occupied the upper terrace. The pool table was as great an attraction as the half-dozen Indian and mestiza whores. Starched straw cowboy hats, sweat and a serious tobacco habit were the common factors amongst the T-shirted truckers, farmers from the Petén, tourist hustlers, shopkeepers and fishermen grouped round the pool table – and that they all had money on the game. A black the shape and size of a wardrobe guaranteed peace amongst the players with a baseball bat.

Bergman kept his back to the wall. At the bar two drunk gringos wore bored teenage whores round their necks and talked war stories at each other. A third gringo recognised a different war and swore continuously at the first two from a cane chair tilted back against the wall. Venom rather than imagination marked his language. His fury hit critical level and he crashed his chair down onto its four legs and exploded to his feet with the enthusiasm of a winning boxer coming out of his corner at the start of the final round. The bouncer leant across the pool table and prodded him back into his chair with the heavy end of the baseball bat. The other two gringos never noticed.

Eight doors opened off the corridor leading back from the bar. A gust of sex, chemical soap and cleaning liquid blew down the corridor as a medium brown whore with long hair and fine features stuck her head out of a doorway and yelled at the barman for a fresh bottle of rum. The barman flicked fingers for the cash and a male head appeared – this one Bergman recognised as a corporal in the unit that had brought the *guerrillero* to the car wash.

Bergman folded two one-hundred-quetzal notes lengthways, poked them across the bar and pointed to the whore. 'Once the señor has completed his pleasure.'

The bills drew the whore fully into the corridor.

'She is from Honduras,' the barman said – whores and automobiles, imports are the classiest.

The corporal yanked the whore back into the room and squared off to face Bergman. 'Whore of a gringo.'

Hardly an insult given the location, Bergman thought. The notes retreated into his palm and he held up the other hand open towards the corporal. 'Please, at you leisure, señor. Or tomorrow night when the señorita is less occupied – it is the same for me. For now I will walk up the road and enjoy the view from the bridge.'

He saw recognition in the corporal's eyes and repeated, even as he turned away, 'Yes, the bridge. Again, my apologies, señor.'

He waited on the apex of the centre span. Upstream, a petrol station and store occupied the south shore. On the north shore a fisherman with a net stood in the shallows below a creek where half a dozen yachts lay to moorings. The moon, low in the west, outlined the walls and tower of Fort San Felipe on the point guarding the entrance to Lake Izabal. The moonlight seemed to slide downstream on the current across the dark water beneath the bridge and out beyond to a small islet on which Bergman could distinguish a frost of egrets nesting in tall mangrove trees. The islet split the moonlight, the left-hand spear cutting across to a marina on the north bank, the right fading into the trees at the next bend. Those living on the river were asleep. Light was a mark of wealth, dim on those yachts anchored out to avoid marina charges, bright at the marinas and brilliant on the private docks of the Guatemalan rich.

Bergman turned back to watch the fisherman gather his net. From beyond the fort came the purr of a powerful outboard motor and the fisherman, ready to cast, hesitated as a big dark-hulled inflatable sped into view. Four soldiers manned the inflatable. The helmsman cut power and the craft dropped off the plane and nosed in to the concrete dock in front of the store on the south bank. Two men jumped ashore, a third pushed the bow clear and the helmsman powered fast across river to the deep shadow at the town end of the bridge. Bergman could hear, above the lap of the river, a soldier scramble up the steep bank. The fisherman rocked back, ready to cast, and Bergman saw the fall of the net hatch the water. Moments later a soldier appeared at each end of the bridge. Silent in jungle boots, the major came striding towards Bergman from the south end. Years of clandestine war had steeped him in the need for watchfulness and he walked like a gun fighter, slim and hard in his camouflage, elbows out, right hand low on his thigh, fingers splayed ready to draw his Colt from its canvas holster. He halted at a distance of ten feet. 'You wished to see me?'

Bergman remained leaning over the parapet. Way below, the fisherman drew the net in through his fingers, searching for fish in the mesh. The fisherman worked slowly and stood a little hunched – an old man, maybe sixty or even sixty-five; and Hispanic; he was the wrong shape for an Indian, too slim and too narrow.

The major was Hispanic and a very minor member of the hundred or so families who controlled Guatemala's internal economy. University professors and journalists on prestigious low-circulation weeklies referred to them as the oligarchy. Bergman simply thought of them as sons of bitches.

He said, 'A beautiful night, Major.' Head back, he breathed deeply, filling his nostrils with the warm scent of the river. 'You can smell the growth. Peaceful. Or so His Excellency the President claims.'

That was the first hint and Bergman let it seep for a minute. Then, the major's curiosity awakened, he said, 'Yes. Sweet forgiveness.'

Bergman betrayed his contempt for politicians with a dry sniff of laughter. 'No scores will be settled. So decides your president, Major. Yes, the new broom. And you and I will be the sacrifice. After all these years they are inquiring again into San Cristóbal.'

He swept the top of the parapet with his fingertips. 'Cleaning? Or simply attempting to hide the dirt under the rug? Look,' he said, pointing to the fisherman bent at the waist to gather his net – a figure from a Chinese drawing. 'Beautiful.'

'Is that why we are here? To watch a fisherman?' The major's voice was surprisingly harsh for a Guatemalan and cold now with suspicion. 'Or is there a destination to this conversation?'

'What conversation?' Bergman wiped his fingers on a handkerchief and folded the handkerchief back into his trouser pocket.

'You recall the attack on the Finca Patricia?' he said to the water, and waited a count of five before adding: 'The attack came after the signing of this peace. Your men were killed by the landslide, and a young officer.'

'Fabio,' the major said.

'Fabio,' Bergman agreed. 'He was trained in Cuba.'

He watched the shadow of a cloud slip downriver towards the bridge. When it reached the fisherman, he said, 'The younger brother of the man who trained Fabio flew into Guatemala yesterday. He will stay for one week.'

'In Guatemala,' the major murmured.

'Yes, in Guatemala.'

Bergman imagined a drop in temperature as the cloud wiped the moonlight from his face. He had it now clear in his mind.

'So many have died because of that training,' he said and nodded approval of his own anger. 'While the Cuban sits there safe in Havana. Tur, that is his name. Estoban Tur. Miguel Tur is the Little Brother.'

The rhythm was important and again he nodded. 'The sea protects Estoban Tur from justice. Doubtless you knew many of those who were murdered at Finca Patricia?'

'Naturally,' the major said.

'And the officer. . . '

'We attended the School of the Sacred Heart in the same years and at the Military Academy.'

'Brother officers,' Bergman said, his voice so low on the second word that only the imagined relationship truly existed – a fraternal relationship to be avenged. On impulse, he walked quickly away, fifteen paces, as if better to see something round the point. A bird, perhaps.

He had established a symbiotic state, sufficiently powerful to draw the major in his wake.

The fisherman let fly and the net drew an almost perfect circle on the water. So awake were his senses, Bergman distinguished the patter of the weights.

'Bait,' he said. 'We grab Little Brother. Let us do it to the son of a bitch.' Except that he used a viciously crude sexual expression that he had learned from a Cuban in Miami: *Vamos a resingarle la vida*.

Bergman had no need to offer the major anything other than Tur. Up there on the bridge, in the fading moonlight, they discussed how many men would be necessary for the snatch and where to hold Little Brother.

Bergman drove fast back to Río Hondo and south through Chiquimula for the second time. A further ten kilometres and he turned east off the main highway onto the dirt road leading to the Maya ruins at Copán in Honduras. Parking off the road a mile outside El Florido, he changed back into his suit. The border with Honduras opened at seven a.m. and he set the alarm on his wristwatch for six fifteen, tipped his seat back and dozed for an hour. A police jeep drove by slowly soon after he awoke and Bergman made a big play of stretching and yawning as he checked the exterior of the car. Parking fifty metres short of the border-crossing, he found a snack stand open and drank two cups of coffee. He wanted to be remembered by the border guards as they came on duty and again he made a show of stretching the stiffness from his neck and shoulders.

A retired US school bus dragged a cloud of dust down the dirt road from Chiquimula. A little later the first minibus arrived from Copán to unload passengers on the Honduran side of the border. A queue formed on both sides of the crossing, mostly backpackers. Many of them were Total Awareness allied to a vacant expression – and in uniform, of course: pseudo dreadlocks, torn shirts, ragged jeans and romantic dirt. Bergman had been poor and thought playing at it an insult to those who suffered poverty.

He let the first few backpackers pass, some to clamber onto the Chiquimula bus while others staggered up the road in hope

106

of a lift. Finally he targeted a man in his early thirties, a little cleaner than the rest, short hair, Timberland shoes and a Gap bush shirt – certainly from the States. Bergman eased his bulk out of the car, blocking the target's way. 'Bergman. From the embassy,' he said, so the target would know from the accent that he was North American. 'Dump the pack in the trunk. I'll give you a lift to the highway.'

The target hesitated, bewildered by Bergman's speed.

Bergman said, 'Move it before we have the longhairs threatening a class action.'

That produced a smile. The target shrugged out of his backpack and dumped it in the boot. 'Thanks.'

'My pleasure,' Bergman said.

The target introduced himself with a man-to-man hand-shake, 'Dave.'

Once in the car, he added that he taught high-school mathematics in some town Bergman had never heard of up in Maine. He had brushed his teeth, which was a plus with early morning backpackers.

'You really from the embassy?'

'CIA Head of Station,' Bergman said, silencing the target for the next fifty kilometres.

Every now and again the target would sneak a quick look at Bergman. Most of the time he stared studiously out of the windows as Bergman pushed the speed over the dirt road that led from lush valley to lush valley, jungle clad mountains on either side, light sprinkling of thatch huts, crossbreed Brahmin cows, a couple of river fords. Only on reaching the hardtop did the target regain his courage. He swung his shoulder round within the seatbelt so as to confront Bergman physically.

'Should you have told me that? I mean, well, the CIA is secret, right?'

Bergman flashed the target one of his grins. 'Secret is what we are from the taxpayer. That's what you get for your tax dollar,' he said. 'Any opposition knows who I am. Cold War, the Russians had a file thicker than Langley. Even had me marked for no further promotion.' A second grin. 'They got that right.'

Bergman thought of adding that Dave was also now marked as CIA. If anybody asked officially where Bergman had been, that was his answer: picking up a freelance at the border. They asked who, Bergman would give them a smile and a little shrug. 'Hey, come on, you know how it is. Drugs. That's strictly a no-names business.'

They pushed the questioning, he would get indignant and tell them to go to hell. Backtrack Bergman's movements and they would discover that he had slept in a hire car short of the frontier with Honduras. Finally they might pick up on Dave. And what could Dave tell them? That Bergman had given him a lift. That, yeah, he knew Bergman was CIA Head of Station; Bergman had told him as much. Everyone would recognise Dave's story as a crock of shit.

For a final touch, Bergman pulled in again at the Restaurant Las Vegas in Chiquimula. He sat with Dave at a terrace table back in the shadows, questioning him on his travels while they breakfasted on eggs, refried black beans and salt cheese. Dave was an ardent student of Mayan archaeology; Bergman, an expert listener, looked up frequently and with interest at his companion's description of one or other find. Their meal finished, Bergman ordered fresh coffee and apologised to his companion for taking notes on an idea that had come to him on the road. He wrote rapidly on a yellow secretary's short-hand pad. To any investigator, the scene was clearly the debriefing of an agent.

The ruins at Tikal in the Petén were Dave's next destination and Bergman dropped him at the petrol station in Rio Hondo. A pair of junky-thin juvenile longhairs hurried over while Bergman was taking Dave's pack out of the boot. Awareness had failed to teach the male longhair that Indian clothes differed in weave for sex as well as tribe and that both the shirt and sash he wore were for women.

'Hey, you going to Guatemala City,' the kid asked, a real charmer.

'Yeah,' Bergman said.

'Great,' the kid said and shrugged out of his pack.

Bergman caught the scent of the day before yesterday's sweat from the kid's armpit. 'The only place I'd take you is an incinerator,' he said and slammed the boot shut. 'Thanks for the company,' he said to Dave. 'You get to the City, call me at the embassy?'

That Bergman was from the embassy was the cream on the cake for the longhair. 'Fascist son of a bitch.'

'Right,' Bergman said and shot the Mitsubishi Lancer back onto the highway. In Cuba long hair had been a crime for many years. Castro had also declared fruits against the law early in the Revolution. The cops had rounded them up and trucked them out to the fields for sexual reorientation – three thousand swishers chopping at cane and no gloves. Imagining the scene made Bergman grin as he passed a train of laden trucks huffing up the next hill. Working with the ballet, Little Brother could be a fruit. Yeah, interesting to see what Little Brother looked like.

Miguelito

Five foot five inches in height and slight of figure, fair skinned and fine featured, Miguel was known to all and sundry as Miguelito – Little Michael. At primary school he had been the national champion at 200 metres and had continued to excel in the first two years of high school. However, he hadn't grown after his sixteenth year, nor had he developed muscle. His mother had accused first the diet and latterly his peasant genes. Ardent revolutionary in her youth, she had succumbed to her wealthy bourgeois origins and lived now off a stipend transferred monthly to the Banco Financiero by her father, a resident of Naples, Florida, who, despite being both a lawyer and banker, was a kindly gentleman and had forgiven his daughter her youthful follies.

Her social life revolved now around those of like background, their preoccupations not so different from that of their cousins in Florida. True, they enjoyed fewer material goods; however, of that available, they devoured a lion's share. The thieves they feared were of government rather than private enterprise, and they devoured cakes baked at home rather than dally in air-conditioned cafés. But this is detail. Their primary preoccupations were identical and found chronicled within *Selecta* magazine and the social sections of the *Diario de las Americas* and the Spanish language edition of Sunday's *Miami Herald*.

Miguelito's mother thought herself more cultured than her Florida cousins because she discussed the arts more often – or, more accurately, the lives of the artists – while censorship, and the resulting lack of books, gave her an excuse for not reading the novels she flayed according to the dictates of leftist European art critics who visited her husband. This second husband was a sculptor who worked in revolutionary-correct intellectual concrete and was prone to explaining the symbolism of his work in phrases as enigmatic as the works themselves and with an enthusiasm otherwise awakened only by the genealogy of a family of the very lesser Navarra nobility arrived in Latin America in the train of Cortés – since when they had attempted to raise cows with greater dedication than success in Peru, Chile, Bolivia, Paraguay, Colombia, Guatemala and, finally, Cuba – a profession from which the revolution had saved them finally through the confiscation of their lands.

Miguelito's stepfather had been responsible for Miguelito's introduction into the establishment circles of Cuba's art world. Miguelito presumed that the stepfather had been responsible also for the miracle of this new employment with the Andaluz ballet and the only dreamed of chance to travel outside Cuba.

Miguelito had fallen in love with Antigua Guatemala in the first few minutes following the ballet's arrival. Founded in 1542, Antigua is one of the oldest Spanish cities in the Americas. At an altitude of 1500 metres, the climate is akin to a permanent European spring; the population remains under

30,000; strict planning regulations have protected the simple colonial domestic architecture, the pantile roofs and flower-covered patio walls.

The buttressed ruins of the splendid baroque churches were familiar to Miguelito – though ruin in Cuba was the result of a revolutionary government's neglect; in Guatemala, earth-quakes were responsible. The cleanliness of the cobbled streets amazed him and that the fountains worked, cooling the tree-shaded squares. With buildings restricted to two floors, the grid system of roads and avenues opened views of the three magnificent volcanoes that dominated the town: Acatenango, Agua, and the always smoking Fuego.

Blossoming jacaranda trees shaded the country lane leading to the Hermitage of the Holy Cross where the Andaluz Ballet of Havana was to perform. The Hermitage lay on the outskirts to the south-east of Antigua and on the opposite side of the road to the Rio Pensativo and of a country mansion with tall garden walls down which spilled sprays of blue petrea blossoms.

Of the Hermitage, only the inner facade of the church had resisted the earthquakes that have shattered much of the grander buildings of Antigua over past centuries. The facade rose in three tiers. First came the main arch some fifteen feet wide by thirty high. Above the arch was an open cross while a crucifix decorated the rounded summit. Where once stood the main body of the church there was now a small open amphitheatre with seating on the flagstone steps facing across to the ruins and a wooden stage erected against the pale ochre plaster of the facade. Miguelito, spellbound, sat on the top step while a solitary dancer strutted a vicious tattoo on the boards.

Andres was both principal dancer and director of the ballet. He had a reputation for fanaticism. On arrival, he had insisted on an immediate rehearsal so that he could appreciate the acoustics of the Hermitage and site the musicians to greatest advantage. When satisfied, he had dismissed the troupe, commanding Miguelito with a cut of his hand to stay behind. For the past half hour he had danced alone to a cassette recorder connected to two big speakers. Tall, with broad shoulders and slender hips, he wore loose black linen trousers and a white sleeveless shirt slashed to a heavy silver belt buckle. Mornings on the beach had burned his skin a deep gold and his face and arms and chest glowed with sweat. Framed within the arch, he appeared demoniac, the stage his battleground. Already the church had crumbled beneath his onslaught. The cross and the crucifix were mere symbols, powerless to oppose his demand for total domination of the auditorium. Each crash of his heels on the wood stage came like the shot of a rifle. A firing squad. Miguelito tied to a stake.

Incapable of movement, Miguelito sat with his thighs clamped together and turned broadside to the stage as if to protect himself from the dancer. There was no defence. Miguelito knew that there was no defence. He had never loved a man, never thought of being loved by a man. Now he was lost. He sat waiting. That was all he could do. Wait for Andres to take him. Possess him. Already he was cut in two by the desire to be used and by shame at wishing to be used. He wanted to run, his legs were liquid. He wanted to weep for mercy and be comforted within the arms of the unmerciful. Most of all he longed for the domination to continue for ever; longed for Andres to accept his surrender into a state of absolute passivity in which he had no choice of action or responsibility for what must happen. Already he felt Andres within him and shuddered at the heels' vicious strike on the boards.

Bergman

'Evil son of a bitch, he's like a goddamn snake,' Bergman said. He and the major had been watching the dancer and Little Brother from the shelter of the white cedar trees planted to shade the coffee plantation that climbed steeply up from the lane north of the Hermitage.

Snakes and rabbits were the territory of Bergman's childhood. With fruits, he was on less secure ground.

Many people in Bergman's line of work avoided homosexuals, believing them dangerous because of their susceptibility to blackmail. Bergman blamed bad law and prejudice for homosexual vulnerability. Gay sex wasn't something Bergman wanted to do or have done to him. What other people did was their affair so long as it was voluntary and wasn't children and wasn't thrust in Bergman's face.

As for Little Brother, 'Grab him the first day, people will think we were ready and set this thing up. Tomorrow or the day after will do okay.'

Miguelito

The music ended. Andres vaulted from the stage and stalked across the amphitheatre. He moved with the arrogant cruelty of the Andaluz gypsy, hips thrust forward, head erect, shoulders square and harder than the stone of the church.

Miguelito was forced to tilt his head back to see up into Andres' face. The line of the dancer's jaw showed dark and harsh against the faded ochre of the ruins. Andres tossed his head back to free his eyes of a sweat soaked curl and salt rain spattered Miguelito. The dancer demanded Miguelito's hand, drawing him to his feet, turning him towards the lane. They walked in step together. Andres' arm lay loose across Miguelito's shoulders and, though heavy as the cross, granted Miguelito strength to walk rather than fall. There were no words between them.

They came to the hotel and Miguelito was blind as they crossed the clipped lawns to Andres' bungalow, blind and deaf as they stood in front of the door while Andres drew the key from his pocket. Last chance of escape yet, in truth, there was no chance. Miguelito had become one of the living dead, powerless to decide and without strength to stand without the support of his master.

The door opened smoothly. The bed lay ahead. Andres ripped back the cover. The sheets were a fierce white that slashed deep across Miguelito's eyes so that he staggered and would have fallen to his knees but for Andres' hand lifting him the last few feet.

10

Miguelito

He awoke to shame. Dawn outlined the curtains. Andres lay against him. Miguelito, careful not to disturb his lover, turned his head to look down the length of the dancer's body, muscles firm even at rest beneath the smooth golden skin. He thought of his brother, Estoban, high official in the apparatus of State. Homosexuality had been proscribed in the opening months of the revolution. So the practice had remained throughout the years of Fidel's rule. The persecution was less overt now, yet the prejudice continued endemic at both official and private levels, homosexuals forbidden membership of the party, excluded from all positions of power and influence.

Miguelito's fall would reflect on his brother.

This was the elder brother who had held Miguelito in his arms while telling him of their father's death in Angola. The difference in their ages had made Estoban more a replacement father than a brother. Often he had fetched Miguelito from school and driven him to the sierra at weekends. He had taught Miguelito to swim at Playas del Este and bathed him afterwards in the shower at Estoban's mother's small apartment, always careful to rinse the interior of Miguelito's ears free of salt.

Such quick snapshots were more real and valuable than the formal pictures and there came to Miguelito early memories of being seated on Estoban's lap in the evening and the smell of Estoban fresh from bathing; memories of the two of them with a book, Estoban following the words on the white paper with a thick brown finger as he coaxed Miguelito to read; memories of Estoban's shirt buttons straining as he squatted with his arms open to welcome Miguelito from school; the sway of Estoban's hips as he danced a few steps on the pavement to salsa playing on the jeep radio; the smile with which he welcomed Miguelito after a race; the surprising strength in his arms as he hugged Miguelito; equally surprising, the evenness of his breathing as they climbed the jagged limestone peaks of the Sierra de los Organos.

Miguelito's childhood had been lit by such flashes of love. He had seen Estoban's delight in his victories on the athletic track. Later there had been no judgement of Miguelito's failure, nor even disappointment. Yet, somehow, they had grown away from each other. Estoban, so changed from the adored elder brother remembered from Miguelito's childhood, had grown distant within the citadels of his secret world – a world in which the sharing of thoughts or feelings was forbidden.

And there was guilt in Miguelito in never confronting his own mother and stepfather, both of whom considered the mulatto half-brother and darker nephews an embarrassment in a society preparing, however surreptitiously, the return to its pre-revolutionary clothing. A further distancing came from Miguelito's closeness to Estoban's wife, Maria. They had built an alliance increasingly on little jokes shared at Estoban's expense; jokes as to his silences, his dedication to the letter of the law. And at how often he worked late at his office so that Miguelito shared with Maria responsibility for the children, accompanying her to parent-teacher meetings, taking one or other child to the clinic, babysitting on staff meeting nights or when Maria was at the theatre.

Estoban's two children were Miguelito's delight. Boys, would Estoban now ban him from the house? Refuse him the right to bathe them? Would he suffer Estoban's eyes following him across the small apartment, read Estoban's suspicions each time he touched one of the boys, kissed them goodnight? And how would Maria respond to the gossip that would fly round Havana fast as a breeze?

And his mother? His stepfather? Having to face them at the breakfast table and at dinner. So much easier if he lived alone; but that was impossible in Havana, where accommodation was at a premium, many families living three generations in the same room and rooms often divided vertically into two. At least his mother's house was ample and comfortable.

Miguelito hid for a moment in thoughts of his own spacious studio. Originally his maternal great grandfather's library, two tall windows gave to the side garden, two more to the rear patio. Many of the pictures on the walls had been liberated by his father in the first months following the Triumph. His father's choice had been catholic, the frames often more impressive than the painting.

Miguelito's stepfather joked as to the misfortune of having power without taste. Yet Miguelito had watched his stepfather curry favour within the revolution's elite in expectation of a commission for which the sole prerequisite was the political correctness of the artist – abstract concrete was always safe.

Miguelito pictured his stepfather: narrow face, cold grey eyes, high-bridged nose, white-white fingers playing with a wine glass, his sarcasm paraded as humour yet always cruel. Now at his mercy, Miguelito would suffer such spiteful mockery at every meal, the thin-lipped chuckles shared sometimes by his mother, often too lazy and innocent to understand her husband's sallies.

The thought was unbearable and Miguelito turned from his shame into the shelter of Andres' arms. The dancer awoke and Miguelito accepted the scrape of the dancer's unshaven cheeks as a prelude to the domination that would again release him from responsibility. The first rays of sunshine shone on the dew as he slipped from Andres' bungalow to his own room. Away from the dancer's strength, the shame returned. He was unable to face himself in the bathroom mirror and was both relieved and fearful when Andres fetched him for breakfast. They walked together across the lawn. As they entered the restaurant, Andres laid his arm across Miguelito's shoulders, a claim of ownership that Miguelito was unable to resist. The dancer deliberately paraded him between the tables where the other members of the ballet sat. Miguelito read a cynical awareness in their eyes; in their little smiles, a spiteful pleasure at his surrender. Laughter followed as he fled.

Bergman

Bergman had been summoned by radio to the Parque Central. Little Brother had been sitting on a park bench for the past half hour. Bergman watched him from the upstairs cloister above the police station housed in the Palacio de los Capitanes. The young Cuban was blind to the beauty and awakening bustle of his surroundings. He sat very still, legs together, hands folded in his lap.

An arcade ran the length of the west side of the square. Bundles of cloth striped in reds and purples and blues stirred in the shade and metamorphosed into tiny Indian women. Descended from the mountain villages, they had slept on the flagstones, wrapped against the cold in the hand-woven shawls and blankets they hoped to sell.

Two old men sought warmth on an unshaded bench close to Little Brother. A security guard unlocked the doors at Lloyds bank above the intersection of 4th Street and 5th Avenue. The dancer entered the square from the corner by the bank and crossed the road diagonally in front of the cathedral. He halted for a moment at the fountain closest to the bench where Little Brother sat. Bergman watched him dab water from the fountain on his temples and on his forehead – for luck, Bergman wondered.

The dancer sat beside Little Brother and tried to put his arm round the young man's shoulders. Little Brother shoved the dancer away and moved to a second bench in the shade of an orange tree. The dancer made to follow, then shrugged and stalked back across the square and up calle de la Universidad towards the ballet's hotel.

'*Que mariconería,*' the major said, his contempt for homosexuals typical of the male Latin American.

Miguelito

People had noticed the scene with Andres. Now they were watching Miguelito. He could feel their contempt. He knew all the names they would call him. He had recited the litany himself when a member of the high-school athletics team: *cherna, loca, ganso, pato, pargo, pájaro* . . .

Here the Guatemalans didn't know him, yet already they were commenting. Miguelito imagined the gossip in Havana. He saw himself taking the elevator up to Estoban's apartment. Reading the knowledge in Maria's eyes. Suffering her affection for him and her understanding. How could she understand? No one could understand. He could already feel her lips damp on his cheeks, their pressure a little firmer than usual, indicating that she would support him and that she wasn't frightened of Aids. She would want details but be shy of asking that which she most wanted to know: was Andres truthfully the first? Or had Miguelito been leading a double life for years? He would meet with such curiosity at every encounter.

His mother would calculate how his sexuality affected her social status while his stepfather would pretend liberalism while avoiding physical contact from fear of Aids.

Aids would be everyone's concern. Friends would shrink from him.

The thought of returning appalled him.

He watched a police car park in front of the arched entrance to the police station on the ground floor of the Palacio de los Capitanes. It was the easiest thing to do. The Americans would take him He was Estoban Tur's brother. Half-brother. No matter that he knew nothing. The propaganda would delight the leadership in Miami. They would protect him. Find him a decent job that paid a proper salary. He could rent a studio apartment of his own, buy a small car, a new car, maybe a convertible – the same pale blue as the MG Roddy de Sanchez drove.

Bergman

From the upstairs cloister, Bergman had watched Little Brother push the dancer, Andres, away. Now he noted a straightening of posture as the young Cuban rose from the bench and walked determinedly across the square towards the Palacio de los Capitanes. For a moment Bergman thought that the Cuban had somehow recognised him. Then he realised that Little Brother's goal was the police station below.

Bergman grabbed the major by the arm, forcing him round towards the stairs. 'Head him off. He's going to request asylum.'

Miguelito

The man barring his way wore civilian clothes. Fair hair and green eyes, intelligent and used to command. And he had a hard look, unlike the other policemen Miguelito had noticed in Guatemala, who tended to the beer bellies and drooping moustaches common to the caricatures of Latin American officialdom in the Cuban press and Hollywood movies.

The man spoke abruptly, his voice harsh. 'What do you want?'

'I am from Cuba,' Miguelito said. He didn't know what else to say. It seemed so obvious to him. His confidence drained away. He couldn't do it. Not to this man.

'It is a beautiful building,' he said. 'I thought it was a museum.'

'The museum is the door further up the square.'

'Thank you.' Miguelito was already turning back to the

street. He was unable to think. His feet took him automatically north out of the square on the same road that Andres had taken. He skirted a group of North American language students, backpacks and schoolbooks. Perhaps he could teach. Impossible. The Guatemalans would never give him a work permit. He had nowhere to go. The hotel was impossible – simpering sadistic dancers gloating. And already someone might be reporting that he had entered the police station. No Cuban would believe that he had mistaken the police station for a museum. He would be punished, perhaps imprisoned, certainly banished from Havana, made to work in the fields for a year, never again allowed out of Cuba.

He found himself on the lane leading to the Hermitage.

He thought that he would walk on past the Hermitage and climb the volcano. It didn't matter which one. He had to die. All other options were closed to him. He felt at ease now that the decision was taken.

Bergman

Language students of all ages hurried across the square to one or other of the many Spanish schools. The Indian women were laying out their wares on the pavement in the arcade. Bergman watched an early customer nod to the armed security guard at Lloyds bank. An Indian in a straw Stetson drove a Toyota pick-up piled with fresh fruit and vegetables down through the square towards the market on the far side of the Almeda Santa Lucia. Little Brother came out of the police station and turned uphill on calle de la Universidad. The major ran up the stairs fast and across the cloister to join Bergman between the arches.

'He said he thought the police station was the museum,' the major said.

'And I'm his grandmother.' Bergman watched Little Brother skirt the students. Right now he was almost certainly wondering who had seen him enter the police station. Defection

121

remained his best bet. Or he could kill himself. The two acts were similar, Bergman thought, as he tried to get inside the young Cuban's head.

Dead, Little Brother was of no use to Bergman. Defection was as bad. They had to move now or face a mess. Everything was happening more quickly than Bergman had planned. He didn't like it. He said, 'We don't have a choice. Grab him now and no witnesses.'

Miguelito

It had begun at the Hermitage. Miguelito thought that he could sit in the small amphitheatre for a while. The lane ran between a high wall to the west and the equally high fence protecting the coffee plantation. A jeep approached from behind. The lane was narrow and Miguelito hugged the wall to let the jeep pass. The jeep was grey. A streak of rust marked the left front wing. A driver and three passengers rode in the jeep. Tough men. Miguelito recognised the type from the *Brigada Especial* in Havana – the same type as the man in the civilian clothes at the police station. Except that he had been an officer. The men were watching Miguelito.

A donkey laden with fresh grass appeared round the next corner driven by an elderly Indian. Two barefoot children of kindergarten age accompanied the old man. The jeep overtook Miguelito and halted at the corner to allow the donkey passage. The Indian hammered the donkey on the rump, forcing it forward on the verge past the jeep and down the lane. The jeep disappeared round the corner.

Miguelito gave the donkey a pat on the rump as it passed and smiled at the children. They looked cute in shirts and skirts striped in yellow on red and blue. Miguelito had thought at first that the native dress worn by the Indian women in the square was to tempt the tourists. However, all the country people kept to their traditional clothes. The children returned his smile and he said, 'Good morning.'

'*Buenos días*,' they echoed.

Miguelito had been led to expect misery yet the children seemed happy. Their hair needed a good comb, probably full of *piojos*, lice.

They passed out of sight round a bend and he was alone again in the lane. He thought of his two nephews with whom lice were an ever-present challenge. Estoban's children. Defecting was a betrayal of Estoban. A hummingbird sucked nectar from blossom spilling over the wall on his right. The volcanoes showed clear against the pale blue of the morning sky. He had been crazy to think of killing himself.

Behind him a driver ground his vehicle into gear and Miguelito looked over his shoulder. A jeep eased slowly round the curve. The driver was in low gear and looked straight at Miguelito who had stepped back against the wall.

It was the same grey jeep.

Miguelito recognised the streak of rust on the left front wing and the four men were familiar. Tough men. Dangerous. They were after him. He didn't know why. But he was sure. Very sure.

He sprang off the wall as he had shot off the starting blocks on the track. He was safe if he could reach the Hermitage.

He could leave the road at the Hermitage and run uphill through the woods where the jeep couldn't follow. He doubted if the men could catch him on the hill. Lighter, he had less weight to carry for the same intake of oxygen and the steep ground would hold him better. It would be a long run and he kept his head up and his chest loose. Only half a mile to the Hermitage. One last corner.

He rounded the corner and saw a second jeep parked short of the entrance gates to the mansion on the right. A second team of four men had dismounted from this second jeep and stood waiting in the road short of the ruins. Miguelito's last hope lay in leaping for the top of the wall. He sprinted straight at the four men in the road. At the last moment he took off from his right foot, turning slightly in the air. He caught a branch of the creeper and swung his feet up. He was almost parallel to the ground when the branch broke. He pawed desperately through the foliage for a fresh grip. Glass ripped at his right palm. He twisted as he fell and landed on his feet, ready to dart left or right.

The men from the first jeep barred the road behind him. One of them grabbed him by the shoulders. Though Miguelito knew that there was no point, he fought because it was the correct action – one against eight.

The garden gate to Miguelito's left creaked on rusted hinges as a boy shoved it open and stepped into the lane. One of the men had clamped a hand over Miguelito's mouth. Miguelito bit hard and tried to shout at the boy to get back inside. He saw the boy stop dead in surprise. Then something hit Miguelito on the head. The hand came away from his mouth and he felt himself falling into darkness.

He thought that he cried, 'No. No, don't. Don't. Please don't.'

He heard the shot crack as hard as Andres' heels on the stage.

Bergman

Bergman and the major had waited upstairs in the cloister above the police station. First came the report of the donkey and the abort.

Now, listening to his radio, the major said, 'We've got him.' Then he said, 'Shit! A boy saw them. They shot him.'

'The target?'

'The boy.'

'Jesus!' Bergman said.

'They say, from the clothes, he wasn't anyone special. Probably a servant's son.'

'Great,' Bergman said. He made no attempt to hide his disgust.

'They put him over the fence into the coffee. Maybe a dog will find him. Otherwise it could be hours. I've told them to get out of town and down to the coast.'

'How old was the boy?'

The major was about to ask via the radio.

Bergman said, 'Forget it. Go on down to your camp. I'll meet you on the bridge. O-one-hundred hours. We need photographs.'

'I've got the Polaroid.'

'Make sure there's enough light so his face shows,' Bergman said. He felt a little sick as he thought of the body tossed over the fence into the coffee bushes. It should have been avoided. Little Brother running out of control had been the main reason; and that Bergman had been ordered to keep his distance from the action. Had he been there in the lane, he might have thought of an alternative to shooting the boy. That is what Bergman thought. It nagged at him as he drove into Guatemala City in the hired Mitsubishi Lancer.

He spent half an hour at his office before heading down to the coast. A car accident would have brought questions and he was content to dawdle behind the lines of heavy trucks on the carretera Atlantico. Workers were blasting at one point and he was delayed for twenty minutes. Local Indians were selling snacks and cold drinks. Bergman bought gum and cashews and from one boy, *tamales* and a coke from another.

He reached the thatched *rancho* beside the car wash in time for a late lunch and gave the gum to the woman's children. The Mitsubishi he parked in the shed at the rear of the concrete building. Having eaten, he went upstairs and showered. The women brought him a fresh beer. He watched her undress. He didn't want her and, when she touched him, lifted her hands away. He wanted to sleep but the dead boy got in the way. He wondered whether the parents had missed the boy and whether the body had been found. He thought that not knowing would be worse for the parents than having their fears confirmed. If the body had been found, the death could be on the evening news. Though, son of a servant, the newscasters might agree with the major that the shooting was unimportant.

Kidnapping of rich kids and major drug busts made the

news, and gangland killings if they were messy enough. Bergman lay there worrying, not about the boy but about the parents – and about Little Brother, caught now and imprisoned at the major's training camp on Lake Izabal. Little Brother must know that witnessing the boy being killed was his own death warrant. Though he had seemed very innocent.

Bergman got out of bed and stood naked at the window. The woman watched him. He had been visiting her for over a year now and didn't know her name. Disgusted with himself, he tried to smile but his face was too stiff. He knew he must make an ugly picture, his belly bulging, body hair plastered flat with sweat.

Though small, Little Brother had been good-looking. Very good-looking. As was the dancer. Bergman wondered whether the dancer would care that Little Brother had been snatched. He hadn't struck Bergman as a carer – too self-obsessed and arrogant.

The woman said, 'Come back to bed.' She lifted the sheet to let him in. He thought that she had lost weight and wondered if she was eating enough. He thought that it would be rude to ask her name after all these months. He could ask one of the waitresses.

He said, 'When they shot your husband, were there debts?'

'Some,' she said.

Visiting her was dangerous, even with the signing of the peace. He hadn't wanted to be alone. Now he wished that there was a chair in the room, somewhere to sit that was less intimate.

She said, 'Do you want another beer?'

'Not now.' He sat on the bed and absentmindedly stroked her back and shoulders. 'Tell me about the debts.'

He watched her calculating what to answer.

'It will be easier if you tell the truth,' he said and she shrugged.

'Thirty thousand quetzals. Ten for the refrigerators and the stove. The rest is on the buildings.'

Five thousand dollars – Bergman's ex-wife spent that on her wardrobe. 'How much do you pay on the kitchen equipment?'

She said, 'Three hundred a month.' Bergman thought that she could manage the payments. 'I'll give you a cheque for the other twenty,' he said.

To free herself from obligation, she needed to thank him and Bergman made no protest as she drew him down beside her and used her mouth. Later he set the alarm and slept.

Half a dozen men were drinking and amusing themselves with the waitresses. Bergman drew their attention briefly as he descended the stairs shortly before midnight. The woman watched from her chair by the kitchen door. The promise of a cheque had given her confidence in the relationship with Bergman. She laid the table closest to the kitchen and set a cold Gallo and a glass in front of him. She didn't touch or speak to him – not even to ask what he wished to eat. Knowing his wishes was part of her new role and she set a bowl of soup on the table before returning to the kitchen to grill a lake fish over the coals.

Bergman had arranged to meet the major at one a.m. He parked the car and walked onto the Rio Dulce bridge with fifteen minutes to spare. Tonight there was no fisherman for him to watch; perhaps Bergman was too early or too late. The same big inflatable rounded Fort San Felipe and sped downstream to the bridge. The major set guards at each end of the bridge as he had the previous night. Joining Bergman, he said, 'There was nothing on the news about the Cuban.'

'Or the boy?' Bergman asked.

Bergman's concern amused the major. All gringos were soft. 'I've told you,' he said, 'There will be no problems in regard to the boy. He was of no importance.'

He passed Bergman an envelope. There were six photographs inside. The lamps on the bridge gave sufficient illumination for Bergman to recognise the photographs' content. All showed Little Brother. The young Cuban looked directly into the camera lens. The soldiers had stripped him naked and tied him over a desk. One soldier was enjoying him while the others waited in line. The photograph didn't show the soldiers' faces.

The major enjoyed Bergman's shock. He said, 'That is what you said we should do. Remember? *Vamos a resingarle la vida.*'

'Yes,' Bergman said. Telling the major that he had meant the phrase figuratively and that he had been referring to the elder Tur rather than to Little Brother would have given the major further pleasure. Bergman slipped the photographs into his shirt pocket and said, 'Thank you. They are excellent.'

He had been ordered in Washington to keep his distance from the operation. Yet he remained responsible. As he had been responsible for cleaning up San Cristóbal.

He said to the major, 'I will be away a few days. Should you require me, leave a message at my office that Roberto has found the keys.'

The woman waited for Bergman. She sat alone in her usual chair by the kitchen. To save money she had switched off all but one electric light. Or perhaps the dim lighting was the setting for an ambush. Bergman drew his Beretta and parked the Mitsubishi alongside the *rancho*.

The woman rose and came to the car and stood with her hand on the driver's door. A gunman trying to kill Bergman would have cut her down.

'Come,' she said. 'It is safer to park overnight in the shed.'

She kept her hand on the door and walked beside the car round to the back. Bergman didn't lock the car and left the woman to lock the shed while he slipped the Beretta back into its holster. He considered apologising for his suspicions, however, there didn't seem much point and he was too tired.

They climbed the outside concrete stairs together, the woman in the lead. They undressed at the same time, washed their faces and brushed their teeth together in the bathroom, lay in the bed together in the dark, side by side, though not touching. After a while Bergman got up and went back to the bathroom. He knelt on the tiled floor to vomit. The woman came to him.

She said, 'The fish was fresh,' and handed Bergman a wet face cloth. 'It wasn't the fish.'

'No, it wasn't the fish,' Bergman said.

Two

11

Bergman

Bergman chartered an air taxi piloted by a retired North American to fly from Fronteras to Cancún, Mexico's premier Caribbean beach resort. Bergman travelled on a US passport issued in the name of Frank David Trautman. The passport was four years old and suitably stamped for an investment and pensions consultant servicing the international expatriate community; paranoia concerning his own finances had made Bergman an expert in the subject.

In Cancún, Bergman bought a seven-day package holiday to the Hotel Inglaterra in Havana from a tour agency for $540. The tour agency issued him a tourist card for Cuba. There was no requirement for a visa. The agency warned Bergman to take cash dollars; US Treasury regulations forbade the use in Cuba of US credit cards and traveller's cheques.

Air Caribe was a Cuban airline and Bergman expected an ancient Illushin. He was relieved to board a Boeing 727 and surprised to find the plane clean and the Cuban cabin staff both courteous and efficient. The immigration officer at Havana's José Martí airport was equally courteous. Hell existed in the customs hall where officers searched every bag off the plane and every piece of hand luggage. Bergman had landed at two thirty. He left customs at four forty-five. A further twenty minutes at the Cubacell office behind Terminal 2 and he was connected to Cuba's mobile telephone system. He had brought his own handset.

The taxi was a new Mitsubishi owned by the tourist off-shoot of the armed forces. The driver spoke what might have passed for English in a downmarket Miami barrio. A dual carriageway led into the city through a landscape of tall weeds and abandoned industrial buildings. The road surface suffered from crater disease. Traffic was light. Prerevolution Fords, Chevrolets and Chryslers were familiar to Bergman from his childhood. Less familiar was the scrap iron disguised as Russian trucks, Ladas pretending to be cars, and bad copies of World War II BMW motorcycles manufactured in communist-period East Germany. A few new Jawas faked they were café racers and there were Chinese-type bicycles, lots of bicycles – and, of course, slogans on every wall. The only fresh paint was on the slogans: SOCIALISM OR DEATH, VICTORY OR DEATH, LIBERTY OR DEATH, HOMELAND OR DEATH.

Get out of the cab or death, Bergman muttered as the driver swerved to the inside lane to overtake a truck spewing diesel fumes.

'No goddamn buses,' the driver said of the hitchhikers waving at them at each street corner. 'Wan' a *novia*, take you pick.'

'I'm on business,' Bergman said.

'From Miami? Helm Burton cut you throat.'

'That's my problem,' Bergman said. He thought of adding that the frontiers of the US extended beyond the municipal boundaries of Miami and even beyond Dade County.

The driver shot into the fast lane to avoid a red Lada stranded at an out-of-work traffic light.

'Is getting there alive an extra?' Bergman asked.

The driver turned to grin, both hands off the wheel. 'Don' wan' a *novia*, why you wan' live?'

'Face the front,' Bergman roared.

'Yeah, yeah, yeah,' chortled the driver. 'You wan' a driver while you here. I have cousin with new Moscovich.'

Bergman said, 'Moscoviches come out of the factory old.'

A concrete phallus dominated an expanse of blacktop to their left. The statue at the base of the phallus represented a moustachioed gentleman in an easy chair, head in his hand, nursing a hangover – or suffering deep thoughts, perhaps concerning Che Guevara, whose portrait decorated the facade of the office block opposite.

'Revolution Square,' the driver said.

Next came the old university, then down through streets of grim mid-nineteenth-century Spanish tenements, black with grime. The driver braked and cursed at a child darting out from behind a Forties Plymouth stripped of its wheels. Four kids screeched abuse from the inside of a rotting Ford. The neighbourhood was a junkyard. So were parts of New York and Chicago; Bergman failed to sense the violence prevalent in US cities.

To his left, he glimpsed dark blue sea and a fortress on a rocky bluff. The driver turned uphill on a street of baroque mansions abandoned to the revolution. Twin lines of Indian laurels shaded stone benches on a pedestrian esplanade running up the centre. A bronze lion had lost a leg and shattered bulbs dangled from the ornate street lamps. The street ended at the Parque Central, palm trees, a dry fountain and another statue of the man who dominated Revolution Square: José Martí, father of Cuban independence. The statue in Revolution Square had portrayed the idealistic philosopher and dreamer. In Parque Central he charged for freedom astride the horse that had carried him on a one-man cavalry assault against the Spanish army. Perhaps he was drunk at the time or had lost his spectacles. Or was simply in search of martyrdom. In which case he was the winner – the Spaniards shot him.

The deep arcade of the Hotel Inglaterra lay on the west side of the Parque with the Teatro Lorca on the next block. A low wall protected the tourists drinking at the café tables. Within the hotel a wrought-iron screen separated the lobby from the restaurant. Blue-and-white Andaluz tiles decorated the walls and continued up the stairs. Bergman's room was vast. The furniture was dark wood and either antique or fake antique. The TV screamed crackle and displayed a blizzard. Bergman presumed that the telephone was bugged. He unpacked and arranged his toiletries in a bathroom with more marble than a graveyard. Even the bath was marble; the massive brass taps would have served Jules Verne as models for the controls of the submarine in *Twenty Thousand Leagues Under The Sea*.

Internal politics both in the US and in Cuba dictate the fiction of severed diplomatic relations between the two nations. Thus the US Embassy in Havana passes under the name of the US Special Interests Section at the Swiss Embassy. The Special Interests Section is housed in an eight-floor office block in a secure compound on the waterfront. The building is a kilometre from the Swiss Embassy. Totally renovated over the past five years, it is now faced with grey green marble and carries the spread-eagle insignia of the US on the main facade, though no US flag.

Some fifty US personnel work in the US Interests Section; one or two of these are diplomats; more are officials of the Department of Immigration concerned with applications for visas, a few are from the Treasury and from the DEA – however, most, quite openly, are employees of the CIA.

Having showered and changed, Bergman called his contact from the centre of the Parque Central and arranged to meet at a bar in the Old City, the Bodeguita del Medio.

'Have a daiquiri at the Floridita first and visit the Hotel Ambos Mundos,' his contact advised. 'Security will peg you as a Hemingway pilgrim.'

In Hemingway's day the Floridita had been a spit-and-sawdust bar. Cuba's Ministry of Tourism had transformed it into a brass-and-fake-leather tourist trap. The waiters considered themselves too important to serve the customers and the price of a daiquiri banished Bergman's thirst.

Map in hand, he strolled on down Obispo towards the Hotel Ambos Mundos. Prior to the revolution Obispo was Havana's principal commercial street. Bank and insurance buildings had been designed to give commerce respectability – thus the ecclesiastical halls, pillared porches and massive doorways.

Now, socialist squalor was the victor and the offices mostly empty.

Ahead of Bergman, a pair of black girls in skin-tight gold lurex swung their buttocks from kerb to kerb of the narrow street – a little more effort and they could have brought down the buildings. A hustler pawed at Bergman with offers of cigars and PPG, a heart pill reputed to restore sexual energy. A couple of grannies sat on a doorstep beside a shop selling nothing – and even nothing appeared in short supply.

Estoban Tur had his headquarters somewhere on the left. Bergman wondered whether the Cuban knew of his brother's disappearance. Losing a member of the ballet was a black mark both against the political officer overseeing the ballet tour and the director of the dance troupe. They would have prayed for Baby Brother's reappearance and kept silent until the final moment.

Bergman turned left at the Ambos Mundos and found the Bodeguita del Medio hidden behind a scrum of black pimps and cigar salesmen two blocks north on calle Empedrado. Fifty or so foreigners were crammed into a bar too small to entertain a string quartet on a diet. The restaurant was behind the bar, tables crammed one against the other. From the kitchen came a stench of pork and chicken and fish all fried in the same rancid cooking oil.

Bergman ordered a *mojito*.

The barman dumped ice into a glass followed by a sprig of mint and added lemonade almost to the top before reaching under the bar for a rum bottle that claimed to be Havana Club. The rum should have been white. Possibly the dim light and the smoke made it appear yellow – Bergman wasn't betting on it.

'If that's mine, you can do us both a favour and start over,' he said. 'First you pour the rum and you take the bottle from the shelf so there's a chance it wasn't distilled in a bath.'

The barman glowered and Bergman watched to make sure he didn't spit in the glass.

A drunk fellow North American slapped Bergman on the shoulders. 'Been around, old buddy.'

'The block,' Bergman agreed.

The drunk introduced himself as Nick.

'Frank. Frank Trautman,' Bergman said.

They talked football for ten minutes and Bergman paid for the drinks. Out in the street the two men backtracked towards the Ambos Mundos and Estoban Tur's office.

Estoban Tur

Estoban Tur controlled a tumbledown corner block where a dozen or so entrances from the surrounding alleys enabled visitors to come and go unnoticed. Estoban's office was on the first floor. Twenty feet square, it was ill-lit and grubby and stank of stale tobacco and sweat. A dozen director's chairs with patched seats stood round a plywood conference table. Coffee cups had left a border of interlocked rings on the tabletop; the table edge had been charred by countless cigarettes.

Estoban sat working at his papers midway up the table. Middle-aged and ten kilos overweight, he was of medium height and of medium brown complexion. His features were nondescript, neither African nor European. He wore a brown double-breasted polyester suit over a yellowing nylon shirt darned at cuffs and collar. His red tie was frayed at the knot; add mismatching nylon socks and downmarket Bulgarian Hushpuppy lookalikes and the overall impression was of an out-of-work bookmaker's clerk – unless you looked in his eyes, deep brown and watchful, very watchful indeed.

He had refused to have air conditioning installed – not because of the expense but because the resulting comfort would insult both his neighbours' poverty and the harsh conditions suffered by most of those Latin American *guerrilleros* whose cause he served. The salt sea air had vanquished the ceiling fan and he had positioned a pedestal fan a little to the left and to the rear of his seat. Greenish pebbles held his papers against the artificial breeze. Typically, he had collected the stones from the beach in Oriente where the two great heroes of the war of independence from Spain had landed in 1893, José Martí and Maximo Gómez.

A soft tap at the door announced Estoban's assistant, Rivas. Rivas was a big man, powerful across the shoulders, and white, as are most Cuban officials at senior administrative level. He stood awkwardly in the doorway, his reluctance to enter reminding Estoban of his own training in Russia years ago at the KGB college, the river cold for swimming even in midsummer for a young man raised in the Caribbean. It was a stupid memory with no place in this new post-Cold War world where alliances shifted like river sand.

'Either inform me of the good news or remove yourself,' Estoban said.

'Miguelito ... he has defected.' Rivas shrugged heavy shoulders to rid himself of the guilt for bearing bad tidings. 'Forgive me.'

There was more to come and Estoban pointed him to a chair.

Rivas put his hands on the table, thick, muscular fingers interlocked over his secret. He was incapable of meeting Estoban's eyes, looking instead into the dark corner beyond Estoban's right shoulder. 'Forgive me,' he repeated.

Estoban smiled. 'Tell me what for.'

'He was in bed with a dancer.'

'That is a crime?'

'Andres. . . '

The fan swivelled and the breeze lifted the corner of the sheet of white paper on which Estoban had been writing. He saw the curves of the two bodies outstretched on the white bed sheet, the dancer's long muscular legs entwined with Miguelito's more slender limbs, the two men in each other's arms, Miguelito weeping inside himself with longing for the father killed in Angola. Estoban recalled the tears from his brother's childhood and the pain of his own incapacity to assuage Miguelito's grief. Even then Estoban had carried the burden of too many secrets. Secrecy and buried emotions were the occupational hazard of his profession. As were suspicion and preparedness – already he was listing the relatives of his superiors – in every family there were those who had deserted or defected. The risk to his own position was negligible. Miguelito was in greater danger. Estoban Tur's brother was a big catch for the Miami Cubans and for the North Americans. There would be pressure on Miguelito to denounce his elder brother. Go public, join the Miami publicity machine. Tremendous pressure. Threats and bribes. Estoban longed to hold him in his arms, protect him, comfort him, tell him to do what he must, do what he felt comfortable with. Estoban had been cast as a villain for too long to be hurt by insult or propaganda.

The telephone rang even as he reached for it. His direct superior, the general, introduced himself, his words bitten short in the way of those from Pinar del Rio.

'I have a report of your brother.'

'In Antigua. Rivas told me a few minutes ago.'

'It hurts.'

'Yes.' The pain of knowing that he might never see his brother again, that was obvious. But there was the other pain, the one to which the general referred; the pain of a believer in the corporate revolution, each loss, each desertion, a part of his own body ripped out.

He said, 'Yes,' again, the general, another believer. *Cuadrados* they were called, squares.

'The Security-Coordinating Committee will meet tomorrow morning, nine a.m.,' the general said. 'I will be in the chair.'

A simple statement of fact? Moral support? A warning that Estoban might need an ally? He had enemies as did anyone in a bureaucracy. In Cuba, there was only the bureaucracy. Each superior was a blockage in the accent of the pyramid.

Many of the younger officials considered Estoban out of date in his commitment to a war that was already lost. However, Estoban had never believed in the Cold War. His was a different conflict, simpler, more direct. The wall of photographs he faced gave evidence of his concerns: an eight-year-old boy sprawled dead in a Rio street; death squad victims on the rubbish heaps of El Salvador; bulldozed graves in Chile. And there were photographs of starved Slav faces huddled against the fence in the snow. Visitors to Estoban's office presumed these to be reminders of Hitler's invasion of the Ukraine. They were wrong. Estoban had taken the pictures with the miniature camera issued him by his masters at the KGB college. The pictures were of Soviet prison camps. No, the Russians had never been on his side, nor he on theirs. They had used each other for a while. That was all.

Pushing his chair back, Estoban rose and reached for a photograph of a mass grave in the Guatemalan jungle; the Indian corpses appeared no more than muddy scraps of ragged detritus. He tapped the photograph with a blunt finger. 'Do we know where he is?'

'Miguelito?' Rivas asked.

'God. . . ' Estoban chuckled softly as he stepped back from his wall to better view the scope of misery. Made in God's image. Disease, famine, earthquakes. 'Yes, Miguelito.'

'He was reported entering the main police station in Antigua. He was there only a few minutes. The police must have documented his particulars, perhaps advised him to change hotels. That was three days ago. He has vanished.'

'They would have referred him to a contact?'

'An assistant undersecretary at their Ministry for Foreign Affairs. This is standard.'

'Did he telephone?'

'They say not.' Rivas shrugged his distrust of anything reported by the Guatemalan authorities. 'The ballet returned one hour ago. Security interviewed them at José Martí airport. Nothing. They would have told the truth,' he said, his contempt for the dance troupe and its homosexuals evident and typical of *machista* Cuba.

'Clearly.' Estoban turned to the window facing down Obispo to the redecorated and newly opened Hotel Ambos Mundos. Hemingway had lived there in a corner room on the fourth floor for several years in the Thirties. Boxer, killer of game and fish, war correspondent – romanticist of violence – *machista* as

Rivas. Estoban fought for concentration but the pain came in waves, pain for his brother, isolated by his shame. The word came to him, *Beloved*, repeating itself again and again. He felt the tears thrust hot at the back of his eyes. Desolation. Never to hold Miguelito again, never to see him in the distance and feel his own belly unzip with a love so strong that he feared he would disintegrate. Yes, *Beloved*.

Miguelito must have gone to the Americans. It was the obvious road; the US Embassy, then Miami to shelter within the exile community.

Any enquiry had to be ministry to foreign ministry. Estoban and his bureau had few allies amongst the diplomats. 'Dig, but be a little careful,' he said.

Alone, he watched an army truck creep round the far corner. Black faces lined the tailgate – illegal immigrants from the eastern provinces; some twenty thousand of them had been repatriated forcibly from Havana to their home provinces over the past months. A group of Spanish tourists passed below his window; bunching behind their guide, their walk was as aimless as the march of prisoners of war chivvied towards an unknown destination. Cuba's new rich circled them, pimps and hustlers darting in and away as did wolves on a wounded bear – black, all of them, hardened by racial insult through their schooldays and thus armoured to withstand rejection. Their clothes marked them: new jeans, Florida T-shirts, expensive trainers worn unlaced to ape the North American blacks they admired on videos smuggled in from Miami.

In company with Estoban's thoughts, three teenagers practised kick-boxing on the south corner of calle Cuba. Thus was the new religion that leaked across the Gulf Stream from the Florida Keys: $100 trainers, kick-boxing and rollerblades. How would Miguelito survive? His lack of English no hindrance in Miami, would he slip into the easy safety of homosexual society? A society sick, not for its sexual orientation, but from its militant exclusion of other values. Waiter in a gay-owned restaurant, a night's tips triple Estoban's monthly salary? Tending bar? Or kept by a lawyer lover, a real-estate broker?

God protect him, prayed the atheist Estoban as he imagined his brother innocent of any experience outside the safety of Havana's streets and now faced with the dangers of Miami: drugs, mugging, senseless street murders. Yet even this infection was spreading to Havana, Estoban accepted as he watched two black teenagers poised in the deep shadows of a doorway, one clutching a bicycle. The smaller was the bag snatcher, the other ready to whisk the thief clear. Estoban had watched them operate. So had the two policemen further up the street – police frightened to make arrests amongst the crowded tenements and theft from tourists ever more common. The thieves were too ignorant to understand that, in destroying Havana's reputation for safety, they destroyed their own future and their children's future.

Such was only a very small part of the evil that accompanied tourism: prostitution, corruption, theft. Worse was the redivision of society into those with access to dollars and the dollar shops and those restricted to their peso salaries, a society in which a car park attendant at a tourist hotel earned fifty times the salary of a brain surgeon.

Estoban could have used his contacts amongst his fellow *poderosos* to secure dollar jobs for relatives and friends. He refused, as he refused to buy petrol on the black market; or even to eat the cheese that came to their apartment stolen by his brother-in-law from the dairy at Siboney; or the hams a cousin smuggled out of the warehouse where he worked; or redecorate their apartment with paint stolen by yet another relative, this one employed by Cubalse, the state agency occupied with the repair and leasing of property to foreign diplomats and businessmen.

Estoban knew that he appeared ridiculous to many; his wife accused him of blindness, even of sacrificing their children – but, no, he saw it all. He chose to live cloistered within his principles. He had no alternative. Violence was his trade. That was the truth and he turned away from the window to face the wall of photographs. So many operations had been planned in this very room. The car bomb in Caracas was one of his; the train derailed by a mine in Peru, rain spattering the bodies scattered down the mountainside; the twisted remains of the twin engine Cessna on the private airstrip in Guatemala, the finca owner's six-year-old daughter beheaded by the blast. These photographs were a daily reminder of what he did.

In directing violence he had to believe. There was no romance in it, no romance at all.

Even one moment of doubt and he would be destroyed as he had destroyed Miguelito. He felt it deep inside himself, the knowledge that had he been less secretive in his life, more approachable, capable of showing his love, then Miguelito would have returned.

Mea culpa, he whispered, *mea culpa, mea maxima culpa*. Yes, he was familiar with the New Testament – know thine enemy. And Pontius Pilate stood always at his shoulder, he thought as he washed his hands in the small restroom opening off his office – a daily routine, as was the twenty minute bicycle ride back to their apartment – a cleansing before he faced his children.

Bergman

'That's your man,' Nick said of a brown ball of sweat dressed up in a brown suit that even Bergman would have fed to the shredder.

Estoban Tur wheeled his bicycle out through the doorway and across the pavement, hopped twice to get it moving, swung his right leg over the seat and pedalled off down the street. His socks didn't match.

Nick said, 'Don't let the image fool you.'

Nick had served fourteen years with CIA Ops, the last three in Cuba. Bergman thought of him as Nick the Greek: dark eyes and short, all nerves and muscle. The Special Interests Section was a haven for old hands. Crazy, most of them, with their dreams of exploding cigars and wetsuits impregnated with poison.

'This thing we're doing isn't legitimate,' Bergman said. 'It goes wrong, dump on me.'

'That's what you said already a half-dozen times,' Nick said. 'Live in Guatemala and you get to sound like a parrot.'

Nick turned Bergman away from the Ambos Mundos and down through the cathedral square to the waterfront. A piece of cardboard against the inside of the windscreen advertised a battered Lada as a taxi.

Nick told the driver to take them up 17th Avenue.

'That's where your man lives,' Nick said.

12

Estoban

Their apartment occupied the north and east facing corner on the eighth floor of an early Fifties concrete tower block on the borders of Central Havana and Vedado. Estoban entered through the garage – the answering system at the main entrance had been broken for the past fifteen years and the doors were permanently locked. Of the service and two residents' elevators, the right hand sometimes worked. Tonight it was jammed on the fourteenth floor. Estoban hoisted his bike over his shoulder and began the long climb up the unlit service stairs.

Exhausted by the ascent, he rested a minute on the landing before letting himself into the apartment. On Wednesdays the children stayed over at Estoban's mother-in-law for their supper. The arrangement was designed to give Estoban and his wife privacy. Half the time Estoban returned late from the office, the other half Maria, a high-school teacher, was busy with schoolwork.

Estoban propped his bicycle carefully against the wall in the narrow entrance passage. A bathroom with shower separated the two small bedrooms on the right of the passage, next came the kitchenette with room for one person to stand at the granite slab. Ahead lay the living room, no door, a poster of Che Guevara the only decoration on the white walls. Four upright metal chairs were set at a round glass-top table. Estoban's wife, Maria, sat at the table, correcting essays.

Estoban could feel her anger flow to meet him as she looked up briefly and gave him a quick nod.

To her right, two cane easy chairs and a cane couch were arranged to allow access to the glass door leading out onto a narrow balcony that faced east to the old city. The dancer, Andres, sat on the couch. He was a head taller than Estoban: blue jeans, a red silk loose-sleeved shirt, high-heeled Mexican boots and a gold neck chain. His eyes were red to match his shirt, the lids swollen.

He blurted, 'We all know what you are.' The We included Estoban's wife. 'You are a killer. A homophobe. Miguelito was unable to face you. You made him ashamed of what he is. You. . .' Andres couldn't find the words. His tears came again, tears of rage rather than sadness. 'Everyone is afraid of you, son of a whore. How does that feel? Or are you above caring what we ordinary people think?'

Even as he let Andres' whip strike, the analyst in Estoban remained active. The dancer's grief was genuine. However, Estoban could scent Andres' pleasure in hurting one of the *poderoso*, the powerful. He saw Andres recounting his attack to his friends, revelling in their admiration of his courage.

'Your children. Do their friends visit here to play? Walking death. Everyone knows. Everyone . . .' Andres jabbed a finger at Estoban's chest. 'How does it feel or are you incapable of answering? Even your wife. Look . . .'

Fresh pain came to Estoban as he turned to Maria and sensed the same desire to hurt. Yet with Maria, he knew that the source of the desire was different; it grew from the need to smash the barriers of secrecy that divided them even as they lay beside each other in the night, not touching, silent, each imprisoned in a small circle of repeated thoughts and longings, words trapped, desires trapped – impotent to communicate in every sense. The pressure was so great that often Estoban lay waiting in the dark for the top of his skull to burst.

He could feel it in her as their eyes met, too real to be denied, too long lived – far more real than the posturing of the dancer.

'Leave now,' Estoban said.

147

'. . . everyone is afraid of you. Everyone . . .'

'Now,' Estoban repeated. He hadn't raised his voice but Andres stopped in full flow.

Estoban accompanied him to the stair head. The dancer's high-heeled boots struck hard on the cement treads, fierce explosions of indignation that echoed up the concrete stairwell.

Maria didn't look up when Estoban returned. Her soft colour and the neatness of her features were Ethiopian as was her body, slim and hard-breasted from daily exercise. Estoban's exclusion from her beauty hurt and he shuddered as he watched her circle a word with her red pencil. He saw a tear drop onto the essay and watched her dab it on the corner of her T-shirt. Ink left a pale blue stain on the cotton. He wanted to cross the room and shake her, hug her, weep for his loss in her arms. He longed for strength to kneel at her feet, beg forgiveness for all the failures; his job held him prisoner, the explanations sealed the far side of the boundary that divided his vocation from his family life.

He said, 'The children will miss him.'

'Yes.' Head bowed, Maria carefully underlined a phrase and printed a comment in the margin.

'The elevator is jammed.'

'Yes.'

He reached for the telephone and dialled Maria's mother half a dozen times. 'The line is dead.'

Maria gave a slight nod that would once have spun waves through the dense springy mass of loose curls. Now she wore her hair wrenched back by a rubber band, severe and controlled. African and Caucasian, bad hair and good – such remained Cuban terminology despite forty years of revolution.

Estoban had bought in la Plaza de Armas a secondhand edition of Gustavo Eguren's collected letters and diaries recounting life in Havana from the city's birth to the revolution. He sat with the book out on the small terrace, though without attempting to read. Car lights threaded through the darkness of a power cut shrouding Central Havana. The light-sprinkled upper floors of the Capri and the Habana Libre pierced the blackness, spacecraft in a science-fiction movie. The rusted exhaust of a Russian Lada crackled along the seafront Malecón. Low to his left salsa pulsed from an open window; flicker of television screens; a police whistle; in their apartment, silence thick as the fog spilling in autumn mornings from the River Moscow. He had been so proud to be one of those chosen for training in the USSR, so very proud. He recalled his confidence that very morning as he swooped down the hill on his bicycle to the waterfront, sea breeze clearing his thoughts as he pedalled to the office. And now, he thought I'm a cripple, a cripple incapable of even weeping for his loss.

Half an hour and he laid the book aside.

The legs of his chair screeched on the tiles. Maria turned her face away to better concentrate on an essay in the pile to her right – corrected essays – Estoban knew her habits. He hesitated in crossing the small living room, irresolute, longing for her to look up. He wondered whether she was crying. He said, 'I will go down to meet the children.'

She nodded.

He said, 'Please.'

The forty watt light bulb above the table flickered, then darkness.

She said, 'Take the lantern.' Rechargeable batteries, twin phosphorescent tubes, 'Made in Japan', stolen from a Caricol dollar shop by one of his countless in-laws. So simple to take it, a peace offering.

'No.' He felt his way down the passage and out to the stairs. Eight floors of blindness. On the fifth he stumbled over an old lady from the tenth marooned by total blackness and wheezing curses.

'It shouldn't be long,' he said.

'Forty years,' she spat, too old to care who he was. He heard her muttering *pig of a mulatto* as he eased past her and on down to the garage.

The powerful headlights of a Nissan rental car dipped into the garage and blinded Estoban for a moment. The internal lights of the car showed two gaudily dressed black girls in their early twenties accompanied by a late middle-aged foreigner – presumably with greater sexual imagination than ability; the girls wouldn't care.

The foreigner cursed as he stumbled over a bicycle – German, so he was probably renting a room from Ricardo Enriquez on the sixth who had studied in Dortmund for his doctorate in engineering before the fall of communism and was fluent in the language. Four tenants regularly let to foreigners and their local lovers – thirty dollars a night came cheaper for a tourist than bribing the security guard at a hotel to permit a Cuban entry. Both Alicia on the tenth floor and Pedro on the eleventh specialised in Italians while, on the third, Jasmine received a steady clientele of homosexual medical doctors from the US. What they did was their affair. Estoban's revolution had always lain beyond the sea.

He sat waiting for the children on the kerb outside the garage – as he had waited in the past for Miguelito to come running from school. In watching his brother race towards him, Estoban had been stunned, not simply by the absoluteness of his love, but by his capacity to love. It was a quality he had doubted in himself.

His mother, marooned and isolated in the strangeness of Havana, had lived only for him and he had accepted her love as his right. In return, his own love had remained automatic and unchanging in its expectations.

Guilt had permeated his love for his father, guilt at his selfishness in longing to deny his father the right to a separate life; and guilt at his jealousy for the revolution that demanded his father's service and loyalty; even jealousy of Che, the adored, and anger at Che for having taken Estoban's father to Angola, Che somehow responsible for the stray shell.

As for Estoban's love life, he had begun by losing his virginity through an accident of the weather to a fellow student at the Lenin school. They had been listing insects for a biology project. Rain had caught them out in the fields beyond the school grounds. A tin-roofed shed had offered shelter.

150

Already practised, she had stretched her arms back so that her nipples thrust at the thin cotton of her shirt. His uncertainty had amused her. Laughing, she said, 'Come on. Let us do it,' and, shedding her clothes, lay on the dirt floor, waiting.

Later had come girlfriends, casual to him and without emotional intensity. Then Russia where, for eight years, he had listened to his tutors lecture on the necessity of hiding his thoughts and feelings. He had been tested. First Irina skidding into him on the ice in his first year in Moscow. Pretending obsession with the difference in their colours, in bed she had purred over him like a cat. Her tongue had left cool trails on his skin. Her questions had come in the aftermath of orgasm. At Naro-Fominsk came Fatima, the Palestinian, who had uncloaked to him the essence of her hate and, in return, had asked of him his own feelings. In the field came the Polish Anya and, later, Manon in Nicaragua.

Unasked-for commitment had embarrassed him. He had ended such relationships quickly and with an absence of finesse that he excused to himself as essential to his vocation.

He had recognised danger in the ease of his resistance and had come to question whether he had been recruited because of this sickness or had become sick through his recruitment.

Then Maria appeared. He had seen her first holding the traffic to allow children to cross the road to her school. The wild swirl of her hair captured him – and an African arrogance portrayed in the depth of her eyelids. Later came his awareness of the warmth with which she greeted her students.

He had warned others always to vary their routine. Yet he found himself on the same road to his office two or three mornings a week. Her absence made him inattentive at meetings. Proficient gatherer of intelligence, he listed her appearances and thus calculated her duty days. He fantasised their meeting, rehearsed dialogue, though without expectation.

He imagined a queue of prospective *novios* captured by her vitality and by her beauty. What chance had he? Ten years older, short, dumpy, and without wit. Two months passed before he dared nod to her; no smile, his lips were frozen.

He considered driving to work; though old, his Lada was a symbol of influence. Then, ashamed, he vowed to avoid her school for ever more.

Ten days' abstinence sapped his determination. Halfway to the office he turned back and peddled fast down the familiar street. The children were already in school. She stepped out of the shadows of a laurel tree. A quick toss of her head spun the mass of tight black curls flying as, hands on her hips, she blocked his way.

He braked hard and skidded to a halt. Putting his foot down, he found a pothole in the road and tumbled sideways.

Laughing, she untangled him from his bicycle. '*Y qué?*' she demanded. And so? 'I believed that you were ill.'

'No.' All the prepared dialogue had vanished from his head. Desperate, he said, 'I am late. *Bolero?*' He meant to ask if she liked dancing but she was already nodding.

'Saturday,' she said. 'We will meet outside the writers and artists union. Nine o'clock. That you should be late will not be forgiven.'

Now, sitting on the kerb, he wondered that he could have destroyed such spontaneity. And Miguelito . . .

The boys were suddenly on him. Mario, eight, was the elder, and Estoban, six, called Tobanito; Estoban had retained the misspelling in memory of his parents, barely literate when they had registered his own birth. Tobanito grabbed at Estoban for attention. Mario, less open and more circumspect, bided his time. Estoban's mother-in-law greeted him with cool politeness, hugged the children and vanished back into the dark.

Estoban led the boys across the garage to the stairs.

'Silly Papi, you should have brought the lamp,' Tobanito reproved.

'Mama needed it for her work.'

Shame for his lie obsessed Estoban. They rested at the fourth-floor landing, Estoban seated on the last step, Tobanito between Estoban's knees.

Estoban confessed into the dark, 'Mama wanted me to take the lamp.'

Mario was behind him. The child threaded his arms round his father's neck. 'It does not matter, Papi.'

'It does,' Tobanito said.

'It does,' Estoban echoed, not for the lamp, but for the pain present in his elder son's understanding.

The lights came on as they reached the seventh floor and Estoban was forced to confront the increasingly present despair in Mario's eyes. It would have been easier in the dark. And easier to enter the apartment.

He shushed Tobanito at the door. 'Mami is working.'

'She is always working.'

Mario said, 'No, she is not.'

'When Papi is here, she is.'

'Please,' Estoban said.

Mario's hand slipped into his. 'It will be all right, Papi.'

Estoban led down the passage, blocking the children's' view of their mother so that she had time to gather herself.

She looked up and smiled with lips stiff as had been Estoban's at their first acknowledged encounter.

Estoban bustled the children out onto the terrace. He held them on his lap and showed them the illustrations in Eguren's book. It was true that the boys never brought friends to the apartment. He wanted to ask why, but didn't dare. He laid the book aside. Carrying the boys through to the bathroom, he helped them undress. They shone in the shower, their skins the colour of caramelised sugar on a baked custard. Their beauty caught in his throat: the trough of their spines, the nape of their necks, their ears so neat and tight against their skulls, thigh muscles springy, their buttocks round. He saw his brother at the same age – all the times that he had bathed him. He reached into the shower for water to cool his eyes. Mario had seen his pain and held his father's face for a moment between his palms.

'What is wrong, Papi?'

'Nothing.' He squeezed toothpaste onto their brushes and counted the strokes as they cleaned their teeth then, waving a towel, shooed them like lambs up the corridor to their bedroom. Light on, he spotted a mosquito on the ceiling and flicked it with the towel.

Mario spotted another on the light cable and Estoban waved it into the air before downing it.

'Story.'

His mind wouldn't clear so he read them a letter from the book they had been looking at out on the terrace – a mother's letter describing her children's progress to her own mother home in Spain.

He fetched water from the icebox and held the tumbler to their lips so that the water didn't spill on the sheets. Setting the fan at the foot of their beds, he switched off the light.

Mario said, 'Please, Papi, hold me. Just for a little.'

Estoban pushed the beds together and lay in the middle, the two boys curled in against him, warm in their nakedness, silky-skinned. They clutched to him, their love unbearable in its power to strip away his protection. In the dark the tears came, silent rivers on his cheeks. 'Tío Miguelito,' he whispered. 'Tío won't be coming back.'

He had expected questions but the boys were tired from the walk home and the climb up the stairs. Mario touched Estoban's cheeks. 'It will be all right, Papi.'

'Yes,' he said. 'It will be all right.'

He listened to the soft stir of their breathing and felt their grip relax into sleep. He wanted to stay with them. Their love was unquestioning, so safe. They made no demand on his courage. Coward, he thought.

Easing out of their arms, he left the door ajar. He could see Maria down the corridor still at her books. Undressing in the bathroom, he washed himself and carried his clothes back to the bedroom, hanging his suit on its hanger before switching off the light.

He lay waiting. The alarm clock on the bedside table noisily ticked away the seconds. He counted, pretending that if Maria came to their room before he had reached one hundred all would be well. He even believed for a while, stretching the seconds as he had done sometimes as a child at night when promising himself that his father would come home from the other house where he had gone to live. Two hundred, three hundred. He wanted so very little. He wanted to hold her, that was all, rest in her, whisper to her his hurt and share it with her.

He heard the creak of her chair in the living room and the click of the light switch. Eyes shuttered, he listened to her slip from her clothes, tiptoe on bare feet to the bathroom in pretence that he was asleep. She drew the sheet back, easing onto the bed, then lay on the very edge so that they didn't touch. He could see her body as clearly as if she were under a floodlight, every slope and curve and crevice familiar to him. Released from its rubber bands, the thick curling mass of her hair would spring out across the pillows, her face tiny in its frame, the swell of her lips generous. He knew the taste of her saliva, of her sweat, of her juices. She felt the shift of the sheet as he moved a hand towards her.

'Don't,' she said.

The disbelieved deception that he slept was his now and he let his hand stay where it was, the angle of his shoulder painful but less so than the pain of being unable to confess and be forgiven.

Bergman

Bergman drove. Four of them were in the Peugeot rental car hired from Havanautos: Bergman, Nick the Greek and two women. They had picked the women up at the entrance to the Marina Hemingway. One of the women was black, the other white. The black woman was the elder, nineteen or there-abouts.

They had told the girls that they were over from Florida via

Nassau for a long weekend. Getting the girls into the marina would have cost a bribe at the gate as would getting them into a hotel. They told the women that a friend had given Bergman the address of an apartment in Vedado on 17th Avenue which the owner let by the night. Nick had four watchers in position, one outside the building, one curled up drunk on the garage floor behind a Sixties Skoda and two on the stairs pretending to be lovers.

This was Bergman's operation and he had taken it back into his own hands. He was doing what he was good at and he was enjoying himself. The women and Nick the Greek waited in the car while he entered the garage. Opening the driver's door of Tur's Lada took Bergman less than a minute. He dropped the envelope with the photograph on the seat. Then he rode the elevator up to the sixth floor and rang the bell to the apartment at the far end of the corridor.

A man came to the door, scratching and ruffled from bed.

'Doctor Enriquez?' Bergman asked and the man nodded.

'I heard you let rooms,' Bergman said.

'Full,' the man told him and produced a cheaply printed card with his telephone number. 'Next time you ring.'

'Yeah, sorry,' Bergman said.

Twenty dollars each cured the women's business disappointment and Nick and Bergman dropped them outside the 1830 disco at the west end of the Malecón by the tunnel under the Rio Almendares.

West of the Rio Almendares and south of Playa, the Kohly district of Havana is much favoured by military *poderosos*. Tur's boss owned a mini-mansion circa 1900 with pillared portico. A hedge of red hibiscus grew against the tall fence facing the pavement and the gates were covered with sheets of tin to prevent passers-by observing the non-egalitarian luxury enjoyed by the general's family.

Bergman had put a weight in the general's envelope and sealed the envelope in a transparent plastic folder with a yellow ribbon threaded through one corner. A flick of the wrist sent the package spinning over the fence.

13

Estoban Tur

The committee investigating Miguelito's defection met in a building beyond Revolution Square. Public transport was always difficult and there might be those on the committee with cars that were broken or who had either sold or used their petrol ration. Driving his own Lada, Estoban could offer such people a lift after the meeting. He fetched a plastic carrier bag from the kitchen drawer and rode the elevator down to basement level. A single bulb stuck out on a wire from the wall opposite the elevator. The light seeped across the garage to his red Lada parked in a corner. He unlocked the passenger door, picking the children's refuse from the floor. He saw the envelope on the driver's seat. White, dangerous.

Slipping in behind the wheel, he bent low to scoop a scrap of old newspaper into the plastic bag. Dropping the bag on the passenger seat allowed him to finger the contours of the single stiff card inside the envelope. He shoved open the driver's door to light the bulb in the door pillar and lay flat across the seat, his head under the dashboard as if searching for something. Then he slid out the card. It was a Polaroid photograph.

Miguelito looked straight into the camera. Estoban saw first the look of pleading on Miguelito's face. He was naked, bent forward over a desk, his wrists bound. A soldier in combat dress stood behind him, their congress brutal. Six others waited their turn. The soldiers' faces were above the camera line.

Estoban dragged the shirt-tails out of his trousers and wiped the photograph clean of his fingerprints before slipping it back into the envelope. He wiped the envelope, replaced it on the seat and covered it with the plastic bag of rubbish. Starting the engine, he immediately switched off. He repeated this routine twice then turned the ignition with his foot flat on the throttle to flood the engine. He kept pumping fresh petrol into the cylinders as he ran the battery flat. Chino from the third floor came over and offered to push, and Teresa from the seventh, owner of the rusty yellow Polaski that never started in the rain. Next came Alejandro and Jenny from the twelfth. Any one of them could be reporting Estoban's reactions to the photograph. He cursed as he got out.

'The gasoline is half water,' Chino said.

Jenny said, 'You have left a parcel on the seat.'

'The children's rubbish.'

Locking the car, Estoban took the elevator back up to the apartment.

Maria had the children ready in the entrance lobby. Pink trousers, short sleeved white shirts, white socks and blue trainers. Mario wore the blue scarf of the pioneers but not Tobanito who was in *pre-scolar* – kindergarten.

Estoban said, 'The car refuses to start. It is necessary that I ride the bicycle. Telephone to Rivas at the office that I shall be delayed for the committee.' He dabbed a kiss at her cheek and, wheeling his bicycle, hustled the boys to the elevator.

Mario sat on the rear carrier, Tobanito on a wooden seat mounted on the bicycle's crossbar. They swooped down the hill to Linea, then right two blocks and up one to the children's school. He could have ridden the road blindfolded, each pothole too familiar to be disguised by the shade thrown across the early morning street by the flamboyant trees. It was a good neighbourhood and there were parents present from other ministries whose co-operation he had sought in the past. He smelt their knowledge of Miguelito's supposed defection. He saw it in the quick shift of their eyes. He had never been popular and in some he divined pleasure at his discomfort. He hugged the boys hard for a moment and Mario whispered to him, 'Do not worry, Papi.'

Estoban knew that the child was speaking to himself.

Revolution Square was uphill and Estoban was sweating heavily by the time he reached the building. A guard checked his papers as if he didn't know who Estoban was, then led him up the steps and across the lobby to a long corridor. The floor hadn't been scrubbed in a year and the off-cream paint on the walls was streaked with revolutionary grime. The guard nodded at the last door. The room was long and low ceilinged, the big mahogany table and heavy chairs filched from some pre-Revolutionary boardroom. Five men sat at the table; they were white, of course. One of them was a surprise – Ramirez, the Spider. Though never holding a position in government, he had been a close confident of Fidel's for fifty years – a member of the magic circle right back to the president's days as a law student. Almost hidden in damp pouches, the pale watery eyes were familiar to Estoban, as was the grey, wispy beard sprouting from the padded cheeks. A fat H Upmann cigar leaked yellowed spittle down his chin and the bald dome of his head reflected the strip ceiling light above the table. Food stained his shirt front and his belly spilled out between canvas braces. To make space for his bulk, Ramirez had moved his chair back from the table and away from his neighbour, the young vice minister of finance, Jorge Mendez.

The minister was less of a surprise. Jorge Mendez and Estoban had been fellow students at the Lenin school, the minister four years younger. He had worked on his figure in the gymnasium and was slim and more obviously muscled than Estoban. Blond hair and green eyes were inherited from his grandparents, immigrants from the Atlantic provinces of Spain. His square face appeared handsome and strong on television. A clean broom and active, he was building a following in the stakes for the succession. Today he seemed nervous as he rose to shake Estoban's hand.

The two men seated across from Ramirez and the minister had fought in the advance on Havana and were grey now, late sixties, one a drinker. Unquestioning loyalty was their hall-mark, brains irrelevant.

The general had joined Fidel earlier, in the first weeks of hiding in the *sierra*, and was classed as a 'Special Friend'. Special Friends did need brains. They were expected to make intelligent conversation at the dinner table and out on the cayos where Fidel loved to scuba dive. The general too was grey. A narrow-faced aesthete, his eyes were hooded by age, liver spots blotched the back of his hands, skin dry and baggy at the knuckles, nails brittle and marbled with chalk. Death sat with him. Estoban could smell it. Cancer of the lower bowel. The general had survived two operations.

The obligatory file lay on the table in front of the general. Estoban was a state secret and there were no copies. The general flicked the table edge a couple of times before opening the cover. He had no need to refer to the contents.

'*Compañero*, we must discuss this matter of your brother,' he began in a dry, clipped voice made small by the pain that castrated his energy. 'We must examine the implications to our national security.'

The grey ones nodded agreement. It was all they would ever do – nod like the wooden dolls Estoban had brought home from Russia.

Jorge Mendez, the minister, said, 'Each one of us has relatives over there.'

There was always Miami.

Since his promotion the minister had taken to twenty-four-hour stubble and wearing T-shirts as proof that he remained one of the people. He fancied himself the pop star of the revolution and the shirts were hand-painted by his groupies. The one he wore today bore an American eagle wreath. The laurel leaves were there but the eagle had been replaced by a plucked chicken strung upside down. Jorge Mendez sat open-chested to insure that his companions appreciated the artwork – rumour had it that he bedded the artists.

The others didn't like him. He was too young, too vital, too thrusting – and far too obviously intelligent and quick-witted.

'We know Estoban's record,' he said. 'This is a charade. Get done with it before it becomes an insult.'

Beside him the old man, the Spider, Ramirez, wheezed softly round the wet butt of his cigar.

The general held an envelope. He took out the photograph and passed it down the table to the minister. Estoban watched the minister's face and there was no disguising the shock.

The minister said, 'Shit!' and came close to blushing as he leant down the table to hand the photograph direct to Estoban. It was a kind gesture intercepted by one of the grey men, who immediately passed the photograph to his companion.

Finally the photograph came to Estoban. He was ready. First he displayed shock, then horror that rapidly changed to a blind rage that permitted him time to assess his position. That they were willing to torture Miguelito made Estoban open to blackmail – they, whoever they were. Vulnerable, Estoban would be suspended from duty. And there would be no way back. Better that he should resign now and keep some small part of his dignity.

He sensed the grey men's pleasure in his fall. They had never liked him. He came from a different background, black blood strained through the cane fields where his father and grandfather had worked and where Estoban would have worked but for the revolution that brought education to the countryside. And not only education, but also the opportunity for a child to excel and leap clear of his birth.

Ramirez sighed and shifted his bulk to better watch as Estoban took the office keys from his pocket. The small brass Buddha on the key ring was designed to deceive a finder of the keys into believing they belonged to an embassy official – not that Estoban had ever lost or even mislaid the keys in his years with G2. Keys had been made sacred for him in early childhood. His family had occupied a shack on the hillside above the cane fields and Estoban could recall the exact slope of his father's shoulders as he knelt at the tin trunk that held their few possessions. He remembered the ceremonial solemnity that accompanied his father's withdrawal of the shiny key on its chain from inside his shirt and the careful fitting of the key into the big brass Yale padlock that fastened the hasp on the trunk and the grate of the trunk's hinges. No, Estoban had never lost a key.

He laid the office keys on the photograph, splaying them so that they pointed at the committee members. 'I possess no others.'

The minister said, 'Estoban, I am sorry, truly sorry. Sons of whores . . .'

Now it was the general's turn. First came the official warning not to leave the city, not to approach his office. Estoban had heard the same instructions issued to others who had become security risks or had fallen from grace.

He said, 'If I can be of help to my successor, he knows where I live.'

'The accounts must be transferred,' the general said. His pain was obvious. Pain only from the cancer? Or was there more? He and Estoban had been friends for fifteen years. The general had fought for Estoban's promotion. Yet now Estoban sensed an unease in the veteran. For how long had he possessed the photograph? Or known that it existed? Had he been instructed not to warn Estoban or had this been his own decision?

The general indicated the minister and, in explanation of his presence on the committee, said, 'The Ministry of Finance will inform you when and where you should attend for the examination of the accounts.'

This definitely was a warning and Estoban gave a slight bob of his head to the older man. 'To serve you, General, has been an honour. *Buenos días, compañeros*.'

He was halfway down the corridor when the minister called after him. Jorge Mendez had paled beneath his tan. A professional politician, Jorge should have been shockproof.

The minister said, 'Listen, Estoban, something will present itself.' He meant a job – one where security and blackmail weren't a problem. Few such jobs existed in a country made paranoid as much by its own system as by the attacks made on it by its all-powerful neighbour, the USA.

Jorge Mendez grabbed Estoban by the hand, his other arm round Estoban's shoulders in an act of genuine warmth, 'It must be them.'

Them was the CIA. And why not? They had plotted to kill Fidel with exploding cigars and poisons and assassins' guns. It was all carefully catalogued in a US Congressional report. Estoban knew much of it by heart.

He said, 'The possibility exists – my gratitude for your support, Jorge.'

'I was of no assistance.'

'They have no affection for us.'

'The old men?'

'The grey ones.'

The minister smiled. 'Grey ones – yes, I like that. They never did shit or believed in shit. You know where I live. Visit at any time. . .'

'Thanks,' Estoban said. Both men knew he wouldn't – good manners forbade non-persons visiting those within the upper strata of the pyramid.

The minister gave him a last hug, then held him at arm's length for a moment, the look in his eyes the same as the one he used on television: straight talker, straight fighter, one of the boys from the barrio. 'We have much need of men like you in government . . .'

Estoban wondered how much of it was rehearsed. Dangerous, another potential dictator.

Bricks and mortar had carried news of Estoban's downfall ahead of him down the corridor to the lobby where the doormen sneered to each other in pretended inattention as they blocked his way to the reception desk.

Estoban grabbed the larger of the two between the legs and twisted. 'Little prick, fight your own weight.'

Self disgust at his violence accompanied him down the steps. He unlocked his bicycle from the tree and stood in the shade on the pavement wondering where to go. He had no office in which to shelter and there was no point in returning home to the empty apartment.

He considered bicycling to the school where his wife taught, telling her now rather than delay to the evening with the children present. He looked the length of the street, wondering which of the pedestrians and bicyclists were watchers from security. Given an excuse, they would arrest him quietly. An error in his accounts would be least scandalous. He would be safer for them in jail and they believed in safety. Above all else they believed in safety. Safety of their own positions, safety of their power. He had never been part of that, never a believer in any ideology. The photographs in his office had supplied his creed: cruelty and selfishness and exploitation had to be fought. He had never expected to win, or even make any difference – however, not trying was the final betrayal, a betrayal of your own life, living without valid purpose.

Now, suddenly, after all the years of fighting, his place in the battle had been taken from him. He swung his leg over the saddle and pedalled down the street beneath the shade of the flamboyant trees. His thoughts had been directed outward ever since he had been conscripted into security. Now he found himself seeing the familiar disrepair of the Vedado mansions from a fresh viewpoint. The pillars moulting plaster, broken windows, lack of paint, holes in the road, sewage bubbling out of a cracked manhole cover into the gutters only for the flow to be dammed by refuse so that it spilled back into the street, a grey sludgy scum covering the cobbles, stinking and fly-infested.

The ruts between the cobbles jarred up between his legs, each thud a reminder of the photograph. He could deal with it now, his brother's desperate pleading. He had turned downhill on calle G. He crossed Linea at the lights, pedalling on past the Hotel Cohiba with its surrounding regiment of available young women. Across the square a 1949 Cadillac convertible waited to have its tank filled at the Cupet service station. A couple of Spanish tourists lolled on the back seat with two final-grade

high-school girls. Little Pepes, the Cubans called such Spaniards, men who played the *hidalgo* for a couple of weeks every
two years, then back to the baking heat of an Andaluz market
garden or a Barcelona factory floor.

The Malecón – Havana's esplanade – lay beyond the petrol
station. Every citizen came to the Malecón in search of cool sea
breeze or love or simply in search of peace from a family
crowded into inadequate accommodation.

Estoban crossed the six-lane highway, propped his bicycle
against the sea wall and stood for a while looking out to sea.
There were no boats. Any craft remotely capable of the voyage
to Key West was long gone, either confiscated or sold to a
potential escapee and left somewhere convenient. Now fishermen bobbed in truck and tractor tubes on the light swell.
Watching them was dangerous. The watchers would report to
the case officer who might conclude that Estoban was contemplating escape. It was equally suspect for Estoban not to look
out to sea because to look was natural and not to look could be
construed as the subterfuge of a man contemplating flight.

So it would continue, this new life.

Bergman

Nick the Greek had six watchers on the target. Their reports
came in by digital phone every few minutes. They had spotted
two of the opposition.

Bergman drove slowly west along the Malecón and window-
shopped the girls strutting the pavement or lolling against the
sea wall. The girls made for good cover and were great to look
at. Outside of a beauty pageant, Bergman had never seen so
many beautiful young women in one place in his entire life, or
such a variety of racial blends.

The target appeared oblivious of the parade. He had taken
his jacket off and sat on the sea wall with his legs hanging
down, one foot on the seat of his bicycle. As a mulatto, it
would have been tough reaching his position, and now his

whole life had gone up in smoke. He would be thinking of his brother and what sort of future he could offer his wife and children. Perhaps whether he could defect. Defection was an alternative that every member of the intelligence community considered when things went bad. Considering it didn't make traitors of them. It was simply an option that existed within the profession. An escape route.

Estoban Tur

Estoban wondered how much he was worth to the Americans. Less and less every hour as the word spread to his agents, and amongst those who had depended upon Estoban for support, that he was cut loose, out of the circuit. In forty-eight hours he would be worth nothing at the operational level, though still a fortune in publicity.

He wondered how long his marriage would last. Castrated by inactivity, plagued by paranoia, a non-person – six months? Perhaps less. In other systems there were alternative careers and employers. In Cuba only the state existed.

But that wasn't true and he had to deal with the truth, confront it. Small farmers were permitted now, as were hairdressers, cobblers, repairers of tires, mechanics, artisans of every kind. And private restaurants were legal in your own home, so long as you never seated more than twelve people, only employed your own family and paid US$800 monthly in taxes – though that option was closed to Estoban by the size of their apartment. In fact he had no options. He knew what he must do. It was the *how* that he had to consider. He had been a controller of agents throughout his career. Now he had to become an agent or recruit one. Preferably the latter. Someone to trust, so someone who would act from conviction. Not a Cuban or any man Estoban had recruited into Cuba's service – or the service of the revolution. All such people would have been warned against him; warned that he was unsafe, not to be trusted, a threat to their security, to their cause . . . whatever the cause.

No, he needed someone who shared his situation, someone who had been cut loose or had cut himself loose. Someone from the past. A Russian from the days before the fall . . . or someone from the opposition, someone no one would expect.

He sat cross-legged on the top of the wall. The flab on his chest and belly offended him. He had cultivated the fat to disguise his proficiency – one more sacrifice to his country's service.

Roddy

Lieutenant Roddy de Sanchez of Cuba's Department of Naval Intelligence had great love for Cuba but little affection for the administration. In this he was similar to the vast majority of his generation. As did his friends, Roddy practised a counterfeit loyalty because there was no easier or more comfortable alternative and he paid lip service to the revolution's successes in education and health service, though even there he was critical, his patriotism leading him to compare Cuba with Scandinavia rather than with its neighbours in the Caribbean and Central America.

Roddy was told of Estoban's dismissal at eleven a.m. His informant was a man of his own age and class or set, the young aristocracy of the revolution. Roddy's father, Admiral de Sanchez, had been shot by Estoban Tur and Roddy's informant presumed that Roddy would be delighted by Estoban's fall from power.

An hour later Roddy heard from his original source the reason for Estoban's fall. He knew Estoban's brother by sight, slight of figure, almost pretty. The viciousness behind the spreading of the news disgusted Roddy. He imagined Estoban's reactions. First the pain for his brother followed by rage and pain on his own behalf. And determination.

Roddy's thoughts went to his own father. The admiral had

been involved in the drug traffic via Angola into the US. Roddy, permitted to travel outside Cuba, had negotiated a deal for the admiral with the American State Department: the legitimising of the admiral's millions in payment for the publicity value of the admiral's defection with his staff officers and a Cuban naval vessel. Estoban Tur had covered for Roddy, saving him from arrest and execution.

Roddy sat at his desk a while longer working things out. Then he went down to records and spent an hour putting names together from the files. Back in his office he made calls to the resident director of the United Nations Narcotics Bureau in the Bahamas and to a Chief Superintendent of the Royal Bahamian Constabulary. Finally he telephoned his superior for an appointment in mid-afternoon. Mid-afternoon was best. His boss would be sleepy and inattentive.

Roddy checked out of the building and crossed the car park to the corner where he had left his powder-blue MG TD shaded by an acacia tree; Roddy's grandfather had presented the MG to Roddy's father on his eighteenth birthday.

Roddy joined the traffic on the avenida del Puerto by the Castillo de la Fuerza, followed the harbour front along to the Malecón and drove slowly along the sea lane of the dual carriageway. There wasn't much traffic. Petrol shortages and the cost of black-market fuel had forced most private vehicles off the roads and the only new cars were owned by foreign diplomats, foreigners involved in business with the state, or rental cars for the use of foreign tourists.

To draw attention to himself, Roddy hooted as he accelerated past slower cars and trucks. He spotted Estoban sitting cross-legged on the sea wall a hundred metres before the roundabout leading round to the Cohiba Hotel and the Paseo. The deposed director of intelligence would be watched, that much was certain. Roddy beat a quick tattoo on his horn and pulled out to overtake a rusty 1952 Chevy running on bare tyres and with a hole in its exhaust the size of a mango.

Roddy turned left onto the roundabout, drove a quarter of the way round and began to cut power. He let the engine stutter and finally stop on the shore side. He started the car again only to come to a halt for the second time facing back the way he had come. He cursed at a driver hooting behind him and leant under the dash as if fiddling with a fuse or a loose connection. Again he started the engine, carried on back down the Malecón and took the first turning right beyond the Cupet petrol station.

Bergman

'Roddy de Sanchez,' Nick the Greek said, pointing to the pale blue sports car stalled on the roundabout. 'You want someone to follow him or you believe in coincidence?'

Bergman had less faith in coincidence than he had in his ex-wife asking him to put her alimony payments on hold.

Roddy

Roddy drove up into Vedado in search of an ex-girlfriend who had once worked at the Partagás cigar factory behind the capitol. Now she had a five-year-old son and an ex-husband and sold cigars stolen by her ex-workmates.

The young woman spotted Roddy's car from the balcony of her family's apartment, waved and charged down the stairs with her son in her arms. She had been fifteen when Roddy had first known her both socially and in the Biblical sense. Now she was twenty-two. Black, short and curved, she had put on maybe a pound in weight over the seven years. She wore a very short flowered dress, white tennis shoes and a white bow in her hair. As she leant across the passenger seat to kiss Roddy, the dress lifted at the back and fell away at the front. Most of her backside was visible. All her breasts were. Her nipples were larger than Roddy recalled, the rest was firmly the same.

She said, 'I am alone in the apartment. We should enjoy ourselves. Half an hour for old time's sake?'

She left her son in Roddy's car while they went upstairs. Eight adults lived in the two room apartment, a reason for marriages breaking. Roddy looked down at his car from the balcony. The boy looked cute, black on white towelling seat covers. The girl pulled the dress over her head with the same fluid ease he recalled from their earlier relationship. One second she was covered, the next she was naked except for briefs that could have been cut from a small handkerchief. The pants came apart at one side and dropped the same way the dress had.

Roddy left the apartment twenty minutes later with a promise of ten boxes of Partagás Lusitanias. Bought legally, the cigars would have cost him $170 a box. Roddy had agreed a total price of $280 and had a contact in the Bahamas happy to pay $2000.

Bergman

'De Sanchez is getting laid – a black girl up in Vedado,' Nick the Greek reported. His watchers had spotted a fourth member of the opposition team shadowing Estoban Tur. Bergman doubted whether Nick's men were that good or the opposition that bad. Most probably the opposition were trying to spook the target.

Estoban Tur

Estoban hadn't moved in the past hour. He continued sitting in the sun down on the sea wall. He was happy that Roddy de Sanchez had come – Roddy of all people – and that Roddy had the intelligence and imagination to use the roundabout as his clock. Quarter to six that evening was too early so Roddy's signal was for half past nine. Estoban checked his watch and dropped to the pavement beside his bicycle.

Bergman

Nick the Greek took the message from the watcher. 'The target's on the move.'

'Don't get too close,' Bergman said.

14

Estoban Tur

Apparently irresolute, Estoban walked his bicycle back and forth for fifteen minutes in the street outside his wife's school. Next he bicycled home. The elevator worked and he directed it to the eighth floor. He pressed the stop button at the fifth and rode directly back to the garage. Getting into his Lada, he tilted the seat back and lay for ten minutes with his hands folded behind his head. Unable to sleep, he brought the seat upright and surreptitiously slipped the envelope containing the photograph inside his shirt. He sat for a further ten minutes with his hands on the wheel and stared straight ahead.

He shook his head a couple of times before getting out of the car. Crossing the garage, he summoned the elevator, changed his mind and unchained his bicycle. He was clearly unsure of what direction to take. Finally he rode back to his wife's school. This time he made it as far as the entrance before retreating. Riding uphill to his children's primary school, he peered over the railings as if trying to catch a glimpse of his sons. Disappointment sent him to his mother's building where he sat on the kerb for half an hour. A couple of times he made as if to enter the building. Finally he remounted his bicycle and rode east a block before turning and braking in the shade of an avocado tree. His indecision was obvious and a middle-aged black man asked what street he was looking for. Perhaps the man was a watcher. Estoban hung his head, bewildered and clearly close to emotional collapse.

'*No es fácil,*' the man said. It is not easy.

'*No es fácil,*' agreed Estoban.

The black man shrugged wearily. '*La lucha.*' The struggle.

'*La lucha.*' Such was the Cuban ritual.

Estoban sighed and pedalled on down the street. A queue waited patiently outside the state bakery on his left. Next came a 1920s house with a pillared porch where four men sat beneath a sign: CDR – Committee for the Defence of the Revolution. There was one such group on every block, informers on their neighbours.

A small crowd spilled onto the street at the state agricultural market on the corner. The stench of rotting tomatoes rose from the refuse beneath three crude wooden display tables, one piled with potatoes on which roots sprouted through a crust of earth. Whatever might have been on the other two tables had been sold.

As a boy, Estoban had known every bump in this street. His best friend at school, Camilo, had lived in a converted garden shed to the rear of the art-nouveau apartment building on the next block

Camilo's grandfather, an architect, had designed and owned the building. The grandfather had fled in the first week of the revolution so the building had been forfeit – including the family's penthouse home.

Estoban had been in Russia when Camilo attempted to escape Cuba on a raft. Camilo had been shot by a Guarda Frontera. The tide had washed him back to the beach at Santa Fe. His legs and his belly were missing, eaten by sharks. On his return from Russia, Estoban had visited Camilo's parents. To do so wasn't safe, of course, showing sympathy for the parents of a *gusano*, a worm – Fidel's word for the escapees and Miami Cubans. Estoban's visits had become increasingly infrequent and finally ceased. The father had become ill, mostly from unhappiness, and had died – happy to die.

As Estoban rode east, the Camilo building was on the downhill side of the street. Estoban glanced sideways as he passed. Nothing had changed. He slowed, then swung his bike round and parked beneath a trumpet tree. He was sure now of three watchers: two women – women were always keenest – and a pseudo-university student, male. Estoban's hesitation confused them. The two women chatted to each other as they passed and he watched them continue for a hundred metres before halting at the agricultural market. The student was already ahead of Estoban. A book fell from the satchel strapped to the crossbar of his bicycle. He scooped up the book and looked back along the street, uncertain as to whether this was his only loss. Estoban watched him search his satchel. Nicely done.

A white Lada with a burst exhaust stuttered by, followed by a '48 Chevy. Next came a Russian truck belching diesel fumes. Estoban sped in front of the truck. Standing on the pedals, he jerked the front wheel up onto the pavement as he had when a boy. His route led down four steps and along the side of the Camilo building to the janitor's quarters. Descending the steps had been automatic once. Now Estoban nearly fell as he back-kicked the rear wheel and shot into the passage leading to the garage.

Abandoning the bike, he sprinted across the garage and out the back door to the square of garden. The corner of the converted shed had collapsed tearing a V-shaped gap in the tin roof. The door was open. Camilo's mother sat in the semi-dark, hands folded in her lap. Wizened by tragedy, she looked ninety.

Estoban blew her a kiss and sped round the back of the shed. A tangle of barbed wire and wire netting separated the garden from a builder's yard piled with rotten timber. Estoban dug into the grass at the root of the fence, heaved up the netting and crawled through. This had been Camilo and Estoban's route as teenagers playing weekend truant from the Lenin school. Entering by the pathway, they would have been spotted by the janitor and reported to the CDR.

Estoban pushed the netting back and combed the grass up. He hoped that he had time now. The watchers would be reluctant to report their failure. They would find his bike. They would check who lived in the building. They would search for connections between Estoban and one of the residents. They might even wait to see what apartment Estoban came out from.

Few Cubans wore suits. He took off his jacket and shirt, transferred his papers and the photograph to his trouser pockets and stuffed the clothes into a broken water tank. It wasn't enough.

In most cities there were public lavatories. Not in Havana. And Cubans weren't allowed in the hotels. Circling, he walked along 11th Avenue. He kept his pace leisurely. Indian laurels shaded the pavement and parked cars added further protection. First came a construction site where the work hadn't noticeably advanced in the past ten years; next the barrio's dollar shop with the normal queue. A fast-food restaurant lay to the rear of the store, dollars, of course. A guard loafed against the solid wood gate and a blocked drain had burst further up the street; flies fed at the grey effluent and the people in the queue breathed through cupped hands.

Four lines waited at the hamburger counter with a fifth at the cash register. The six waitresses and the cashier were deep in discussion as to whose turn it was to do something or other that had nothing to do with serving the customers.

There was only one queue for the lavatories; their filthy state kept the line moving.

A police siren screeched along Linea and turned uphill, perhaps towards the Camilo building. Estoban could hear two more squad cars in the distance. He listened to them grow louder – no doubt as to their destination. The speed of the reaction surprised him. And the noise. Usually the defection or arrest of a *poderoso* was hushed up. Unless they were bent on a show trial. Show trials ended automatically with execution. They. . .

Estoban's turn came for the lavatory. He cut off the legs of his trousers below the knee with his pocket knife and double folded the edges to hide the jagged borders. He took off his socks and packed them and the trouser legs into a plastic supermarket bag. The people in the queue were too preoccupied with their bladders to notice Estoban's change of dress.

He strolled now, taking his time, in appearance one of the myriad of Cubans with jobs that existed only to falsify the employment statistics. A dozen men waited at the barber shop on 14th Street and Linea. Estoban took his place on the bench with his back to the pavement. The conversation was the usual list of complaints. Food headed the list – or the absence of it. And the exorbitant prices in the dollar shops when compared to peso salaries.

Roddy

Dollars were on the mind of the director of Naval Intelligence, a captain. He had lunched well in the senior officer's cafeteria. Dozing at his desk, he dreamed of a mulatta secretary new to headquarters. Given his rank and official car, the dream was attainable.

High-heeled shoes made an irresistible present. The captain could buy the shoes at a quarter of their dollar-shop price from a cousin in Customs at the container wharf. The captain had sold ten litres of petrol from his official car for six dollars; ten litres a month was all he could risk. Even delaying payment on the shoes, he was looking at another two months' frustration.

Lieutenant de Sanchez knocked and entered. Roddy, with his looks and youth and sports car, never had to buy gifts.

'What do you want?' the captain barked.

'Permission to fly to Nassau.' Roddy laid a file on the desk. 'There's a few names the police and UN drug man over in the Bahamas wish to discuss.' He drew the requisite flight application from the file.

The captain brightened. 'What do you have?'

'Partagás Lusitanias, Captain. Eight boxes. It will be necessary for me to stay in Nassau overnight.'

The captain was already signing the application. 'Splendid.' His fifty per cent cut on the cigars guaranteed him the

176

secretary and he could keep his wife sweet with a gold chain. 'There's an old saying, Roddy. All women have buttocks but only Cuban women have arses. And their tits fall . . . from heaven.'

Estoban Tur

'Children,' Estoban complained when his turn came at the barber's. 'All they bring into the house is lice.' He ran his hands back through his wiry hair. 'Shave it.'

The job done, his scalp itched and he hardly recognised himself in the mirror. He picked up a copy of *Granma*, the party newspaper, from the barber's counter.

A young black man in a Chicago Bulls T-shirt grinned at Estoban. 'You wish to wipe your arse?'

'It is not possible to wipe your arse with shit,' joked an older white man.

'Perhaps he is a student of fiction writing,' suggested the barber as he handed Estoban his change.

Estoban felt safe with his head shorn and in shorts and singlet. Furtiveness drew attention. He stayed in the open, shifting slowly down 5th Avenue from park to park, reading *Granma* on the park benches, always picking the closest bench to one of the police sentry boxes that stood at every major intersection. Fidel lived out at the far end of 5th Avenue and there were always police ready to clear the traffic for his convoy of armoured Mercedes.

Bergman

Bergman and Nick sat in the rental car, sipping cold Cristal beer bought at the Cupet petrol station. Wherever they parked, women would come over and make their pitch. When the women became persistent, Bergman would drive on a couple of blocks.

Nick's team had lost Tur – the Cuban had made his break. Police had entered the building where Estoban had his apartment. Three squad cars came first, followed by the unmarked white Ladas of State Security. The delighted informant reported that an electricity cut had forced the police and officers of State Security to climb the stairs. A further two cop cars were at the apartment building where the target had disappeared and Roddy de Sanchez was in Havanatur's offices at the Malecón end of La Rampa.

Estoban Tur

5th Avenue possessed a facade of normality foreign to the rest of Havana. The State Housing Corporation had restored many of the mansions to their pre-revolutionary splendour, renting them to embassies and to the foreign investors honoured to work in partnership with the state. New Volvos, Peugeots and Mercedes sped in from the diplomatic enclaves in Siboney and Playa and there were rental Nissans, Mazdas and Suzuki jeeps from the seafront hotels and from the Marina Hemingway.

Dusk and Estoban watched two young black women rollerblade hand in hand. Cracks in the pavement pounded their breasts for release from white halter tops, and their white shorts were cut in a steep V to display the lower curve of their buttocks. Estoban watched them pirouette alongside an open topped rental jeep halted at the traffic lights. *Jineteras*, Cubans called such women – jockeys – for the number of men they rode. Fidel had ordered a clean-up back in August. Rollerblades had returned the girls to business. The police were unable to catch them. Anyway, few of the police cared. All Cubans were on the same side – the side of survival, of getting by.

The two tourists in the jeep were Italian. The girls clambered over the tailgate and were embracing them before the lights changed to green.

'*Negras,*' a plump middle-aged white woman said to her pale mulatta neighbour queuing at the bus stop to Estoban's left. 'They're all thieves. They ought to lock them up.'

The black policeman in the sentry box heard and Estoban saw his shoulders stiffen at the familiar racism.

On the other side of the avenue, a slim blonde girl in a cotton frock watched the jeep's rear lights dwindle. She flagged without confidence at a Mazda saloon then, in shame, quickly crossed the road.

Estoban wondered whether she was ashamed of her attempt or of her indecision.

She sat at the far end of his bench – perhaps waiting for the disguise of total darkness. Estoban's wife, Maria, owned a similar dress, Russian cotton in a printed pattern of tiny roses, buttons down the front. The girl plucked at the bottom button. Then the top two buttons. Estoban pretended not to notice. Her nearness disturbed him. Having decided to escape, he had barred the children and Maria from his mind. The security police would be at their apartment. The boys would be frightened and asking for him. Estoban felt their fear. Helpless and empty, he fought back the tears. And Maria, who knew nothing of Miguelito's rape – perhaps rage at being abandoned would give her strength as she faced the investigating officer.

Estoban imagined her shouting at the investigator, 'What do I know? Estoban and his secrets. You imagine that he talks to me?'

And the children listening.

Estoban saw Mario's face break open and all the fear burst out. The pain was too great and Estoban turned to the girl the other end of the bench. The inner slope of her breast was visible, pale and tender.

He said, 'There is no need to expose yourself. You are already beautiful.'

He walked the few yards to the sentry box. First the quick jerk of his head in the direction of the plump white woman in the bus queue.

'Fat cow. You heard?'

'Nearly forty years and nothing has changed.' The policeman spoke in the accent of Santiago – most policeman came from the eastern provinces. The people of Havana were contemptuous of their speech and their supposed slowness of thought – and, of course, that they were black.

Estoban stabbed his thumb at a passing tourist taxi, the driver white. 'Where there are dollars, it is a white colour job.'

'Who can blame them,' the policeman said. He was talking of the two black *jineteras* who had boarded the rental jeep. He had done his mathematics. 'One hour in a clean bed or six months cutting cane in the fields.'

'For the bed I'm too old and the wrong sex,' Estoban said.

The policeman chuckled. 'What arses,' he said, returning to the black *jineteras*. 'Sweeter than sugar.'

'And confident,' Estoban said. 'Confidence is necessary. The girl on the bench must be new. You could do her a favour. A tourist, not too old, not too bad looking.'

The policeman hardened. 'What are you? Her pimp?'

'In such clothes? And I am the wrong colour to be her father.' Estoban dug into his trousers for his identity card. 'Truck driver. The truck has been broken for nine months. Gear box,' he said.

'Russian?'

Estoban nodded.

'True to life – made of shit.' The policeman clambered down from his box and waited for the lights to turn red. A blue Peugeot rental was third to halt. The driver was alone, late thirties, winter white, and dressed for a business meeting. He looked up at the lights as the policeman approached, hoping for them to change. Scandinavian or German, Estoban guessed, and nervous of authority in a communist state, perhaps nervous of black people.

The policeman rested his hand on the door and called the foreigner señor. *'Por favor, señor, podria llevarla hasta el final de la carretera?'*

'He's asking you to give the girl a lift,' Estoban said in German.

The policeman was already opening the passenger door and beckoning the girl. 'Think of me when you buy new shoes,' he said as he handed her into the car.

'We are all pimps,' he said to Estoban as the car drove on. '*La lucha*,' Estoban said.

'Shit on *la lucha* – that's what my ex-wife says,' the policeman added in protection of himself.

'We live with my mother-in-law. She won't let me in the house till my wife returns from work.' It was a typical story.

'White?'

'White.'

'Screw them,' the policeman said. He had no interest in Estoban's identity card. They were on the same side. 'Until the next time.'

Estoban cut down through the park to 3rd Avenue then across to 1st and along to the open shore two blocks north of the Russian Embassy. The breeze blew cool off the sea. Flat rocks offered a meeting place for courting couples, privacy for the jilted.

Bergman

Roddy de Sanchez had visited his black girlfriend up in Vedado a second time. Nick's men had discovered that the woman was in the tobacco business and Roddy had descended from her apartment carrying two plastic bags. Now Bergman watched Roddy drive west on 1st Avenue, top down on his powder-blue MG and salsa booming from the speakers behind the seats.

Roddy drove with one hand on the wheel, grinning and flipping the other hand to locals on the pavement and beating time to the salsa on the outside of the car door. The de Sanchez compound faced the sea; a black gardener swung open the garage doors in answer to Roddy's horn. Bergman thought that it was quite a lifestyle, getting laid whenever, big house on the seafront, pool in the patio and a drophead sports car. He wondered what loyalty impelled Roddy to put it all at risk.

Bergman waited five minutes before ringing the doorbell.

He didn't threaten. He said, 'We have a friend in common,' and handed Roddy a Polaroid of Little Brother.

Roddy cursed once, a charm to keep his nausea under control. Then he looked up from the photograph. 'You did this?'

Bergman had been safe while playing a game with Nick the Greek for the past two days. Now it was real. 'No,' he said. It was half-truth or half-lie. Not one he could repeat, and he looked away, out to sea, and said, 'I want you to give your friend a package.'

The shopping bag he offered Roddy contained dollars and pesos in small bills, a sleeveless T-shirt, workman's shorts and a pair of trainers. The trainers were bottom-range Nike and available in the dollar shops.

Bergman said, 'Do that for me and there's a chance I can help your friend get to wherever he wants to go.' Again it wasn't a lie. Not quite. 'I'm sorry,' he said.

He knew that Roddy believed he was apologising for this blackmail. Roddy had his airline ticket in his pocket, the cigars. Add an anonymous denunciation and he was done for.

Searching for the rhythm, Bergman said, 'Your friend won't make it without help.'

Roddy looked out across the pool to the sea where the white sails of a lone yacht showed on course for the Florida keys.

'You have a plan of your own, that's fine,' Bergman said. 'It had better be good.'

He felt the rhythm now and watched for its effect on the young Cuban.

'He gets caught, he's going to talk. Everyone talks.' There was the threat. 'I'm sorry,' Bergman said. 'We both know it's true.'

He allowed a count of ten. Then, 'You think I like doing this?' he said, man to man, members of the same profession with godawful superiors to whom they had to answer. 'You're doing something noble,' *noble* a word Cubans loved.

'There's no point in useless sacrifice. I'll do my goddamn best to get him out. You have my word.' Bergman stressed the *my* – no bosses present to get between the two men. 'Give him the package, that's all. Tell him I've been here and he won't accept. Then we're back to wasting our time. And our lives. Yeah,' Bergman said and grinned at Roddy. 'That's where it's at. We screw up and my ex-wife won't have anyone she can sue for a raise in alimony payments.'

15

Estoban Tur

With an hour to wait before his meeting with Roddy de Sanchez, Estoban remained on the rocky shore in front of the Russian Embassy. The slap and suck of the waves reminded Estoban of his grandfather supping corn porridge over his gums. Estoban had visited the old man only once after the move to Havana. His father had taken him in the second year of the revolution. They had ridden on horseback up from the railway station, Estoban seated in front of his father on a smooth leather saddle liberated, as was the pinto stallion, from the stables of a plantation owner.

Estoban's grandfather had believed the revolution would give him the dry patch of hillside rented from the sugar plantation where he had cut cane every harvest for forty years. Instead the plantation had been expropriated by the state. Estoban's father was on the committee that implemented the law. Estoban recalled the vicious argument, his grandfather cursing his son as a betrayer of his class, of the *campesinos*. The two men stood face to face in the harsh sunlight, fists balled, rage sculpting their narrow faces fierce as axeheads.

'You think, because I am your son, that I will protect you,' Estoban's father shouted.

The old man spat in the dust and carved the edge of his boot twice through the phlegm, the sign of the cross on which to swear: 'You are no son of mine.'

Watching, Estoban had seen the two men as strangers to his

own life, their white skins died deep red by the sun, pale eyes, lips dragged thin with hate.

Estoban remembered his grandmother weeping and his own fear as his father spurred the stallion slithering back down the hill. Having returned two days later to his mother's small apartment in Havana, Estoban had crept into her arms in the night: plump arms, plump breasts, dark skin soft and smooth, odour humid and fertile as a freshly watered garden.

His mother had understood. 'Go,' she had said each weekend, pushing him out of the door to visit his father and stepmother. The big grey stone and marble house in Miramar had been built by his stepmother's family before the revolution. His father's alliances had protected the house from expropriation. A lesson in power structures. As were his mother's strictures.

'Remember your colour,' she warned time and time again. 'You must work twice as hard, fight twice as hard, be always in the first three of your class.'

Estoban knew that he was searching for memories to absolve his desertion of the revolution. Fidel's revolution. A revolution of ideas that took no account of man's most basic desire.

To Estoban's grandfather those few acres of dry hillside had represented a dignity of ownership that would have made him the equal of the grandest rancher or planter in Cuba

The revolution, drawing its power from a pyramid of patronage, recognised equality as the enemy. Every Cuban must depend on the pyramid. At the top sat Fidel. *El chullo grande*, the young of Havana called him – the big pimp.

As a schoolboy, Estoban had been proud of Fidel, proud that Fidel had put Cuba, a small island, on the world stage. However, as a member of the intelligence community, he had gained access to too much knowledge. He knew that the Soviet Union had paid for everything; that Cuba had received sufficient aid to build a paradise. All those billions had been wasted – government by caprice. And Estoban knew that Cuba was of no importance.

Fidel could strut and preen, stroke his beard, lecture Cubans for hours on television. Yet, in reality, his only power, beyond Cuba's frontiers, was that of a bright and mischievous school boy to disrupt the class and bait the teacher.

Estoban had never spoken of his own achievements or of his aims. He had faith neither in communism nor capitalism. His aims were simple: to gain for each peasant in Latin America his own few acres to do with as he wished. Estoban believed that he could break opposition to land reform by forcing down the price of agricultural land. The big estates were his target, fear was his weapon, his methods were direct and bloody.

Estoban accepted that guilt drove him – guilt for his grandfather, dragged down from his hillside and finally incarcerated in a psychiatric hospital; the logic was faultless: an antirevolutionary was clearly antisocial; to be antisocial was proof of mental illness.

The old man had died in the hospital. Estoban's grand-mother had come to live in Havana in the Miramar house. Estoban recalled the scratchy feel of her dry stick fingers on his arm, dragging at him, demanding of him that he remember.

'He loved you, Estoban. You must remember.'

Yes, he remembered.

He remembered walking with his grandfather down the hill and through the cane fields to the one-room village school. He recalled waiting after school until his grandfather had finished work at the plantation sawmill where, too old to cut cane, he swept and cleaned the blades. Estoban remembered the smell of warm sawdust. He remembered his grandfather holding him quiet on the path home lest he frighten birds or animals and his grandfather teaching him their country names. He remembered his grandfather squatting to show him plants and explain their qualities, whether healing or harmful. He remembered the evenings and his grandfather hacking at the hard earth of the hill and sometimes drawing lines along the hill to show Estoban the contours.

'Estoban, with victory the land will be ours and we will build terraces to protect the soil.'

Waste of land had obsessed his grandfather.

Now half Cuba was abandoned to weeds. The KGB instructors at Naro-Fominsk had awakened Estoban to reality. They had sought to make him one of their own. Shown him the figures. Exactly how much aid and where it had been spent – or wasted. He turned now to look at the Russian Embassy. The Soviet Central Committee had demanded a building that would dominate the client state. The architects had designed a massive humanoid robot. Fifty metres square at its base, the body stood twenty floors high, then came heavy shoulders protruding on all sides followed by a narrow neck of a further three stories supporting a massive head capped by a bristle of radio aerials. No limbs, the sad creature was immobile, stranded. Even its sight was limited by heavy concrete lintels and buttresses surrounding the windows in the head. It was a caricature, funny and tragic. Estoban loved the building, not for itself, but for the architects' perhaps involuntary statement of the special relationship between the old USSR and Cuba.

A squad car drove down from 5th Avenue and stopped at the rocky beach. The police summoned a middle-aged mulatto and checked his identity card. Estoban didn't hurry but rose casually, strolling back along the rocks towards Miramar before turning inland towards 5th Avenue. Half past eight and he walked quickly now, anxious to get home, either from work or from an assignation. He checked his wristwatch frequently, Russian and heavy as a hammer. Time was critical and he turned down towards the sea with seven minutes to spare. Danger lay here for Estoban. This was a residential area favoured by the old guard of the revolution rewarded with property seized from those who fled the Triumph. Now many of these *poderosos* rented to foreigners for US dollars and there were diplomats with houses on lease from the state and both protected and spied upon by police. Hedges of hibiscus and bougainvillaea hid the houses and the pavements were shaded by almond trees and pines which scented the air with their resin.

Prior to the revolution, the de Sanchez family had been richer than that of Estoban's stepmother. The Miramar house had been built on the shore side of 1st Avenue in the mid-1940s for a younger son. Street lamps lit the high wall facing the road. Double gates, clothed to their full height in green-painted aluminium sheeting, gave entrance to the property. A tourist hotel and an apartment building stood left and right of the house. A line of dollar taxis waited at the kerb outside the hotel – all drivers of tourist taxis reported to the Department of Security within the Ministry of Interior. Plain-clothes security officers loafed in chairs by the hotel entrance. Demanding $30 to $50 from tourists to allow a girl up to a room, these were the true elite of a society in which governmental whim made paupers of all but the corrupt.

Estoban crossed to the shore side of 1st Avenue, fifty metres from the apartment building. He turned towards the de Sanchez house with two minutes to spare. As he passed the end of the apartment building, the gate nearest to him swung part open. He slipped into the vee of shadow and the gate closed. Roddy de Sanchez had turned off the lights on the road side of the house but illumination came from the apartment building and from the hotel and he hurried Estoban across the paved courtyard to the shelter of the pillared entrance porch and into the house.

'My mother and sister won't be back for an hour,' Roddy said. He didn't remark on Estoban's dress and shaven skull.

The hall opened to a large living room with a mahogany-topped bar in one corner. The array of different bottles was impressive; however, most of them were empty. Roddy poured Estoban a straight tot of rum from a green Havana Club Añejo bottle. Añejo rum is dark and this was white. Roddy grinned at Estoban: 'Rough day, *compañero*, but the rum is safe. Filched from the hotel. Please seat yourself.'

His attitude was very casual, yet, caught harbouring Estoban, Roddy would be shot. He indicated a pair of leather armchairs facing out to a garden shaded by palms and two sea grape trees. The moon threw shadows of the trees across a swimming pool and speckled the sea beyond with silver. A Rottweiler sprawled on the paving stones leading to the pool.

188

Ten boxes of Partagás were arranged in twin towers on the coffee table separating the armchairs.

'I fly to Nassau in the morning – price of my exit visa,' Roddy said with another grin. 'Fortunately my superior believes that I have only eight boxes and that I paid thirty-five dollars each rather than twenty-five, so the profit is reasonable.'

He placed a plate of sandwiches in front of Estoban. 'You must be hungry. I have uncles in the US and in the Dominican Republic. They are generous,' he said in explanation of the food. 'Please help yourself.'

He shrugged, uncomfortable at mentioning Estoban's difficulty. 'Forgive me, but there are few Cubans who would risk trying to get you out of the country. I thought perhaps a foreigner. One of your old colleagues. If I can be of help. . . '

'You are very kind,' Estoban said. He wanted to be sure that Roddy acted freely and understood what he was offering. 'Roddy, I shot your father.'

Roddy took his own glass back to the bar. Estoban thought him very young. Miguelito and Roddy were of the same generation, enjoyment their only object. Miguelito had found joy in the children – and perhaps in Andres – Roddy in his car and his women and in his tennis.

Both young men gave pleasure simply with their presence. Estoban had seen so often the sudden lightening of the atmosphere at Miguelito's entrance to the apartment, laughter bubbling from the children and Maria made vital as she had been in the first months of marriage. Often he would sneak from the apartment for fear of destroying their happiness.

Roddy said, 'My father destroyed those he touched.'

Much as he had done, Estoban thought, not only in his war but in his private life. The pain of Mario's fear hit him suddenly, emptying him of energy; Mario whispering, *It will be all right, Papi,* the words for himself, a charm to halt disaster. Estoban longed to close his eyes. Instead he saw Miguelito bent over the desk, eyes pleading for succour.

'You gave me my freedom,' Roddy said. 'Possibly you believed that there was something in me that was worth saving.' He grinned again, ashamed to be thought serious. 'Let me return the compliment.'

'There is an Englishman,' Estoban said. 'He was involved with me in the affair of your father.'

'Trent,' Roddy said. 'You used him.'

Estoban smiled at his innocence. 'Roddy, that is something that is done in the world that the Englishman and I inhabit. Rancour is not part of it.'

He bit into a sandwich, cheese and ham. That both had been purchased with dollars on the blackmarket no longer mattered. He was out of it. Dismissed. The children would eat better.

'We ate breakfast in my home, Roddy, after the affair of your father. The Englishman brought sausages and bacon from his yacht.' Estoban recalled the sizzling in the pan and the scent of cured pork rich in their small apartment and Maria smiling at the Englishman as she set their plates on the table. 'I know no one else,' he said. 'Perhaps you would talk to him? We were on opposite sides in the Cold War. However, in a way we are friends. Or perhaps I should say that it is possible that he considers me a friend.'

He took the photograph of Miguelito from his pocket and placed it on top of the cigar boxes. 'I think we would be friends over this.'

16

Bergman

There was little sport in spotting a tail in Cuba. Early morning and Bergman had left messages with the reception desk at the Hotel Inglaterra that he would be driving out of the city for a couple of days, maybe stay in Vinales. For company he took his IBM laptop and an overnight bag. He followed 5th Avenue west towards Siboney before cutting south to the Pinar del Rio autopista. Two miles out on the highway and he had over-taken two horse carts, one truck and a Forties Chevy and had passed a red Lada stranded on the side of the road with its bonnet up and half a dozen may-be mechanics arguing a cure that didn't require unobtainable spare parts. The traffic head-ing into the city was as light and the only police were those at the highway entrance trying to hitch a ride. Bergman pulled a U-turn across the grass and drove back into town. Nick the Greek stepped out of the shrubbery on 11th Avenue midway between 70th Street and 82nd.

Nick the Greek took the wheel while Bergman opened up his IBM. The laptop was identical in appearance to any other ThinkPad and behaved similarly unless you knew the codes. The codes loaded a detailed road map of Cuba onto the colour screen. A blue star marked the trainers Bergman had left with Roddy de Sanchez. Nick the Greek's watchers reported that Estoban Tur was either inside the de Sanchez house or had taken a long underwater swim.

Bergman recalled his first meeting with the Brit at the Zoo and the Brit casting an imaginary fly to a trout. Waiting to see if Estoban Tur had put on the trainers was much the same as waiting for a fish. Maybe a little more nervous, Bergman thought. He and Nick the Greek had little in common beyond the Tur operation. They had expended mutual friends, acquaintances and enemies within the Agency as a source of conversation. Now they remained silent as they cruised the streets of Playa.

The blue star moved at 10:32. A further two minutes and Bergman received the report from Nick's watcher outside the de Sanchez house. The target was on the street heading south on foot. Roddy de Sanchez had reversed his MG drophead out of the garage and was also heading south.

Bergman told the watchers to pull back.

Estoban Tur

Estoban had spent much of the night working out his route. He had imagined the conference of those assigned to hunt him down. Some would have been his students at the Punto Cero guerrilla warfare school in the Sierra de los Organos and would have learnt from his lectures on escape across hostile territory. The rules were simple. Never be surreptitious. Always appear to have a reason for being where you are. Never look like a traveller. Be wary of bridges. And avoid public transport – impossible to flee from a crowded bus halted at a road block or from a train.

Estoban walked on the shady side of the street. He had smeared cement and water on his hands and arms and on his shorts and vest. He carried a bricklayer's trowel in his left hand and a quarter sack of cement on his shoulder. A plastic bottle of water and three sandwiches in a plastic shopping bag dangled down his back on a piece of old cord. The neck of the bottle protruded from the bag. The clothes were Roddy's and

Roddy had provided the trowel and the cement from his garage and had pressed on Estoban a hundred US dollars in small bills and a hundred Cuban pesos. He had let Estoban out into the street when leaving for the airport in mid-morning.

Roddy had offered to drive Estoban to the western edge of the city. Estoban had declined. He distrusted cars. They moved too rapidly. On foot he would spot a road block and have time to change direction without awakening suspicion. Fellow pedestrians would presume that he was a builder's labourer, walking from one job to another.

Estoban's goal was a creek on the north coast. The creek was 500 kilometres east from Havana by road. Estoban thought that he could make it in three days. He tried not to dwell on what would happen if Roddy failed to contact the Englishman or what would happen if the Englishman was disinclined to help. And he tried not to think of the children or of Miguelito. Success lay in concentrating all his energies on achieving a simple objective. He had to keep alert and aware of his surroundings – especially of the people.

Where to cross rivers was Estoban's greatest concern and where to sleep – walking at night was too conspicuous and suspicious. The cane fields were safe and the woods. He needed to be well clear of the city.

The security forces would expect him to run west into the Sierra de los Organos where he had taught guerrilla warfare and knew every fold of the land. The coast in both directions was sprinkled with blockhouses sited to confront the long awaited invasion from the US. Extra patrols would have been posted to search and cordon the coast. Thus an attempt to follow the shore was doomed and all roads would be watched.

Estoban cut south-east. He took his time, never walking more than three consecutive blocks in a straight line. A little after three in the afternoon, he was in sight of the railway line heading east to Santiago de Cuba. Estoban turned east parallel to the track.

The first raindrops fell as Estoban neared a curve in the rails.

Though this was still the outer suburbs of Havana, a tangle of grass and scrub grew waist high on both sides of the track. One of the revolution's many warehouses or factories abandoned in mid-construction preceded the bend; this one had no roof and half the concrete blocks had been stolen from the walls.

In general, Cubans have few clothes and can't afford to get wet. Added to which, Estoban was carrying a precious quarter sack of cement. It was natural for him to seek shelter. He chose the tin porch of a squatter's shack opposite the abandoned building and one street back from the railway. The shack looked to be deserted. The street was dirt; the potholes would have swallowed a pig.

An airliner flew high overhead and Estoban checked his watch. Roddy would have landed in the Bahamas. Estoban wondered whether he would find Trent.

Bergman

Bergman had fished for marlin a few times off the pacific coast of Guatemala. It wasn't his sport. A quarter of a million dollars of boat plus all the equipment struck him as way too much money to expend on catching a fish for fun, particularly in a country with a per capita annual income of $400.

For the past hour Bergman had been estimating the cost of this present surveillance: airline tickets, hotel, rental cars, the IBM laptop and its special features, the different telephones and the time. Time was the biggest item. Nick the Greek would invoice for himself and his team. Add Bergman's own time and the time of everyone else involved and the cost had to be way higher than the lost interest on capital invested in a good game fishing boat.

Bergman tried sharing his calculations with Nick. Nick was more interested in the rain clouds and in what manner the approaching storm would affect their equipment. For the moment they had the target pinpointed.

Estoban Tur

The rain curtain was solid with cloud stretching to the horizon; lightning snapped ahead of the rolls of thunder. Estoban watched the rain chase a black cyclist up the street. The cyclist spotted Estoban. Wanting company, he leapt off his bicycle and sprinted with it into the shelter of the tin porch. The rain hit and they couldn't hear each other's greetings above the drumming on the tin. Estoban had hoped to be alone – however, the black was unshaved and wasn't dressed like a cop.

Visibility shrunk to a few yards. Lightning spat through the deep purple murk and thunder followed, smashing down on the two men; the echo returned in wave after rumbling wave, until finally it faded away only to recommence with the next massive explosion. In seconds the rain had filled the potholes and flooded the street. No police driver would risk his Lada on a dirt road in such a downpour.

Conversation was impossible. Estoban tore one of his sandwiches in two and offered one half to his companion. Food was always short and the black man would have been discourteous to accept without first being pressed. They stood shoulder to shoulder, communicating their companionship with grins and shrugs.

Bergman

Bergman had watched the clouds gather all afternoon. He had as much faith in electronics functioning in a storm as he had in his dentures remaining comfortable all of one day. Meanwhile the target had halted a hundred metres short of the railway track leading east. Bergman had moved Nick's team up along the track.

Lightning came first, then thunder. The image on the screen shivered. Bergman looked up at the almost solid rain curtain racing down the street. He looked back down at the screen as the rain hit. He had to yell above the beat of the storm on the car roof. 'We've lost the son of a bitch.'

Estoban Tur

Breaks came in the downpour, the rain less relentless for a few minutes and the sky lighter. Then fresh thunder would announce a further onslaught. An hour passed and then another half hour. Finally, through the beat of the rain on the tin porch, came the clank and creak and clatter of a train creeping towards the bend. The diesel locomotive appeared through a gap in the concrete walls of the abandoned factory. The driver leant out from the footplate, hand shielding his eyes. Freight cars followed the locomotive.

Estoban slipped his cement into the plastic bag containing the remaining sandwiches and water bottle. Grabbing the black round the shoulders, he pulled him close, shouting in his ear, 'Good luck, *compañero.*'

He had memorised the potholes and crossed the street at a run – running was normal in the rain. He ducked through the gap in the factory wall. The concrete floor had become a lake spotted with islands of rubble. Estoban kept his eyes on the train. Some of the doors to the freight wagons were open. If any soldiers or police were guarding the wagons, they were keeping well back out of the rain. Estoban slipped through the undergrowth on the side of the track as the last wagon passed. Grabbing the iron handle on the corner of the wagon he scrambled up onto the steel buffer. He sat astride the buffer to recover his breath before hauling himself up the supporting diagonals to the roof. Flat on his belly, he inched across the slippery curve to a wooden ventilator. He gripped the ventilator with both hands and waited, face pressed against the galvanised tin. He thought the rain would continue for another half hour and dusk would be settling on the countryside. He had stressed so often in his lectures that trains were dangerous. Perhaps it was the one way they wouldn't expect him to travel.

Bergman

Rain beat down and the car windows misted up. Bergman had switched from high technology to a tourist road map and had split Nick's team two ways along the railway track on each side of the target's last confirmed position. The tall weeds growing along the track had enabled Bergman to bring them in close. Now one of the watchers reported the target astride the steel bumper on the last wagon of a freight train. The next watcher reported him halfway up the back of the wagon. The train was heading east.

Bergman gave Nick the direction to drive. At this stage of the operation Bergman was on Estoban Tur's team. Tur was a clever son of a bitch to have used the rain.

Estoban Tur

Vibration from the unevenness of the rails together with the cold of the rain numbed his fingers. The numbness spread up his hands and into his forearms. The rain eased as dusk fell and he was tempted to raise his head to see where they were. Someone could so easily spot him in that one second: police, armed forces or simply an ordinary civilian indoctrinated by state-controlled TV and radio to watch for spies, saboteurs and assassins from Miami.

Forty years' minimal maintenance of both locomotives and track had tripled pre-revolutionary journey times. The train advanced at no more than fifteen miles an hour and even then had to slow at every bend. The crash and clanking as the cars struck each other or lunged at their couplings was as continuous as the crack of the wheels into the gaps between the rails.

The breeze dried Estoban. The roof of the freight car was less slippery and he risked easing over onto his back, hands above his head still gripping the ventilator. The first stars showed through light cloud. He thought that he had done well and he thought that Mario would be proud of him. *It will be all right, Papi.*

He always thought of Mario first, not because he loved him more than he loved Tobanito, nor because he believed Mario more sensitive than his younger brother. It was simply that Mario more obviously suffered from the increasing tension between his parents and that Estoban, in turn, suffered both with his son and with guilt for being the cause of the suffering. Estoban accepted that his own feelings of guilt were a contributing factor to the child's insecurity. For a while he had considered consulting a child psychologist, yet he had known that the insecurity was based in reality.

Mario and Miguelito, both of them had expectations of him beyond his capacity. As perhaps Estoban did of the Englishman and Roddy.

Roddy

The flight from Havana had landed at Nassau, capital of the Bahamas, at ten minutes to three in the afternoon. The guest house where Roddy stayed was stipulated in his itinerary. Roddy expected the owner of the guest house to report his movements to Havana. There would be other watchers; perhaps the cab driver who had picked him up at the airport and volunteered his services day or night.

And the Americans would have a team hunting ammunition for blackmail.

All this was standard for a Cuban intelligence officer travelling abroad under his own identity. Estoban's Englishman was an extra. The Englishman had worked for both the British and the CIA. His telephone might be tapped; to be reported in his company would be fatal.

Roddy completed his official business by early evening. Cubans abroad save their hard currency travel allowance by picnicking in a park or eating in their rooms. Roddy bought two bread rolls, a tin of corned beef and a can of beer. He chose the apex of the toll-bridge connecting Paradise Island to Nassau for his picnic. With no cover on the bridge, he could be seen to be innocent. Two big motor yachts lay out in the channel and there were four marinas within view. Interest in yachts was healthy in a young man. He crossed the bridge and visited the marinas one by one.

Sleek power boats appealed to Roddy rather than sail – again this was typically Cuban. A Sunseeker Superhawk named the *Yellow Submarine* gained his greatest admiration. She was close to fifty feet in length and driven by triple Arneson surface drives rather than propellers. The engines were installed beneath a sun deck aft. A wetbar and a U-shaped couch and table furnished the vast cockpit. Twin racing seats faced the helm and a varnished walnut console set with gleaming dials.

Roddy imagined racing out to sea in such a boat, 100kph and a couple of *novias* in almost nothing basking on the sun deck. His fantasy was obvious to any onlooker. He stumbled as he turned away, banging his arm against a plastic trashcan on the dock. The clatter, together with a few choice curses, covered the drop of the weighted envelope he tossed into the cockpit of the neighbouring catamaran.

Roddy continued his tour of the marinas for a further hour before returning to the guest house to negotiate with the owner the sale of his cigars. All Cubans sold cigars when travelling. To do so was safe unless the seller made a political error. In which case he would be arrested for the contraband cigars . . . thus the deliberately blind report that there are few political prisoners in Cuba.

Trent

The Bahamas archipelago spreads across the Caribbean to the north of Cuba from a point approximately sixty miles east of Florida's West Palm Beach to within fifty miles of Haiti, a distance of 600 miles, and comprises 3,000 coral islands and islets.

The total population marginally exceeds a quarter of a million, of whom 200,000 live in and around the only two towns – Nassau on New Providence and Freeport on Grand Bahama. Nassau is the capital. Tower blocks are forbidden and much of the architecture dates back to the nineteenth century. Duty-free shops and the casinos on neighbouring Paradise Island tempt two million tourists annually off the cruise liners that lie sometimes three deep at Prince George Wharf.

Financial services is the second most important contributor to the Bahamian economy. Lawyers, bankers and accountants are drawn mainly from the remnants of a white colonial oligarchy, the Bay Street Boys. Bay Street runs parallel to the shore and is Nassau's main shopping thoroughfare.

The Abbey Road Investigative Unit was a Japanese agency specialising in marine insurance fraud. Its Bahamian offices occupied the top floor of one of the few modern buildings in downtown Nassau. The branch manager lived aboard his fifty-foot catamaran, *Golden Girl*.

Anglo-Irish, he had been christened John Patrick Mahoney. However, John Richard Trent was the name on his British passport and on his business cards.

In the days of the Cold War, Trent had been employed by the British Secret Intelligence Service. His expertise was in infiltration of terrorist groups and he had been leant by his Control, Colonel Smith, to the CIA for those missions prohibited by congress, 'wet work' in Langley parlance. One of these missions was responsible for the incident at San Cristóbal de los Baños. The target was a Guatemalan general and presidential candidate financed by Colombians.

Trent had read in the newspapers of the guerrilla attack on Finca Patricia. In the old days he might have been summoned by Colonel Smith: 'Guatemala. This man, Fabio. The cousins want something done. Get him for me.'

Bergman was Head of Station. NAFAC's demands for vengeance would come with promises of patronage backed by threats to have Bergman skinned by the Senate committee. Deliver Fabio or lose his job, his pension. Perhaps Bergman would use one of the new non-governmental organisations staffed by the detritus of the Cold War: ex-KGB, ex-Mossad, ex-CIA, ex-Stasi, ex-SAS.

Though Trent was out of that now, his past retained its threat, not only in nightmares, but in files at Langley and in Moscow and London. And he featured high on the death lists of those terrorist organisations which he had infiltrated. Therefore he was watchful and very careful indeed.

He was below in the galley in the starboard hull when a passer-by stumbled against the dockside trash can. Whoever it was swore in Spanish and Trent thought that he heard something strike the cockpit deck. Rather than go directly to the cockpit, he made his way across the saloon that connected the catamaran's twin hulls and made his way forward, crawling through the sail locker and onto the deck via the sail hatch. A dozen or more pedestrians showed beneath the lights illuminating the various arms of the marina. Any one of them could have been the stumbler. Trent first checked the warps to his mooring boys. And he checked the fenders port and starboard as he made his way aft. His performance was very casual and natural in a sailor.

Twelve feet square, the cockpit of the catamaran would have been described as a patio by a New York real-estate broker. Cushions covered the lockers aft and on each side and two director's chairs were drawn up to a teak table to port. Trent ignored the brown envelope that lay in the corner of the cockpit. Instead he checked the stern warps before returning to the galley where he filled the Italian cafeteria with bottled Malvern water and freshly ground coffee.

Trent returned to the cockpit with his coffee and a file of papers on which to work at the table. One of the sheets blew loose and he scrabbled for it across the cockpit. He felt the stone in the envelope – one sheet of paper. He worked on the file for a further fifteen minutes before going below to refill his mug.

Unobserved In the galley, he opened the envelope. The message was written with a black ink ballpoint and in capitals on a page torn from a notebook: HI, HOW ABOUT JOGGING TOMORROW MORNING? 6 A.M. The message was signed, *Ari*.

Trent set the paper alight and dropped the ashes into the trash bin beneath the galley counter. Back at the cockpit table he continued work on the file for a while. If the stumble was deliberate, so were the curses in Spanish. Closing the file, he sat looking up channel.

Hi was high.

Ari was short for arriba, Spanish for above.

The apex of the toll bridge was the highest point in the Bahamas. Slitting his eyes merged the lights on the bridge into a crescent. Once on the bridge, he would be committed. He visualised a shooter the far end and his own small Suzuki jeep reaching the apex. A vehicle would be the only practical cover for the shooter. A parked vehicle would be obvious and Trent could drop to the floor. The engine would protect him. And he would be safer knowing the purpose of the message. Ignorance was always dangerous – and, by habit, he turned on the radio and listened to the weather report.

Estoban Tur

A second storm had swept in from the south. The rain beat Estoban into the roof of the railway wagon so that he was flat now and very thin. And he was cold. He hadn't been prepared for the cold. He had thought only of walking across Havana, the shorts and the T-shirt given him by Roddy perfect camouflage for his role as a builder's labourer. Lightning spat at him, followed immediately by a massive strike of thunder that shook the train and left Estoban's mind numb of everything but images of himself clipped from ancient black and white movies, his body stretched crucified to the train's roof. Movies were his passion.

Bergman

The active colour screen on Bergman's IBM displayed great colour and that was all. 'Where in hell has the son of a bitch got to?' Bergman cursed. This was the second time that they had lost the target.

The wipers swept rivers from the windscreen, the rain so thick that it reflected the beams of their own headlamps, blinding Nick within a ball of light so that he was forced to creep to the right across the apparent infinity of the autopista in search of the verge. Shadows loomed out of the rain at most a couple of metres in front of the bonnet and Nick braked, slewing the car sideways across the sheet of water towards a pair of oxen stopped with their heads down into the rain.

One of the oxen found the energy to moan, the other remained silent.

Nick eased the car into reverse, detouring round an empty wagon with two men crouched sheltering underneath. No lamp, no nothing, and this was the only freeway in Cuba.

Nick said, 'Keep driving and we're going to get killed, Bergman. Your man's on the train. We wait till the rain stops.'

17

Estoban Tur

Estoban awoke to the shock and crash of iron on iron as the driver braked and the freight cars pitched against each other, the wagons old and the springs in the buffers feeble. Lights shone each side of the track. A hundred soldiers might be lined either side of the train. Estoban tried to press himself into the roof of the wagon. He had warned against this a hundred times: the agent blind to his surroundings and unable to run.

The locomotive jerked forward and the freight cars opened out only to slam together again at a set of points. Floodlights crept towards him as the train approached the yard of a power station or a sugar factory. With a power station there would have been the whine of turbines, so it was sugar, quiet in these months between harvests. During the harvest he would have been able to smell the boiling sugar at a distance of ten miles.

Estoban wanted to roll over and face the lights. He didn't dare. He didn't dare look even at his wristwatch. The light slid over him. Blind in the glare, he lay outstretched, an insect on the dissecting table. A second floodlight passed and a third, then a factory. Signals, and the train shook and clanked over a second set of points. The glare faded to a soft yellow as the locomotive drew the freight cars out again into the countryside.

Estoban wanted to leap clear of the train and hide in the fields. To do so made no sense. He was out of danger for the moment. He rolled onto his stomach and looked down the length of the swaying roofs. For a moment he thought that he imagined the man at the locomotive end of the train. Only head and shoulders were visible. Then the whole man appeared and a second followed.

The men held guns and wore uniform. Estoban couldn't tell what uniform. His stomach fell out through his loins and he was left empty and helpless. The indignity of arrest and transport back to Havana frightened him more than death. Followed by the cells. Sealed in solitary confinement with the memories of his brother and his sons. Listening to steps in the corridor, wondering if this was the day or the next or the next. Finally the sense of total helplessness as he was led out to the courtyard, blindfolded, tied to the stake, the last few minutes of waiting in the hot sun. Knowing that he had failed in everything, failed Miguelito, failed Mario. He wasn't frightened of the pain but of being so demeaned. Far better to die now while in command of his actions, quickly, and by his own choice.

He had expected the men to shout at the driver to halt the train. Instead they approached cautiously along the swaying freight cars and paused briefly at each gap, always one of them covering Estoban with his rifle while the other jumped. They were soldiers, Estoban saw, black, and young enough to be conscripts.

He spread his arms wide, so that they could see that he was unarmed. Then he struggled to his knees, not upright but sitting back on his heels, so that he would appear to them defenceless and defeated.

They stood over him. They were ordinary military rather than police and Estoban sensed that they were unsure of themselves and how they should act.

He said, 'I was working in Havana. Look.' He used the accent of a simple labourer from the eastern provinces and the soldiers had to lean forward to hear above the clatter and creak of the wagons.

He opened his carrier bag, so they would see the cement and the trowel. They would know of the enforced repatriation of people from Havana to the provinces. Black themselves, they would have thought about the new laws, possibly even discussed the laws amongst themselves.

'I wasn't legal, that's all,' Estoban explained. He tried to sound both indignant and pathetic. 'The police came to where I lived when I was at work. Everyone was taken. At my age it is not respectable to be sent home like a criminal. I thought to go on my own.'

He reached into his pocket and brought out the envelope containing his identity card and his work permit and the peso bills Roddy had pressed on him.

'Look,' he said and held the envelope open to the nearest of the soldiers. The wind spread the envelope at the moment that the soldier took it. It was gone on the wind, the contents fluttering in the red tail light of the train.

Estoban's despair was absolute. 'I have nothing else,' he cried.

He leapt from the train. His right foot struck a rock and he tumbled sideways only to struggle quickly to his feet. Despite the pain in his ankle, he ran a few steps back along the line, not running away, but crouched low in search as he swung his head and shoulders left and right, arms wide to grasp at the lost dream that had drawn him to Havana.

He spotted the envelope in the track and dropped to his knees. Swinging his upper body round to face the train, he waved the grubby white paper high as a victory banner. Then back he bent, crawling on all fours as he patted desperately along the verge for the peso bills. He waited for the bullet. Or the screech of the train's emergency brakes. Instead the chatter of the steel wheels on the steel rails faded slowly into the distance.

Bergman

They had driven fast for eighty miles east along the autopista and had nearly died up the back end of an unlit truck and again at finding the highway blocked by a herd of cows. Nick swore they were well ahead of the train. He spun the car off the highway down a side lane towards the railway track. Sugar grew ten feet tall on each side of the lane. Rain on the slim leaves and on the stalks reflected the headlight beams and they drove through a tunnel of light so bright that Bergman thought they must be visible for a hundred miles.

Nick the Greek must have had the same idea. 'American passports, we're the goddamn enemy,' he said. 'Cubans stop us out here in the middle of the night, they're going to give us a hard time.'

'Reasonable of them,' Bergman said.

Nick glanced sideways at him. 'Hey, just whose side are you on?'

'Reality,' Bergman said, though he knew he should keep his mouth shut. He and Nick had been cooped up together in the rental car too long. 'All I'm saying is that we're trying to screw their system, so it's reasonable they get pissed.'

'The system stinks,' Nick said.

'So they should change it.'

Nick braked hard and swerved to avoid a hole in the road. 'I never picked you for one of the new boys. Clean hands, all that shit. I mean what are we doing here?'

'Hey,' Bergman said. 'Cool it.'

'Cool it, bullshit,' Nick said. He was driving bunched forward over the wheel as if he was about to eat it. 'Next you'll be handing me a goddamn flower.'

'Or going on a diet,' Bergman said, attempting to make peace. 'That's the new order. Crushed oats, vitamin pills, and working out at the gym.'

A hundred yards further and they came to a flood. Bergman shed his shoes and socks, rolled up his pants and waded to the far side. At its deepest the water was less than a foot. Nick eased the rental car through the water with Bergman walking behind. Up ahead, crossed wooden arms painted in red and white warned of the railway track. Half of one arm had fallen off.

Nick crossed the track and searched for a side road that enabled him to turn. Back at the crossing, he fetched the jack from the boot and the spare wheel and arranged them, so that he would look busy to anyone on the train. The mosquitoes were already busy – Nick and Bergman were a foreign aid offering. Bergman dived back into the rental car for a spray can of Otan repellent.

Twenty minutes and they heard the *tickity-tickity tickity-tickity* of the locomotive. Bergman shaded his eyes against the beam of the headlight as the train crept round a curve. Its approach was so slow, it had to be suffering from asthma – and it swayed side to side, almost brushing the cane.

Nick and Bergman waved because, whatever the country, everyone waves at engine drivers. It is something people learn to do as kids and drivers wave in return. This driver added a grin that showed his teeth in the light of the overhead bulb.

The wheels hammered and the couplings banged and clattered, the planked sides groaning as the wagons lurched over the crossing. A red lantern hung on the rear wagon and the IBM showed a total blank.

Nick said, 'He's headed back for the Oriente with the rest of the *negros*, so maybe he threw his shoes off.'

Bergman thought of calling Nick a racist son of a bitch.

Nick said, 'That's kind of a Cuban joke.'

'So you aren't Cuban,' Bergman said. He had to concentrate on the target and Nick was getting in the way. In all probability the target had been caught.

Bergman imagined him in the cells. Castro would want a confession. Deciding what confession best suited the cause and extracting it could take a couple of weeks. Meanwhile Bergman's role and career would be finished. He thought that he shouldn't be considering his career with Estoban Tur in the cells. Given that the operation had worked, there was some reason in what he'd done. Failure was a true mess and not something he was prepared to contemplate.

'We need to backtrack along the line.'

'Crap,' Nick said. He dumped the spare wheel and the jack

back into the boot and stood beside the car with his fists balled and his head in a thick halo of mosquitoes. The mosquitoes were trapped between a desire for Nick's blood and a horror of the Otan. Nick was trapped between saving his hide and loyalty to Bergman. His hide won.

'If we keep driving round in the night, we're going to get caught,' Nick said. 'Like you've told me a hundred times, Bergman, this thing isn't official. I still have a career and I've got a wife and a kid that like to eat.'

'Yeah,' Bergman said. 'Okay.'

Back to Havana, Nick drove through Santa Fe to the Marina Hemingway. He dropped the car keys into Bergman's lap outside Papa's disco. 'Take care of yourself.'

'Yeah, thanks,' Bergman said. So far he'd got a nice kid raped, the target in the cells and lost a friend. He said, 'I wouldn't have got this far without help.' His meaning was right, so maybe the way he spoke was wrong.

'Go screw yourself,' Nick said and paid his entrance fee to the disco.

So much for his wife.

Estoban Tur

Estoban sat in the track and watched the red tail lantern of the train fade into the distance between the walls of sugar cane. He sat with his head at a slight angle and with a hand cupped to his ear as he listened for the sudden screech of brakes. He continued to listen despite knowing that there would be no brakes. He wanted to cry and to laugh.

He had travelled 100 kilometres out of 500. It wasn't enough and he couldn't rely on further miracles. Already his ankle was puffy and he would have to walk later down the footpath that zigzagged through the woods to the creek.

Crawling along the line, he found a twenty-peso bill. He didn't find his identity card or any other bills. He limped two hundred metres before sitting with his back to the cane. A further train was his only hope. He wondered when the Englishman would reach the creek and how long he would wait. Estoban thought that it would be funny if the Englishman left before he reached the creek. He wondered whether the Englishman would leave a message and, if so, whether he would find it. Then he wondered why he presumed that the Englishman would come at all and why he presumed that, if the Englishman did attempt the rescue, that he would reach the creek without being caught by the navy or by the Guarda Frontera. And he wondered why he should think that Roddy would find the Englishman or even look for him. And he thought it funny that many Cubans believed that mosquitoes didn't bite people with black genes. A cloud of insects had risen out of the cane. Cubans had learnt to queue for everything. Not so Cuban mosquitoes.

Fidel had spent four days hiding beneath cut cane almost immediately after landing in Cuba to raise the flag of revolution. Faustino Pérez, who was hiding with Fidel, reported that Fidel had talked for the entire four days. Estoban wondered whether the mosquitoes had bitten Fidel.

Within the cane there would be even more insects. For now Estoban sheltered in the fringes of the field. A freight train clanked past, but from the east. An hour before first light a second came from the same direction, this time a passenger train but almost empty; probably one of those in which the illegals had been shipped from Havana back to Oriente Province, the train now returning for a fresh cargo.

Estoban drank a little water before squeezing in through the clumps of root from which this year's cane grew. He crawled backwards, so that he could rearrange the dry lower leaves to cover his tracks. He thought that twenty metres into the field was far enough. He crawled east, parallel with the rails for a further twenty metres. The downpour had left the earth soaked and sticky. Estoban built himself a nest, never ripping more than a single leaf from the same stalk, and he slanted sufficient stalks in over his head, so that he couldn't be seen from the air. He had betrayed himself on the train by falling asleep. Now he determined to remain awake. He had no distractions within the cane and the throb of his ankle increased with boredom.

Bergman

Politicals are held in jail in Marinau. Cubans report beatings, torture and starvation as commonplace in the jail. Bergman drove down two sides of the compound. That the target didn't show on screen proved little. He could be in a police truck or held at an army camp or in one of the many houses the Ministry of Interior kept for interrogating special prisoners. He could have lost his shoes or had them stolen. The transmitter might have malfunctioned.

And the target could be hiding someplace along the track. Why, Bergman didn't know. However, it was a possibility.

He was nervous of falling asleep at the wheel and keeping an eye on the IBM added an extra danger to the autopista. He took each exit that led to the railway track without making contact. Around dawn he drove on over the track to the coast and found a rocky beach where he swam and dried himself on his shirt.

He wanted a cup of coffee and he wanted something to eat. In almost any other country in the world he could have found a café. Not in Castro's Cuba. Restaurants and cafés only existed in the major towns and tourist resorts.

Finally Bergman found a bar run by an agricultural co-operative on the left side of the autopista and he parked beside a truck and a Lada. Four men sat on stools at the bar and two men stood behind the bar. No light in the glass-fronted cold cabinet signalled a power cut and anyway the cabinet was empty. Nor was there anything to eat – not even a packet of cookies.

Bergman stomped back to the rental car and drove on a dozen miles before pulling off the road into the shade of a yellow trumpet tree. Sliding the seat back, he dropped the back down. The seat was too small for Bergman and made a lousy bed. He thought that Roddy de Sanchez over in the Bahamas was the only man so far involved in the operation who might be enjoying a little comfort.

Roddy

Roddy jogged for an hour six days a week in Havana; there was nothing suspicious in his doing so in Nassau. He reached the toll bridge shortly after six in the morning. He marked time for a few minutes at the apex, as if admiring the view. Wanting to be seen, he wore white shorts and a white T-shirt. He headed off the bridge onto Paradise Island. He kept to the main road and ran with his head down, oblivious to the few pedestrians abroad on the street.

A couple of delivery vans passed and a bus carrying hotel staff, then a small Suzuki jeep.

The jeep returned and took a left two blocks ahead of Roddy.

Roddy suffered a bad attack of stomach cramps as he approached the intersection.

He stopped at the intersection and stood with his hands on his hips and bent double so that he could see back along the main street. With no one behind him, he turned right and jogged down the side road for a further quarter of a mile. The jeep stopped beside him. The driver shoved the door open. The passenger seat was folded forward. Roddy scrambled into the back and the driver pushed the seat upright to hide Roddy from the road.

Roddy said, in Spanish, '*Gracias, señor Trent.* I bring a message from Cuba.'

The Englishman picked up, one-handed, the white envelope containing the photograph of Miguelito which Roddy dropped over the back of the seat.

The Englishman spoke quietly and without apparent surprise. 'Who is he?'

'Miguel Tur, the younger brother of Estoban Tur – half-brother.'

212

'Where?'

'Guatemala.'

The Englishman had turned left and left again onto the main road. 'When?'

'We believe last Friday, señor.'

A cab overtook the Suzuki, followed by a tour coach, then another cab. A plane must have landed.

Roddy spoke rapidly. 'The Andaluz Ballet of Havana performed in Antigua, señor Trent. Miguel was responsible for public relations. First he attempted to defect. Then he disappeared. The photographs were delivered three days ago.'

'Who to?'

'That we know of, one to Estoban Tur and one to the director of military intelligence.'

The Englishman turned the jeep left up a lane beside a lagoon and parked in the shade of a jacaranda tree. Turning in his seat, he looked at Roddy for the first time and Roddy was able to see his face. Within a thick black beard there was nothing to read. Bland, Roddy thought – bland as an Englishman.

'The general remains the director of military intelligence?'

'The same, señor. The general presented the photograph to the committee investigating Miguel Tur's disappearance.'

'So now everyone knows.'

'Those of importance, sí, señor Trent. It was necessary for Estoban Tur to resign his position.'

A rat, black eyes shiny as glass beads, peered out of the mangrove on the lagoon side of the lane. The little animal's nose twitched and puckered in search of danger. Belly low to the ground, he scuttled across the lane and disappeared into a clump of pink oleander beyond the jacaranda.

'My name is Sanchez,' Roddy said. '*Compañero* Tur said that I should inform you that Admiral Sanchez was my father. Thus the *compañero* said that you would know what he will do.'

'He said when?'

'He has already departed, señor.'

'They are looking for him?'

'It is to be expected, señor.'

'*Mierda. . .* ' The Englishman wound down the window and Roddy breathed the thick foetid scent of the mangrove swamp edging the lagoon.

'I must get back to the road, señor,' Roddy said.

The Englishman knew the communist system of surveillance. 'Clearly,' he said and drove on up the lane in search of a place to turn.

'Señor Trent, I know something of your past and I have much respect for you.' Roddy laughed despite himself. 'This may not have the appearance of a great compliment, coming, as it does, from one hiding on the back seat of a small jeep.'

'A Japanese jeep,' the Englishman said.

'Yes, a Japanese jeep.'

'My employers are Japanese.' The Englishman reversed at a gate and drove back towards the main road.

Roddy owed Estoban one last effort. He said, 'I have no desire to appear to you melodramatic, señor, However, *compañero* Tur depends on you. These are my words, señor Trent.'

'You are a good friend,' the Englishman said.

'If you would leave me before the corner.'

Roddy ran fast to make up the time he had spent with the Englishman. He had done his duty for a friend. He had sold the cigars. He was young and fit and handsome, and he was running towards a hot shower in a clean bathroom followed by an ample breakfast.

Estoban Tur

The heat within the cane field increased as the sun rose, steaming the previous evening's rain out of the ground, so that Estoban lay dripping within a Turkish bath. Water became his major preoccupation. Without sufficient water he would dehydrate. His sight of the sky was limited by the cane; he sensed the cloud build again to the north-east.

Midday and he heard voices to the east and the kick of boots on the aggregate between the rails. The voices moved on past his hiding place. He determined five voices – perhaps there were others, silent. The accents were from the region; judged by their vocabulary, the men were white: railway workers, or field hands taking a short cut – not army or the accents would have been a mix of regions. Rural Guard was a possibility.

The men passed the spot where Estoban had entered the cane. One of them shouted in excitement. He must have found one of Roddy's peso bills and Estoban cursed himself. He had warned those he had trained against exactly such carelessness. A second shout followed the first and Estoban imagined the men scrabbling like crabs along the line. Then came a different shout and now the men's voices were muffled from him as they formed back into a group. Estoban thought they must have found his identity card. The boots of a single man ran west while the others split into two groups and beat along the cane in both directions, searching for his point of entry. Twenty minutes later they abandoned their hunt.

Estoban listened to them talk amongst themselves, though without being able to discern the words, and he caught the faint scent of burning tobacco. One of the men walked back from the group and his urine spattered on the cane leaves. Dark cloud slid overhead, the weight imprisoning the heat and humidity.

Estoban imagined the scene at whatever headquarters had been set up to co-ordinate the hunt. He could have lost his documents getting onto the train as easily as getting off it. They would check what trains had headed east through the night and perhaps those that had passed during the day.

Estoban expected them to send helicopters and possibly dogs. Dogs reminded Estoban of North American movies and the hunt through the swamps for escaped slaves or escaped prisoners wrongly convicted. That was the movies and sometimes the victims escaped. Not in real life; if they sent dogs, Estoban was lost. This time there would be no miracle to save him.

He knew why the soldiers had let him go.

They had let him go because they were black and he was at least mulatto and because they believed that he came from Santiago.

Estoban had watched on television the director of the state housing agency explain to the leaders of the Popular Front in Santiago the expulsion of the illegals from Havana. The director was white, of course – and the leaders of the Popular Front in Santiago were black or mulatto as were most of those thousands now named illegals by the government. The director hadn't apologised for the lack of food and work and the opportunity to better themselves that had driven families to abandon Santiago for Havana in the first place. Nor did the director apologise for the condition of the slums to which they were being forced to return or that there were floods in Santiago and a dengue fever epidemic. He had simply called the repatriated blacks, illegals and claimed that Havana couldn't absorb them. The leaders of the Popular Front had looked glum and Estoban had reaped the reward of an injustice perpetrated by the administration of which he had been, until the previous day, a powerful member.

He saw the irony. He thought that it was something he could tell Trent and that Trent would be amused. Thinking of Trent helped, and of the big catamaran. He would lose hope without an immediate target.

Trent

Trent sat at the cockpit table on *Golden Girl*. He held the photograph of Miguel Tur between his fingertips and his hands shook as he absorbed the look of pleading in the young man's eyes. It was a look Trent had lived with each day since his father's death.

Trent's father had managed a Gulf sheikh's racing stable. Trent was eight years old. He had scampered down the passage on the way to the stables and glanced into his father's office. His father was at his desk, service revolver in his square

216

horseman's hands and, in his eyes a desolation and plea for forgiveness too painful to confront.

Ten steps across the wooden floor and Trent could have saved his father simply by hugging him. Instead he had fled to the stables and was found squatting dry-eyed in a corner of a stall two hours after the shot. Arms crossed on his chest, he had been holding himself together for fear of disintegrating. He had known that if he cried, he would never stop.

Even now Trent had to bite on the inside of his lower lip.

And he took shelter in analysing the kidnapping.

The CIA must know of it – Guatemala had been a client state for more than half a century.

Perhaps Bergman was trying to save his career with a publicity coup.

Next came the Miami Cuban leadership; confession by Estoban Tur to state-sponsored terrorism would strengthen their hand against liberals and the business lobby, both of whom supported the normalisation of relations with Castro's Cuba.

The right-wing senators, Helms and Burton, greedy for votes and directed, in their old age, by emotion rather than intelligence, might well approve. As might some in the House, eager to curry favour with a segment of their electorate or merely fund-raising.

The purpose was obvious: bait for Estoban Tur. Trent knew where Estoban hoped to be picked up. The Cuban had set a trap for Trent once at an inlet on the north coast; Admiral de Sanchez had been involved – hence the message and the messenger. Estoban had been fortunate in young de Sanchez. Suspiciously fortunate. And asking help of someone he hardly knew, someone who had been an enemy for twenty years?

It was too pat, too well planned.

The smell was there of something more.

Estoban's confession to state-sponsored terrorism? Or could the object be Trent's own confession to his past activities?

Fidel's continual attacks on the United States earned Cuba friends amongst the like minded: Iran, Iraq, Syria, Libya, North

217

Korea. Would one of these reward Fidel for Trent's capture? Would Fidel sacrifice Miguel Tur or was the photograph a piece of theatre?

Trent dropped down through the saloon to the port hull. The area forward of his cabin served as a dark room. He had bolted an angle-poise lamp with a magnifying glass to the bulkhead. Dragging a stool out, he sat staring into the young man's eyes. He discerned no resemblance between the half-brothers. The age gap must be fifteen years.

Was the younger brother an intelligence officer? A spy?

Service to the secret world was often a family affair – a common background presumed a common belief in the general morality of the national cause.

Trent wasn't sure that he had ever believed. MI was something that had happened to him. Mostly he had been fearful of betraying his side – as he had betrayed his father. And he had been ashamed of not believing.

Estoban had struck him as a believer.

And the emotion in the photograph was too strong to be theatre.

Crossing to the galley, he made fresh coffee and carried a cup out to the cockpit. He could smell the sea and the palm trees and the freshly watered lawns. A pair of young lovers leant against the wooden railing outside the clubhouse. From the saloon of a Grand Banks trawler came reggae and laughter, followed by the dull tap of an ice tray against the galley counter. A fishing launch with a forward cuddy slipped into a berth at the next dock and Trent watched the owner and a temporary girlfriend walk up to the clubhouse.

Cubans were forbidden access to their own cayos and required security clearance to fish off-shore. In the hunt for Estoban every road would be checked and police and army would scour the countryside. Estoban would be lucky to reach the creek on the north coast.

As for getting out of Cuba, Trent took a last look at the photograph before calling his office manager. He had no choice.

Bergman

Bergman awoke to the familiar roar and wind-slap of a helicopter low overhead. His back ached; his eyes were gummed; his mouth felt as if it was packed with dirt.

He struggled into a sitting position and fumbled for the lever to bring the seat upright. Sliding his legs to the ground, he stood and stretched and tried to work the crick out of his neck. Then he fetched his washbag from the boot and dry-scrubbed his teeth. He still felt like shit and black cloud hung over the countryside.

There was nothing for him back in Havana apart from a told-you-so Nick the Greek. A further fifteen miles would bring him to the intersection with the road to Varadero, Cuba's main beach resort. Given that the Guatemalan Visa card issued to Frank David Trautman was acceptable to the Cubans, he could sing his swan song at a plush hotel with a good restaurant and a pool. Though, given the approaching rain, the pool wouldn't be much use.

He was only half a mile short of the intersection when he spotted the helicopter put down on the edge of a cane field. It was the same model as that which had woken him.

Estoban Tur

Estoban had been crawling through the cane away from the railway track for the past half hour. He hadn't got very far. The cloud had been building steadily, deep grey and threatening to burst. Estoban heard the roar of the helicopter engine and the smack of its wings on the air as it passed overhead.

The men up the line were shouting at the helicopter – as if the pilot or crew could hear; almost certainly the men were Rural Guard with little experience of aircraft. The engine revolutions dropped as the pilot set down on the rails. Through the beat of the propeller came the baying of dogs and bellowed instructions.

The dogs headed down the line in Estoban's direction. He needed to urinate. And he wanted to run. The helicopter was airborne, hovering above the hunting party. The swot of the propeller tore clouds of pollen from the flower canopy. The mixture of pollen and aircraft exhaust confused the dogs and the helicopter rose high and peeled away to wait 400 metres to the east of the hunt. The sky was almost midnight mauve as the dogs picked up the scent again. The bark and bay of the dogs awoke movie images: escaped slave, men with whips and antique shotguns hunting him through the bayou. Fear drained Estoban's bladder and he crawled in his own water.

18

Bergman

The helicopter lifted to fly a search pattern between the autopista and the railway. Bergman grabbed for the IBM. The screen grew in brightness and the road map steadied. The beginnings of a blue star shivered down by the railway track. Thunder exploded directly above the road. The rental car shook and the screen went blank. Bergman cursed and hammered one fist on the steering wheel. He saw the cane bow and disappear as the rain beat across the open fields towards the road. The hot tar smoked steam under the first rain drops. Then the storm hit and forced Bergman to the verge.

Estoban Tur

The dogs were gaining. Then came a sharp scrape and clatter of dry leaves as the rain swept in across the field. Drops stung Estoban's cheeks as he looked up into the breaking storm. The scent of the rain reached his nostrils, fresh and filled with the promise of new growth.

The voices of the dogs were lost in the sweep of the rain curtain. Then came the full roar of the downpour and one of the dogs howled.

Estoban heard the soldiers blunder in search of his track. The helicopter swung back and dipped low, the pilot using the blast of the propeller to part and flatten the stalks. Move, Estoban told himself. He had to keep moving.

Pylons marched across the field in the distance, the cables connecting the sugar factory's sub-station with the power station at Matanzas. The spread of the power lines would protect him from the helicopter. He crawled on all fours, ignoring the cane leaves cutting at his face and slicing across his arms. As he crawled, he suddenly saw himself through his son's eyes, Mario's eyes. Crawling like an animal, he wept, not with fear now, but with shame for his fear. They had destroyed in him all he had made of himself.

His dignity, his loyalty, his beliefs, all were shattered.

He wanted vengeance and would have been exultant had the helicopter hit the cables. Instead the rain forced the pilot to the ground.

Estoban crawled in fresh mud, the rain piercing the canopy. They had too few men to cordon the field. They would bring in troops. Trucks would already have left the nearest barracks – if the trucks were in running order and if diesel was available. For once the shortages were to his advantage.

Every train would be searched. He was incapable of walking far enough or fast enough. With the rage in him, he thought he should take the fight to the enemy. At this moment he could have killed easily. He didn't care that the enemy were his own people. Trent was the only person he could trust. He had to trust Trent or give up.

Trent

He had opened a chart on the navigation table in the saloon. The chart showed a section of Cuba's north coast and the Old Bahama Channel that divides Cuba from the Great Bahama Bank. The tiny Lobos Cay on the south-west edge of the bank was the closest land to Cuba. Cayo Hermoso was the closest Cuban land to Lobos Cay and one of a string of small cayos

that protected the main body of the Archipiélago de Camagüey. A current made four knots west up the Cuban edge of the
Old Bahama Channel and the prevailing wind blew from the
north-north-east.

Twenty-three miles separated Hermoso and Lobos cays.
Trent would then have to work his way through the man-
grove-studded waterways of the archipelago and across a
further ten miles of open water to the creek which lay in a
solitary wedge of hill cut off from the main body of the Sierra
de Cubitas.

He would have to cross the channel under cover of darkness.
How long the crossing took would depend on the seas. He
might well have to hide the next day inside the archipelago
and run into the coast the following night. On a previous trip
into Cuban waters, he had hidden *Golden Girl* within a small
inlet surrounded by mangrove. However, there hadn't been a
manhunt in operation. The hunt for Tur would bring helicopters sweeping the cayos, coastguard and navy patrol boats.

The way in was aboard something fast and small and
unlikely to register on the antique Russian radar. Trent owned
two Zodiac inflatable tenders; a nine-foot rigid-hull, which
hung in davits aft of the cockpit, and a fifteen-foot-five Futura
with an inflatable floorboard which he used for diving
expeditions and carried on *Golden Girl* athwartship on the
trampoline forward of the mast.

The same 40hp Yamaha outboard powered *Golden Girl* and
the big Zodiac. A 9hp powered the small tender. Four five-
gallon tanks gave the big Zodiac a range in smooth water of
200 miles at a cruising speed of twenty knots and eighty miles
at thirty-five knots.

Tur had been on the run now for forty-eight hours. The
Cuban had to travel 500 kilometres. On foot, the journey
could take him a fortnight and he would never make it. Cuba
was too narrow. Soldiers, shoulder to shoulder, could sweep
the island from one end to the other; not even a mouse would
escape. Manpower was available, Cuba had an army of 40,000
plus the Rural and Coast Guard and a massive police force.

Fortunately for Tur, a manhunt required organisation and infrastructure – say a minimum of three days to get the men in place.

If Tur moved fast, he would keep ahead of the sweep: motor-cycle, car, truck, train, bicycle. No, even bicycle was too slow.

And forced to hurry, Tur would make mistakes.

Bergman

As the thunder eased, the picture steadied on the IBM. The target was six miles away and moving very slowly north by north-east. Rain cut visibility to fifty metres and the target would be hidden from pursuit. However, he was moving far too slowly to be saved by the storm. Bergman was helpless. Headlights on, he eased the car back onto the road and crept closer, not because he could do anything, but as if drawn by a magnet. Tur had ceased to be the target and become Bergman's man. The helicopter was responsible. Bergman had used helicopters to track guerrillas in Guatemala.

He had listened to the crews brag the way that weekend hunters did, of how a guerrilla had looked as he ran and weaved and looked up in terror at the helicopter and tried to hide, only to be winkled out from wherever he went to ground. Surrender was inevitable as was the transformation of the man, by fear, into little more than a domestic animal herded to the abattoir. Beaten and trembling, the guerrilla would wait to be led away. Sometimes the prisoner's face twitched and some begged and cried; men who, under different circumstances, had shown great courage. It was the remorselessness of the helicopters that defeated them.

Estoban Tur

He broke out of the sugar at a narrow lane that ran with rain water. Beyond spread rolling countryside that had been ranch land before the revolution but was now mostly *marabou*, a tall, tangled evergreen scrub that smothered the grazing.

Estoban crawled for some four hundred yards before spotting a pair of clapboard shacks in a grove of fruit trees. The shacks hadn't been painted in years. The rain had driven everyone to shelter and the *marabou* gave Estoban cover. The scene reminded him of the opening shots of a black and white movie from the Thirties shown wide-screen on a square TV: the fields flat, colour washed by the rain from the sodden vegetation; cloud solid, grey and very low; the gap between land and sky no more than a slit; endemic poverty.

A fence marked the end of the *marabou* twenty metres short of the shacks. Beyond the fence the soil was tilled and built into raised beds to protect neat rows of lettuce, tomatoes and onions from seasonal floods. Estoban had been raised in such a shack, a well out the back and an outhouse. The only improvements were the electricity cables and the TV aerial.

The rear end of a pick-up protruded from a tin-roof shed. The truck had started life as a '37 Chevy sedan. The back end of the body had been replaced by a flat-bed with wood sides. A bicycle leant chained to the side of the truck. A few sad-looking chickens roosted on the side of the flat-bed. Half a dozen pigs penned behind the shed had churned the ground into a mud and crap wallow. A horse that was mostly bones stood with its head low and its rear end to the breeze in the shelter of the mango trees behind the shacks.

Estoban judged from the cloud that the rain would continue for a further hour. The pilots were grounded and troops on foot would be unenthusiastic. The closest communications radio and telephone line must be back at the railway track.

Estoban circled the shed and approached the shacks from the rear. The shacks were identical at the back with two wooden-shuttered windows each and a door sheltered by a sloping porch. A padlock hung locked on the hasp of the door of the nearer shack. On the second shack the door stood open. Shadow hid the interior.

In flight, Estoban's safety had already depended upon an accurate reading of enthusiasm for or opposition to the revolution. The *campesino* families living in the shacks had resisted pressure to surrender their land to a co-operative or to the state. To Fidel their class were the enemy of progress; they had been castigated with forced labour and taxes on their produce; their living conditions had deteriorated drastically in the years since the Triumph. Here, in the province of Matanzas, they were probably white. Were Estoban white, they might help him. Mulatto, he was more doubtful.

He untied Roddy's dollars from the cloth in his carrier bag. He thought that forty dollars would be enough. Holding the bills between his teeth, he tied the rest back into the cloth and inched his way out from between the pig pen and the shed. Pigs' faeces had overflowed in the rain and spread across the wet slippery clay and the surface of the puddles that separated him from the horse. The stink of the faeces and the feel of it against his bare chest and legs made him retch. He gained the nearer mango tree, rose to a crouch and reached for the horse's halter. His fingers were numb and awkward and the knot on the rope refused to loosen.

A scream of fury came from the open door and an old white man armed with a garden fork charged out of the shack.

Estoban opened his mouth to shout and lost the two twenty-dollar bills to the breeze. Grabbing at the money, he slipped and skidded on his belly. The old man leapt after him, fork poised.

Two small blonde girls ran from the shack to join the old man. One spotted the twenty-dollar bills and snatched them from the mud.

'Mami,' the child cried at a woman with long fair hair who had appeared in the doorway. The woman took the money.

Flat on his back and with the fork at his throat, Estoban pleaded, 'My intention was not to steal, only to borrow the animal.'

The woman held the twenty-dollar bills up. 'You intended to leave these?'

'On the tree,' Estoban said.

She believed Estoban but not in fortune. 'A buzzard would have stolen them.'

The old man spat in a puddle. 'Better a buzzard than a bearded son of whore. As for you,' he said to Estoban. 'You look like a black pig and you smell like a black pig.' He hadn't moved the fork from Estoban's throat.

The woman said, 'Let him up, grandfather.' And to her children, 'Go in to the house.' She pointed Estoban to a gutter draining rain from the shed roof.

The rain ran pig faeces and ochre clay off his body. He watched the woman through the water. All bone, she looked to be in her mid-thirties and was probably ten years younger. Aged seventeen she must have been a beauty. Now one of her front teeth was black and broken. Bruises marked her cheek and her upper arm and she wore that air of permanent exhaustion which goes with lack of hope.

'Are you a thief?' she asked.

'Not yet,' Estoban said. 'The government are hunting me.'

The old man said to the woman, 'Then your shit of a husband will shoot him.'

'My husband is of the Rural Guard,' she said.

'And of every other shit of a guard.' The old man spat again.

'Please, grandfather. . . ' She said to Estoban, 'What will they do to you?'

'Shoot me,' Estoban said. He shook the water out of his hair and wiped his face on his hands.

'Why?'

'Because I ran.' No, it had begun earlier. Before Miguelito. He felt the weariness heavy on his shoulders. 'I don't know. It is who I am rather than something that I have done.'

'You are a *poderoso*?'

'Until yesterday.' He looked into the rain driving across the *marabou*. 'I am sorry that I came to your house.'

She shrugged. 'Grandfather will chase you into the field. We will go inside. Wait five minutes before you return for the horse.'

'Chasing the pig will be a pleasure,' the old man said.

He reminded Estoban of his own grandfather and Estoban smiled. 'My ankle is hurt. It would be a kindness if you would chase me slowly. Also if you would permit me to steal a hoe and perhaps a knife.'

Estoban rode bareback due north through more *marabou* down the side of a long field of cane. For the first fifteen minutes he kept the horse to a canter then slowed to a trot in hope that the horse would survive until the rain stopped. He was aiming for the highway leading from Matanzas to the beach hotels at Varadero.

Bergman

At first Bergman presumed that the target had stolen a bicycle. He was moving too fast to be on foot. However, the rough terrain demanded a mountain bike. Perhaps he had stolen a tractor or a horse. And he had a chance now while the rain kept the helicopter grounded. Bergman wanted to hug the son of a bitch. Then he recognised that he was considering only the immediate situation. The security forces knew where Tur was. Somehow he had to escape from Matanzas Province. He was heading now for the highway leading into the expanding resort town of Varadero. Perhaps he thought that he would be less visible amongst the construction workers. However, Varadero was a peninsular and the security forces would seal it off.

Bergman drove carefully along the Varadero highway and found a flooded dip in the road. He braked midway across the flood and switched off the engine. Taking his sandals off, he stepped out into the water, opened the bonnet and loosened a connection from the distributor. He stayed out in the rain for a further five minutes before getting back into the rental car.

Few Cuban vehicles have effective windshield wipers and Bergman had been parked for ten minutes before the first vehicle appeared, a grey Lada that eased into the flood and drew up alongside. The shoes manufactured in Spain and sold for dollars in Cuba are factory rejects that melt in the rain and the Cuban driver was reluctant to get out of the car into the water. Window down, he called across to Bergman, asking whether he required assistance.

Bergman said he was fine. 'Water in the electrics. Once the rain stops, I'll dry it out.'

A further ten minutes and a police car came from the opposite direction. Again the flood water protected Bergman from interference. Tur was only a mile short of the highway. He was moving more slowly now, so either the tractor had a problem or the horse had run out of wind.

Estoban Tur

Beyond the cane the soil changed from dark to pale grey and he rode across fields of sisal cactus overgrown with long, straggly grass. The rain thinned as he approached the dual carriageway and he saw the sea at last, grey and dark as the clouds. An hour of daylight remained. He pegged the horse in a patch of grass close to the road – a loose horse would have aroused suspicion. A helicopter swept over the sisal fields as Estoban limped along the road edge, hoe over his shoulder, a labourer on his way home. The highway climbed a low ridge and curved to the left at the top.

Estoban sat on a rock at the top of the ridge. He could see a mile down the highway in both directions. Behind him the sun slipped beneath the cloud. The light struck the raindrops trapped in the feathery flowers of the sugar cane beyond the sisal and transformed the vast field into a shimmering sea of pale, silvery pink. A delivery truck raced by on its way to the tourist enclave. Five minutes passed and a Suzuki jeep followed the truck. Then came two rental cars on the way back to Havana, Ladas, an ancient Ford Fairlane, nothing for a few minutes, then a Tropicola truck. The truck reached the ridge as a Peugeot rental car appeared from the opposite direction.

The truck passed Estoban. The truck and the Peugeot were the only vehicles in sight. Estoban jammed the fork into the dirt, drew the old man's knife and opened the blade. Then he lay in the road with his left arm twisted up his back and his right hand under him. The scent of the warm wet tar was strong and he heard the Tropicola truck driver change gear on the next rise. The Peugeot came up the hill and round the curve. The engine was smoother and quieter than any Lada – even a new one straight from the factory.

The driver saw the body sprawled in the highway and stamped on the brakes. The tyres screeched. A door opened and Estoban saw foreign sandals walk towards him. Never before had Estoban been so interested in feet. These were male, white and big. A corner had broken off the nail on a big toe and the skin on the heels was dry and flaky. The tourist squatted beside Estoban and took his wrist, feeling for the pulse. Very professional – perhaps the tourist was a doctor or a male nurse.

Bergman

Theatre was part of their profession. Bergman thought that the target looked the part sprawled on the tar. He hoped that he looked equally good checking the target's pulse. He wasn't surprised when Tur rolled over onto his back and stuck a knife at his belly.

In Spanish, Bergman said, 'I was informed that there is no violence in Cuba.'

Tur said, 'I require to be driven, that is all.'

A helicopter flew inland with a second one beyond it. They were flying a pattern and Bergman saw the desperation in Tur's eyes. Fear had already marked his face, narrowing it and cutting lines into the cheeks that had been smooth and plump when Bergman had first seen the target leave his office.

Helping Tur wouldn't be easy. The Cuban had to believe Bergman a friend, and friendship had to be earned.

Frightened of the helicopters, Tur no longer saw Bergman as the immediate danger and relaxed. Bergman was surprisingly fast and Tur found his wrist pinned and a knee across his throat.

'They are looking for you?' Bergman asked.

'Yes,' Tur said. 'Yes, they are hunting for me. I am sorry.'

'To be hunted? Or that you put a knife in my belly?'

'Both,' Tur said.

'What are you? A murderer?'

'It is political,' Tur said. 'It would be a great kindness if you would give me a ride. I am heading east.'

Bergman rocked back on his heels. 'Get in behind the seats.'

He grabbed his camera out of the car as a helicopter approached and waved to the pilot before crossing the highway to photograph the car against the background of the sea. Returning to the car, he said, 'Perhaps taking photographs is a crime.'

Tur said from the floor of the Peugeot, 'For tourists, the only crime is not to spend.'

Bergman got back into the car and started the engine.

Estoban Tur

There was little dignity in lying behind the seats. A previous passenger had stubbed a cigarette out on the floor; the carpet smelt of burnt plastic and chemical deodorant and Estoban was worried about the horse. Estoban could see, through the gap between the seats, the tourist's foot on the accelerator. 'You will help me?'

The American chuckled. 'Why not? How far do you hope to get?'

'Four hundred kilometres.'

'They want you badly?'

'It appears so,' Estoban said. 'No doubt there will be roadblocks, so it is required to drive with care.'

Bergman

A helicopter flew low over the road; too low for Bergman. He said, 'I will stop under the next tree. You must hide in the trunk.'

The helicopter returned and hovered briefly over the Peugeot.

The blossoms of a coral shower tree showed beyond the next curve. Bergman halted under the tree, got out of the car and walked out into the field to a rock standing proud of the sisal. Facing away from the road, he pretended to urinate. The helicopter swept in from behind him, the blast of the blades twitching the top of the sisal canes. Bergman waved and tucked himself back into his trousers with the other hand. Then he walked slowly back to the car and drove on down the road.

The helicopter followed him for a couple of minutes before dipping away towards the sugar fields and from the next rise Bergman spotted the flashing blue lights of a police car way to his rear. He drove fast, hoping for another flood in the next dip. He wasn't worried for himself. Tur was his man and Bergman was determined not to lose him. The next two dips the road were dry and the police car was less than half a mile back. Bergman drove up the next slope and saw a skim of water below. The moment he was into the water, he knew that it was too shallow. He accelerated fast out and up the next slope and again saw water ahead. The water looked deeper and Bergman was already braking as he hit the flood. He came to a stop facing out from the verge toward the centre of the road at an angle of thirty degrees. He cut the engine and paddled round to open the boot.

'Police,' Bergman said to his passenger. 'Make yourself small.'

Leaving the boot open, Bergman hurried to the front of the car and lifted the bonnet before the police car appeared over the rise. Bergman hoped that it was a different Lada or, at least, a different crew.

The police drove carefully into the water and pulled up next to the Peugeot.

Bergman looked out from under the bonnet and shrugged. 'Water. It is the second time.'

The police driver was in the middle of the flood and made no move to leave the Lada. The policeman on Bergman's side craned out of the window and stuck his head into the Peugeot. He could see down to the floor, front and back. He glanced at the boot. Had the tourist anything to hide he would have shut the lid.

The helicopter lifted over the ridge ahead and dipped towards them. The pilot would look straight into the boot.

The downdraught hit the flood. The sheet of water smacked Bergman and drenched the policeman's shoulder.

Furious, the policeman waved the helicopter away.

Bergman stood dripping in the flood.

The policeman said to Bergman, 'You should drive more slowly.'

'That pig of a comedian should use his brains,' Bergman said.

'That also,' the policeman admitted as he dried his face. 'Be careful of yourself,' he said and nodded to the driver. '*Vámonos.*'

Bergman watched the police car disappear over the next slope. Then he walked round the back of the car and looked at the target cramped in the corner of the boot.

'God is on our side – if there is a God,' Bergman said

Tur looked up out of the boot, a new tension apparent. 'Our side?'

'Of the righteous.' Bergman said.

'Or you are a professional in such matters?'

It was said now, though without force. Forcefulness was difficult when curled in the corner of a car boot – even of a splendid rental car rather than of a Lada.

Bergman retrieved the previous day's shirt from his bag and wiped his face. 'Are you so important?'

'It is you that we are discussing,' the target said. 'Who are you?'

'Trautman,' Bergman said. 'Frank David Trautman. If I appear expert to you, perhaps it is because I was a marine – in Vietnam. In those days I was not so fat. Now I sell retirement pensions,' Bergman said. 'Yes, to self-declared experts who earn high salaries for advising countries whose experts earn low salaries.'

'Or you aid politicals.'

'One political,' Bergman said. 'And at your choice.' He stepped back from the Peugeot and glanced east and west up the road. 'The way is clear, *compañero politico*. You are free to descend.'

The target uncurled a little and wiped his forehead on his arm. 'Perhaps I am too suspicious.'

'Perhaps that is not possible,' Bergman said. 'Should you wish our relationship to continue, I believe that it will be safer to travel by day. There is a culvert here where I will collect you in the morning. I advise that you find thick bush in which to sleep.'

Trent

Golden Girl slipped quietly south round the tip of New Providence Island. Ahead lay the Tongue of the Ocean, a mile deep, the seas lumpy and the dark waters foreboding. Sailing single handed, Trent had set the smaller of his genoas. The wind was directly aft and he carried the genoa to starboard with the mainsail vanged out to port. Even in light breeze *Golden Girl* made eight knots. Sails set opposite each other, the big catamaran resembled a vast butterfly ghosting over the waters.

The breeze strengthened as he cleared the shelter of New Providence and he brought the catamaran round on to the port tack, the bows slicing through the short steep seas of the bight. After an hour he could make out the low spine of Andros Island quivering above a layer of molten silver spilled by the heat across the western horizon while ahead lay the surf which marked the edge of the vast shallow underwater plateau that spread from the edge of the Old Bahama Channel north to within thirty miles of Miami Beach.

The water over the limestone was seldom more than three metres deep and many reefs and coral heads touched the surface. Navigation was by sight, experienced helmsmen judging depth by colour of the water and from memory as much as from the charts. Trent had cruised these waters for six years and knew them well. *Golden Girl*, lightly loaded and with her twin dagger boards raised, drew eighty-five centimetres.

Trent had an hour of daylight in hand when he slipped between the walls of surf at Magic Gap and across the flats towards the settlement of Green Creek on South Andros. The settlement was little more than a peppering of clapboard houses spotted amongst the sea grape trees and coconut palms that shaded a crescent of pale gold sand at the head of a shallow bay. Mangrove sprouted in the north corner of the bay with a steep ridge behind. Feathery pines grew along the ridge and along the main spine of the island behind the settlement. A wooden jetty stuck out from the beach towards a line of brown coral heads almost awash.

The coral protected the settlement from the huge waves hurled out of the Tongue of the Ocean and across the outer reef by summer cyclones. The water within the inner reef was as calm as a village pond and a dozen island skiffs lay to moorings. Other skiffs were pulled up on rollers into the shade of the trees. A couple of fishermen were hanging their nets between the trees while a pair of frigate birds, too lazy to hunt their own food, floated gracefully overhead.

Trent rounded the inner reef and sailed his anchor hard into the sand before coming up into the wind to drop his sails. He stood on the cabin roof to furl the main. The scent of burning charcoal, pigs, coconut oil and pines drifted to him across the water. He was known in the settlement. Villagers were gathering on the beach and children came swimming out to the cat.

A square black man dressed in shorts and a wide-brimmed red felt woman's hat rowed amongst the children. His wooden skiff was smeared with pitch and he kept his distance from the yacht. He was over sixty years in age and a rim of grizzled curls showed as he tipped the hat back from his face. His smile displayed three yellow teeth. He had a barrel chest, bow legs and toes splayed by years of holding the mesh taut as he repaired his nets. Deaf at birth, he welcomed Trent with exuberant waves of his arms and with a high-pitched squeaking from the back of his throat.

Trent pointed to Dummy and to *Golden Girl*, then south towards Lobos Cay. Finally he pointed to the sun and demonstrated three days by swinging his hand from eastern to western horizons and showing Dummy three fingers

Dummy nodded happily and asked when by pointing first to the sun, then indicating different angles in the sky.

Trent indicated urgency by pumping his arms as if running a race.

19

Estoban Tur

Estoban hid in the culvert and waited for dusk. He didn't believe in the American. Frank, he had called himself. Frank David Trautman, ex-marine, specialist in retirement investments.

Or an agent of the CIA?

Why should an ordinary tourist take the risk?

And, with the best of intent, what could the American do? Drive east with Estoban lying on the floor or curled up behind a wall of suitcases in the boot? Estoban would be discovered at the first roadblock, hauled out of the car, shoved into the back of a State Security Lada or helicopter. Cells. Bullet.

Or did they want a confession from him? To a plot invented by the State Security as more proof of US duplicity and aggression?

It had happened. But why now and to him?

The hunters had time to think. The quarry only had time to run. That was the name of the game. And fear. He had been frightened in the past – when in Latin America. However, there his death would have had purpose. He would have died for the cause – or so he could have told himself.

But how would he act when led towards the stake?

The deliberateness of such a death appalled him – that he would have lost all control over his actions. Though under general supervision, he had run his department as a fiefdom. The same was true of his directorship of the guerrilla warfare school. Now, as he crouched in the culvert, he realised that his sudden change of status horrified him in part because he saw himself through his son's eyes. That his father should be helpless was both the embodiment of all Mario's fears and identical to Mario's own situation of being unable to halt or change his parents' drift towards separation.

Mario.

Mario on the stairway in the dark. Mario holding him in bed.

The child's face so small and marked with such depth of misery.

Estoban doubled up in the culvert, retching with his own misery and guilt. Yet little had changed – merely the spread of his incapacity from his family life into the public domain. And that now he shared fear with his son and with his brother.

He had been frightened for three days.

And he could achieve nothing without first escaping. He had to escape. Why had he allowed himself to become dependent on the fat American? He had to retake control. Yet there was nothing he could do. In the dusk he was unable to distinguish between a rental car and a private vehicle or one belonging to the state. His ankle made a return to the railway impossible.

The heavy rain had washed the highway and he filled his bottle from a runnel spilling over the lip of the macadam. Stepping always in the water, he hobbled a hundred metres down the watercourse that flowed from the culvert. He left the watercourse at a slab of limestone and picked his way carefully for the first fifty metres, choosing rocks as footholds in the hope that dew would wash away his scent. A dense barrier of *marabou* had rooted in the loose soil at the base of a low rise. Estoban built a nest deep inside the thicket, interlocking the branches to form a cage that would protect him against sudden assault. He tried to eat the last sandwich but the bread was too dry. The American was probably ordering a *Cuba libre* at the hotel bar before dinner. He would have had a hot shower and would sleep between crisp sheets. In the morning he might feel a twinge of guilt as he made his way to the hotel pool or to the beach. Perhaps it would rain.

Bergman

He had booked into the best hotel on Varadero beach. Europeans of mixed race are attracted to Cuba for its supposed lack of racial prejudice and Bergman found three such men at the bar. Two were Brits, noisy and difficult to separate. Bergman concentrated on the third, a German in his early thirties.

Karl Jonas

Karl Jonas had studied English at school and at technical college. Now he sat tapping time to salsa and listening to the fat American tell stories at the downstairs bar in the Varadero Beach Club hotel. Thirty-three-years-old and a Volkswagen-trained car mechanic, Karl had been conceived in Wiesbaden, the Federal Republic of Germany. Karl's mother had worked at a truck stop. Karl's father was a black corporal in a US transport regiment. Informed of Karl's conception, the corporal had admitted to a wife and three children home in the US. Karl's mother moved to Bielefeld. A Catholic, her religion forbade her an abortion. Karl showed his gratitude to the church by attending mass ten times a year.

Karl lived with his mother, worked for the main VW dealer in his home town and drove a four-year-old VW Rabbit which he handwashed and wax-polished every Sunday. In four years he had been late for work once. He had neither stolen as much as a sweet nor cheated in an exam; neither had he been stopped for speeding nor for running a red light. One solitary parking ticket scarred this blameless record.

Karl had chosen Varadero for his summer holiday after

watching Cuban athletes on TV compete in the Atlanta Olympics. The athletes were black and he had presumed that so were most Cubans. He had also read that Cuban women were beautiful and available. His fantasy of Cuba was white sand and sun. Reality was different.

First, Varadero was for tourists and guests were forbidden to invite Cubans to the hotels.

Secondly, hotel jobs, however menial, were amongst the most prized in Cuba for the tips earned in US dollars. Jobs went to those with influence – thus employees were almost exclusively white.

Thirdly, Cuban women were beautiful; however, they were no longer available in Varadero. Those who had enjoyed foreigners' company in the past had been arrested. Heads shaved, they had been held in a courtyard without shade for two to three days before being shipped home to their provinces for further punishment.

Fourthly, Karl had seen nothing but rain, rain and more rain.

He was initially suspicious of this American who introduced himself at the bar. However, the man was jovial and told a good story. He said his name was Frank Trautman and that his paternal grandfather had emigrated from Munich to Milwaukee. He knew Cuba well and was sufficiently affluent to afford a rental car, a Peugeot. He had a girlfriend with a younger sister in Matanzas.

Karl and the American drank three *mojitos* at the bar before deciding to visit the sisters.

The American said, 'You need your passport. The Cubans beat the shit out of you if you don't carry identification.'

Karl had been confident when leaving the hotel. In the car the American told him of disasters that happened to tourists in a communist state – tales of police brutality and the innocent held in solitary confinement for months. A half dozen such tales and Karl wished that he had watched TV in his room.

Four policemen and four soldiers manned the roadblock at

the exit to Varadero. The American braked smoothly and handed up his documents and car papers to an officer.

Karl was patting his pockets in panic. He could have sworn that he had left the hotel with the wallet containing his passport. He had been up to his room to fetch it and had brushed his teeth in preparation for the younger sister. He got out of the car to search under the seat. Perhaps the Cuban policemen suspected that he was reaching for a gun.

'Keep cool,' the American shouted as a Cuban grabbed Karl by the shoulder and yanked him back.

The American was out of the car. There was a lot of shouting from the American and from the police and military and the American bulled his way round the car to protect Karl. Karl couldn't understand what happened next except that he was on the ground and his face hurt, specifically his left eye. The American stood astride him, holding back the Cubans.

The American grabbed one of the policemen by the arm and yelled something in Spanish. Whatever he yelled calmed the Cubans and he heaved Karl to his feet and helped him into the rear seat of the Peugeot.

Two policemen sandwiched Karl. An army officer sat in the front beside the American. The American drove back to the hotel.

The police accompanied Karl to the reception desk where he asked if anyone had found his wallet and they followed him up to his room where he searched the floor under the bed and in the bathroom where he also examined his left eye in the mirror above the hand basin. The eye was swelling and would be shut by morning.

The police accompanied Karl back down to the lobby where the hotel manager and the staff swore that he was who he said he was. So did the representative of the Cuban tour agency and the German rep from LTI.

The American insisted that the police issue Karl a certificate confirming the loss of his passport and tourist card. The American also demanded the police apologise in writing for having hit Karl in the face. The police claimed Karl had hit himself on the car or when he fell. Finally the American settled for the certificate and a version of events that simply stated that Karl had been hurt getting out of the car at the roadblock.

'At least it will explain your eye to your people back home,' the American said. 'You don't want your boss believing you were in a drunken brawl.'

The American had business in Havana the following morning and promised Karl that he would take the documents to the main police station and to the German Embassy and return to the hotel with something official which would let Karl out of the country at the end of the week. Meanwhile he suggested that Karl sun himself in the morning way down the beach by the marina. The American would send his girlfriend's sister.

'If she isn't working, she'll get a lift out with the workers. Otherwise she won't be free till late afternoon. She's worth the wait,' the American said.

They arranged that Karl would wear a yellow sports shirt and blue shorts so that the sister would recognise him. The American would drive him down to the marina end of the beach.

Karl was deeply grateful to the American.

Bergman

Head of Station, Bergman seldom had the chance to exercise his talents and was proud to have retained his touch. He emptied the young German's wallet and spread the contents on the desk in his hotel room: passport, identity card, driving licence and parking permit, a letter from a girlfriend and a couple of receipts from a supermarket in his home town, and a used train ticket with a telephone number written on it with a black ballpoint. Karl was younger than Tur by some twelve years. However, a swollen eye made good camouflage. And the file on Tur reported him fluent in German.

Estoban Tur

Nightmares haunted Estoban's sleep. The cry of an owl jerked him awake, and he found himself wet with sweat. The breeze whispered through the *marabou*. He listened to the scuttle of rodents and lizards and for the spill of the sea on the beach half a mile away. Sipping water from his bottle, he thought of carrying a glass through to one or other of the children disturbed by a dream. And he thought of his wife. He needed Maria. Above all else, he needed Maria.

He left his hiding place before dawn and retraced his steps, hobbling stiffly up the watercourse to the highway where he squatted shivering in the culvert. The first grey signs of day seeped in from the east. Estoban hoped that someone had stolen the horse or that it had got loose and found water.

The dip in the highway restricted his view. He thought that early morning was too suspicious a time to attempt the second hijacking of a car. Drivers would think him a drunk passed out on his way home. Midday offered the best chance. No air conditioning in Ladas, Cubans avoided driving in the noon heat. And a foreigner was essential – any Cuban with the courage to risk arrest on behalf of a fellow Cuban had built himself a raft and had drowned at sea or lived now in Florida.

Estoban decided to wait an hour for the sun to dry his clothes so that he would look less of a tramp. Then he would walk up the next rise in hope of finding a better vantage point. He had no expectations of the American. This time he would use the knife with greater authority.

Bergman

Soldiers were visible a mile away advancing either side of the road. Parking on the verge, Bergman slammed the Peugeot's door and scrambled down the bank to the culvert. Tur crouched inside. Bergman slung him a plastic shopping bag containing blue shorts, a yellow sports shirt and white socks.

Telling Tur of the soldiers would have made the Cuban nervous and slowed him. Standing with his back to Tur, Bergman unzipped his trousers and once more pretended to urinate. Soon the Cuban security forces would mark him down as suffering from an enlarged prostate.

'How do I look?' Tur asked.

Bergman turned to inspect him. 'Good,' he said and slammed the Cuban hard in the left eye.

Estoban sprawled on his back.

'Sorry,' Bergman said. 'The eye's your disguise.' He dropped Karl's leather wallet on the grass between Estoban's legs, together with the envelope containing the police reports.

'Who you are and why you have a black eye.' He grinned and said, 'So call the eye what you want. The man in the police reports had it first and he is a German mulatto.'

'Thank him for me.'

'He doesn't know about you,' Bergman said. 'He believes that I am doing him a favour.' He thought that Tur was a little short on humour. Perhaps it was the circumstances.

In the car he said, 'If there is a roadblock, it is your decision whether you attempt to walk round or use the papers.'

Tur was watching the soldiers along the crest.

Estoban Tur

The rain had saved Estoban by the railway track. And the American. Impossible for the American to wait while Estoban crept half a dozen miles round each roadblock. The American would be noticed and ordered back to Havana for investigation. Estoban doubted whether the American's cover would hold up.

The slam in the eye had convinced Estoban that he was CIA. Estoban's suspicions had been awakened on the previous day. The American was too cool to be an amateur.

Estoban could surrender him to State Security – a bargaining counter.

The comfort of the Peugeot delayed his decision. The whirr of the fan in the air conditioner was audible above the purr of the tyres and the murmur of the engine. He pictured himself the previous day crawling on all fours through the cane, the baying of the dogs and the helicopter overhead.

They were hunting a half-animal terrified of being seen.

Impossible for such a quarry to confront a roadblock.

'I'll take my chance on the autopista,' Estoban said. They won't expect me to have found help.'

Bergman

Bergman approved of the Cuban's decision. The Cuban had held up well under pressure. Bergman said to his companion, 'Many young black Germans wish to appear as black Americans. Confidence is important and to be relaxed – even with police, or especially with police.'

Tur pushed his seat all the way back and put his feet up on the dashboard. 'This is sufficiently relaxed?'

'Excellent,' Bergman said.

Liking the Cuban hadn't entered into his calculations.

Estoban Tur

Exile in Russia had turned Estoban into a film buff, an attribute he had found comforting through the solitude of his years as a courier in Eastern Europe and Latin America. At the guerrilla warfare school he had used films in developing his students' ability to identify with character and so meld themselves into a variety of covers. Now he was in a road movie and police and Special Brigade manned the roadblock up ahead.

They had set the roadblock under the bridge east of the junction between the road south from Varadero and the autopista. Special Brigade trucks blocked the outer spans while two white Ladas of the police cut the centre span into a dog leg. A third white Lada, unmarked, blocked the exit from the bridge.

The American opened his window as he drew to a halt. The police might have been depressed. The sight of Estoban cheered them up – perhaps because he had a badly swollen face. One of them drew a pistol and grabbed the door as Estoban lowered his window.

Estoban said in German, 'What the shit do you want?' and to the American, in Hollywood English, 'I've had enough of these motherfuckers.'

The American had his own documents out and passed them up to the policeman on his side of the car. Laying a hand on Estoban's shoulder, he said, 'Relax, Karl.' And to the policeman on Estoban's side of the car, 'Last time we were stopped, a policeman hit my companion.'

The policeman was unconcerned by past incidents. He took his time examining the American's documents. The American pushed his door open, forcing the policeman to retreat. The American was taller than any of the Cuban police and broader across the shoulders. Estoban heard him say in his coarsely accented Spanish, 'Before there are further errors, I suggest you telephone to your headquarters in Varadero. Or don't you have a telephone?'

Estoban pushed his own door open. One of his Russian instructors had joked that the freedom of the individual could be calculated in reverse proportion to the number of police required to read a man's documents. Two police were reading the history of Karl's eye with a further four men craning over their shoulders.

The policeman holding the American's passport had turned it upside down to read an old entrance or exit stamp. His lips moved as he tried to pronounce the city or airport to himself.

The American was smiling with great condescension.

A typically supercilious gringo, Estoban thought.

Of all the men, only the officer of State Security had power, the man in the unmarked Lada parked in the shade. The officer had tilted his seat back and was apparently asleep. His forehead with a lock of fair hair were visible and the tip of his nose. A hand pushed the hair back and he sat up, drawing the seat straight. He glanced across at Estoban before settling mirrored sun glasses on the bridge of his nose – a single look, pale eyes blank, uninterested. Estoban wondered how he would react when told that the American was CIA.

Alighting from the car, the officer wriggled the stiffness from his shoulders. In his early thirties, he was slim and white. He wore the uniform of Cuba's white upper class, a class which officially didn't exist: faded jeans, a red sports shirt, white socks and clean trainers. Miguelito had dressed the same way, as did Roddy de Sanchez.

Disdainful of his surroundings, the officer stepped out of the shade and glanced at the sun in disapproval. An inadequate salary added to the small demands placed on his intelligence would have made the officer idle and arrogant – such frustration sometimes led to sadism. Standing beside Estoban, he flicked fingers for the reports on Karl Jonas and scanned them quickly. Then he turned to the American's papers, studying them with equal speed.

The American stood leaning against the Peugeot, arms folded on the roof. His arms were heavy and a little red from the sun. He wore a watch with buttons and small faces within the larger one. The strap was black plastic and had made his wrist sweat so that the blond hairs were dark and stuck together. He looked very confident and very bored.

CIA and arrogant, Estoban thought. Now, he thought. It was the right moment. He said, '*Compañero*,' to the officer. The word was drowned in the slap of the American's open palm on the car roof

'Well?' the American demanded. 'You have read the account of what was done to my companion. We wish to visit Trinidad and see the architecture. Is that permitted?'

'The road is open.' The Cuban dropped the American's documents on the car roof and prodded them across the glossy paintwork with one neat finger. Then he tapped the reports on

Karl's identity and misadventure. 'First there are some small formalities.'

'Small?' The American chuckled softly. 'We had hoped that one day would be sufficient for the excursion. If we are to be stopped every few kilometres we will require a week.'

'You should forgive us our enthusiasm.' the officer said and, switching to German, and to Estoban, 'We are searching for a Cuban criminal. It happens that he speaks German.'

'And is black?' Estoban responded, the bitterness only half theatre as his role in the play took command. 'I pity him – considering what you do to an innocent tourist.'

'The Varadero police write of an accident,' the officer chided. He had laid the reports concerning Karl Jonas on the roof of the rental car. Now he poked the sheets apart with one finger, separating the pages. 'I would be happier with a photograph.'

'In case there are two black Germans with swollen eyes?' Estoban asked.

'Or one German and one Cuban who speaks German. Please, you will accompany me,' the officer said to Estoban. He led the way to the white Lada of the State Security and opened the front passenger door for Estoban. 'Unfortunately there is no air conditioning, however the shade is more comfortable.'

'Than what?' Estoban asked.

The officer took off his dark spectacles. 'A dry riverbed in the Sierra de los Organos.'

Estoban wanted to vomit. He sat in the car empty, as if scooped out. The blade dug between his legs and the pain and the emptiness spread back to the base of his spine and up the spinal cord, the flow slow as hot tar spilled into an open drain. He breathed because to do so was automatic. He wanted to pray, however, prayer wasn't automatic and he didn't believe. He wanted to believe – and he recalled words whispered almost in shame by his grandmother in the atheist house of her son, servant, as was Estoban, of a revolution which had locked the churches and forbidden belief. Succour me, Oh Lord.

The officer was speaking into the car radio: 'Varadero. You

had an incident last night at the roadblock with a black German. Kindly verify that he is at his hotel.'

After much crackling of atmospherics, a voice replied, 'The hotel seldom answers the telephone.'

The officer raised his eyebrows in mock despair and smiled at Estoban. It was a smile of complicity, of frustrations shared by the intelligent when faced with stupidity. 'Precisely. Were they to answer, I would myself telephone.'

'Then what should I do?' crackled the small voice, offended by the sarcasm.

'You drive there,' the officer said. 'This should take you five minutes – ten should your require associates to push the car so that it will start – fifteen should it become necessary for you to bicycle.'

A drop of water hit the bonnet of the Lada and both men craned their necks to look up at the underside of the bridge. Tendrils of iron oxide leaked from a sodden patch caused by rain penetrating a fissure in the concrete. A yellow and black butterfly alighted on the bonnet and touched the water with its proboscis.

Estoban looked across to the Peugeot. The American appeared so calm.

'I knew this Cuban criminal when he was younger,' the officer said. 'Not well, you understand. More what one might call a passing acquaintance which he would be unlikely to remember. He was the instructor while I was merely a pupil. Thus I was in the riverbed while the criminal remained on more comfortable ground.'

The officer's smile was thin and dry. His eyes were pale and expressionless.

Estoban looked away. He thought that three days of fear was enough. One word and it would be over. Then shame took him that he thought always of himself. What they had done to Miguelito was a hundred times worse. A thousand times worse. He was incapable of saving Miguelito. He wanted to reach him, that was all, touch him so that Miguelito could gain comfort from the assurance of how much he was loved. It seemed very little to ask.

Now he was no more than a spectacle for the *campesinos* who had gathered along the bank of the road junction. Most were middle-aged men and women, lean and prematurely worn by toil. Even the children were muted by the presence of the Special Brigade. Love gave confidence to a young couple sprawled in the shade of an acacia. Short shorts displayed their legs; a halter top left the girl's stomach bare. She was darker in skin than her *novio*, though not as dark as Maria, and her hair lacked the wild spring. Her *novio*'s right arm lay across her shoulders

Closer at hand a grey older man leant on a bicycle. His chest showed hollow as a cave in the open shirt, cheeks sunken and covered in white bristle. Estoban wondered what the old man carried on the rear carrier of his bicycle. The package was the size of two thick hardcover books and was wrapped in clean white cloth, probably a piece of bed sheet. The boy let his hand slide up the side of his girlfriend's breast. Estoban thought of them making love, all that was ahead of them. He wanted to weep. He wanted the officer to finish with his theatre. He thought that he could run straight down the open road, forcing them to shoot him. He saw his body buckle and sprawl on the black tar. Black to black. To have it over with. This selfishness of desire was so tempting. To have people think well of him. To die with his pride intact.

The officer said, 'Were I you, I believe that I would be less calm.' He nodded in agreement with his own thoughts. 'Of course a German would have no need for anxiety. Even a black German.'

The radio crackled and the same voice from Varadero enquired for the officer.

'The black German is with his friend. An older man, fat. An American. They left early this morning in a rental car. A Peugeot.'

'He is not in his room?' the officer asked.

'No. I have told you. Neither tourist is here. It is believed that they drove to Trinidad.'

'You are certain of this'?

'I have talked to both internal security and to the room maid and to the reception desk. Also to the security guards in the car park and at the gates into the hotel. All saw the two tourists depart.'

'You enquired what they are wearing?'

'Naturally. The *negrito* wore a yellow shirt and blue shorts.'

'And he departed with the fat American?'

'As I have told you.'

The officer replaced the microphone on its metal slide. The officer didn't look at Estoban. He looked ahead down the autopista. For a while he drummed lightly on the steering wheel. The heat pressed down, air still as a steel slab. Even the Lada seemed to hold its breath.

The pressure on Estoban's bladder approached disaster.

Finally the officer sighed and said, '*Negrito*. Charming.'

He eased himself in his seat. 'This Cuban criminal – I know his half-brother. The half-brother's mother and my mother are friends. Such friendships are common in Havana amongst the older generation of what was once described as the professional classes. Fortunately the Triumph has made us equal and there are no classes.' He turned then to look at Estoban.

'The Americans require laws that demand employment of people of different races and sexes. In Cuba we require no such law. That there are no black ministers in our government is evidence of the revolution's liberalism.'

Estoban recognised the officer's smile. Automatic as the flash on an instant camera, the smile was a hallmark imprinted on graduates from the Lenin School, insurance with which to cover themselves for any rash statement they might have made: *I was only joking. . .*

'Tell me, were you an investigating officer, would you judge that I have exercised due care in the matter of your identity? I ask only because it would be unfortunate for me should this criminal be captured and confess to having passed this way.' The officer gave a little shrug. 'You understand? Because of my friendship with his brother. A connection might be established.'

'As an investigating officer, I would judge that you have acted correctly,' Estoban said.

'And as a revolutionary? Though, as a German you would have no criteria by which to judge.'

'Fervour?' Estoban suggested.

'Fervour? Yes, indeed.' The smile flashed again. 'Your eye suggests a certain fervour, Herr Jonas. I wish you pleasure in Trinidad. A very white city. Also the only city in which there was no revolutionary committee prior to the Triumph.'

The officer fitted his sunglasses carefully and led Estoban back to the Peugeot.

'My apologies,' the officer said to the American. 'You will sympathise with my need both to be considerate of visitors and to do my job. The police in Varadero have confirmed Herr Jonas' appearance and that he accompanies a fat older American.' The officer gave the American a small bow and a smile. 'I merely repeat their description, señor. I will inform all police on your route to Trinidad. Hopefully you will suffer no further delays.'

20

Trent

The Old Bahama Channel skirts the southern edge of the Great Bahama Bank and offers a gateway along the north-east coast of Cuba to Haiti, the Dominican Republic and Puerto Rico.

A hundred yards long by fifty wide, Lobos Cay lies half a mile back from the edge of the channel and rises some twelve feet above the high watermark. A metal tower a hundred and fifty feet in height houses the light. Painted in black and white bands, the tower sprouts through the roof of a colonial-style bungalow shaded by verandas and built originally to house the lightkeeper. The Bahamian coast-guard station is a concrete building with radio aerials and a flag mast. Two huts serve fishermen as a camp and store for their gear and two palm trees lean with the prevailing northerlies. The closest land to Lobos Cay are the south tip of Andros Island in the Bahamas forty miles to the north and the cayos of Cuba's Camagüey Archipelago fifteen miles to the south.

Mid-afternoon and *Golden Girl* lay to anchor within the protection of the reef in water silky calm and a pale transparent blue above the white of the coral sand. Though less than half a mile to the west, Lobos Cay was barely visible, the light tower twisted by the heat and the buildings mere shadows forming and reforming within the mirage. To the south the cool deep waters of the Old Bahama Channel showed dark and lumpy and flecked with white. Seven merchant vessels sailed within sight of the saloon roof where Trent sat, two tankers, a bulk carrier and four container ships. Trent had been listening to the weather report broadcast on short wave from Florida: wind a maximum of ten miles an hour and smooth seas. Smooth seas for cargo ships could be a rollercoaster for an inflatable tender.

Trent and Dummy had positioned twin spinnaker poles and halyards as an A-frame on which to hoist the big Zodiac overboard and the grey inflatable drifted now at the end of a painter off the transom with two fuel tanks and both 40hp and 9hp Yamaha outboards mounted. Three more fuel tanks remained in the shade of the cockpit awning with the ice chest loaded with rations for four days and ten water bottles strung together by the neck. Trent had made simple duplicate tracings of his proposed course in through the cayos to the coast with latitude and longitude marked – depth of water was unimportant to the Zodiac – and had sealed the tracings into transparent plastic envelopes. His dive compass and a hand-held Magellan GPS were his navigation instruments. With six satellites overhead, the Magellan would supply his position to within six feet.

The Bahamian sat forward watching the channel, his face hidden beneath the red felt hat that an American woman had given him more than fifteen years ago and which had become his banner, visible for miles across the reefs where he fished for lobster. The hunch of his shoulders betrayed Dummy's anxiety, the same anxiety he had betrayed when Trent and a marine biologist girlfriend had made night dives along the wall of the Tongue of the Ocean, the mile-deep trench off the coast of Andros.

Trent dropped down into the cockpit and through into the saloon to check once more the equipment for the trip: thirty metres of light line, foot pump and repair pack for the Zodiac, dive knife, fins, snorkel, two torches, sun block, insect repellent, life jackets and distress flares, medical kit. The medical kit included antibiotics, antihistamine cream, sutures, wound pads and a couple of spikes of morphine.

Trent had pictured the entry into Cuban waters and the

alternatives. The Zodiac and its equipment were difficult to hide. Either Estoban was at the rendezvous or Trent would have to retire to the cayos and hide amongst the mangrove until the following night. Danger would increase with each approach to the creek: that he showed on the radar screen aboard a Navy or Guarda Frontera patrol boat or that a fisherman spotted the Zodiac or heard the outboard And mostly he sensed that the whole scenario was too structured: the young brother kidnapped in Guatemala, Estoban Tur resigned, de Sanchez able to visit the Bahamas, and him on board *Golden Girl* and connected to Bergman through San Cristóbal. Complicated, yes, but patterned, and the pattern possessed a nagging familiarity.

Bergman

They left the roadblock at nine a.m. Tur sat silent and Bergman didn't look at him. Two hundred miles of autopista to Ciego de Avila lay ahead, say three hours, and a further hour to the north coast – with no delays, eight and a half hours in total, which returned Bergman to Varadero at five thirty.

He had warned Karl Jonas that the younger sister might not reach the beach until after work. Sex was the best incentive and Bergman thought that Karl would wait until six or even six thirty.

Tight but possible, Bergman thought.

Tur, nervous that Bergman would hear his fear, cleared his throat and swallowed. 'The officer,' he said. 'The one from State Security. He recognised me.'

'The guy with the sunglasses?' Bergman said for something to say while trying to think.

'He will have issued instructions that we should be watched for at the entrance to Trinidad,' Tur said. Trinidad lay on the south coast, beyond the Escambray mountains. Quite a detour. An extra three or four hours on the journey. Bergman couldn't make it.

'You understand? The officer will wish to protect his decision,' Tur said and relapsed into silence.

Bergman didn't understand a damn thing. Two cows had strayed onto the autopista ahead. Bergman slowed the Peugeot to a crawl and glanced at Tur.

'Why did he let you go?'

'His mother is a friend of my stepmother.' Tur lowered his window and the heat off the tar exploded into their air-conditioned sanctuary. One of the cows found sufficient energy to kick up its rear hooves as Tur yelled and slapped the side of the door.

'That is what you believe?' Bergman asked.

'Not entirely,' Tur said.

Bergman jinked round the rear end of the second cow, changed up and slammed his right foot to the floorboards. 'What in shit does that mean?'

'I thought perhaps that you would tell me,' Tur said.

'What would I know?' Bergman protested. 'The first time I've been in Cuba and you are the *poderoso*. Or meant to be.'

'Was the *poderoso*,' Tur corrected.

'Yeah, okay, *was*,' Bergman said. Blaming someone was the easiest escape from the mess churning round in his head. Or hitting something, or cursing. Or driving too fast. He eased his foot back a little off the throttle.

They passed yet another compound of abandoned road machinery, monuments both to lack of maintenance and the poor quality of Russian manufacture. And mile after mile of land had been surrendered to weeds and a thick thorny scrub which clambered over trees and up banks and over rocks.

'The scrub,' Bergman said. 'What is it?'

'*Marabou*,' Estoban said.

'I thought you people were short of food.'

'It is your embargo,' Estoban retorted, his anger automatic at criticism from the enemy. 'Helms Burton,' he said as he watched the abandoned fields race by – good fields – while his grandfather had died in the psychiatric hospital from love for a scrap of hillside forbidden to him by the Triumph.

The American said, 'Castro, does anyone listen to him?'

'Everyone,' Estoban said.

The American didn't bother hiding his disbelief and Estoban pictured his own apartment, the children on the floor, Tobanito drawing while Mario read. The look of exasperation on Maria's face as Fidel appeared on the screen and the children disappointed because they knew that the speech would continue and continue and continue and delay transmission of the Brazilian soap opera to beyond their bedtime. To ensure maximum exposure, Fidel's speeches always came on the evenings of the soap.

'No, nobody listens,' Estoban said. Confessing to the enemy was less painful than confessing to his own kind. And less dangerous. He recalled the American leaning against the car at the roadblock. Impossible for him to have been that tranquil within himself – unless it was Estoban's paranoia that presumed the gringo an agent of the CIA.

'I thought of giving you away,' Estoban said. 'Bargaining.'

'Yeah, I know,' Bergman said. 'When I slapped my hand on the car roof.'

'Yes,' Tur said.

'What would you have told them? That I'd stolen the German's papers?'

'And that you were CIA.'

'CIA, I wouldn't drive a *poderoso* round the island,' Bergman said.

They turned off the autopista to Cienfuegos on the south coast and headed for Trinidad. On the outskirts of Trinidad, a police car pulled out of the shade of a flamboyant tree and followed them into town.

'We have to stop,' Tur said. 'Pretend we are true tourists.'

Bergman parked beside a rummy parking attendant with rotted teeth. Bergman's guide book referred to Trinidad as a perfect relic of sixteenth-century Hispanic Caribbean architecture. There were no trees to shade the narrow streets and the sun roasted the cobbles and smashed light off the whitewashed walls of the colonial houses. Open doors gave glimpses of inner patios, fountains, palm trees. A street photographer caught the two men crossing the main square in front of the church – except that there were no street photographers in Cuba and this one was shooting film in an East German Leica.

In Guatemala the police and the military were on Bergman's side. True, he had been a target for assassination from his first day in Central America; being hunted was different and he was out of practice by fifteen years.

He said, 'Shit,' because to do so was habitual and because, way back in his early years with the Agency, he had thought that it sounded cool.

'Let's keep it casual,' he said. 'I'm the guide. Otherwise they'll pick you for a local pimp.'

Shouldering his way into a restaurant one block from the square, Bergman ordered two cold Cristal beers at the bar. They found a table on the far side of a patio packed with sun-red tourists tapping time to a bossa nova quartet playing medium-live in the shade of a royal palm.

Seated facing the entrance, Bergman said, 'How will they get the photograph to Havana.

'Road. Fax won't give sufficient definition. An advantage to having a brown skin,' Estoban said and grinned.

'And a black eye,' Bergman said. If the photograph went by road, they had three hours. However, if they left Trinidad in a hurry, they would confirm police suspicions.

Bergman watched Tur turn his can of Cristal round on the table. The can left overlapping rings of condensation on the plastic marble. Tur's eyes were dark and deliberately open as he looked across the table. 'They will arrest you.'

'Yeah, I know.' It was about all Bergman knew. He had a bad feeling that the operation had reversed itself and that he had become the target of a Cuban sting.

'Is there someone who will pick you up?' he asked.

Tur shrugged. 'It is possible that someone will pick me up.'

'Maybe that's as good as you get in your situation.' Bergman was trying to be positive. He opened the guide book. 'Tourists visit museums. You choose. Art, Romantic, National History?'

'Romantic. I am a revolutionary,' Tur said.

A plain-clothes policeman pretending to be a clerk tailed them back to the main square where the Museo Romántico was housed in a colonial mansion beside the church of Santisima Trinidad. Culture didn't fit their image and the two men showed boredom and joked to each other as they wandered through the displays of porcelain and glass and ornate furniture.

The car park attendant had changed from rum, grime and too few teeth to clean jeans, a white T-shirt and polished boots. Bergman complained of the heat and asked directions to the Motel Las Cuevas a couple of miles out of town. At the motel, he parked in the shade at the far end of the car park, tipped the guard five dollars while mopping the sweat off his face and asked whether the bar stocked cold beer.

'With certainty, señor,' the attendant said, a lie given that this was Cuba.

Bergman and Tur booked into an air-conditioned chalet facing the swimming pool and ordered fried snapper with salad from room service. Tur arranged Bergman's toiletries in the bathroom while Bergman spread his clothes over both beds, opened his laptop on the desk and pressed the three keys that wiped its memory and programmes. The police quarrelling over his possessions might delay the chase for fifteen minutes.

A waiter, who considered himself too superior to serve (probably an economist or a sociologist), kneed the door open and dumped their food on the desk rather than on the table.

Bergman grumbled about the heat and asked for the *Do Not Disturb* sign. They gave the waiter five minutes to report their siesta to the police. Then they ducked round the rear of the chalets. As Bergman had hoped, the attendant had taken his five dollars in search of a drink. Both men buckled their safety belts and Bergman put his foot down on the highway to Sancti Spíritus. Skirting the Escambray mountains, the road ran straight across a coastal plain planted with sugar. Cloud had gathered in from the west to cut the earlier glare and Bergman kept the speedometer quivering around the 120kph mark.

Tur spread a road map on his knees. Familiar with the country, he directed Bergman off the highway fifteen miles east of Trinidad.

The dirt road cut between the Escambray mountains and the Heights of Sancti Spíritus. The way led over spurs of rock. Between the spurs the surface was mostly clay, slippery from the rains. The road hadn't been graded in a few years and rainwater disguised the depth of the potholes. Bergman fought to keep the car on the road and the needle on the 80 mark. He lost the rear end twice in the first five miles and slid broadside into sugar.

In movies, cars chased cars for miles down open roads. In real life, helicopters did the search and pursuit. They probably had thirty minutes at most before the hunt began and driving the Peugeot was as obvious as beating a drum and flashing a light on the roof of a bright yellow double-decker bus.

'We have to change cars,' Bergman said.

Tur merely nodded and kept his eyes on the map to avoid looking at the road and the approaching corner. Bergman slid the Peugeot round the corner and hit a crater. Tur rammed the flat of his hands against the roof. Bergman said, 'Shit!' and fought the car back onto a straight line for the next spur.

They sped over the spur and spotted a lump of rusty blue creeping towards them between the cane.

'Fifty-two Chevy,' Tur said.

Bergman hit the brakes and skidded the Peugeot to a halt blocking the road. Opening the boot, he tossed Tur the jack handle, then went round the front of the car, stuck his head under the bonnet and removed the distributor cap.

For noise, the Chevy could have competed with a World War I tank and its tyres would have made a new billiard ball look rough. A driver in his early twenties tried to focus through the rum he had exchanged for brains.

A siren pierced the hammer of worn bearings and exhaust

explosions. The police car appeared over a ridge less than a mile away, the blue lights on its roof flashing bright against the dark background of rain cloud spread now to the horizon. The driver of the Chevy took to the sugarcane to pass the Peugeot. Tur had disappeared.

Any moment could signal the discovery of their flight from the motel, their description broadcast to all squad cars. Bergman considered flight back the way they had come or hiding the Peugeot in the fields. He hadn't the time. Wetting his finger, he moistened the inside of the distributor cap.

Two cops manned the white Lada patrol car; a young driver and a sergeant in his late forties. The driver switched off the flashing lights and the siren but kept the engine running, probably because of a dead battery.

Both policemen dismounted. The sergeant was tall and tough, though courteous in addressing Bergman.

'There is a difficulty with your car?'

Bergman showed him the distributor cap. 'Wet electrics.'

The sergeant handed the distributor cap to his driver who wiped the contacts on his shirt. Bergman and the sergeant leant forward over the car wing to watch the driver replace the part. Tur crept barefoot from the cane. He struck the sergeant across the back of the head with the jack handle and grabbed his pistol from its holster. The driver hadn't time to defend himself.

The sergeant sat on the ground dazed and mumbling curses. Tur demanded his uniform, holding the pistol to the driver's head while the sergeant stripped.

Tur's speed and the efficiency of his violence had taken Bergman by surprise. His picture of Tur had been formed in Havana; the Cuban dressed in his brown suit, plump and sweating as he mounted his bike.

Tur kept the policemen covered while Bergman cuffed them back to back on the rear seat of the Peugeot. They found a track through the sugar and hid the Peugeot in the deep shade of a laurel tree. They hadn't time to camouflage it.

Tur had dressed in the sergeant's uniform. He drove the

squad car while Bergman sat in the rear and read the road map. A few tractors and a couple of trucks were the only traffic for the next ten miles. Lightning flashed across the horizon accompanied by the first rolls of thunder. The radio officer at the police station called them a few times. Tur answered with harsh noises and tapped and scraped the microphone on the dashboard in imitation of the atmospherics brought by the storm. They were short of the autopista by five miles when an officer from Sancti Spíritus broke in with an all-stations alert for a rental Peugeot driven by an American and with a Cuban passenger.

'We need to change cars again,' Bergman said.

The road improved as they approached the autopista. They passed a chicken co-operative without chickens attached to the Cuban version of a communist-period East German housing project (the Cuban version has broken wood slats in the windows instead of broken glass), a sugar factory and one of those Cuban warehouses that have never stored anything. This one had lost half its roof.

Next came a village with a horse-drawn bus and bicycles and residents walking the pavement as if they wanted to be elsewhere. A rusted Moscovich had collapsed up a side street and two American wrecks stood on concrete blocks. Laurels shaded the standard village square and the statue of José Martí with his back turned on a workman's cafeteria that served stale air. Another mile and there was more sugar on the left of the road.

A dozen men and women in search of a ride stood disconsolately at the foot of the bridge spanning the autopista while two policemen checked the documents of a black cyclist.

The clouds were low and dense as an eiderdown.

The first spits of rain sent the hitchhikers cowering into the shelter of the bridge as Tur crossed over the autopista and turned down a dirt track. Ten metres of mud and crushed grass separated the end of the track from the highway. Tur parked on the autopista's verge. Two farm trucks and a military canvas-top passed their side of the autopista. Then came a white Lada with both headlights shining. The tyres spun as Tur accelerated. He pulled alongside the Lada before switching on the flashing lights. The driver braked and Tur parked in front of him. He got out of the squad car and walked back in the beginnings of the rain.

Watching Tur through the rear window of the squad car, Bergman was reminded of police movies and the barely restrained aggression of Los Angeles cops. It was all there in the hunched shoulders and the manner in which Tur carried his weight forward a little, the deliberate loosening of his neck muscles and, for reassurance, the fingers tracing the butt of the holstered automatic.

The Lada was as new as a Lada could be and the driver and his companion were middle-aged overweight *poderosos*. The rain beat on the cars as Bergman stepped into the storm. Tur tossed him the keys to the *poderosos'* Lada and Bergman opened the boot. A sack covered half a pig wrapped in a plastic sheet, three hams and a box of five-kilo bars of processed cheese from the creamery in Camagüey.

Tur ordered the driver and his passenger out.

The *poderoso* cursed him and told him to be satisfied with one of the hams or pass the next twenty years cutting cane.

Something snapped in Tur. Grabbing the driver by the shirt collar, he brought his knee up between the *poderoso's* legs and, as he buckled, clubbed him across the mouth with the butt of the sergeant's automatic.

The full force of the storm was on them now with visibility down to a fifty yards and thunder continual. Tur was breathing heavily as he hustled the two men through the field. He forced them against a tree, the classic execution. Bergman had seen it a hundred times in Guatemala and he recognised the knowledge in the faces of the *poderosos* as Tur confronted them, his dark skull glistening wet and his chest heaving.

21

Trent

He had found a Cuban radio station: rain was forecast along the island from mid-afternoon and through the night. Rain would aid Estoban Tur and Trent would be hidden as he slipped through the archipelago to the main island.

The late afternoon sun was meek after the midday blaze. Ahead lay the inner fringe of coral heads within the surf which rolled from the deep to explode against the edge of the Great Bahama Bank. Trent watched a fresh roller swell dark and steep against the side of the trench. The roller broke first to the east. The line of foam spread fast and the dark wall collapsed and spilled forward as if it were the innards of some vast serpent laid along the reef and gutted by a razor.

Trent was in no hurry. Steering the big motor for twenty miles across the swells of the Old Bahama Channel would have left him exhausted and he used the 9hp Yamaha. The roar of the surf drowned both the purr of the small outboard and the screech of gulls quarrelling above a fishing boat alongside the dock over on Lobos Cay. A narrow cut in the reef gave access to the cay and more birds sailed and swooped and dived at the mouth of the cut where the surf faded for fifty feet.

As he headed out into the channel, Trent set a light rod in the stainless steel holder mounted on the inside of the transom. Releasing the brake on the reel, he ran out 150 feet of line. Surf, slamming the coral on each side, spewed froth across the dark blue swells that curled round the mouth of the cut and effortlessly lifted the Zodiac. The twin walls of wave towered over the inflatable and shrunk it to the size of a grass seed. The unharnessed power made Trent shiver for a moment as the breeze drew a curtain of spray across his course. Then he was through the cut and into the channel with half a mile of water beneath him. Evening sunlight shimmered on the western face of the waves and on the small curls of foam that broke free of their crests. The scent was less salt than in the shallows, less rich, and the breeze brushed cool off the sea.

A fish hit the yellow and scarlet lure and the ratchet screamed as the line sped from the reel. Trent slipped the Yamaha into neutral and grabbed the rod. Deprived of power the Zodiac tipped and rolled with the swell and Trent slid to the inflatable floorboard, bracing himself against the side tubes. Tightening the brake, he snapped the rod back to imbed the hook. The rod bowed under the strain and the fish leapt clear of the water, a vertical streak of silver flailing against the golden sunset. Trent guessed that Bahamians watched from the cay and he played the fish carefully so that his audience would believe sport his reason for sailing the channel. Finally the quarry lay close, a kingfish ten or twelve pounds in weight. Trent slid his hands down the trace to pry the lure free and he supported the kingfish beneath its belly for a minute while it regained its strength. A flick of its tail and the fish was gone. Mounting the rod in its holder, Trent snipped the hook free of the lure and slipped the Yamaha into gear.

He headed now up the edge of the channel. The tin roof of the lighthouse bungalow glowed beneath the sweep of the light while, to the west, the sun swelled against the sea and dyed the underside of the clouds with streaks of orange and of crimson. The swells rose higher with the approaching dusk. A container ship followed an empty tanker up-channel towards Florida, while sailing east towards Haiti, the Dominican Republic and Puerto Rico came two laden cargo ships, a bulk carrier and a tanker deep in the water.

As the sun melted into the sea, the last spills of old gold

glistened across the face of swells that were almost black in the twilight. The lure skipped on the surface as Trent reeled in his line and a gull dived only to scream at the deception. Trent turned towards the reef with the last of the light and held his course for a minute before swinging the bows round, the dark grey of the inflatable now invisible to any watcher on Lobos Cay and to the radar that licked across the sea from the ships and from the coastguard station and from the shores of Cuba. Enemy territory. The fear was familiar, the sense of isolation magnified by the minuteness of his craft and the depth of water.

As always there came the desire and the temptation to abort the mission.

Estoban Tur

He had fought for three days to hold himself together against the fear. Rage that he should be made to suffer had cohabited with his fear. Discovery of the pork and hams and stolen cheese in the Lada snapped his control. Both *poderoso* wore gold chains; one wore a watch on a gold strap and the silver top of a fountain pen protruded from the breast pocket of his shirt. Despite the cleansing rain, Estoban could smell the imported soap and deodorant. The stolen food was all that he had denied himself and his wife and children – the comforts that accompanied power: good shoes, clothes, extra food, the bigger apartment.

Stripped of power, he suspected that egotism alone had made him deprive his family. The pain was too great and he focused on the two men as he drove them through the sugar to the tree. Stepping back, he aimed between the elder *poderoso*'s eyes and he wanted to laugh into the rain as he saw a stain flow from the man's trouser zip.

The gringo shouted. 'Don't kill the sons of bitches. All we need is the car.'

Bergman

Bergman didn't care who they were or what they were. He watched Tur cuff their wrists so that they faced away from each other, their backs to the tree trunk, and he made no move to help as Tur gagged them with bits of shirt.

Tur spat his contempt and limped to the squad car, reversing it down the track into the cane. He splintered the head lights and the windows of the car with the jack handle, opened the bonnet and smashed the distributor cap and coil. Vengeance was the only aim of the destruction.

Bergman waited in the *poderosos'* Lada. The rain beat on the roof and humidity fogged the windows. Bergman rolled the window down and the rain drove in cold on his cheek.

Finished his fun, the Cuban opened the boot and retrieved a ham and a cheese. He was breathing hard as he slid in beside Bergman. He said, 'Head east up the autopista about a mile. There's a side road that bypasses Sancti Spíritus.'

Bergman started the engine and eased the Lada forward. The wipers were inadequate and the windshield became a sheet of water while the rain drew a curtain round them. Out of sight of the verge, Bergman lost all sense of direction. The Lada seemed poised on a black disc of water. He expected the Lada to fall off the disc – or a truck to smash into them. Grass sprouted ahead. He drove into the grass and found it was the centre strip separating the traffic into east and west. Turning at right angles across the strip, he drove straight until he hit the far verge where he turned up the autopista against the flow of traffic. Peering from the open window, he followed the verge at little more than walking pace.

'We will never find your road,' he said.

'Americans have no right to be pessimists.' Tur had drawn a knife and was sawing slices off the ham. He fed a slice off the blade into Bergman's mouth.

The ham tasted of chemicals and truck grease. Bergman spat it into the grass. 'In Cuba everyone has the right to be a pessimist.'

'It is possible that the cheese is more palatable,' Tur said and reached back to the rear seat. He peeled the red cover off the cheese and carved Bergman a wedge.

The cheese tasted only faintly of chemicals.

An army truck loomed suddenly out of the murk. Bergman swerved off the road and cursed as the left-hand front wheel smashed into a rock. Looking back over his shoulder, he saw soldiers drop from the truck's tailgate. Bergman's clothes would betray him as a foreigner and he rammed the Lada into reverse and let out the clutch. The rear wheels spun in the mud.

'Show calm,' Tur warned as he stuck his head out of the window and shouted at the soldiers to push the Lada in reverse.

Perhaps the soldiers were impressed by his sergeant's uniform. They were ten in all under the command of a corporal. They gathered at the front of the Lada. A single heave shoved the Lada back onto the roadway.

'The tire is punctured,' a soldier said.

Tur got down from the Lada, walked round and kicked the wheel that had struck the rock. He showed no interest in the soldiers.

Bergman felt under the passenger seat in hope of finding the spare automatic. Tur must have locked it in the boot.

'There is no interest in all of us becoming wet,' Tur said to the soldiers. 'Continue on your way and we will change our own wheel.'

The corporal stooped to peer into the car. He spotted the ham and the cheese on the rear seat. The rain beat on his back. His comrades were retreating to the truck. He made to follow. Then changed his mind. His posture hardened as he peered at Bergman and he drew his forearm across his face to clear his eyes of the drips.

Tur tapped the corporal on the back. Thunder rolled and grumbled round the two men as they confronted each other in the downpour. The corporal was white and thin and fierce while Tur appeared complacent in his brown plumpness. He held a pistol against the corporal's belly and he said quietly, 'Should such be necessary, I will kill you. Follow me with care to the other side of the car and kindly order the two soldiers behind you to change the wheel.' And to Bergman, he said, 'Open the boot.'

Their corporal's back to them, the two soldiers were unable to see the pistol. They watched sullenly as Bergman fitted the key.

Lifting the boot lid, Bergman expected to see the second automatic. Apart from the spare and tools, only the half pig and the hams and cheese were visible. He dragged out the spare and passed the jack and the brace to the soldiers. Then he carried a ham and a bar of cheese to the truck. Dusk had added its shade to the rain and cloud cover. The soft glow of cigarettes supplied the only light beneath the canopy and the faces were featureless ovals shiny with sweat.

Bergman passed up the ham and cheese over the tailgate. Dividing the food would keep the men occupied.

Meanwhile one soldier had levered the punctured wheel free. Bergman bowled it to the rear of the Lada and heaved it into the spare's slot on the left side of the boot. He almost missed the pistol. Tur had wedged it behind the petrol tank filler pipe. Bergman felt more confident now that he was armed. He thought that the corporal was dangerously immobile and unprotesting – probably nerving himself.

Bergman slapped the corporal on the back and smiled and opened his billfold and withdrew a twenty dollar bill. He held the bill so that the two soldiers watching over the bonnet of the Lada could see it.

'You people have been more than kind,' Bergman said and folded the bill into a neat square and slipped it into the corporal's palm.

The one soldier lowered the jack and carried it round to the boot while the second soldier finished tightening the wheel bolts with the brace. Bergman thought that Tur was foolish in not talking to the corporal. The tension between the two Cubans was too obvious.

Estoban Tur

The American had failed to placate the corporal. The corporal leant a little forward and the line of his shoulders remained rigid against the rain. Estoban knew that he ought to do something. Shooting the corporal seemed his only option.

His finger tightened on the trigger.

Bang, he thought.

Bang and it was over with.

In his mind, he fired this second shot at the American. Gringos always used dollars.

Bang, he thought

Though not yet. He needed the American to help him down through the woods to the inlet.

The gringo rolled the punctured tyre round to the boot and heaved it in.

Estoban leant a little closer to the corporal. 'Pinar del Río will take the championship. They have Omar Linares,' he said, naming the Pinarenio who pitched both for Pinar and for the national team. 'And Raoul Jiminez and Pedro Ruiz, the two Lasos and Jose Ariel Contreras.' As Estoban listed the Pinarenos, he sensed the fight go out of the corporal.

The line of the corporal's shoulders eased; he wiped his eyes on his palm and watched as the American tipped the two soldiers five dollars each.

Gringo dollars and Estoban felt the familiar anger. He smiled deliberately and said to the corporal, 'There is half a pig in the trunk that you may take.'

The two fives together with the twenty in the corporal's own pocket would be forfeit in an enquiry. And the meat was too tempting. The corporal carried the side of pork over his shoulder. Estoban walked with him to the truck and stood aside as the corporal clambered into the cab.

The corporal swept the rain from his face and looked down at Estoban. Lightning lit the two men as he gave Estoban the finger. 'The next tour, your players will defect. Central will win.'

Estoban got back into the Lada. 'Drive,' he said to Bergman. Perhaps it was because he held the police sergeant's pistol but he felt very confident and in control for the first time since hearing of Miguelito's disappearance. And he was very sure suddenly that the Englishman would come.

Trent

Trent wore a grey wetsuit against the spray and had slung his mask and snorkel round his neck. The 9hp Yamaha slid the Zodiac smoothly over the swells. Three hours out from the Great Bahama Bank and the sway of Trent's body matched the rise and flow of the waves. Only the passing cargo ships destroyed the rhythm, vast monsters towering out of the dark to splay their wake across the pattern of the sea. A half moon shone sharp-edged and the stars blinked brilliant against a clear sky overhead and to his north. The spit of the lighthouses on the Camagüey archipelago was barely visible to the south where lightning flickered within a curtain of cloud drawn across the horizon. The cloud was dangerous within Cuban waters, camouflaging the silhouette of any waiting patrol boat, and Trent strained to see into the dark as he made his approach.

Guarding the main archipelago, the outer cayos were mere scraps of dune-capped coral. He checked the Magellan GPS every five minutes and marked his position on the first of his home-drawn charts before adjusting his course against the luminous dial of his dive compass. First he heard the swells break. He found the pass in through the reef and saw a pale curve of sand. Shifting the tiller to port, he followed the beach until he came to the passage between two cayos.

The sea was smooth within the reef and he slowed the Zodiac to avoid drawing a wake of phosphorescence. Thunder rolled along the mountains and lightning drew the outline of the outer cloud bank. He smelt the rain fresh and cool on the off-shore breeze. Then came the beat of the rain on the sea and he changed from the 9hp Yamaha to the 40hp, opening the throttle wide to lift the Zodiac onto her twin keels, then dropping the revs down until he heard the fast jet cut out.

Safe within the rain, he sped west in protected water at twenty miles an hour. The shower ceased after a quarter of an hour and he switched back to the small motor and turned south, seeking for a cut between the main cayos. A twin cylinder diesel hammered and he heard voices and spotted the single pale electric light of a small Cuban fishing boat. Too late he saw the black wall that was a patrol boat's hull rear above him. He rammed the tiller over and hit broadside. An officer shouted and the beam of a searchlight licked across the sea and trapped the fishermen setting a net. Netting was illegal within the cayos and for a moment Trent thought that he was safe. Then a spotlight spat at him. He was already lowering the big Yamaha.

A warning shot cracked over Trent's head as he hit the start button and a sailor yelled at him to raise his hands. The Yamaha fired and he snicked it into gear and opened the throttle wide. The propeller bit and he threw his weight forward to hold the bows down. Surprise was his best defence and he swerved the Zodiac back towards the patrol boat and was already hitting thirty miles an hour as he raced under its stern. He heard the sailors swear as they stumbled over the after cabin in pursuit. Then came the chatter of a Kalashnikov as Trent zigzagged the Zodiac due south towards the shelter of the cayos to the south.

A bullet hit the port hull and a second hit one of the spare fuel tanks. Searchlight and spotlight beams traced his wake and Kalashnikovs stitched the water. One more bullet and the petrol flooding into the Zodiac could explode. The port tube was leaking; the Zodiac was difficult to steer and losing speed. The spotlight caught the stern of the inflatable for an instant as Trent hurled the punctured tank overboard. He had to hide. A smoke screen. Or destroy the sailors' night vision.

Desperate, he grabbed a flare and fired it back towards the patrol boat. Bullets sought him as he swerved the Zodiac away from the flare trail. The searchlight caught the sheen of floating petrol as the flare died in the water. He fired a second flare and rammed the tiller hard to starboard. The flare hit the petrol and a fringe of small flame grew briefly. The roar of the patrol boat's engines beat at him, a third flare lit the vicious bow wave and a heavy machine gun mounted on the foredeck pumped tracer across his track. A single explosion preluded a brilliant white flare floating overhead on a parachute. The Zodiac was a rabbit now in an open field, one leg wounded and speed Trent's only defence as he zigged and zagged in his race for the mangrove.

To maintain speed, Trent favoured the starboard tack, lying along the stiff tube to keep the weight off the punctured port hull. A fresh flare soared high and the bow wave of a second patrol boat burst from the shelter of a channel through the cayos to Trent's west. He was trapped between the two patrol boats with half a mile to the shallows.

Again he sought for surprise, curving the Zodiac fast on its starboard hull and heading straight for the pursuing patrol boat so that the gunners on the second boat were forced to delay fire or risk killing their own men.

The combined speed of the Zodiac and the patrol boat approached fifty miles an hour. Luck alone could enable a marksman armed with a Kalashnikov to hit the inflatable while the acute angle of depression silenced the machine gun. Trent fled down the side of the patrol boat and cut a tight circle on his good hull before heading south-east in a gentle curve to starboard. The coxswain began to swing the patrol boat in Trent's wake. At thirty knots the Russian-built patrol boat had a turning radius of four hundred metres and the skipper must have screamed at the coxswain to change course back away from the shallows. This outer circle gained Trent extra seconds and took the patrol boat across the line of the second pursuer.

A fresh parachute flare from the patrol boat lit the first patch of mangrove a bare quarter mile off Trent's port bow. Balanced on his starboard hull, Trent would miss the mangrove by a hundred metres. The half-deflated port hull slapped the sea as he drew his dive knife and cut the lashing holding the spare fuel tanks against the port hull. He heaved the tanks overboard and the ice chest. The machine gun smacked fountains out of the sea as Trent spun the Zodiac again on the starboard hull. The skipper of the patrol boat out-guessed him and laid a barrage across the new curve that would take the Zodiac into shelter.

Trent thought that it was a very stupid way to die and he thought of Estoban Tur at the inlet and whether the Cuban could hear the gunfire.

22

Trent

Shells from the machine gun chopped the water. Trent was dead if he stayed in the Zodiac. Both hulls had been hit and a second fuel tank. He cut the engine and dived overboard with the coil of light line. He fastened one end to the bow, dived and swam carefully away from the boat towards the mangrove. A searchlight caught the Zodiac and held it, the hulls sagging and the engine stopped. The light lingered a moment then criss-crossed the sea in search of Trent. Impossible for the sailors to know whether the infiltrator lived or had been killed.

Trent reached the end of the line, turned and slowly drew the Zodiac in his wake. The first spits of a shower patterned the sea with interlocking circles. The second patrol boat joined the first in the hunt and the two cones of light slipped backwards and forwards across each other as the boats edged ever closer to the shallows. The boats probably had a draught of eight feet and the outer fringe of mangrove grew in less than five feet of water.

He swam a further thirty metres and again dragged the Zodiac forward. He knew that they wouldn't destroy the Zodiac – the contents were spoils of war.

He swam towards the cayo and, reaching the end of the line, probed with his feet for the mud. The rain fell more heavily and one of the searchlight operators, nervous of losing him, held the Zodiac in mid-beam while the second searched the edge of the mangrove. Something moved, perhaps one of the indigenous rodents, and a nervous gunner chopped the surrounding growth to slivers. The gun stilled and Trent could hear the rain beat hard on the sea; the inflatable had become a faint blur. He drew it in faster now and swam the length of the line careless of the searchlights spotting his shoulders. His feet touched mud and he could smell the swamp.

The creak of a winch pierced the rain and he heard the thud of a tender being lowered against the side of one of the patrol boats. He doubted whether the tenders were equipped with outboard motors – and if they were, it was unlikely that the motors worked or had fuel. Humphrey Bogart and the *African Queen*, he thought as he dragged the Zodiac into the shelter of the mangrove and turned west in search of a cut into the swamp. Behind him came shouts and the creek of oars in their rowlocks and the splash of blades.

The second patrol boat had run down the cayo before lowering its tender. Trent was caught in a pincer movement. Night exaggerated the drip and grate of oars and the orders shouted by the commanders of the hunting party. Heralding the main swamp, scattered patches of mangrove sheltered Trent from the searchlights and only the weaker beams of the spotlights mounted on the tenders reached him between the branches. He dragged the Zodiac by the stern to hide the engines from his pursuers. The rain was solid and blinding, the mud slippery along the border of the mangrove and roots caught at his feet. With his free hand he searched for a channel into the heart of the swamp and snapped branches beneath the water, tossing them into the Zodiac. The inflated floorboard and the twin keeltubes running fore and aft beneath the floor were the sole sections of the inflatable unpunctured and the Zodiac floated low in the water, grey and formless. At a distance and at night and in heavy rain, it might be mistaken for a mangrove bush; however, the two tenders were closing steadily and discovery was inevitable.

Death had seldom frightened Trent, rather it promised an end to the fear with which he had always lived: of failing those who depended upon him – as he had failed his father. He pictured Estoban Tur's half-brother weeping in terror of the next sexual assault and Estoban waiting at the head of the creek. Estoban would have heard the shooting and perhaps seen the parachute flares float above the cayos.

Twice Trent thought that he had found an opening into the swamp only to hit a dead end. He discovered a third opening, narrower than the others. Mosquitoes rose in clouds as he forced his way between the scrub and the Zodiac snagged on a branch. Twenty feet into the swamp and the channel cut to the right. A further few feet and he confronted an impenetrable tangle. The closest tender was less than fifty yards from the cul de sac. Slashing beneath the water, Trent dragged at the branches as they came loose and waded back to the narrow entrance. Too late to weave the branches into the surrounding vegetation, he stood with them in his arms. The tender approached and he ducked beneath the surface, breathing through his snorkel. The water glowed as the beam of the spotlight slid along the edge of the undergrowth. He heard the oars dip and tap the branches only feet from his head. The flat of an oar smashed down on the branches he held and the bows of the tender swung into the alley and rammed him face down in the mud. He was blind in the mud and already desperate for air and he felt and heard the hammer of the machine gun beat through the fibreglass hull.

He eased sideways and up the side of the tender. He expected to see the Zodiac caught in a flare and diced fine as fried onions. Instead he found the gunners facing away from him. They had shredded a deer or a wild pig or perhaps a turtle. The slap of wings above the swamp heralded the panicked exodus of a colony of egrets and Trent heard the shriek of gulls and of oystercatchers. Anxious to view their kill, the coxswain shouted at his oarsmen and the oars dipped and scraped against the skinny trunks of the scrub as the tender retreated from the cut.

Bergman

A fresh squall swept off the sierra. The headlights of the stolen Lada pushed dulled beams between the walls of cane and the windscreen remained awash despite the sweep of the wipers. Bergman had been driving for more than two hours since leaving the autopista. Most of the roads had been tarred in the past but were now mostly dirt and potholes. Bergman had feared a cordon cutting them off from the east. The corporal and his men must have held their tongues while the storm would delay until daylight the discovery of the police sergeant and his driver and the two *poderosos*.

Another hour and Tur directed Bergman to park on a country lane.

The Cuban took the wheel and turned onto a track that climbed over a rocky ridge of mountain with thick woods covering the north face. A white owl burst out of the trees near the crest, then came a sharp left bend along the lip of a cliff that plunged sheer some three hundred feet to the sea.

Tur brought the car to a halt, switched off the lights and opened the windows. Bergman collected the last ham and a cheese from the boot while Tur hobbled into the woods and found a stick. With the Lada in first gear, Tur wedged the stick against the accelerator while keeping his foot on the clutch. He dived sideways and the Lada jerked forward and vanished. The car smashed rock twice on the descent. Then came the smash and splash as it hit the water and the engine died.

Bergman watched the car sink. Way out to sea a light fell slowly. Given the rain, it had to be a very bright light. A parachute flare. Tur remained on the ground, massaging his ankle. Bergman carefully cleaned the tyre marks off the cliff edge before helping the Cuban to his feet. Supported under the shoulder, the Cuban hopped and hobbled back along the track to a narrow footpath that dipped through the wood.

The path was steep and slippery. Without help, Tur would have found the descent impossible. The trees thinned as they approached the sea. A cascade spilled into an inlet some thirty metres wide and a hundred long. The inlet lay between the steep sides and was sheltered from the surf by a bar that the sea had built into a small strip of beach below the outer tip of the near bank. A narrow track led up from the beach to a wooden hut built on a natural terrace, which had been widened to encompass a vegetable patch. The door of the hut hung open on one hinge and the vegetable patch was overgrown with weeds. Bergman lowered Tur into the shelter of a ceiba tree and drew his pistol before crossing the terrace. The hut was empty, the only furniture a chair with one leg missing and two broken clay pots. He retrieved Tur from the trees and helped him down the track past the hut to the top of the bank above the beach. The distance to the nearest cayo in the archipelago was less than five miles and they could hear, despite the rain, the sputter of a machine gun.

'Your man,' Bergman said.

Tur said, 'Yes.'

Perhaps half an hour passed before the firing ended.

They sat listening, waiting. Suddenly came renewed firing that rose in seconds to a crescendo. Silence returned. Small waves sucked at the beach and at the rocks and Bergman could distinguish the soft patter of the rain from the fall of the heavier drops that had collected first on the leaves.

'Dead,' he said.

'He is not easy to kill.'

Tur tossed a pebble. The pebble hit a rock before bouncing into the sea. The two separate impacts were clear and sharp. Thunder rolled round them and a sheet of lightning cut across the sea. Bergman imagined that he saw the outline of the cayo. The shadow drawn by the lightning faded out of his eyes and he saw the sea again below, small curls of white against the rocks and on the sand. The temptation to ask the Cuban for forgiveness was very strong – for all of it, for Little Brother.

'He will come tomorrow night,' Tur said.

Bergman helped Tur to his feet and they retreated up the path until they found a rock that enabled them to step clear of the track without leaving scent. Bergman settled Tur into the bushes above the cascade. Returning to the inlet he clambered down and marked the sand both with his sandals and with his bare feet. Then he drew in the sand the track of a boat dragged ashore and relaunched and he walked backwards off the beach to the track up to the hut.

He wasn't sure how to handle Tur. The Cuban had been on the run too long. His rescuer was almost certainly dead and he was incapable of walking far. Abandoning him was the obvious solution. Reach a telephone and Nick the Greek would collect him in a car with diplomatic plates. He would leave Cuba on a diplomatic passport issued to a lookalike who would report the passport stolen once Bergman was gone from the island. Routine. Except that Bergman knew that he wouldn't do it. To abandon Tur would be a sacrifice of the Cuban's life to no purpose and even a bad purpose was better than no purpose at all.

Leaving the track at the same rock he had used with Tur, he climbed up through the trees and crossed the stream at the head of the cascade. The Cuban sat propped against a tree. Shoulders hunched and shivering, he reminded Bergman of a wet pigeon. Bergman squatted beside him.

They had water and cheese and a ham. The rain was on their side, washing away their scent. Perhaps the soldiers would miss them. They had to wait for the hunt to end – three or four days – perhaps a week. Then he could plan a new escape route for Tur. For the moment Bergman had forgotten why he wanted the Cuban out.

'It could be worse,' he said.

Way in the distance a pale white glow showed through the rain and the harsh chatter of machine guns came to them again across the water.

Trent

The Cubans fired at anything that moved. Trent lay exhausted against the mangrove. His present position was on the outer flank of the channel between two cayos. The further he entered into the shelter of the channel, the wider would grow the mangrove. The sheltered south coast would host a true swamp extending perhaps a mile from the shore and with canals winding through the scrub.

Fresh water limited his options. He had water for three days. He wasn't concerned by Tur's predicament. Gunfire would have warned Tur that Trent had been delayed. Already he would be looking for a hiding place.

Trent's breathing steadied and he re-entered the cut and camouflaged the Zodiac more thoroughly. Taking two bottles of water, he followed in the wake of the tenders. He swam dog paddle, his hands always below the surface to avoid swirls of phosphorescence, and he kept his feet clear of the bottom so as not to disturb the mud.

The tenders had joined forces at the entrance to a shallow inlet. The gunners had sliced swathes out of the swamp and the surface of the inlet was coated with wood chip. Trent eased past the boats. An hour took him through the channel and he turned east along the southern edge of the swamp. Now he searched for a canal running deep into the wilderness. The first cut looped back, dead mangrove blocked a second. The third ran straight for fifty yards into a small lagoon from which three exits led deeper into the maze. Seeking a spur of mangrove between two exits, he cut branches below the surface. He cut a final branch above the water and at an angle so that the cut would show in the shade. Then he dragged the severed branches one by one and buried them separately within the mat of underwater roots.

With first light he drew himself into the undergrowth. No trace of mud marked his path as he slid like a serpent between the trunks of the mangrove trees and over the roots that pierced the surface, and he sniffed the air, the scent of a colony of snowy egrets giving his course. He heard the rumble of diesels in the distance as the patrol boats quartered the channel and, with dawn, the softer purr of outboard motors.

He was close to the bird colony. The lime stink of their

281

droppings stung caustic in his nostrils and their cries came sharp and irritable. He shouted and shook a tree. A panicked smack of wings and the colony lifted, white and screaming, above the swamp. Within minutes a helicopter thrashed in from the south.

Trent eased his way back to the lagoon. Two launches raced in from the sea, ski boats expropriated from a tourist centre by the Guarda Frontera, four men in each launch. The boats separated at the mouth of the canal and Trent watched them hunt the edge of the lagoon for his tracks. At a distance, the scrub seemed as solid as the baize-covered cushions of a billiard table. A guarda spotted the branch Trent had cut at the head of the spur. The Cubans checked underwater and discovered the sharp tips of the other severed branches. Their voices echoed across the lagoon as they reported by wireless. A Bertram 32 sports fisherman with a tuna tower sped up channel and curled in to block the canal to the sea. Next came a pair of Boston Whalers powered by outboards.

The swamp was a mile deep with a thousand hiding places and boats bunched together, the crews planning the hunt. They sought a big inflatable rather than a man and Trent had little fear of discovery as he dragged himself back through the tangle of mangrove to the entrance canal. He had been in the water for six hours and his skin was pale and wrinkled. Mosquitoes whined round his head. The sun sliced through the slim leaf canopy and the heat stirred the thick stench of stagnant swamp water. The helicopter dipped to the boats and swept away to search the mainland coast.

23

Bergman

Immediately above the waterfall the stream flowed over layered slabs of yellowish grey rock. The rock held the pines at bay and Tur and Bergman sat drying themselves in the morning sun. The tumble of the stream· over the stone and down into the pool gave them an excuse for silence. The night's rain had cooled and washed the air and the outline of distant cayos floated cleanly on waters dyed pale brownish green by sediment carried on the spate. The black dot above the cayo closest to the inlet was a helicopter flying a search pattern and Bergman saw two white specks disappear into the centre cayo. Perhaps Tur's man had survived. Bergman was tempted to question Tur as to who the man was. However, silence protected them from antagonism and he kept his peace.

Tur spoke finally. 'He's alive.'

'Or they haven't found the body,' Bergman said.

Trent

The mangrove trees thrust eight to twelve feet above the sea. The trees sprouted aerial roots that arced out and down from the main trunk so that the swamp resembled a vast dump of interwoven parrot cages shaded by a grey-green canopy. Trent had cut his hands while dragging himself through the mangrove and the torn skin was white and puckered and he was tired, very tired.

Shadow camouflaged him as he swam slowly up the western fringe of the cayo. He stopped every few minutes, covering his face mask with his hands to keep the sun from flashing on the glass. With only his head above the surface, he listened and searched the surrounding waters. Patrol boats quartered the channel between the cayos. More dangerous were the rowing boats manned by marines, and he was forced to retreat twice into the mangrove as they scoured the swamp edge. In mid-afternoon, three jet skis commandeered from a tourist resort sped by to join the whalers in the lagoon. The capture of an infiltrator promised the Cubans a propaganda coup and Castro would forbid abandonment of the hunt. Trent could only hope that the search remained centred on the swamp.

Bergman

Two helicopters flew in from the cayos and began a slow search of the coast. Slipping into the water, Bergman and Tur sluiced the rocks before heading upstream to the next pool where a tangle of thick bush overhung the bank opposite the forest path. The two men ducked below the surface and eased themselves under the branches. The water was waist-deep where they knelt within the undergrowth. They listened to a helicopter hover above the inlet. Later, voices approached through the trees – soldiers – and a dog barked below the falls. Bergman was unable to decipher the soldier's words against the background of the cascade. He heard a soldier kick the hut door off its one hinge. The door smashed against the plank floor and the dog barked again. Next the soldiers would clamber down to the beach and attempt to read the tracks Bergman had drawn in the sand.

Bergman imagined one of the soldiers kneeling to touch the dry crust left by the rain. The soldiers would look out to sea, to the cayos, then back at the sand; push their hats back, scratch their scalps, spit. The officer or NCO in command of the party would turn to face the waterfall.

A helicopter returned and hovered over the inlet before rising over the fall. The downdraught beat the bushes and leaves trembled against Bergman's face. He had been a hunter all his professional life, one of those red-coated horsemen who directed the hounds across the meadows in Brit paintings. Now he was the fox and he made a conscious decision to be amused by the reversal of roles. The alternative to humour lay in memories of being the after-school quarry of a pack of older boys shouting, *Pa's an alky, Pa's an alky*. Bergman had been more afraid of hating his parents than of the boys.

Uncomfortable with recollections, he touched his companion on the shoulder and smiled encouragement. The shade hid Tur's expression but Bergman felt the blast of hate that exploded from the Cuban. There was no disguising the hate.

Estoban Tur

A helicopter lifted away over the trees and Estoban heard a command shouted down by the hut below the fall. Impotent, he crouched within the bushes. Movies and TV serials played in his head: helicopters as movie stars, while Vietnamese peasants cowered in the paddy or were driven from their villages by shadow aircraft; napalm splashed flames over the huts; explosives blasted babies from their mothers' arms – frail skinny arms, eyes dragged wide to show the whites of terror, white teeth embroidering the screams. Vietnamese were spectacle; the protagonists were gringo. Happy evening sprawled on the living room couch.

He wanted to club the gringo to pulp. Better, drag him out into the stream and display him to the soldiers. Show them the truth. Tell them the truth. The enemy.

He cupped water to his face to disguise his tears. The tears

were of rage, and for himself rather than for Miguelito –
Miguelito who had betrayed them all with his naivety. Then
came shame that he should blame his brother.

And more hate for the gringo.

And for Trent, the Englishman, stupid and careless to have
been discovered.

Trent

He reached the Zodiac in early afternoon. The boat appeared
abandoned beneath the camouflage of mangrove branches,
crumpled tubes buckled backwards by the weight of the two
Yamahas. Four bullets had pierced the port hull and the bow
and starboard hulls had been hit once. Fortunately the Cubans
had been armed with solid ammunition and both entry and
exit holes were small.

Trent clambered into the Zodiac and lay on his belly
beneath the cut branches with the twin keeltubes and the
inflated floorboard supporting his weight. He unlashed the
Zodiac's foot pump and repair kit from beneath the small bow-
canopy. The repair kit contained twenty aluminium clam-shell
clamps fitted with rubber gaskets and wing nuts. Forcing a
clam head through the closest bullet hole, Trent tightened the
nut until the hull fabric was sealed within the clamp by the
rubber gasket. He worked slowly and methodically, five
minutes to each bullet hole. The sun burnt through the
camouflage of branches and stirred the stench of rotting
vegetation. The whine of mosquitoes and buzz of outboards
hunting the swamp mixed with the heavier throb of patrol
boats quartering the channel. From the north came drifting
the faint rhythm of surf bursting on the reef. To the south,
helicopters searched the coast, evidence that Tur remained at
liberty.

Estoban Tur

The soldiers must be climbing up from the inlet and the gringo faced into the bank to hide the white of his face. Estoban crouched beside him in the water and watched the path the far side of the stream. The sun skidded light across the swirling flow of the stream and steamed the scent of pine tar from the forest and the foetid stench of rotting vegetation. Dragonflies sped and jived across the water and the inevitable mosquitoes hid in the shade of the bushes. The bushes bore small yellow trumpet flowers and Tur watched a scarlet crested humming-bird dive its long curved beak into a blossom. The whirr of the tiny bird's wings reminded him of a cat purring in the morning sun. Within the forest, pine needles carpeted the sodden earth and he was unable to follow the soldiers' progress up the path.

Finally, the path led the soldiers out of the trees above the falls and down to the river bank. Here their boots struck patches of rock and the heavy breathing of the men carried across the stream as did the panting of the dog as it dragged against its leash. The rain had washed any scent from the path and the dog was useless.

The soldiers halted on the edge of the stream. Two of them knelt and scooped water into their faces and over the back of their necks and the dog drank. Part Rottweiler, the dog was heavier in the chest and muzzle than a pedigree Doberman. Its tongue lolled over white teeth and its head swung as it sniffed for scent, eyes searching across the stream to the far bank where Tur hid. He could see the twitch of the black, wet nostrils and he imagined that their eyes met. The fear was strong in his bowels and in his bladder and he touched the gringo beneath the water, searching, even in one he hated, for companionship. Faced in opposite directions, the two men knelt in the water and held hands and barely breathed. The shrill of a single mosquito screamed loud as a security alarm.

Bergman

He was very conscious of his looks: a white moon hidden within thick undergrowth. A mosquito landed on his cheek.

Mosquitoes had driven his wife to divorce. Or so she had claimed.

Bergman had claimed that her desertion had left him desolate. In fact he had eaten his weight up to 220lbs in the hope that she would leave him for a lover rather than sample lovers indiscriminately from amongst the available MAG, Aid and diplomatic personnel. Perhaps her departure had saved his life.

He thought of Senator Joe McCarthy and the anticommunist witch-hunts in the 1950s. Here he was hiding under a bush and holding hands with Castro's prime bullyboy.

Estoban Tur

Theirs was the only hiding place along the banks of the pool. The lieutenant commanding the search party shoved the dog into the water and pointed to the thicket. A soldier picked up a rock and hurled it across the stream. The pool was sixty feet across and the rock fell short. A second rock, smaller, plunged into the thicket almost exactly above Estoban's head and slithered down through the branches. A third rock thrown by a different soldier fell midway between the dog and the bushes and the officer swore as the dog retreated.

The soldiers cursed and leapt away as the dog clawed up the bank and shook itself. In the bright sunlight, spray, flung from the dog's coat, painted a tiny rainbow against the dark background of the pine trees.

The lieutenant grabbed at the dog, missed and aimed a kick at its rear end. Then he picked up a flat stone and pitched it skimming across the water directly into Estoban's face. The stone slapped the water twice before striking the bush. Soldiers hunted for more ammunition and soon the thicket was under a barrage of skipping stones. Estoban's face was the bull's-eye. Forced to remain motionless, he watched each stone race towards him across the water and strike the branches. The stones shredded the leaves and slivers of sunlight pierced the deep shadow and licked at his face and across the ripples stirred by the bombardment. The slow and deliberate stripping of their camouflage was accidental and that their unmasking would be unintentional added pain and fury to his fear.

Fear made him hyperventilate and he had to fight against dizziness or lose his foothold. The gringo tried to remove his hand from Estoban's grasp and Estoban realised that he had been gouging his nails into the gringo's palm.

Bergman

His hand bled into the water. Facing away from the soldiers, he was blind to the action on the opposite side of the stream. The dog barked excitedly and Bergman imagined it prancing on the river bank. He heard the soldiers shouting and the slap of flat stones on water. A stone fell through the branches and slipped down his scalp into the water and minute waves spilled against the matted roots which protected the bank from the current. The shadows had grown less dense and he watched a worm wriggle free of the wet earth and slither over a root. A small black beetle fumbled amongst the trail of dead leaves abandoned by the night's flood six inches above the present waterline. Bergman had grown numb inside. He wanted to be afraid – or at least feel something. Anything.

Thinking of his wife and of their life in Guatemala City was less painful than thinking of the evil he had committed against his present companion. He had resisted his wife's desire for the classy social life which she had considered her due. He could have pressured the Guatemalan generals and government ministers to have their wives accept his wife's invitations. His wife would have been happy – or less unhappy.

And their two daughters might have had upmarket Guatemalan playmates rather than play only with the children of other staff at the embassy. The Guatemalan children would have been accompanied by bodyguards and his daughters would have required bodyguards. Bergman trusted bodyguards as little as he trusted generals.

A second stone ricocheted through the branches and struck him on the back of the head. Stoned to death, he thought. He saw himself kneeling to vomit in the bathroom at the car wash and the almost accidental tenderness in the mestiza woman as she proffered a damp cloth. He thought that he ought to check what schools were available within reach of the car wash. He wondered whether Tur's children were at school. Or had they stayed home in the apartment? He saw their bright tears quiver on dark skin. He wanted to turn and walk out into the pool and face the stones.

Estoban Tur

The gringo was lucky in facing away from the soldiers. A stone flew straight and low across the pool. The stone skipped four times on the water and Estoban fought to remain motionless as it pierced the thicket and struck him below the eye on the right cheek. He had been hit four times and he felt very visible beneath the torn leaves as he watched a tall black soldier pitch a fresh missile. Only three soldiers continued what had become a pitching contest. The rest had grown bored and sweaty and sat now sharing a cigarette in the shade of a pine. The officer leant against the tree and the dog had fallen asleep. A soldier offered the cigarette to the officer.

The officer took a final drag and flicked the butt into the water before ordering his men to their feet. Estoban expected the men to cross the stream by way of the rocks at the falls end of the pool and follow the bank up to the thicket. Instead the officer led them directly uphill along the bank.

Relief caught Estoban by surprise and his bladder emptied. Embarrassed, he nudged the gringo and nodded upstream. The gringo turned carefully and the two men watched the search party.

The handler kept the dog close to the bank and the soldiers on point held their Kalashnikovs at the ready. Two automatic rifles were ample armament to bring down two fugitives and the rest of the soldiers betrayed little interest in the hunt.

Estoban relaxed for the first time that day.

Then the roar of a helicopter rose from the beach and struck the mountain. The helicopter resembled a huge black bug as it lifted over the falls. Sunlight shattered the windscreen into fragments of diamond and Estoban was unable to see into the cockpit. The pilot hovered a few feet above the drop as if to peer beneath the bushes. Then he flew low up the pool and hovered short of the army patrol. A passenger dropped to the ground.

The passenger landed bent-kneed, one hand clamping a straw hat on his head while the blast of the propeller flattened his blue sports shirt. Pale skinned, he was thin and short and wore faded jeans and trainers that were very white. The slope of his shoulders was familiar and the tilt of his head as he addressed the commander of the search party. Estoban knew him from the old days at the Naro-Fominsk school for illegals in the USSR. From Naro-Fominsk the newcomer had graduated directly to Fidel's personal security detail.

The soldiers backed away and their officer's body language was deferential as he went into a huddle with the new arrival. The two men clambered into the helicopter and the pilot lifted off and peeled away down over the falls to the beach. Estoban guessed that they were re-examining the marks the gringo had drawn in the sand. Fidel's man was too expert to be deceived.

A further fifteen minutes passed, then a whistle shrilled from below the falls. The soldiers gathered their packs and headed downhill into the woods. Estoban imagined the officer planning his ambush. Estoban saw no way of warning Trent.

Trent

The bullet holes in the Zodiac were sealed. However, sound travels far over water and the puff and gasp of the foot pump would have disclosed Trent's position. He had slept in the semi-deflated Zodiac while clouds built through the late afternoon. Dusk brought a mist of mosquitoes. Slipping overboard, Trent eased the tender free of the mangrove and out to the edge of the swamp where he waited for nightfall. The hump of the sierra showed deep mauve above the undergrowth and lightning spat veins of brilliance across the underside of the approaching storm. Soon rain would spread down to the coast and he imagined Estoban Tur crouched somewhere in the woods. The Cuban would be wet and chilled, perhaps hungry, all this augmenting the persistent dread of capture.

Infiltrated into terrorist cells, Trent had suffered years of fear. He had learnt to split from his active self a watchful guardian ready to forestall the temptations of the territory: the desire to end it all, to act without sufficient thought, take risks, disclose himself, surrender.

Had he been in command of the hunt he would have set launches in ambush along the edge of the mangrove and he moved silently, first swimming the length of the line, then hauling in the Zodiac.

He headed north towards the coral barrier that protected the cayo from the Old Bahama Channel. Stars spat daggers of light across a sea silky smooth within the reef. Then came cloud to draw wisps of curtain across the stars. An offshore breeze grew cool with rain and Trent inhaled the scent of storm-thrashed cane fields blended with the forest's tar and the cloying odour of rotting leaves. Thunder rolled across the sierra and the soft rumble of surf swelled to a broken roar through which he listened for the whisper of a patrol boat's petrol engines or the diesel thump of a fishing boat.

The surf drove a short steep lop inshore off the reef, the

mangrove thinned and a patch of beach showed pale above a white border of foam. Mud gave way to a sand bottom and Trent waded a first few steps in water up to his chest. Waves slapped the deflated bows of the Zodiac as he hauled in the line. Rain spattered as he stowed his fins and mask in their nylon bag beneath the mangrove branches that disguised the inflatable. He found his plastic beach sandals and ducked underwater to pull them on. Perhaps instinct held him. Or a childhood habit of counting the seconds that separated lightning from thunder. The flash sliced across the sea. He paused to count and thought that he saw, in the extremes of his peripheral vision, a shadow on the water to his left. Unsure, he froze and pushed the Zodiac gently back towards the nearest mangrove. Then he bent his knees until his chin touched the water. He strained to hear through the surf. The rain swept hissing across the shallows followed by fresh lightning and he recognised the dark shape of a patrol boat's tender low in the silver froth of broken droplets. The marines were lying in wait for a quarry to be outlined against the beach. Trent eased the Zodiac in against the bushes and rolled on board and lay curled flat beneath the branches he had cut for camouflage. Then he waited.

Bergman

They had waited for nightfall before daring to leave the water beneath the thicket. Their scent would have betrayed them had they sheltered in the woods, so they lay side by side on the flat rocks above the cascade and the rain beat on their backs and spilled fresh rivulets into the stream. A second divided the thunder into two parts: first a vicious crack followed by a massive hammer blow that reverberated off the sierra.

Hours in the water had drained Bergman's energy. He watched the clay-stained stream slide beneath the lightning. And he thought that he was mad to be where he was. He wondered whether loyalty or debt or blackmail drew Tur's man to the inlet. He recalled standing on the bridge at Fronteras and being confronted with the photograph of Little Brother.

Thunder pressed him into the rock: a thunderbolt hurled by the God conjured by the minister at the church he had attended in his childhood, a church where confession was made in public rather than in the safe secrecy of those screened sentry boxes in which his wife sought forgiveness for her sins.

Bergman wanted absolution from himself rather than from God. In God he remained a very marginal believer – even when awakened by acute heartburn in the middle of the night in an unfamiliar hotel and unable to find the bedside light switch.

He imagined clambering down to the beach. Not now, but when Tur's man approached. Warning him that soldiers were probably hiding in the woods.

Trent

The stars and moon were hidden and the sea slipped velvet black away from the Zodiac towards the Cuban marines who waited in the patrol boat's tender one hundred metres off-shore. The Cubans would be armed with Kalashnikovs equipped with night sights and they would have night-vision enhancers. If so, any movement should have betrayed Trent, even against the muddled backdrop of the mangrove swamp. Perhaps the vision enhancers had malfunctioned. The puzzle stayed with Trent as he rolled over the floppy side tube into the sea.

He backtracked south some two hundred metres before turning out into the channel. He took his direction from the burst and tumble of surf out on the reef; the rain sheltered him as he swam and he swam with his hands beneath the surface and with his face turned away from the tender. He expected a shout or a warning shot and thought, once, that he heard a boot or an oar knock against a fibreglass hull. Perhaps the Cubans were dozing or sheltering from the rain which fell steadily while lightning flickered faintly in the distance and the last low rumbles of thunder rolled back from across the Old Bahama Channel.

The line to the Zodiac cut across his shoulders and his eyes ached with the strain of continually searching the darkness. He cut north towards the outer reef and felt the push of the sea strengthen. The tide was out and the sea sucked across the ragged surface of the coral heads. The lights of a cargo ship showed beyond the surf – heading towards Florida. A faint breeze brought the scent of deep water. Emptiness.

Close into the reef he dived with the Zodiac's small grappling anchor and imbedded it beneath a coral head. Spray drifted across his face as he dragged himself on board and he could see the white line of rollers rise and burst. The crash and roar of the surf drowned the wheeze of the foot pump as he filled the bow and hull compartments.

The small outboard started and he motored slowly westward away from the hunt and close to the reef for a further half an hour before cutting inshore to round the next cayo. The rain had ceased, the first stars appeared and a sprinkle of lights showed on the cayo, a beach resort with comfortable beds. Had the lighter sleepers been awakened by gunfire the previous night? Had the day's lack of jet-skis disappointed the tourists? Had the resort management organised a beach barbecue? That was the smell Trent remembered always from San Cristóbal de los Baños; the cloying perfume of roasting meat that had accompanied him downriver to Lago Izabal and greeted him again on the approach to Fronteras, barbecue parties at the waterside vacation homes of the rich down from Guatemala City for the weekend – the rich deliberately ignorant of how their police and special forces controlled the countryside, just as these tourists were deliberately ignorant of the fear that ruled Castro's Cuba . . . and were oblivious of Estoban Tur.

Estoban Tur

The rain had filled the stream and the roar of the cascade drowned any movement of the soldiers hidden in ambush. Estoban lay on the rock above the fall. The gringo lay close to him so that they could communicate by touch.

The cold had sapped Estoban's anger and he possessed nothing else with which to fortify himself. He lay watching the foam and waiting – though not for Trent. The distance between them had grown too great and the Englishman had lost substance. Reality was this waiting for dawn and the sun rising over the hills to the east. The sun would rise whatever Estoban's circumstances. Estoban had no control over it.

Perhaps he had been sleeping, even cried in his sleep. He saw the inlet again and the gringo had his hand on his shoulder, shaking him. The gringo wore a watch with a luminous face. Estoban turned the gringo's wrist inward. Confused by sleep, he required time to decipher the positioning of the two hands: 03:50 – first light in two hours. Fatigue muddled his thoughts as he tried to envision the Englishman's options. He found that he was shaking his head against the pain and a moan escaped his lips as, for a moment, he almost saw the Guatemalan soldiers waiting in line behind Miguelito.

Trent

The inlet was Estoban Tur's territory. The spur of high ground behind the inlet grew into the sierra. Trent approached the coast two miles to the west. The surrounding sea paled and a thin beach grew out of the darkness. Trent slipped overboard and lowered his feet to a sand bottom. Dragging the Zodiac into the shallows, he waited, listening as he studied the long wispy grass bordering the beach and the scrub beyond and the few stunted casuarina pines.

The sky seemed washed by the rain so that the stars were very clear and isolated from each other. The waves and current were too feeble to reach the black line of dried seaweed which indicated the high-water mark. Rain had melted any footprints.

Trent used the inflated floorboard as a walkway across the tide line to the soft sand and snapped off the tips of two casuarina branches to sweep up the dried seaweed. Then he walked back fifty metres into the scrub. Mosquitoes rose in clouds, however, there were no tracks nor path and, reassured, he searched for a hiding place. First he hid the two outboards and the remaining fuel tanks in the bushes. Next, he deflated the twin keels and hull compartments, rolling the Zodiac into a sausage which he carried over his shoulder. He spent half an hour camouflaging the Zodiac with branches and smoothed out his tracks to the cache.

Returning to the beach, he pushed the floorboard into the sea. Then, kneeling in the water, he sprinkled the small pile of dried seaweed into place. Satisfied, he paddled the floorboard parallel to the beach for a quarter of a mile. He used the floorboard as a bridge again to cross the sand to the scrub where he squatted looking out to sea while picturing his approach to the inlet.

24

Trent

Properly sited, one machine gun on either promontory or on the high ground above the waterfall made the inlet a killing field. Trent approached the inlet overland through the trees. The waterfall drowned any sound and the night limited Trent's vision. Dependent on his sense of smell, he tilted his head back so that his nostrils faced forward and he drew in the air in small quantities, searching within the scents of the forest. The rain had left the air fresh and Trent expected to smell wet ashes or, in the case of an ambush, the smoke from a cigarette. He found no trace of man: perhaps Tur had been captured – or possibly a disciplinarian had set an ambush, an officer for whom the soldiers' fear was greater than their desire for tobacco. Trent hated the not knowing.

He climbed up through the trees to the head of the pool above the waterfall. The flat rocks on the edge of the drop gave the best view of the inlet and he spotted two men lying close together. The roar of the cascade covered his approach as he slithered to within twenty feet of them. The paler of the two wore shorts and a short-sleeved shirt. The other wore uniform with a sergeant's stripes. Trent's memories of Tur fitted into the uniform as did any other man of medium build and a trifle overweight. A rifle would have been visible had the men been in ambush.

A further half an hour took Trent to the end of the second promontory where he clambered down the rocks into the water. He swam carefully out from the rocks and then in a gentle arc back across the mouth of the inlet. As he swam he checked both the shore and out to sea so that a waiting patrol boat would have shown against the sky. Having crossed the mouth of the inlet, he headed in to the beach with only his head above the water. Finally, he grounded in the shallows where he stayed on his belly close in to the slope. The moonlight was sufficient to show tracks on the sand that suggested a body of men and the parallel furrows left by a helicopter.

He considered climbing back up to where Tur lay and asking the Cuban who his friend was. And asking why they were hiding up there rather than waiting for him down by the shore. There was only one reason. They believed soldiers were watching the inlet.

Which brought him to the hut.

He had checked everywhere except the hut.

The hut scared him with its abandoned patch of vegetable garden and shadowed doorway. Once committed, he had nowhere to hide and he paused at the edge of the terrace to the rear and searched for a small round pebble before easing out onto open ground.

A hint of rum greeted him at the hut. He lay along the wall with his head at the open door so that he could listen as he flicked the pebble indoors. The pebble rolled across the wood floor. He waited and waited. No response . . .

Perhaps there were explosives hidden beneath the floorboards and triggered by a trip wire or pressure pad, or by something more sophisticated. He imagined the boards bursting upwards, piercing his belly. That was the danger, that not knowing would act as a catalyst on the imagination.

He crept round to the front of the hut where the roof extended to form a dirt-floored veranda facing the inlet. The door was shut; both windows were open. Trent lay a little to the left of the second window. One thrust of his legs against the wall would launch him onto the slope down to the water. The hut sheltered him from the scent of the forest and the smell of rum was more distinct together with a trace of sweat. A man crouched against the wall, frightened to breathe. And perhaps without the nervous strength to take a grenade from his pouch and drop it out of the window. Grenades were more frightening than bullets.

Trent's fingers seemed clumsy as he undid his dive-belt. He slipped the end back through the buckle to form a noose. 'My companion is at the back door,' he began. His tone of voice was soft and conversational and he heard a quick intake of breath. 'Behind you. He holds two grenades,' he continued. 'You should extend your hands through the window so that I may inform my companion that you are unarmed.'

An hour that was only a few seconds passed before hands showed pale against the wood.

'Now your head,' Trent advised quietly. He dropped his belt over the soldier's head, drew the loop taut and stood on the end with the soldier bent forward over the sill. To his own imaginary companion, Trent said, 'One man secured.' And to his captive, 'Reach in with your left hand for your rifle, hold it by the end of the barrel and lower it through the window to the ground.'

He scooped up the soldier's gun – a Kalashnikov – and checked the magazine. At least one more man must be inside the hut, perhaps two. Trent said, 'Instruct your companions to approach the window.'

The soldier said, 'There is only one.' His voice was young – though less nervous than Trent had expected. 'Lazarus. He sleeps. He brought with him a bottle of rum.'

Trent ordered the soldier out through the window and employed him as a shield while entering through the door leading off the terrace. He closed the shutters on the front windows before using his torch. The second soldier, a mulatto, lay asleep in a corner. He was older than Trent's prisoner, dressed in a vest and in need of a shave. His head rested on a pillow made of boots wrapped in his shirt. An empty bottle lay beside him, corked. A backpack and a communications radio stood against the wall as well as the older soldier's Kalashnikov.

Trent ordered the younger man to tie the drunk's hands with one boot lace and his feet with the other. The drunk sighed and his mouth fell open. A moment later a snore erupted and, half awake, he groaned and rolled his head against the floorboards.

'Now remove your own laces,' Trent told the young soldier. He chopped the soldier with the side of his hand at the junction of the neck and the Cuban crumpled. Trent lashed his hands behind his back and tied his feet, checked the drunk's bonds and sliced his shirt into strips to make a rope. The drunk had discovered his situation and lay cursing and spitting. The younger man seemed in shock. Perhaps this was the first time he had been hit. Trent dragged him to the far end of the hut from the drunk and sat him against the wall. Squatting to face the young man, he shone the torch in his eyes. The soldier was Caucasian and medium blond. His hair was long for his rank and his fingernails were too clean. He pushed with his feet against the floor the way a frightened patient does against the footrest on the dentist's chair when trying to escape the drill, and every few seconds he looked across at the drunk. A scared kid and a drunk made a fine ambush.

Cubans were reared on TV tales of CIA assassins stalking the island.

'I am an Englishman,' Trent said by way of reassurance. 'I have no desire to harm you.' He nodded to the radio, 'Do you call or does your superior call you?'

'We call,' the young man said.

'At what intervals?'

'If a boat should enter the inlet.'

'And when will you be relieved?'

'In two days. We have rations for two days.' The soldier indicated with his nose. 'In the backpack.'

Trent dragged the drunk over and sat him back to back with his companion. Knotting the strips of shirt into a rope, he looped one end round the drunk's neck and the other end round the young soldier's neck with sufficient slack to prevent the soldiers choking.

Trent put the radio into the backpack and slung the pack over his shoulder and he took the Kalashnikovs. Stepping out through the doorway, he held a whispered discussion with his imaginary companion. Then he followed the path down to the beach. He was thinking of Tur and of the younger half-brother and what Tur would be prepared to do to get his brother out. Who or what the Cuban would be prepared to betray. Friendship? His beloved revolution?

Reaching the beach, he turned slowly to face the waterfall. The sky was lighter to the east and thin tendrils of mist rose off the sea. He thought that Tur would be able to see him.

Bergman

Bergman saw him first. The first hint of dawn showed the shape of the hut below the falls and the trees of the forest edge behind the small terrace. Beyond the terrace a thin mist rose from the water and disguised the tip of the promontory within the backcloth of sea and sky. A pale comma of sand grew slowly out of the backcloth followed by the shape of a man poised on the comma – not a real man – more a clay cast of an Oscar statue, smooth and featureless, grey rather than gold. The statue's movements were slow and any sound was drowned within the tumble of the cascade. Bergman expected soldiers to open fire.

Estoban Tur

The gringo was on his knees. He held a rock and Tur watched in horror as he hurled it out over the falls. Grabbing at the gringo, he tried to wrestle him flat. The gringo struck him and they knelt face to face, flailing at each other. They were too tired and too cold and too undirected to do each other harm. Finally they stopped and leant against each other panting.

'Your man's here,' the gringo managed.

Tur looked down and saw the Englishman on the beach. The Englishman wore a wetsuit. He must have circled the inlet before disclosing himself. This was the manner in which he had been trained and the discipline with which Estoban had attempted to train his own people. Few of them had been sufficiently patient and most were dead or captured. Fabio in Guatemala was an exception.

'If there were soldiers,' he said, 'they would have shot him. Or perhaps he has silenced them.'

Bergman

Tur was very certain of his man's prowess. The Cuban had lain on his belly all night and the shape of the pistol in his waistband was imprinted on his wet shirt. He grunted with pain and nearly fell as he thrust his weight on his injured ankle. Bergman grabbed him and supported him down the path.

The newcomer watched them appear out of the trees. His eyes were black and separated by a hawkish nose with a small scar across the bridge. A thick mop of dark curls and a full beard disguised the rest of his features and the wetsuit camouflaged his muscles. He wore a single string of red coral beads round his neck, a diver's watch, and a black-handled knife in a sheath on his right calf.

Bergman expected the two men to greet each other with Latin warmth: hug, kiss – despite the ankle, dance a few steps of salsa. Instead Tur came to a halt when still ten feet from the newcomer. The two men stood eyeing each other in silence – almost as if they didn't know each other, or were enemies.

Finally Tur found a rock to lean against. 'Frank Trautman,' he said, pointing to Bergman and with no attempt to hide his lack of belief in Bergman's alias. 'American – he helped me escape.'

The newcomer nodded to Bergman. 'Gregorio. I was intercepted by a patrol boat the first night.' This last was an apology to Tur for arriving late at the rendezvous. 'There is a drunk and a kid tied up in the hut. Soldiers.'

Trent

Trent wanted to add that the mulatto was only a fake drunk and that the kid was almost certainly a fake soldier. And he wanted to ask Tur whether fake ambushes were standard Cuban tradecraft and have the Cuban judge what department employed the two men. Trautman's presence stopped him. Trent hadn't expected Tur to have a companion and certainly not an American – a pro of some sort, a cop. The US spawned competing law enforcement agencies faster than the old Soviet Union: Federal, State, City, County; add in a dozen intelligence services and specialists from Customs, Immigration, Treasury and the DEA and unravelling what type of cop required a manual with a fashion supplement thick as a New York telephone directory and a gypsy woman with a glass ball.

'If we get off the beach,' Trent said, 'they may believe that we have escaped.'

Tur spoke first. 'Where is the boat?'

'Hidden,' Trent said. He smoothed a patch of sand at the tide mark the width of the Zodiac's bows and retrieved the soldiers' pack. He dug his feet deep into the sand as if pushing the boat off the beach and waded straight out twenty metres before turning west and waiting for the American who supported Tur. The sea floor shelved gradually and they waded round the tip of the promontory and parallel to a rocky shore below the forest. The forest continued for a mile then came a cliff; beyond the cliff the land fell away to swamp and stunted scrub and the stands of casuarina pine where Trent had cached the Zodiac.

Never betray your escape route; never trust your companions. These were rules of the trade and Trent kept his distance from the Zodiac, searching instead along the forest shore for an overhang amongst the boulders that would protect them from aerial search. Birds sung their morning chorus and the sea lapped gently at the rocks. A perfect morning to fly-fish for tarpon, Trent thought. And he thought that the commander of the two men in the hut must know that no rescuer would make landfall by daylight; thus radio silence was unnecessary and the commander would call the two men for a situation report.

The first helicopter swatted east along the coast and Trent heard it land at the beach below the hut. Almost immediately the boats barricading the lagoon withdrew from the mangrove and spread out through the cayos. A second helicopter joined in the hunt and a pair of single-engine Russian Androv biplanes droned north across the reef to check the Old Bahama Channel.

Both the American and Tur were munching stale sandwiches from the soldiers' backpack and had turned to warm themselves in the first rays of the sun. Before they could grow too contented with life, Trent said, 'I have insufficient petrol to get us back. We require petrol and we require another tank.' The blame wasn't his. 'It was necessary for me to throw three tanks overboard.'

The American appeared unconcerned. Overweight and with thinning hair, he was the type of good ol' boy non-Americans mistook as soft. Trent had learnt to place greater trust in such men than in his own people. They didn't suffer from the British disease of forming committees to agree on an indecision. Contemptuous of the suits in Washington, they made their own rules and were loyal to their field agents. They sent a man in, they got him out.

Tur equated with the men from Washington or London. Safe for too long, he had been unprepared for the fall from power: the pain of his brother's kidnapping, guilt at being the cause, perhaps lack of understanding as to the whys of what was happening to him and even ignorance of who was pulling the strings. In these conditions everyone was suspect. Such paranoia was standard fare for field agents. For Tur it was foreign territory. He bottled the turmoil inside, disguised behind a deliberate vacancy of expression and in the apparently relaxed manner in which he rested against a boulder, eyes shuttered against the sun and the muscles in his face slack. All his muscles were slack – as if he were about to melt into the grey of the stone.

Trent watched a helicopter quarter the cayo out to their north-west. Closer to shore a dozen gulls quarrelled over a patch of detritus while a frigate bird floated above against the bright steel of the sky. The breeze carried the throaty rumble of a patrol boat's diesels, a goat bleated beyond the forest and Tur stirred, rolling against the boulder so that he faced Trent.

'We dumped a Lada with a full tank of petrol over the cliff back there,' Tur said. He had been on the run for five days and spoke in a whisper more from practice than from fear of being overheard.

'What do you suggest?' Trent enquired placidly. 'That I raise the Lada or suck the petrol up a pipe we don't have?'

Watching Ladas being repaired competes with baseball as Cuba's major spectator sport; Trent's ignorance took Tur by surprise. 'The tank is held in the boot by a steel strap,' he said and sketched the layout in the damp sand. 'Only a spanner is required, and pliers to seal the fuel pipe and the air vent.'

A fuel spill would have been spotted from the air. 'You blocked the air vent?'

'The *auto* is on its roof,' the American said.

The American's accent was Mexican and auto avoided confusion between *coche* and *carro*, respectively the Spanish for car and farm wagon and reversed in some Latin American countries, including Cuba.

'Daylight will be necessary,' Tur warned.

'Let me sleep until midday,' Trent said.

Trent slept while the American and Tur stood sentry. Whoever directed the hunt had determined that Tur had escaped from the main island and the search remained offshore. Biplanes returned to refuel, helicopters hovered, boats sped from cayo to cayo. With the sun directly overhead, the sea had become a mirror and there was little chance of Trent being spotted as he first waded and then swam close inshore. The sea deepened below the cliff and rain had muddied the waters. A thin skim of oil led Trent to the Lada.

Trent piked and straightened so that the weight of his legs came clear of the water and forced him smoothly down some twenty feet. The bottom sloped steeply away from the cliff and the car lay upside down, engine facing the shore, and balanced on the rear edge of its roof and the rear edge of the boot. The sea floor was soft mud and an air bubble trapped inside the car provided sufficient buoyancy for Trent to be able to rock the car. He surfaced and lay hyperventilating for a minute before diving again. Wedging his fins against a rock provided purchase and he managed to pivot the Lada six inches. A further ten dives brought the Lada parallel to the shore and the weight of the engine tipped it slowly off the boot and onto the bonnet. The movement had stirred the mud and Trent was swimming blind as he felt for the boot latch. The boot was locked.

On the next dive he reached into the Lada and found the keys. Everything heavy in the boot had been resting on the lid. With the boot open, they slid to the sea floor. Trent fumbled in the mud and found first the jack and then the Lada's steel toolbox closed with a padlock. He lugged the jack and toolbox into the car for safe keeping and surfaced again. On the next dive he was able to feel for the bolt closing the steel strap retaining the petrol tank. The nut was small and octagonal.

Trent broke surface. An airliner drew a grey trail towards the Bahamas and a biplane droned inshore from the cayos. Shifting the Lada had released more oil and a blue-and-gold sheen glistened on the surface of what had become a pool of mud. No pilot could miss the signal and Trent watched the biplane bank five degrees. With a single 1000hp radial engine, the Antonov seemed of a different age to the sleek jet, however, a range in excess of 500 miles and a minimum safe flying speed of under sixty mph made the biplane a dangerous hunter and Trent clung to the shadow of the cliff.

The pilot circled and flew a pass over the Lada so low that the draught from the big propeller blasted patterns across the water. The side door was open, the observer peering down. The pilot banked away and swung inland to refuel at Ciego de Ávila.

Swimming out of the shadow, Trent dived again and unlocked the toolbox and felt for pliers, screwdriver and small wrenches. He had dived perhaps fifty times; his chest and lungs ached and he needed to think.

A pair of oystercatchers digging for clams along the water edge took flight as he approached the shore between the end of the cliff and the Zodiac. The storm had washed dead leaves and seed pods down the beach and hermit crabs had etched their trails in the brittle crust left by the rain. Trent crawled ashore beneath a sea grape tree bent forward over the water. Sandflies swarmed off the tangled roots and mosquitoes rose from the long grass as he crept inland to a stand of casuarina pines. The heat steamed the flat swampy land. The two stroke engine of a motorcycle shattered the silence as it passed a quarter of a mile inland along a track bordered by a wall of cane frothed with blossom. Long streamers of black cloud lay against the peaks of the distant sierra. Rain offered cover and, given a full tank in the Lada, they had ample fuel to cross the Great Bahama Channel with the 9hp Yamaha.

Trent sketched the rear of the Lada in the sand: first undo the strap holding the tank, remove the petrol cap and pry the tank free so that he could reach the fuel line and vent pipe. He would need to tilt and turn the tank to draw it through the gap between the lip of the boot and the part open lid.

Crawling to the Zodiac, he cut a length of fishing line from the reel and took a patch from the repair kit. He risked walking back to the cliff through the long swamp grass. A patch of thick scrub provided a hide with a view of the water. An hour passed before an army truck halted at the top of the cliff. First an officer and a non-com peered down at the stained sea. Two soldiers were ordered towards the forest; two more were left stationed on the cliff edge. The truck ground on down the slope and braked fifty metres back from the shore and within view of Trent's hiding place. The officer stripped to shorts and the driver helped him into scuba harness while the non-com led two men along the shore searching for tracks. They passed close by the scrub where Trent hid. The soldiers had sweltered beneath the dark canvas top in the rear of the truck and carried with them a sour scent of sweat and unwashed socks. Trent had little hope of the stink on the other two soldiers warning Tur and his North American. They weren't field officers. He should have warned them to keep awake and hide in the scrub and trees immediately above the boulders.

Bergman

Each boulder weighed several tons. The boulders had tumbled free of the hillside way before the existence of the forest and now formed a barrier against the northerly storms. The stone trapped the sun and the air between the boulders was oven hot. Bergman and Tur had been wet too long; the rain and cold of the night remained in their bones and they welcomed the heat as they had welcomed the newcomer, Gregorio, abdicating to him responsibility for their escape.

They heard voices first, two men. Then came the familiar scrape of metal on rock and of leather boots that accompanied a patrol. Fear was instant and physical: pain in the solar plexus, the desire to vomit and defecate, so that Bergman was already short of breath as he hefted the backpack and clawed his way up the steep bank. The soil was red clay and wet in the shade above the boulders. Bergman's weight on his knees transformed the clay into a slide and he grabbed with one hand at the uncovered root of a bush. Looking down for a foothold, he saw Tur faced toward the approaching soldiers. The Cuban had made no effort to hide. He had drawn his revolver and stood in a marksman's crouch with the pistol held two-fisted. Bergman hissed to get his attention and thought from the blankness in Tur's eyes that the Cuban would shoot him. Bergman gauged the distance separating them from the soldiers as one hundred metres; enough time to escape, and he beckoned urgently and pointed uphill. The pointing undid him and he slipped. As he tumbled, he grabbed at the Cuban and they fell sideways against a boulder, Tur beneath him. Bergman's weight added power to the blow and the Cuban slumped slack in his arms.

Tur was too heavy for Bergman to drag up the bank into the trees and he couldn't abandon him. Blood flowed from a cut along the Cuban's hairline and oozed from a scrape on his left cheekbone. Bergman was nervous that he would groan or regain consciousness and curse or cry out. He knelt over him and retrieved the pistol from the sand. Cleaning the sand from the breach and out of the barrel was automatic.

The soldiers were close.

Bergman crouched waiting.

He thought that it was a mess. A stupid mess. And they had come so close to success. His duty was to the Cuban, both to protect and deliver him beyond protection. Bergman had controlled field agents; he had never worked as a field agent, not as a man of action. He saw himself as too fat for the role and too clumsy. Falling on top of Tur was typical; and, earlier, throwing the rock down the cascade to warn of an ambush which Tur's man had already neutralised.

The soldiers weren't much better. One of them had lost his footing and cursed as the sea spilled over the top of his boot. The second laughed. They were casual in their approach, confident. Bergman thought that he might be able to infiltrate behind them. Tur's man, Gregorio, had disarmed two soldiers in the hut.

Gregorio's accent could be Uruguayan – perhaps a Tupamaro. As for his name, all names were false – Gregorio, Trautman – such was the way of their world. Bergman pictured the scar across Gregorio's nose. Cut in a knife fight? Or perhaps a childhood fall from his bicycle. Bergman had never learnt to ride a bicycle. When at grade school, he had wanted a bicycle more than anything else; to be able to ride to school rather than walk. He had walked rather than have the school bus pick him up at their trailer home and have the other kids see his dad and the way his mother dressed.

Bergman had moved almost as an automaton and crouched now closer to the soldiers and with his back to them and protected by a boulder. Tur appeared dead except for the wet blood. Dead men didn't bleed.

Twenty metres.

Bergman peeked at the soldiers. They had halted at a flat rock while the one with the wet foot emptied the water out of his boot.

Bergman had spent ample time on the pistol range and knew that he could drop them both. To be certain, he calculated each move:

Pistol up.

Left foot out and swivel onto the right to face the soldiers. First take the soldier standing, then the one with his boot off.

Death would be instant for the first soldier. The one with the boot off would have seconds in which to be surprised. He would die frightened, screaming inside himself.

Bang, Bergman thought and he did it coolly and cleanly. Except that he hadn't moved. The action was in his head. Like a movie.

The soldier standing on the rock took a box of matches and a flattened cigarette pack from his breast pocket and shook out a cigarette. The cigarette had been smoked a third of the way down. The soldier scratched the burnt scab off the tip and studied the inside of the matchbox a moment, counting the matches before lighting up. Such routines of poverty were familiar to Bergman from his childhood.

The one soldier handed the butt down to his seated companion who studied its length, calculating how many drags remained, and he inhaled with the enthusiasm of a Pink Floyd fan. Yeah, it was all familiar – though Bergman hadn't been welcome amongst the cool set; fat had been downmarket, as were trailer homes and parents everyone avoided. Except for Mex kids. Mexicans were familiar with disaster; they kept their own tragedies within the family rather than dump them on the County, and Bergman's Mexican friends from school were quietly polite to his father, hunkering beside him while waiting for Bergman.

These soldiers were pale mulattos. The cigarette passed back and forth and Bergman watched the smoke trickle away on the breeze. He had hoped that they would have advanced before Tur regained consciousness, however, Tur stirred now and a low moan bubbled the spittle on his lips. Bergman moved instinctively, sitting on him and clamping a hand over his mouth. Tur twisted and kicked and Bergman could hear his own heart.

The soldiers were hidden from him

He heard the one soldier say, '*Vámonos*,' to the other and he heard boots on the stone.

One of the soldiers spat and Tur bit hard on Bergman's hand.

Bergman clubbed him across the jaw with the pistol.

25

Trent

He watched the officer settle his mask and wade out towards the Lada. The water closed over his head and bubbles marked his progress. Five minutes and the officer had seen enough. The driver waited on the shore and supported the tank while the officer shrugged free of the straps. The two men returned to the truck and the officer beat a tattoo on the horn.

Bergman

Bergman was incapable of understanding the horn as a signal. He crouched between the boulders in an isolation of spirit that might have permitted him to kill the soldiers had they advanced. His own death hardly concerned him, rather it was the continually increasing pressure of responsibility for what had seemed almost a game in its beginnings.

Tur stirred on the sand and groaned. Blood caked with sand formed a crust down one side of his forehead and on his jaw. Slowly his eyes focused; hate came into them and he forced himself to his knees.

Shadow spread across the boulders and Bergman looked up at the first scraps of black cloud creeping out above the steep hillside. The shadow between the trees seemed very dense. He looked back into Tur's eyes and wouldn't look away. He wanted Tur to know that he accepted the hate and the blame.

The same tattoo on a horn sounded and this time Bergman understood.

'They've gone,' Bergman said. 'The soldiers. You would have killed them.'

He held the one pistol. Now he took the second pistol from his waistband and hurled both weapons out to sea. The rings spread out over the water. Bergman watched the small waves lift through the rings and fall finally and gently at the feet of the boulders. 'I'm sorry,' he said.

Trent

The officer beat the horn a second time. The non-com and his two men jogged back along the shore and Trent watched them clamber over the tailgate. A further two men boarded at the cliff top. Trent listened to the truck grind away up the road and halt again to collect the final two. The casualness of their attitude suggested that they were merely collecting evidence in support of Tur's escape.

Thunder ripped thin scraps of cloud free of the sierra. A squall tailed down and rattled through the cane field and on across the sea toward the nearest cayo. Trent swam out to the Lada. With petrol lighter than water, none could escape while the tank remained upside down. However, each action was complicated by being in reverse and lung capacity governed how much he could achieve on each dive.

First he loosened the bolt fastening the retaining strap with an adjustable spanner. Next he unscrewed the filler cap and levered the tank back six inches into the boot so that he could slip the patch from the Zodiac repair kit over the mouth of the filler pipe. On the next dive he closed the filler pipe with the patch and secured it temporarily with a noose of fishing line. He required a further three dives to lash the patch firmly in place. A double loop of line closed the rubber feed pipe to the engine and he used pliers to squeeze the vent pipe shut. Finally he cut the feed pipe and slid the tank out. The tank took him to the surface and he held it upside down for the swim along the cliff. Once into shallow water he was able to reverse the tank and he carried it up the shore and into the long grass. Looking back, he saw that rain had scattered the skimpy trail of petrol droplets.

Bergman

Tur had permitted Bergman to clean the blood from his face. Now, in the last of the twilight, Bergman watched the rain draw small tails from the wounds. He sat with his back to a rock while the Cuban lay curled on his side at a distance of two metres. The need for action might have galvanised them, however, the arrival of Tur's man had left them without purpose and neither man had moved in the past hour. Bergman wondered whether Tur planned a final assault, perhaps with a rock – or would order his rescuer to use his knife on Bergman. He had been stupid in throwing away both pistols.

Trent

Regaining the Zodiac, he sat with the tank supported on his knees and released the lashing round the rubber feeder pipe. More than a litre of water drained from the tank before the petrol ran pure. A few litres of petrol remained after he had topped up one outboard tank and filled the second. In the last hour of daylight thunder rolled down the sierra and the beat of rain in the cane drowned the mechanical wheezing as he pumped each compartment of the Zodiac tight. A small fall of rainwater spilled from the edge of the track, enough to fill the water bottles. Now for darkness to shelter them . . .

Beneath the thick cloud night fell early. Half past seven and Trent fetched the inflatable floorboard, pumped it taut and dragged the Zodiac into the water. He mounted both engines and loaded the two outboard tanks and lashed the Lada tank upright.

A single flash of lightning could betray them to a patrol boat and he swam with the Zodiac along the beach and under the cliff to the boulders below the forest. Anchoring the Zodiac to a rock, he waded to the boulders and whistled softly.

Bergman

The whistle stirred Bergman from his lethargy. He hefted Tur to his feet and supported him at the armpits so that the Cuban served as a shield. Thunder shook them. Lightning followed and Bergman saw their rescuer, Gregorio, outlined between two boulders. Sea and rain had plastered the newcomer's hair flat and he had closed his eyes against the flash. Bergman was blind in the aftermath of the lightning. In his blindness he sought the feel of danger or antagonism. In Tur and in himself only weariness remained and Bergman could sense neither good nor evil in the stranger; Gregorio was a presence – a tool. That was all.

Estoban Tur

The gringo shoved him from the shelter of the boulders and the other one, the Englishman, grabbed at him. Rain pock-marked the sea and Estoban saw the grey flat shape of the inflatable and the two outboard motors. He would cease to exist once he was in the boat and he struck suddenly at the two men attempting to save him, struck at them and struggled to free himself.

Caught by surprise, they let him go. His ankle buckled and he collapsed sideways. The Englishman caught him under the arm and the American was there, behind him, propping him up. The indignity was unbearable. To be helped by this

American whom he had intended killing, this American who had plotted his downfall – of this Estoban was certain. He and Miguelito were pawns. And rather than being rescued, he was being delivered into the hands of the enemy.

'Leave me,' he said. His lips were dry and perhaps they didn't hear; and perhaps he didn't want them to hear.

They lifted him into the Zodiac and settled him curled up aft on the floorboard. Old women fussing over his comfort, a couple of *maricones*. The cold and the rain made him snuffle and he wiped his eyes on his forearm.

'I have the fuel from the Lada,' the Englishman said. 'We move now, the storm will cover us.'

Trent

The Cubans would be waiting at the reef. Trent had marked three gaps on his charts. The big Yamaha might have been heard despite the rain and Trent used the small engine to motor out to the westerly corner of the swamp where the Cuban had abandoned the search that morning. For the approach to the reef he needed to be able to hear and he shut off the engine once they were in the shallows by the mangrove. His passengers would be visible against the dark background and he ordered them to lie flat. Slipping overboard, he cut mangrove branches as camouflage. Then he waded with the Zodiac up the side of the cayo. The nightlife of the swamp plopped and splashed: fish, frogs, rodents – and an owl or a hawk seized some small animal that squealed against the fierce beat of the bird's wings.

The rain eased as they approached the seaward shore. Here the patrol in the whaler had nearly trapped Trent and he boarded the Zodiac and paddled out into deeper water. They were close now to freedom and the three men strained to see into the dark and listened intently through the soft hiss of the rain on the sea.

The surf built into a steady rumble. They could distinguish

the burst and suck of individual breakers across the coral and the reef drew a faint white border. Soon the sand showed pale in the shallows close to the reef and Trent waded again. By daylight he might have found a passage, too small and shallow to be marked. By night he was faced with the choice of one of the three channels he had drawn and he visualised the chart and checked his GPS. The American leaned out over the sidetube to question his intentions. Heads close together, they spoke in whispers and must have appeared as conspirators to the Cuban who struggled to sit upright and get between them.

Trent tried to calm him with explanations. Given rough weather, any patrol boat would be inside the reef. However, the seas were calm and a skipper could anchor across the seaward mouth of a channel, silent, no lights, the shape of the boat masked by the spray from the surf.

'So what's the solution,' the American asked.

'There isn't one,' Trent said and he thought that Tur smiled. 'We take the next cut. They spot us, we run.'

The channel showed as a dark margin to the sand. Trent boarded and lowered the big motor. Connecting the fuel pipe, he squeezed it full and drew smoothly on the starter cord three times to fill the carburettor. Then he pulled out the choke and switched on the ignition. A sharp drag on the cord and the Yamaha fired. The initial roar of the engine softened to a gentle burble as he closed the throttle and adjusted the choke.

The noise and size and power of the breakers would terrify those unfamiliar with the sea and he touched his passengers on the shoulder, warning them in a harsh whisper, 'Hold hard and keep still. We're going out.'

Engaging the gears, he eased the throttle open. To each side of them, the waves rose black out of the deep, higher and higher and curving forever forward until they fell over themselves and exploded along the raw edge of coral and flung foam across the deeper water through which the inflatable crept seaward. The channel was a black blade piercing the whiteness. The slap of the Zodiac's bottom on the unpatterned waves seemed loud as pistol shots. Crouched low over the tiller, Trent sought to see through the spray and rain.

Suddenly there was a different shape. The long low shape of a boat. The patrol boat lifted high on a wave then slipped away sideways, the rhythm repeated.

Within the channel the Zodiac remained invisible. Instinctively, Trent closed the throttle. Deprived of power, he was unable to hold the bows into the surge, a surge that threatened to spin the inflatable broadside to the sea. A fresh breaker exploded off the edge of the reef. The taut hulls shuddered as the Zodiac lifted to the spilling race of the wave. Spray curtained them within the thunder of the surf; impossible to think; impossible to hear or see.

And Trent had given all his concentration to the passage.

A light spat from behind them.

They were caught.

Trent had no time nor space for manoeuvre.

In desperation, he opened the throttle wide. The Zodiac rose to the next wave like a horse to a jump. Trent yelled at the American and at Tur to get their weight forward to hold the bows down. A second light caught them. From the boat ahead. Knitting needles and they were as vulnerable as a ball of wool. Trent steered straight for the boat. The boat was less than a hundred metres ahead. The boat astern the same. If the Cubans fired, they risked damaging each other with ricochets off the water. However, once clear of the channel, the Zodiac could be cut to shreds. And no hiding place. Unless . . .

The Zodiac was a small target and speeding at over twenty miles an hour. As the inflatable tore free of the maelstrom within the channel, Trent pushed the tiller over and shot up the seaward side of a roller about to break onto the reef. He held the boat for a moment on the very pinnacle of the wave before darting down and out to meet the next roller. Again the Zodiac lifted to the wave. Again Trent raced along the crest and down the back and up to meet the next. Every part of him was concentrated to the feel of the sea and, in the very thunder of the surf, he was deaf to gun fire.

Perhaps for a mile he raced, nip and tuck with the breaking rollers. Then he pushed the tiller over for a last time and sent the Zodiac racing straight out into the Old Bahama Channel, his course drawn by the loom of the lighthouse on Lobos Cay.

Three hours and Trent eased the Zodiac in to the dock.

Three men in a boat.

They were reluctant to face each other.

The American busied himself holding the inflatable off the concrete. Tur sat hunched against the port hull, hands between his thighs. Continual drenching had bleached the skin surrounding the scabs on the Cuban's face and his eyes seemed shuttered.

The light beam circled smoothly overhead and illuminated the striped metal tower and the lightkeeper's colonial bungalow, a concrete store and shed. The few palm trees were angled by the prevailing wind.

'Bahamian territory,' Trent told the American. 'We leave you here.'

The American dragged himself upright. The seawall came midway up his belly. He managed to raise one knee onto the dock and scrabbled for a hand hold. The Zodiac slid from under him and he flopped forward flat on the concrete. He pushed himself up and stood looking down at Estoban Tur. He appeared about to say something to the Cuban. However, all he did was nod and turn away and walk up the dock towards the bungalow.

Trent snicked the Yamaha into gear and spun the Zodiac clear.

Three

26

Washington

Bergman wasted a day writing fiction for Bahamian official-dom on why he had been put ashore on Lobos Cay. Catching a late evening American Eagle flight to Miami, he called his departmental chief at home and reported that the target was out and in transit. He expected congratulations, dinner with Clif some place with real beeswax candles and a lengthy wine list, even the offer of a bed for the night. Instead Clif ordered him to New York and a meeting in the open air.

Half six the following morning and the car park at Washington's airport was nearly empty. Glen, adviser on terrorism and golf partner to the president, parked his forest green Cherokee jeep on the top level. Clif drove his own Buick rather than an Agency vehicle. He drew up alongside the Cherokee. Glen nodded to him, which was some sort of notice coming from a member of the White House staff. Clif locked the Buick and climbed in next to Glen.

The two men hadn't talked since their meeting in the rain. Glen poured coffee from a stainless steel vacuum flask into a red plastic cup for himself and for Clif into the steel cap.

The cap was hot and difficult to hold; Clif didn't like to sit it down where it might mark the leather and shifted it from hand to hand and from knee to knee.

'Bergman got the Cuban out,' he said. 'The Guatemalans should have him in the next few days.'

Great would have been good. *Good* would have been okay. All Glen did was watch the way Clif held the coffee.

Clif fumbled in his trouser pocket for a handkerchief. 'I thought you'd like to know,' he said and folded the handkerchief into an oblong pad which he laid on his knee. Setting the cup on one end of the handkerchief, he folded the rest up the side of the cup and held it between thumb and forefinger over the rim. 'I'm meeting with Bergman in New York . . . Today,' he said.

Glen said, 'You want to drink your coffee while it's hot. Real beans. I grind them myself.'

The cup burnt Clif's lip. He said, 'Bergman needs to fly down to Guatemala tomorrow. There's a Brit TV journalist here wants to interview him which we need to avoid.'

Glen remained bored.

'Concerning San Cristóbal de los Baños,' Clif said. A jumbo lifted off the end of the airfield; the surface of his coffee trembled.

The roar of the jets faded and Glen said, 'San Cristóbal. That's something that happened under the previous administration.'

'Right,' Clif said.

Glen flashed one of his best smiles. He preferred his gold Omega to the clock on the dashboard. Lifting his shirt cuff, he said, 'Six forty-five already.'

Clif swallowed the rest of the coffee before handing Glen the cup.

Glen gave him a second smile. 'This thing of yours seems to be going well. Call me when you have the interview on videotape.'

The sun shone on New York's Central Park. Bergman waited on the third bench west of the red maple on the north side of the path. A pair of short-haired male fitness addicts in aviator shades and matching tanktops held hands as they swooped down the slope on roller-blades. Bergman wondered what they did that paid for the gym and the caps. Maybe they worked for an escort agency – or *The* Agency, new-breed escorts for Bergman's boss who appeared at the top of the slope.

Clif sat on the far end of the bench. Five years back he would have produced a pack of Camels and patted his pockets for matches before turning naturally to Bergman for a light. Now the *Washington Post* served as an introduction and Clif scanned the front page of that morning's early edition for a headline on which to comment. He wore a new upmarket lightweight blue suit that fitted his new shape and his new masters, a white button-down shirt and a wavy stripe tie trapped mid-journey between hip and conservative club. Most of the time Clif's feet were under a desk and he had saved money on his loafers.

'The shoes are a mistake,' Bergman said. 'Even with wool socks.'

Clif said, 'I didn't fly all this way for you to be a pain in the arse.'

All this way was sixty minutes on the shuttle.

'Try crawling across Cuba and back in the rain,' Bergman said.

Clif flashed a false grin. 'So now you want to give me heroes? You were trying to save your job.'

The truth hurt. And the lack of justice. 'I got him out, the director of G2. So I expect to be flavour of the month and this is what I get? A meet in the park? Like I'm some Third World defector with terminal leprosy.' Bergman shook his head in disbelief. 'Clif, what did I do?'

They watched a pensioner scuff by in trainers that would have shamed the refuse downtown on the lower Lower East side.

'San Cristóbal de los Baños, that's what,' Clif said. 'There's a Brit TV company set to film a one-hour special with a couple of the Senate aids you insulted taking star parts.'

The pensioner had turned and tottered back. He faced them from the far side of the footpath, silent and without raising his eyes, simply waiting in hope or without hope. Such was the manner in which Bergman's dad would have begged.

Bergman handed him ten dollars and the old man shuffled

back the way he had come. At the top of the slope he turned and gave them a smile that faded before it could establish itself.

'You should have given him your loafers,' Bergman said.

'Who's to say he isn't an undercover billionaire?' Clif patted his pockets as had been his habit through twenty years of cigarette addiction. 'You want to tell me what happened?'

Bergman narrated his and Estoban Tur's escape. 'Tur's on a yacht with his friend.'

'Heading for Guatemala. You did good,' Clif said. 'Pick him up and get his confession on tape. Do that and you'll be in great shape.'

Bergman had doubts that he had done good or was in great shape.

A blonde teenage divinity wafted by on the arm of a Puerto Rican boyfriend tall enough to play pro ball.

Clif said, 'What happened to our youth?'

'Mine I escaped,' Bergman said.

Clif said, 'What you haven't escaped is San Cristóbal. May be you should tell me the truth.'

'You read my report,' Bergman said.

'It didn't say shit.'

So Bergman had got something right in his life.

'That way you're safe. You can't answer questions and no one gets to inspect what remains of the town.'

'A whole town. No witnesses?'

'That's right,' Bergman said.

A couple of twelve-year-old black boys sprinted down the path and round the corner. They should have been in school. Bergman wondered whether they were habitual truants or whether today was a one-off with the weather fine and the flowers out in the park. Nature lovers?

Clif said, 'This administration doesn't give shit what happened before they were voted in and you aren't sufficient target. Yet someone's orchestrating a scandal. Maybe the Company is the target. Another witch-hunt. Sweep up the last of the old guard.'

Hence the new suit, distancing himself.

A man their age dressed in Wall Street banker's drag had taken off his jacket and sat reading a newspaper on the grass to their right – probably the *Journal*. Perhaps he had dressed that morning and come up to town in pretence of a job he had lost – kissed the wife and kids goodbye, told them to have a good day, even that he might be late back. In Japan there were agencies designed to support the executive employment myth; answering services that said always that the subject was in conference or at a meeting. The idea frightened Bergman: falling out of what you thought of as your own existence and then abandoning reality.

'This is something that ought to have gone away,' Clif said. 'This Brit producer – why is he interested? The pressure's coming from outside. That's my guess.'

He waited a while for Bergman's answer before saying, 'It would help if you helped. Like even in Cuba you have to make enemies.'

Bergman was sure the man in the suit's newspaper was the *Journal*. Perhaps the man was a fund manager and liked to do his research out in the fresh air. 'Nick the Greek? What did he say?'

'Write,' Clif corrected. 'That you were playing private games on his turf and behaved like a prize prick.' He turned half round on the bench so that he faced Bergman who was forced to accept that Clif was talking to him rather than to some newly recruited no-relationship from the office.

'We're meant to be friends. That's what this thing is about,' Clif said. 'Most people are trying to get by. They're not trying to change the world. That's something you've never under-stood. So now you're trying to save your job and it pisses you off. That you're down at our level. Down there with a jerk like me who's worked at keeping his job and gets promoted. You could have had my job. You didn't want it. You wanted to stay on down in your little kingdom. You've been down there too long,' Clif said. 'It's like you've regressed to where you started out.'

'Trailer trash,' Bergman said before he could stop himself.

Clif sighed. 'I was thinking of the permanent outsider,' he said. 'That's something that doesn't fit within an organisation.'

They sat in silence for a while. Not yet the lunch hour, those they watched were the sad and the irresponsible and a very few of the very fortunate.

Finally Bergman said, 'You're right, Clif. This thing's turned me into something I don't like.' He kicked at a bubble in the tar then pushed himself up. 'You want to walk a little?'

'In these loafers?' Clif asked and the two men chuckled together, though with insufficient confidence for Bergman to discuss what had happened to Little Brother. And Tur's kids – how it must be for them at school suffering the other children's mockery at having a father on the run and an uncle who took it up the arse.

Bergman looked away across the grassy dell at the great trees of the parkland; majestic, yet with none of the jungle exuberance with which he had grown familiar. Five days on the run together and he and Tur had shared nothing of themselves. More and more secrets and thoughts that he couldn't disclose, that was the direction of his life. Back in Guatemala he was used to it. Clif was different. Clif was his people. They had been friends for twenty years. How to tell an old friend that the only place he, Bergman, belonged was a Central American car wash.

'Vorst,' he said. Vorst, the enemy. Which was another secret. 'I have a meeting with him.'

Bergman had called Vorst from Nassau and demanded a face-to-face on grounds that what he had to tell couldn't be said over an open line. He had set the meeting in a midmarket Salvadorian diner with high-back wooden booths and scarred tables. Ninety per cent of the customers were dark Latino, the women mostly a little gaudy by WASP standards, their men in sharp suits or jackets with wide shoulders and lapels; fifty per cent were certainly illegal; every one of them could scent cop. Bergman stood inside the entrance where he would gain maximum attention and took his time selecting a bench. He knew the picture he projected, not exactly cheap but a little down-at-heel and a little furtive. He sat crammed into a corner where Vorst couldn't spot him from the door. The financier arrived precisely on time. Vorst's clothes and his presence marked him out. Bergman rose from his corner and raised a hand. He guessed what the other customers must imagine, a private detective with a rich client. Which made Vorst a cuckold.

Bergman had been cuckolded by his wife with every blond American she had been able to wrap her legs around in Guatemala City. Confronted, she claimed that it wasn't the sex. Rather it was her need to feel desirable and that she counted as someone in her own right.

She didn't hide her infidelity – she said that being married to him had made her hate secrets. Their daughters knew and the Guatemalan servants. Bergman paid the rent and the bills and the wages and was treated with contempt.

'Don't you care?' his wife demanded.

Had he replied in the affirmative, she would have repeated the infidelity to hurt him the more.

He replied in the negative and she would do it again even more openly so that he would be forced to notice it.

Screw some other man.

Not make love to another man; the act had nothing to do with whoever she took to bed. She was screwing Bergman, attempting to get through to him, a weird sort of cry for help which he had been unable to answer. With the clandestine war at its height, he was out at all hours and all over the country. He was seeing things and being implicated in things that didn't exist outside horror books. He slowed down, he had time to think. In bed he lay awake all night with his eyes closed so that she wouldn't know and ask questions or ask to be made love to.

The making love was worst. As if he had rights and as if their life was normal and he wouldn't be summoned out of bed to inspect the results of what the Guatemalan army reported as a successful anti-guerrilla action which meant bodies scattered amongst the tin-roof huts or down the hillside or along the banks of a stream: small brown bodies of both sexes and of every age from infant to great-grandparent, and naked because the soldiers sold the clothes off the dead in the market. A successful guerrilla action looked the same.

Bergman's responsibility was to end the violence. He had thought to do so with training and discipline and US aid harnessed to political and economic reform. He had been in a hurry back then. His years in Guatemala had taught him that anything worth the effort demanded a great deal of time and patience – and would be rewarded with a great deal of pain.

He had learnt to cope with the pain by distancing himself. Clif had called him an outsider. Being an insider was too fearful.

Standing to greet Vorst was awkward with the bench against the back of his knees and he was forced to lean forward across the table to make room for his belly.

Vorst was as slim and neat as ever in a charcoal grey suit and white Oxford shirt. He checked the bench for dirt before sitting down and cleaned the top of the table with a paper napkin.

'Food's genuine and the menu's my price,' Bergman said. Taking control, he ordered for both of them: *pupusas* stuffed with home-made sausage and cheese followed by charcoal-grilled squid served with rice and a lettuce and avocado salad.

Vorst was polishing his table knife. His fingernails were already polished and the cuticles trimmed in perfect crescents. Bergman wondered whether Vorst's manicurist was a looker and whether Vorst noticed.

Bergman leant forward a little, invading Vorst's space. 'The man you want is out of Cuba. We should pick him up in the next few days.'

Vorst nodded in agreement with his own thoughts. 'That's something you could report over the phone. What do you have to say that required we meet face to face, Mister Bergman? And on your territory?' he added as he inspected the diner with its smell of garlic and onion, beans, fried fish and fried sweet peppers. He laid his cleaned knife back on the table, selected the fork and smiled at Bergman as if genuinely interested.

'You don't like me, Mister Bergman. Is that personal or is it what I represent? And which do you resent most? That you *need* my help or that I *can* help?' He had placed each question as neatly as a piece in a delicate jigsaw. The final picture was of Bergman and his prejudices.

Bergman lost his cool. 'Your promise of support in Washington, Mister Vorst, was dependent on my getting Tur out of Cuba. I should have told you to go screw yourself.'

'Or words to that effect,' Vorst agreed with a cool smile.

Even the financier's teeth were perfect. Bergman wanted to hit him. 'You already owed me support,' he said. 'I got to Guatemala, the country was run by military hoodlums. We had a clandestine war, Indians getting massacred by both sides; few owners or managers dared sleep a night on the plantations or even visit without an armed escort. Now there's a ceasefire, a democratically elected president and reasonable labour laws. Tur or no Tur, you owed me.'

Vorst had been working a napkin between the prongs of his fork. Holding the fork up against the light, he said, 'I'd agree that you did well and that NAFAC owes you support, Mister Bergman. Unfortunately NAFAC and I are not always synonymous.' He laid the fork down, set his elbows on the table and steepled his hands against his chin. His wristwatch was a slither of gold on a polished leather strap. The cuffs of his shirt were whiter than white and steam pressed.

A bishop – or a cardinal. Bergman and Tur had come from similar backgrounds. Bergman wondered where Vorst had started out. A house with ample hot water. Or was he reacting against messy parents? Or against poverty? Was he a third side of the same coin, differing only in the solution he sought?

Perhaps Vorst read his mind. 'The suit confuses you, Mister Bergman. And the corporate jet. I'm an instigator of policy and an administrator, nothing more. Power lies with the banks and the fund managers. A cabal on the board has doubts in regard to the special relationships I've developed in Cuba with the young technocrats. The attack on Finca Patricia supported their position. That made you and me two of a kind, Mister Bergman. Despite being good at what we do, our jobs are at risk. Tur's confession is your insurance. The Cubans sacrificing Tur is mine – if that's what they did?'

'They gave us Tur's brother,' Bergman said.

The Salvadorian owner of the dinner intervened with their *pupusas*, setting the plates on the table: '*Que aproveche.*'

Vorst cut the stuffed corn tortilla in quarters and cut one quarter in half. Raising a piece on his fork, he paused to look at Bergman. 'I've built NAFAC. I'd hate to lose it.'

Vorst's finickiness irritated Bergman. 'I've been in Cuba the past week,' he said. 'This NAFAC investment, that's a joint-venture project with the state? Mind my asking what you pay the workers?'

Again the smile, a little mocking. 'Bergman, the believer. We aren't authorised to pay labour directly. We'll pay the Cuban government – approximately four hundred and fifty dollars a month per man.'

'As against six fifty in Guatemala,' Bergman interjected.

Vorst gave a small shrug. 'That makes me the villain? Or the Cuban government who will pay NAFAC's workers the equivalent of fifteen dollars a month in pesos? That's why Castro permits foreign investment: hard currency for slave labour. It's a system many companies are already exploiting, Mister Bergman: Spanish investment, Canadian, Mexican, the Israelis, Dutch, French, British. And that's in a traditionally US trade area from which NAFAC is excluded by the Helms-Burton Act.'

Vorst paused to eat. He seemed hardly to move his jaw as he chewed.

A young woman had been watching them from the next table, fading pretty, fake pearls and a twinset leaking threads at the seams. Seeing the pause in their conversation, she held out a cigarette and asked for a light. She wasn't confident and neither Bergman nor Vorst smoked.

Vorst cut off another quarter of the stuffed tortilla before continuing. 'Unfortunately politicians think as far as the next election, Mister Bergman. Nationwide, you've got under thirty per cent of voters bothering to vote in a presidential election. A million Cubans in Miami and they all vote. That gives the Cubans a value close on four to one and buys them the blockade.

'If the blockade rid Cuba of Castro, I might approve, Mister Bergman. It hasn't and it won't. It strengthens him. It gives him an enemy to blame for the economic chaos he's created. That's a truth anyone who studies Cuba is aware of – including the politicians who passed the Act.'

Finishing the tortilla, he set his knife and fork together. The woman made a second attempt, this time requesting the salt. Bergman fed warmth into his eyes and told her, 'Later, señorita. For the moment we are occupied with a discussion.'

She wasn't interested in Bergman.

'Guilt,' Vorst said quietly of Bergman's attitude to the woman. 'I like that. You want a job, call me. Guatemala, Dominican Republic, even Cuba if this deal comes off.'

Bergman had thought NAFAC's deal was signed.

'Even signed, it's worth only how Castro feels on the day, Mister Bergman. Government by caprice. If I ran NAFAC that way, I'd be voted off the board and be out of a job in the first week.' He permitted himself a faint irritation. 'Cuba's a rich island, Mister Bergman, and the US is the only country with which it can't trade. At NAFAC we suffer European Community quotas. I find other markets, Mister Bergman. That's my job.'

The Salvadorian brought fresh cutlery with their grilled squid and Vorst repeated his polishing. 'Cleanliness and tidiness, qualities that mark our plantations, Mister Bergman, and the families who work for us,' he said. 'It starts right at home with the houses we build the workers and the school uniforms. Something they can be proud of – that marks them out from the surrounding squalor.'

'A cattle brand.'

Vorst ignored the interjection and Bergman tried again, 'It's what Castro promises.'

'And hasn't delivered,' Vorst said. 'Work for me, Mister Bergman. In three months you'll have lost weight and be wearing a linen suit. Why? Because you'll be proud of what you do.'

The Zoo

Mid-afternoon and the president's adviser on terrorism parked his Cherokee jeep in the shade outside bungalow 4. The two men sat out on the terrace facing the fourth fairway. Pink bougainvillaea protected them from the sun. Glen preferred coffee. Colonel Smith offered him China tea and a cucumber sandwich with the brown bread cut wafer-thin. It was a game, of course – and Glen retaliated by relating the minutia of a recent golf game with the president.

The colonel listened in apparent interest. And he lit an Abdullah, drifting the pungent Egyptian tobacco smoke in Glen's direction so that it caught in the American's lungs.

Glen coughed and the colonel apologised profusely and reached for the silver teapot. 'Another cup of tea?'.

Glen's refusal would have won the Brit another point. 'Half a cup,' Glen said and sipped almost delicately. 'Tur's out.'

The Brit acted puzzled for a moment. Then, 'Ah yes, the Cuban. Splendid.'

'Right,' Glen said. He leant forward, unable to restrain his glee. 'Once we have the videotape, we'll have it on TV. Meanwhile it's Bergman freelancing with the senator's support. It goes wrong, the senator burns. Yes,' he said, uncharacteristically eager to share success. 'Your idea and it's earning you points right where it counts.'

'Splendid,' the colonel repeated. He lolled back in his chair, ankles crossed, brown brogues brilliantly polished. Withdrawing a white handkerchief from his shirt cuff, he dabbed his forehead. The acting was perfect. 'Wonderful weather, something I'd miss dreadfully in England.'

Glen gave the colonel one of his best smiles, young and open and honest and all-American. 'This thing works out, it'll be like old times. You'll be back and forth like a yo-yo.' He looked away across the fairway, for the moment unwilling to meet the colonel's eyes. 'You can depend on me. That's fact.'

There was more, of course.

Out on the golf course one of the colonel's fellow prisoners hit a ball to the centre of the fourth green. The ball bit and held on the slope and a magpie took flight. The colonel clapped silently and waited.

Glen was very casual. 'Remember San Cristóbal? There's a journalist you might like to speak with.'

In passing, the golfer glanced towards the two men and the colonel acknowledged him with a slight wave.

'A fellow Brit. TV,' Glen said of the journalist – as if it didn't matter and he wasn't interested.

The colonel wasn't fooled. San Cristóbal occurred under the previous administration. Now came a nice little scandal orchestrated to coincide with the lead-up to the presidential elections – professional class voters wondering whether they could entrust power to such people. In the end it was always politics with those who lived in Washington. Washington politics. The size and power of the United States made them view everything beyond their frontiers as immaterial.

The colonel watched the golfer cross the green and sink his birdie put. Extraction of the Guatemalan general had been a favour the colonel had done his allies – people with the same beliefs, committed to the same fight.

'No,' the colonel said. 'That's not something I'd do.'

'That could be a mistake,' Glen said. He stood up and stretched and gave the colonel a last smile from the door. 'Give me a call when you change your mind.'

Estoban Tur

The dumb Bahamian had taken the second Zodiac home while Trent had sailed directly up-channel in international waters and rounded the western tip of Cuba, Cabo de San Antonio. Starlight speckled the sea and the half moon drew a pale silver strip down which *Golden Girl* swept towards Mexico's Yucatán coast.

Estoban lay on the trampoline and watched the unravelling of the seas ahead. The lift and roll of the dark smooth swells reminded him of the heavy velvet curtains at the Lorca Theatre, home to Cuba's national ballet. Estoban had found the ballet uncomfortable. Maria had accused him of being enmeshed in prejudice. She and Miguelito were the aficionados, their minds freed by culture, while Estoban had been harnessed by his Russian tutors to the party and the service, his imagination castrated – so Maria had argued in the days when they had retained the energy to argue rather than hide in silence.

The sea and silence were strangers. Estoban listened to the creak of stressed timber, the spang of tensioned rigging, the suck of the wind against the sails and the surf cleaved beneath the bows. Streams of phosphorescence spilled from the bows and sucked his gaze further and further aft into the deep shadows beneath the bridge deck. His brother lay imprisoned within the shadows.

He pushed himself up and carried his pain aft to the cockpit where the Englishman, Trent, sat with his back to the varnished wood bar connecting the twin tillers. The saloon sheltered them from the spill and hiss of the torn waves.

Tur said, 'The photograph . . .'

27

Trent

Heavy rubber ties held the laminated ash bar connecting the twin tillers and the *Golden Girl* steered herself. Running at fourteen knots, the light hulls of the catamaran rode over the sea and left twin dark trails pressed in the foam. A steady force three wind fetched them round Cabo de San Antonio. Despite nightfall, Trent had kept the big genoa headsail set to carry them across the three-to-four-knot current that drove out of the Atlantic and north up the Yucatán Channel into the Gulf of Mexico.

The Yucatan Channel is the main shipping lane connecting the southern United States with Central and South America and the navigation lights of a dozen ships were visible. Trent had little faith in the marine law that power gives way to sail. The sailors on watch first had to be aware of *Golden Girl's* presence. Trent took sights of the ships every few minutes, marking their positions on a compass rose printed on a plastic board. Another part of his mind catalogued and searched for change in each familiar breath and movement of the yacht, speed and pitch and heel, pressure on the tillers, the feel of the wind on his ears, the hiss and rush of the torn waves down the sides of the hulls, slap of water against the underside of the bridge deck and the suck of the transoms each time they dipped into the wake.

Set to port of the saloon companionway, repeaters from the array of instruments above the navigation table gave him the force and angle of the wind and the catamaran's speed through the water and Trent checked their position every thirty minutes on the GPS. Their progress over the ground rather than through the water gave the current's speed and direction and enabled him to adjust their course for a landfall south of the Mexican border at Belize's Ambergris Caye.

Estoban clambered along the side-deck and dropped down into the cockpit. Trent had insisted he wear a life jacket and safety line while on deck

'The photograph,' Estoban began, then cursed as the line caught round his foot. 'You have turned me into a monkey,' he complained and unshackled himself, coiling the line on the seat.

The two men were uncomfortable together. They had been enemies for the eighteen years of Trent's service with Military Intelligence. Though they had made peace, there was no trust between them and Estoban had avoided a discussion of his brother's predicament. They had been at sea for the past forty-eight hours; between short spells on watch, the Cuban had slept, or pretended to sleep. This reaction was familiar to Trent, for whom fear had been a natural habitat throughout his years in the field. He had thought himself free.

'Coffee?' the Cuban asked.

Trent nodded and sheltered his eyes as Estoban ducked through the companionway to switch on the shaded light above the galley counter.

While they sipped their coffee a cloud slid across the moon. Estoban shifted awkwardly on the cockpit bench and watched the shadow speed across the water. 'Inside myself there was always the certainty that you would come,' he said in self-exculpation for his lack of faith.

Fear bred the field agent's mistrust and even hatred for those on whom he depended – such had been Trent's territory. He said, 'I understand,' and busied himself, taking fresh bearings on the ships within their area. The bearing on a tanker to port remained unchanged, proof that they were on a collision course, and Trent eased the helm to pass astern.

'The photograph,' Estoban repeated. 'The soldiers' faces are hidden from the camera so that there is no evidence against them.' His tone suggested that this was a fresh revelation; on the run, his need had been for hope and purpose, thus the necessity to blind himself to the obvious.

'Only the victim can recognise the rapists,' Estoban said as he watched the approaching tanker. The tanker would pass some four hundred yards ahead of them on course for the refineries in Venezuela. With its bunkers empty, the ship rode high in the water, an immense black cliff surmounted by a pimple of lights aft while, forward, moonlight glistened on the great curling vee of foam smashed clear by the ship's bows.

'The victim will never be permitted to bear witness against his persecutors,' Estoban said and looked now at Trent for the first time, 'They will kill him.'

Victim because Estoban was unable to speak his brother's name.

'Yes,' Trent said. 'Yes, such is clearly their intention.'

The smell of the tanker came to them across the water, of wet steel and petroleum and they could hear the deep hum of steam turbines through the crash of the bow wave bursting along the hull. The ship sped by and the white wall of its wake raced towards them. Trent brought *Golden Girl* up into the wind, first cutting speed by spilling wind from the sails before paying off to meet the wave squarely. In driving across the sea's pattern, the wake carried with it the splash and suck and rolling rustle of a river in flood. Foam spewed forward as *Golden Girl* lifted to the white wall and Trent shifted the helm, sliding the catamaran down the back of the wave at an angle that obviated the possibility of the yacht burying her bows.

Unfamiliar with the sea, Estoban had been holding his breath while gripping tight to the cockpit coaming.

Trent was already entering the bearings of the remaining ships in sight.

'This thing is complicated,' Estoban said – not *this matter of my brother* nor *this kidnapping* nor *gang rape*. *Thing* was his and Trent's language.

Estoban was an analyst of intelligence as much as he was a controller of agents and operations. He chose his words carefully now, marshalling his thoughts for Trent's approval.

Miguelito, with no connection to the ballet, had been chosen for the trip to Guatemala. In Cuba such jobs were precious for the foreign currency which could be saved out of the cost of living allowance. Such jobs went to relatives or friends of the directorate . . .

'Or to one chosen by the Ministry of Security,' Trent suggested.

'*Sí, claro.*' Yes, clearly.

'Your brother was chosen?'

'No,' Estoban said. And, after a pause, 'No, not by my department.'

Trent took the empty coffee mugs below to the galley before reading off their position and entering it on the chart. Back in the cockpit, he took fresh bearings on the ships surrounding them. A laden freighter had changed course ten degrees and Trent flashed gratitude on the spotlight. Shackling a safety line to his life jacket, he made a tour of the catamaran to check rigging and sails. There were no further delays that he could manufacture.

Sitting in the opposite corner of the cockpit to Estoban, he said, 'I have read reports that exit visas in Cuba are forbidden to close relatives of senior military or intelligence officers.'

'Exceptions exist,' Estoban said, 'Trusted members of the party . . .' He fell silent and turned away to watch a cargo ship cross their wake at a distance of half a mile. The bridge door was open with a figure outlined in the light; probably watching the moonlit genoa through binoculars; dreaming, perhaps, of how it would be to navigate the Caribbean under sail, dive the coral waters, make love on the sand.

Estoban had been a trusted member of the party; Colonel Smith had belonged to the right class and clubs. They were the instigators, the Controls, while Trent had been merely a weapon to be discarded when inconvenient; meanwhile to be kept in ignorance and at a distance, lest he dirtied his superiors with the blood of his métier.

A servant, he thought and felt the familiar anger. 'Miguelito was a party member?'

'No.'

Estoban examined his hands, perhaps searching in the lines for an explanation of his ignorance. 'There are things that one knows without accepting that one knows,' he said. 'My brother is small, slim, beautiful. Yes, *beautiful*,' he repeated, placing the word as carefully as he would have a cut-glass goblet or a porcelain cup on a narrow shelf. He looked to Trent for understanding – a small shrug, 'The party prohibits homosexuals from membership and perhaps there were always those who suspected.'

The subject was uncomfortable and Trent squinted through his compass at the closest ship and checked the bearing against the previous reading. 'Apart from G2, there are other intelligence agencies.'

'Miguelito recruited? I would have known. Or suspected. Yes, certainly I would have suspected.'

Trent imagined Estoban receiving the news of his brother's appointment to the ballet and hiding his incredulity. And he would have been suspicious of whoever had authorised the appointment; mutual suspicion was endemic within the hierarchy of any dictatorship.

'We are half-brothers,' Estoban reminded Trent. 'Miguelito is white. I thought perhaps that there had been an error at immigration – or special circumstances. Miguelito's step-father has influence within the Ministries of Culture and of Education and at UNEAC, the artists' union.

'To travel for the first time outside Cuba. It was a dream. He was so happy. And Maria. Both of them. I did not wish to investigate. It was Miguelito's opportunity to be free. Yes,' Estoban said, 'of what I represent.'

'Bait,' Trent said, 'Your brother was used as bait.'

Estoban wished to be precise. 'Sacrificed as bait . . .'

The concept was too painful. In need of an antidote, Estoban sought the familiar target, 'The American was CIA.'

'Or some other agency,' Trent said.

'It is possible that we were permitted to escape.'

'The bullets were real enough.'

'Not all would have been involved. A few . . . at the summit.' Estoban looked back across the sea to where his homeland lay beyond the horizon. 'They would have been nervous of scandal. A touch here and there – at the roadblock, at the inlet. They would trust in our competence to avoid the others. Had we failed, they would have demanded our confessions to something equally suitable.'

'The American?'

Estoban was thinking of Miguelito. And of his own children. Children playing war games in the bath. Making waves that swirled their toys hither and thither and without direction.

'Perhaps we are toys.' He had no better explanation and he followed with his eyes the line of moonlight on the water.

'We will be off San Pedro before first light,' Trent said. 'Then a further twenty-four hours south to Guatemala.'

Estoban remained silent.

His apparent apathy irritated the Englishman.

'They are raping your brother,' Trent said.

He felt Estoban's anger as the Cuban looked across the cockpit. Anger was further self-indulgence.

'You need help. Information,' Trent pressed. 'Who can you trust?'

Estoban shrugged. 'One man – yes, possibly one man. A *guerrillero* commander.'

'Out of all the people you trained,' Trent said.

Fabio

The yellow Ford bus had worked ten years ferrying pupils to and from elementary school along the quiet shaded streets of a middle-management Atlanta suburb. For the past three years it had made this daily return journey each weekday between the village of Yepocapa and Antigua Guatemala. Rain fell steadily. The rubber on one of the wipers had torn and the bare metal screeched against the windshield.

Prior to the end of the clandestine war, fear of ambush and robbery by either *guerrilleros* or the army would have held the passengers silent as the bus lurched and slithered up the dirt road. With peace the Indians chattered in their high-pitched voices of illness and scandal and the cost of fuel and of the low prices paid them for the fruit and vegetables and chickens and pigs they had brought to market.

Grey wisps of cloud leaked down the mountainside between the trees and down a cart track that lay ahead and across the road. Fabio waited in the shadows beside the cart track. He had left his men at their camp high on the flanks of the volcano.

The bus halted at the intersection and one fat old man clambered wheezing from the bus. Clearly he suffered from toothache or perhaps of a cancer and a bandage covered much of his face. What showed of his skin suggested that he was of Spanish descent, perhaps a retired teacher or a priest who had lost his faith or been banned by his church for too public a frailty. A black binliner served him as a poncho and he wore a straw hat with a torn brim and cheap blue draylon trousers with frayed cuffs draped over green rubber over-shoes and he carried a straw shopping basket.

The bus driver accelerated away in a cloud of diesel fumes. Fabio waited for the bus to disappear before stepping out of the shadows. Twenty metres separated him from the old man. Fabio knew him as the Spider and would have preferred fine weather for the meeting; the rain gave the Cuban an excuse to hide his right hand beneath his makeshift poncho.

Nervous, Fabio touched his Adam's apple as if feeling the words of greeting unique to Cuba. '*Cómo anda?*' How does it go?

Squatting in the centre of the path, he picked up a pebble and tossed it from one hand to the other so that the Cuban would see that he was unarmed.

'What news?'

'Good,' the old man said. He had walked less than fifty metres up the hill yet already sweat ran down his forehead and stained the grubby bandage. He set the basket on a flat stone in the track and freed his right hand from beneath the bin liner. Pushing his hat back, he wiped the sweat on his palm and dried his hand on his trouser leg.

'It is the altitude,' Fabio said.

'Yes, I am not accustomed to the altitude.' A fit of coughing shook the Cuban and he hawked and spat phlegm. 'The attack on Finca Patricia was successful.' He nodded to the basket. 'I brought cheese and wine from the city.'

The Spider unpacked the food and drew the cork on a bottle of rioja. They ate the cheese off the blade of their pocket knives and drank from paper cups. As always on his visits, the Spider withdrew a Kodak envelope from within the folds of his old clothes and shuffled the dozen prints which gave witness to the major barbarities of Fabio's career. Only the final print was new and showed the Cuban who had trained Fabio in the school for illegals in the Sierra de los Organos and was now director of G2 – Estoban Tur.

'A traitor to the revolution,' the Spider said. 'We have permitted his escape. He will come to Guatemala. Clearly he will contact you. Kill him.'

The Cuban retrieved the photographs from Fabio and replaced them in the Kodak envelope. The cold of the mountains made him shiver and he coughed once into his fist. His eyes watered and he wiped them on the back of his right hand. 'You will kill him before he falls into the hands of the army. This is clear to you? Very clear?'

Fabio nodded his assent.

The Spider tucked the Kodak envelope back into his basket and pushed himself upright. The effort made him gasp. He wiped his lips on the back of his hand and looked at Fabio slantwise. 'Age has me in its grip. You remain young, Fabio. Do this last service for the revolution and you will be permitted to retire.'

Always the same lie . . .

'A house on the beach at Varadero.'

Bergman

Siesta hour and Bergman lay dozing in the big bed upstairs at the car wash. The woman knocked. Her children wished to thank Bergman for his support – please, would he cover himself.

The children came to the bedside shyly and presented Bergman with a paperback edition of a novel by Graham Greene: *The Quiet American*. They had discovered the book on a market stall in Morales and had bought it for the title.

The older child pointed to the cover, '*Americano*'.

'*Sí, americano,*' Bergman agreed. He was nervous that the children should discover his nakedness beneath the sheet and his lips were dry as he pecked their cheeks – such inadequate miserly Protestant kisses, he thought.

The woman herded the children down to the care of a waitress. Closing the door, she stretched the stiffness from her shoulders before unbuttoning her dress. She said, '*Uno momento,*' as she disappeared into the bathroom.

One moment – as if Bergman's needs were even more urgent than in his teens.

He listened to the taps run and the familiar female washing. He had brought a packet of Oral B toothbrushes from the city and she brushed her teeth and gargled before returning to the bedroom. Walking naked across the room, she closed the shutters on the single window. She made no attempt at sexuality, neither temptation nor titillation. She was his to use when she reached the bed. Or he was hers to use her when she reached the bed.

'*Disculpame,*' he said, 'that I am so badly educated as not to know your name.'

'Manuela.'

'Manuela.'

She touched him, anxious that he should finish so that she could sleep an hour before the restaurant filled with her evening custom.

He said, 'Forgive me, I am inadequate.'

Prayer was his wife's solution for all problems: a quick word to St Antony to find the car keys; to St Christopher to make sure she didn't get a puncture on the way to the airport in the tyre she should have changed; St Juste helped the soufflé rise; St Michael was responsible for the amount owing on her credit cards, St Jade for their daughters' studies.

Dear God, vouchsafe me an erection and an orgasm so that this good kind woman, Manuela, will be satisfied that I am satisfied and so can sleep before taking up again the burden of her labour.

The prayer worked and Manuela turned contentedly onto her side, her buttocks slippery with sweat where she pressed against him. Flaccid stomach muscles loosed her belly on the sheet and she snored gently. God and Bergman had done their duty. Bergman reached for *The Quiet American*. The fan stirred the furled mosquito net and a cock crowed.

Manuela slept for an hour. She kissed Bergman much as she would have rewarded the children with a sweet for good behaviour. He watched her cross to the window and open the shutters before heading for the bathroom. Stretch marks patterned her sides and a broken vein showed on the back of her right thigh. She lifted her breasts on her forearm to scratch at a mosquito bite. The areolae were big and dark and the nipples prominent and well chewed. Bergman imagined the children suckling while Manuela lay on her side, her mind filled with the mental arithmetic demanded by the car wash. Her life was a tale of struggle and disaster and her courage and competence touched him. An hour with Graham Greene had been sufficiently depressing and he threaded a red ribbon between the pages; it was a neat habit for one so careless of his appearance. He laid the book on the bedside table and smiled at Manuela as she returned fresh from the shower, 'I will be down shortly to eat. Then I must drive to Fronteras.'

Disclosing his plans added to the security risk of staying at the car wash. He no longer cared for himself. However, the woman concerned him – Manuela – and her children. Bergman opened the book and tied a knot in the ribbon to remind himself that he must drive into Morales in the morning to check the schools.

The operation had the senator's support which made it as official as such things ever were. Bergman was using his own car. He crossed the bridge at Fronteras and turned left down to a clapboard restaurant on the river bank where he played with a cold beer and watched passing boats scatter the reflections of the town lights on the water. He was the only customer in what was normally a popular haunt for local Guatemalans.

Two soldiers manned the black inflatable that sped into the wooden dock. The major jumped ashore. He wore civilian clothes and he straightened his sports shirt and adjusted the pistol inside the waistband of his chinos before entering the restaurant. The kitchen was divided from the main room by a half wall and the major nodded to the cook before seating himself facing Bergman.

Bergman's Toyota was parked at the door and the major said, 'Advertising?'

'The Cuban has no information as to what car I drive.'

The major said, 'He knows when you crap and how many sheets of paper you use. He even knows how you fold the sheets and which way up you screw your woman.'

Bergman didn't give a damn. Three days at the most and it would be over. 'Everything is prepared?'

'Nothing is prepared,' the major said. 'I have been amusing myself these past weeks pissing in the river. Is that what you think?' He banged the handle of his knife on the table and a waitress scurried over with fresh beers.

Bergman thanked her and asked the major, 'How many men do you have?'

'Do *we* have,' the major corrected. 'This is *your* operation, *Americano*. And, yes, there are men watching the river from the bridge and on the waterfront. Also on Main Street and by the bus stop.'

The cook placed a steak that overlapped the rim of the plate in front of the major together with a salad and a second plate piled with French fries. Bergman watched with envy as the major cleared his plate. French fries turned Bergman into a balloon – one more injustice. He knew that the major wanted him to ask where they were holding Tur's brother. Bergman already knew. He had known from the beginning. The major had taken Miguelito to San Cristóbal de los Baños.

Both the gang rape and the place of imprisonment were plays in a game the major enjoyed, a game of vengeance, not against Tur, but against Bergman and against the United States. Bergman had ordered the kidnapping; the major intended that he should suffer responsibility for all the consequences rather than restrict himself to the benefits of Tur's confession.

Bergman had murdered the boy in the lane in Antigua. Bergman had raped Little Brother. Bergman would capture and torture Estoban Tur. Bergman would kill both brothers. And the United States would stand at his shoulder.

This was the major's vision.

And that Bergman and the United States should judge themselves guilty rather than lay the blame on the major as they had done at San Cristóbal.

28

Trent

Estoban was convinced that his American accomplice, Frank Trautman, was involved in Miguelito's kidnapping. The American was certainly either Agency or DEA and would have reported his own and Estoban's escape from Cuba. Estoban would be expected to enter Guatemala by boat – illicitly because he had no passport and because he knew that his brother was bait in a trap – and probably in company with a bearded Latin American so Trent shaved his beard.

Few yachtsmen, particularly when single-handed, would sail directly from the Bahamas to Guatemala; to do so would have drawn unnecessary attention to *Golden Girl*.

Sandwiched between Mexico's Caribbean province and Guatemala, Belize comprises a narrow strip of coastal swamp and rainforest. The longest barrier reef in the northern hemisphere protects the shore from all but the worst of hurricanes. The reef lies at an average of twenty miles off the mainland. The shallow waters within the reef are scattered with islands that have grown out of the mangrove.

Entry and exit from Belize was easier than Trent had feared. He had gained the sheltered waters at first light via a cut midway between the two northernmost cayes, Ambergris and Caye Caulker. Estoban, dressed in swim suit and T-shirt and equipped with mask and fins and a bottle of drinking water, slipped unseen into the sea and swam to the uninhabited southern tip of Ambergris while Trent sailed up the island's coast to drop anchor off the only settlement, San Pedro.

Dive boats, fishing skiffs and gaff-rigged sailing barges lay alongside short wooden jetties. The houses were of lapstrake pine in pastel colours, each with a neat veranda facing either to the unpaved street or to the beach. Pots of flowers added colour to the verandas while coconut palms and sea grape trees shaded the small gardens. The native population appeared a mixture of every race known to man. The tourists were mostly North American in their twenties to early thirties and on Ambergris to dive the reef or cast for bonefish. Shorts and T-shirts were uniform, bare feet, cans of iced Belikin beer.

Trent was obliged to pay the $70 return air fare for a customs officer to fly out from Belize City. While waiting, he had his hair cut short. Formalities completed, he collected a half block of ice from the fish market and sailed south to anchor a mile off the point of the caye. Once darkness fell, he ran in with the Zodiac to collect Estoban.

At first light they sailed south between the surf and a string of cayes that lay between a quarter and half a mile inshore of the barrier reef. The lighthouse on English Caye marked the ship channel into Belize City. South of the channel the waters were more open and the trade wind strengthened through the afternoon. Aided by a southerly current, they averaged eight and a half knots to anchor inshore of a loop of small uninhabited cayes and mangrove patches.

Trent put Estoban ashore on a caye at dawn and sailed into the township of Dangriga to clear out of Belize. He had Estoban back on board by mid-afternoon. *Golden Girl* made 14 knots under genoa and main and they passed a mile inshore of the light on the south tip of Glovers Reef. The seas darkened and grew in length and height with foam flecking their crests and the wind backed from north-east by east to north-east. A further hour and Trent changed course to pass Hunting Caye light which marked the end of Belize waters.

With daylight fading, he brought *Golden Girl* up into the wind and exchanged the genoa for a jib. Despite the shortened sail their speed seemed to increase with darkness. Coral extended south beyond Hunting Caye light and Trent allowed ample room before coming onto a course of 245°, which brought *Golden Girl* past the Cape of Three Points at the entrance to the bahía de Amatique. A lighted buoy ahead marked Ox Tongue shoal. The lights of the small port of Lívingston showed eight miles beyond the shoal on the north bank of the Rio Dulce; two further buoys marked the channel into Guatemala's major port of Barrios tucked into the southeast corner of the bay.

Trent shortened sail, timing his arrival off the mouth of the Rio Dulce for an hour before dawn. Leaving *Golden Girl* to sail herself, he called Estoban up from his cabin. They sat side by side to study the chart. The two men were awkward with each other. They had conversed at length only once on the sail from Cuba. Now Trent pointed to a short stream flowing into the bay two miles up the coast from the port of Lívingston. The stream had its source in the limestone hills abutting the coast and the purity of the waters in its upper reaches were renowned.

Trent sketched the footpath that ran from the stream through thick jungle. The path forked half a mile from Lívingston, the major path leading into town while the lesser circled round behind the hill on which the town stood and down to an old pier a mile upriver.

'You know the country well,' Estoban said.

'I did a job here.' Trent ducked out to the cockpit to check their course and for other ships before dropping down to the galley.

Estoban watched him fill the kettle and light the stove.

'You killed a man?'

'That was my job,' Trent said. He measured instant coffee into two mugs.

'One of my men?'

'No, not one of yours.' Trent filled the mugs and brought them to the table. The tracery of minute surgical scars on his fingertips was very obvious against the white porcelain –

351

mementoes of another rescue in which he had been employed as a weapon. He said, 'We don't have to like each other, Estoban.'

Service to the party had trained the plump, smooth brown face in secrecy. Only the eyes were alive and even there the depth of Estoban's despair was hidden beneath his anger. Anger against Trent because he was available. Any target would have sufficed.

'Why did you come?'

'For your brother,' Trent said. Returning to the deck, he inspected the sails and rigging. Their course was 212°.

Few yachtsman would risk navigating by night the sand bar that extends across the mouth of the Río Dulce. *Golden Girl*'s saloon and navigation lights were visible from the shore as Trent tacked back and forth a mile to seaward of the town. Gradually he extended each tack to the north-west. With her lee boards raised, the catamaran drew less than three feet of water. Estoban had packed clothes in a sealed plastic bag and he wore a pair of Trent's plastic sandals. Trent held the catamaran into the wind as the Cuban dropped overboard. The two men didn't speak.

Lívingston flew the Guatemalan flag, however, the town's character was Caribbean rather than Latin American. Absent were the discipline of architecture, the sullenness of an occupied population, the weeping of sadomasochistic music. Instead the black and mulatto population projected leisure and pleasure as pre-eminent goals; even at sun up, the rhythms of Jamaica, the Dominican Republic and Cuba blared from the jumble of wooden houses that mounted the hill. Fun for a party, hell to live with.

On anchoring, Trent had raised the obligatory quarantine flag and the Guatemalan ensign and mounted the 40hp Yamaha outboard engine on the aluminium frame that swung down aft of the cockpit between the hulls. Two hours passed before a launch motored out from the town dock with a boarding party of three customs officers, three policemen, port captain and health inspector. Mestizos, none of these officials were native to the town. Their aggressiveness was typical of those who rule by fear. Ruinous to an impecunious community, their greed was merely tiresome to Trent who could afford the expected bribes.

Motoring ashore in the Zodiac, he changed US dollars for Guatemalan Quetzals at the Chinese grocery, paid the officials and bought a fresh papaya and a dozen oranges.

Raising the anchor, he motored a mile upriver to a small marina managed by a multinational coven of penniless optimists. The custom was equally penniless: backpackers taking the ferry to or from Belize. Neither management nor custom remarked Estoban as he strolled down the dock and boarded the big catamaran.

Mosquitoes had breakfasted on the Cuban as he waded up the stream and followed the path through the jungle. Trent found a bottle of camomile lotion in the medicine cupboard.

'There may be watchers on the river,' he warned. 'You should stay below.'

The river narrowed above the marina into a canyon with walls towering 300 feet. The walls were hung with great curtains of trees, creepers, bromeliads. Frangipani scented the air; kingfishers and hummingbirds darted amongst the blossoms; egrets, cormorants, pelicans and herons fished the water's edge.

The wind blew directly down river and Trent was forced to motor. He kept to the outer side of the bends with up to sixty feet of water showing on the depth sounder. The river provided the only connection between Fronteras and Lívingston. Entire families motored or paddled canoes with bare inches of freeboard. Honda outboards powered a fibreglass tourist launch. The wake of the launch almost swamped a child in a canoe no more than five feet long and too narrow to encompass the child's rump. A fisherman cast a net from a canoe shaded by the undergrowth and Trent spotted a snake swimming upriver under the opposite bank. Roofed over with jungle, tributaries flowed into the main stream from cuts in the cliffs. Sunlight pierced the shadow and caught the brilliant yellow wings of butterflies and the emerald green of king-fishers. A French-registered Tahiti ketch lay to warps against the north bank, the crew bathing in steaming water that gushed from thermal springs. The walls fell away and the catamaran emerged into a shallow lake some two miles wide by nine miles long. A fair breeze blew across the lake and Trent set main and genoa and lifted the motor.

A further ninety minutes brought *Golden Girl* to the end of the lake with five miles of river remaining before the bridge at Fronteras. At first the banks were mangrove and virgin jungle. Then came the occasional house set back from a private dock. The further upriver, the larger the houses, some with boat houses shading motor cruisers and marlin boats, lifts for speedboats and jet-skis. Difficulty in transporting materials governed the architecture and these holiday homes were constructed of wood and palm thatch. The homes and small marinas and hotels were separated one from the other by patches of jungle and mangrove and by tributaries of the main river. Yachts lay to anchor; speedboats and jet-skis inter-mingled with wooden skiffs and canoes.

The road bridge lay ahead. Trent eased *Golden Girl* west round a mangrove islet and into a dead-end creek some three hundred yards across. Half a dozen yachts rode to anchor out in the clear water. To starboard a tall black man waved from the cockpit of a Jenneau catamaran flying the stars and stripes. To port lay a wooden ketch with a sweet sheer and a modern GRP sloop.

Trent sailed the Danforth anchor hard into the bottom before coming up into the wind and dropping the sails. The cabin roof was a good vantage post and he took his time furling the main. Astern the town leaked down the south shore to a quay where a dozen or so skiffs waited for passengers. The boat handlers squatted in the shade of a mango tree, their faces sun darkened beneath smooth mats of black hair. Next came a tumbledown or never-come-up bar-restaurant on piles, a downmarket yachties' habitat, judging by the dinghies tied to the lower step. A market filled the adjoining street. The head of the creek was mostly mangrove while midway down the north shore a Japanese-style bridge connected two arms of a timber jetty parallel to the shore. A pair of cat-rigged ketches lay stern-to at the jetty together with a bigger ketch and three sloops. A small launch and an aluminium skiff were tied up at the arm of the jetty leading back from the Japanese bridge to what looked to be a bungalow-style hotel. The roofs were thatch and the reception area open to the breeze. Tall mangrove grew to one side, palm trees and an acacia on the other. An aerial flashed a red light on top of the hill behind – part of a cellular telephone network.

A gringo ponytail shot the skiff out from the Japanese bridge. A couple of young backpackers sat amidships. The ponytail gave *Golden Girl* a cursory inspection but didn't come close. Trent watched the backpackers clamber ashore at the town quay. Two Indian families slipped by in a thirty-foot tree-trunk *cayuco* powered by a Mercury; the women wore shawls, the men straw cowboy hats; shopping packed the narrow hull. An inflatable rounded the point by the road bridge and pulled in astern of a hard-chine ketch flying the Swiss flag. An Indian cast a weighted net out from the point. Trent watched him haul the net in and club a fish over the head. Special forces waited to do the same to Estoban. Trent couldn't spot the watchers.

Finished furling the mainsail into its cover, he dropped from the cabin roof and unshackled the genoa. He laid the sail out along the port deck, then rolled and lashed it with cotton thread before hoisting it back up so that the white nylon sausage lay against the stay.

The ponytail with the skiff powered back. This time he didn't even look at *Golden Girl*. Only the black man was dangerous. Keen on multihulls, he would visit. Trent knew the conversation:

'Hi. Nice boat. There's a good butcher in town. Beer and vegetables you buy at the Chinese. The food's fair at the Three Anchors (or what ever the name of the local yachties' haven).

Butane bottles you fill at the Esso station. Maria takes laundry.' Then the wait to be invited on board.

Ducking into the saloon, Trent folded and stowed the charts. The door was open into the guest cabin. The Cuban lay on his back on the double bunk. Hands clasped under his head, he pretended to be at ease.

Sound travels far over water and Trent kept his voice low. 'There is an American on a catamaran. Better that I invite him over so we know at what time he will visit.'

Estoban didn't risk looking at Trent. 'We can ask him where my brother is.'

'Right,' Trent said. He filled the coffee pot and cut bread for a sandwich. 'You wish me to telephone your man?'

'Employ that Castillano lisp, they will laugh at you.'

'They will understand me,' Trent said. He sliced ham from the cold box and spread butter and mustard on the bread. Passing the sandwich to Estoban, he said, 'It is not advisable for you to cook while I am away from the boat; both the smell and the sound of the water pump will betray you. The same is true of the bathroom.'

'And I should keep away from the windows,' Estoban said.

Trent thought the Cuban might spit on the carpet.

Estoban controlled himself. He said, 'You dial thirty-two naught, six sixty-three in Guatemala City. You ask for Doña Maria and whoever answers will say that you have the wrong number. You say that it is a message that you have for Pedro Mantua. That is the nephew of the cook, you say. You tell them the truck broke down wherever you want to meet. The days are reversed and the time is six hours ahead. Thus noon the day before yesterday is six o'clock in the morning on the day after tomorrow. For the distance you switch direction and double the mileage. Once they have the message they will replace the telephone receiver. You should continue to talk, then curse when you realise that they have cut you off. You call twice more and finally they will say that you must stop calling which means they agree to what you have told them. Take great care in deciding where you meet.'

'There is a doubt as to trust?'

'You I trust,' Estoban said.

'*Gracias.*' Blind meetings were never easy. 'Your man can travel freely?'

'My department,' Estoban began – but he wasn't part of it any more and he stopped and lay very still, all his energy taken in fighting the pain and rage back under control.

Trent searched for something that might encourage the Cuban; there wasn't anything. Through the window he watched a white inflatable skim east towards Mario's Marina. A heron stood frozen in the shallows. A flight of egrets rose off the water into the mangroves on the islet. He wanted to say to Estoban, 'Don't give up.' To do so would have been impertinent.

'The G2,' Estoban said. He spoke carefully, choosing his words with the care of a sailor navigating inside a coral reef. 'They have the only photographs taken of this man in the past fifteen years. Most of that time he has lived in the jungle. There is a doubt as to whether his mother would recognise him. The photographs are standard procedure. They guarantee that the department maintains control.'

Trent had suffered the same type of blackmail. He continued to suffer it. The past wasn't something you could run from – no matter how many changes of name and location. If a new hierarchy wanted him back, back he would go or have his photograph and alias circulated amongst his ancient enemies. His death would be an example to others who dallied with dreams of safe retirement, a country cottage, roses in the garden. Trent had owned such a cottage once: with a view over the Beaulieu river, library, more than a hundred opera recordings. He recalled the hospital in Ireland and Colonel Smith telling him that Patrick Mahoney was dead and buried, his home up for sale. Trent had always been Patrick to the colonel – Paddy was his father.

Trent said, 'This thing with your brother. We are alone. We have to look at it together. I have to know what thoughts you have in your head.'

The Cuban's small smile was as familiar to Trent as his own self-camouflage.

'My brother is in my head.'

Trent steadied himself as the wake from a passenger launch rocked *Golden Girl*.

'Go,' Estoban said.

Trent scooped his pack off the chart table. 'Lock the door.'

'I will lock the door,' Estoban said. 'I will avoid the windows. I will refrain from cooking. Should I wish to shit, I will contain myself.' He smiled then – as if he were really in control and didn't give a damn. 'There is a further matter,' he said. 'Do not tell me that you are sorry. That also I already know.'

'Right,' Trent said. First he hung fenders port and starboard, then swung down into the Zodiac. Casting off, he motored slowly over to the Jeannau cat.

The black man was fiddling with a dismantled electric pump at the cockpit table. 'Jefferson,' he said. He had a big smile and a small beard, mostly white. 'Nice boat. yeah, like an elongated Iroquois.'

'Same designer,' Trent said. 'Drop over later. Say six o'clock?'

'Six? I'd like that. For supplies there's the Chinese beyond the bridge. Fuel dock's next door. Butcher's left at the head of Market Street.'

'How about renting a car?'

'There's a Brit. Nothing new but people say they run. He's the same end of the bridge as the Chinese but the other side. Iguana Azul.'

Trent dropped the Zodiac's anchor well out from the town quay. He clamped a five kilo lead weight on a line to the anchor warp twenty feet inboard from the anchor, ran on in to the quay and made fast with a loose line. Once he was ashore the lead weight dragged the Zodiac out clear from the other boats.

He walked up past the yachties' watering hole. On main street he dodged between a bus and an overloaded Mazda truck. Reaching a cold drinks kiosk demanded a steeplechase over piles of earth and lengths of plastic water conduit laid beside a trench dug on the road edge. An awning shaded six plastic chairs in front of the kiosk. The breeze off the river curled cool round the end of the bridge and Trent sipped a cold Gallo beer in the shade.

The pollution of revving engines and hooters, of North American pop and rap and Mexican sob blaring from radios and tape decks smashed whatever tranquillity remained from the voyage. Trent had breathed sea air. Now he inhaled the stink of diesel and petrol, of sewers, and of rotting fruit and vegetables from the market.

This was Ke'K'chi country and the indigenous people were short and square, bow legs, broad faces, little or no neck. Since Trent's previous visit, tourism and television had further influenced the young women and skirts cut mid-thigh were the norm. The men remained more conservative with only a few teenagers sporting sleeveless T-shirts, long hair, tattoos and earrings. Picking a plain-clothes cop out of the crowd demanded time in which to assimilate the human patterns.

A duckling a few days old ran between his legs. The bar owner caught the bird and sat holding it on his lap. A couple of *campesinos* began loading sacks of cement over the tailgate of a Mazda pick-up across the street. Trent counted twenty people packed shoulder to shoulder at the cab end of the cargo flat. Five were squashed in the cab. The bonnet slanted up at twenty degrees.

Trent said, 'Should the driver strike a ridge in the road, the front tyres will lose traction.'

'It happens.' The barman stroked the duckling. 'From where do you come?'

'From England.'

Central America, Mexico, the US and Canada meant something to the bar owner. The rest of the world was a vague blur. He said, 'Ah, clearly,' and to the duckling, 'The road is dangerous, little one.' Then again to Trent, 'Spanish is spoken in your country?'

'By some.'

'But not as we speak here.'

'And how is it here?' Trent asked.

'As always.' The Guatemalan shrugged. '*La lucha.*' The struggle.

'Such is life,' Trent said.

The breeze dropped for a moment. San Cristóbal de los Baños was only a few miles up the lake and Trent came close to vomiting at the whiff of roasting meat that drifted from a charcoal grill.

After paying for his beer he set off to cross the bridge. Short on battery power, four rusty pick-ups and an equally ancient Beetle were parked facing downhill on the ramp. Two conscripts lounged in the guard post. Trent watched them check the inside of a Nissan Patrol. The inspection was either cursory or they were looking for something hard to hide – perhaps the size of a man.

Trent judged the spans to rise some eighty feet to the summit. Two men lent against the left-hand parapet, a third man on the right. Rayban replicas hid their eyes. In their late twenties, they were a little taller than the men in town. They wore lightweight windbreakers over white T-shirts, good jeans and trainers. Perhaps they were up here on their own because they didn't like women. Maybe they belonged to an Athletic Club.

They answered politely when Trent bade them good afternoon. He joined the two looking downstream. The water stretched away to El Golfete.

'A truly magnificent view,' Trent said. He pointed to *Golden Girl* just visible to the north. 'My boat. I am English. Trent,' he said, offering his hand to the closest of the two.

Trent thought of asking whether the Guatemalan earned his living chopping logs with his bare hands. Or queuing up to rape Estoban's brother.

Instead, he said, 'I am told that tarpon pass through the narrows. The strongest fighting fish in the world.'

Crossing to the other side of the bridge, he said '*Buenas tardes,*' to the third member of the team. West he could see the fort the Spanish had built to protect Lake Izabal from pirates and from the British privateers.

The first man had followed him. He leant against the parapet beside Trent, very relaxed, very confident. Trent scented the arrogance endemic to Third World cops; they wrote their own laws and no one argued, neither judge nor even presidents. Especially presidents – presidential survival depended on the cops' goodwill. This type of cop. The name didn't matter: Special Forces, Guardia Civil, Gendarmerie. In Guatemala, the *Kaibiles* were the jungle elite while the DIT controlled the urban areas. DIT – *Departamento de Investigaciónes Tecnico*.

The cop said, 'You speak good Spanish.'

'Ten years in Spain,' Trent said. 'From there I acquired the *theta*. In Mexico, they mock me as a lisping *maricon*.'

The questioner smiled.

'Or a little Pepe,' Trent said. 'It is painful to be insulted for one's education.'

'You sailed from Mexico?'

'Belize. The diving is stupendous. You dive, señor?'

'Sometimes,' the Guatemalan said.

'Perhaps you dive the caves, the *cenotes*?' Trent said. 'To do so is beyond my courage.' He had a knack of seeming smaller than he was, shy and hunched. He blinked in the fierce sunlight as if in memory of his fear. It was a very North American performance, showing the inner man, and an attitude which Latin Americans held in contempt.

The cop clapped him on the back. 'To remain calm is the secret.'

'So I have been informed. Perhaps I will make the attempt once more in Honduras, the Bay Islands.' Trent was incapable of hiding the self-doubt and the Guatemalan laughed and said something fast and low to his companion.

Embarrassed, Trent turned half away. 'My intention first is to attempt the catching of one of your tarpon here in the river or off the Fort San Felipe. I like to fish.'

'But not in caves.'

'No, not in caves.' Trent pointed to high thatched roofs nestling in the jungle behind a smart wooden dock and boat house shading a Bertram sports fisherman. 'A considerable house.'

'A banker,' the cop said – one of those who survived and exercised power by cop consent; the relationship between wealth and force was symbiotic. The cop had lost interest in Trent. Raising pocket binoculars, he watched a dinghy head in from a newly arrived sloop flying a blue ensign oversewn with the insignia of the Cayman Islands.

He was probably a sergeant, Trent thought. Over-confidence and contempt for civilians were the weaknesses, and not bothering to hide his interest in the waters both sides of the bridge.

Trent found the Iguana Azul travel agency in the shade of the bridge. He signed the hire contract for a one-year-old Hyundai with air conditioning that worked. The petrol station was on the main road out toward the highway that linked Puerto Barrios with Guatemala City.

Four miles short of the intersection he hit a long straight that crossed a hill. A cut some fifty yards long at the crest of the hill divided a small coffee plantation shaded by trumpet trees and a coral-shower tree stood on one side of the cut.

Trent turned right at the intersection and almost immediately left to Morales, once the capital of the United Fruit Company. The telephone exchange occupied a modern building on the right fork of the main street opposite the tin roof of the old United Fruit commissariat. Trent called the Cuban's contact number. Trent's accent was Nicaraguan, nasal and abrupt in comparison to the treble fluting common to Guatemala. The place of the accident set the meeting midway down the long straight on the road back to Fronteras. Pedro Mantua's van had hit a coral-shower tree. Trent gave the time of the breakdown as six a.m. two days back, which gave Estoban's man thirty-six hours to reach the rendezvous. On the fourth call a different voice answered, a woman. She said, 'What is this? Yesterday, an accident, you say? Yesterday? Yesterday? What nonsense. We have no Pedro Mantua in this house. You must stop calling.'

29

Trent

On boarding *Golden Girl*, Trent checked the anchor warp and the fenders before going below. Estoban lay on his bunk with the curtains closed. A slight movement of his head against the pillow indicated that the Cuban was awake.

Trent leant against the bulkhead by the door. 'I asked for a meeting the day after tomorrow – in the morning,' he said. 'Your man – from where must he travel?'

Estoban yawned to show his lack of interest. 'He has a camp in the mountains.'

Guatemala was mostly mountain.

Trent waited and finally Estoban added, with reluctance, 'The central highlands.'

'He has sufficient time for the journey?'

Estoban had made the calculation. 'Yes, sufficient.'

Except that the meeting was set for the following morning. Possibly the *guerrillero* commander was in the city rather than in his camp – or perhaps even closer to Fronteras. Trent wondered whether the Guatemalan was alone or with his men. And what urgency demanded that the meet should be set forward by twenty-four hours? 'Perhaps you would give me a name,' he suggested.

Sitting up, Estoban swung his legs off the bunk. 'Fabio.'

'*The* Fabio? The one who attacked the NAFAC finca?'

'The same.'

'He will have been notified of your situation.'

'That I am a traitor?' Estoban dropped off the bunk and smoothed the bed cover. 'Your American with the catamaran will visit shortly.'

Trent said, 'Yes.'

Estoban squeezed past Trent and into the head. He left the door open while he rinsed his face and brushed his teeth. 'The sail locker is a convenient place to hide?'

'Adequate,' Trent said.

Estoban dried his face and nodded agreement with his own thoughts. 'All those that I have directed and with whom I have co-operated in the struggle will have been notified. Warned,' he corrected, bitterness in his smile as well as in his eyes. 'So, yes, certainly Fabio will have been informed.'

Raising the wood lavatory seat, he turned his back on Trent while urinating. 'I trained him.'

'He is a friend?' Trent asked.

'Are there friends?'

Estoban finished flushing the head with the hand pump and Trent followed him to the forward cabin.

Estoban clambered onto the double bunk which occupied the full width of the hull. He wore one of Trent's tracksuits. The suit was too tight at the waist and drooped at the wrists and ankles. Opening the hatch that led forward into the sail locker, the Cuban turned on his knees to face Trent. It was a position of little dignity.

'I am attempting to help,' Trent said.

'Help?' In his anger, Estoban was contemptuous, 'It is finished, *compañero*. Even the struggle is finished. What we have now is a madness of self-deception.'

He backed into the sail locker on hands and knees, a loose-coated dog into its kennel.

'I was speaking of your brother,' Trent said.

'Not of great ideas? *Compañero*, you disappoint me,' Estoban said and slammed the locker door shut.

Trent set tumblers on a tray together with a bottle of fresh lemon juice from the icebox and a bottle of Jamaican rum. Carrying the tray up to the cockpit table, he poured lemon into one glass, uncapped the rum bottle and sat waiting at the cockpit table for the owner of the neighbouring catamaran.

In the early evening electric light bulbs glowed dimly beneath the eaves of the shacks on Market Street and at the yachties' haven. Launches and inflatables, dinghies and canoes hustled across the waters with men and women heading home from work or to bars and restaurants or merely yachtsmen visiting each other. Someone attempted Bach on a guitar at the small marina with the Japanese bridge. The tall trees on the islet aft of *Golden Girl* were frosted with snowy egrets and Trent heard a fish rise close by. Perhaps there were watchers on the water as well as on the bridge, police and special forces manning the net for Estoban who crouched in the sail locker, Estoban stripped of his faith.

And what of Estoban's man, Fabio?

The *guerrillero* had been hunted for ten years or so by Guatemala's special forces. Survival proved Fabio's cunning and that he was very careful and suspicious to the point of paranoia. Lucky, of course – though planning created its own luck. So he was a planner and certainly obsessive in his attention to detail. And patience was essential, the ability to wait and watch, silent and motionless, hour after hour after hour . . . though not for this meeting. If Fabio came, he would be nervous of betrayal and of being surrounded. Given that his men were available, he would post an advance guard. He would arrive close to the hour or even late. Expected to approach from the west, he would travel past the rendezvous point and backtrack . . . probably on foot rather than risk being trapped inside a vehicle.

Trent thought a moment more before going below to the port hull and opening the sail locker. Estoban peered out at him.

Trent said, 'I will go ashore with the American and return in the morning.'

'You wish to warn me not to use the lights?' Estoban enquired with his fake smile.

'Hang yourself if you wish, though preferably not on my boat,' Trent said.

Back on deck Trent watched the Afro-American cast off from his yacht in a small red inflatable. Trent spilt a few drops of the strongly perfumed Jamaican rum on the table and rubbed more round the edge of his glass. Finally he swilled a little rum over his tongue and spat in the river.

The Afro-American boarded and they drank in the cockpit before going below to inspect *Golden Girl*'s accommodation. Typically of catamaran sailors, they discussed their crafts' ability to tack under varying conditions, what speed they had averaged, weight distribution and methods of anchoring. Trent slurred his word slightly and mentioned that he had money waiting at Lloyds Bank in Puerto Barrios and intended catching a late bus over to sample the nightlife. He stuffed a dark-green sweat shirt and matching chino pants into a small backpack, along with a rolled-up Panama, toothpaste and brush, lavatory paper, insect repellent, his binoculars and three bottles of water.

He left his Zodiac for safekeeping at the agency from which he had rented the hire car and walked back across the bridge. Two of the same breed of cop as those with whom he had conversed earlier in the day were watching the river while two sentries manned the guard post.

Trent bought a dozen ripe pears off a fruit stall at the head of Market Street. Pears were safe while the scent of citrus was dangerously strong and Cold War myth reported a field agent betrayed to an East German frontier patrol by the crunch of his teeth on a crisp apple. Myth. Trent felt trapped in a myth of Estoban's making.

He caught the last bus to Morales and bought a ticket to the national highway connecting Puerto Barrios to Guatemala City. At the road junction a tall stand of poplars shaded a score of mud and wattle stores stocked with cigarettes, soft drinks and coconut cookies. Trent shared a wooden bench at the bus stop with an old man and two plump sisters in their mid-thirties. With the next bus to Puerto Barrios due in five minutes, Trent became obviously anxious, fidgeting and clamping his thighs together. Finally he headed up the slope behind the shacks into the trees.

The old man called after him that he would miss the bus.

'Better than wet my trousers,' Trent called back and the two sisters giggled.

Once into the trees, Trent changed into the dark green chinos and sweatshirt and he doused the rolled Panama in water, moulding it so that the brim turned down. Thus camouflaged, he slipped through the trees, circling to rejoin the road to the Río Dulce half a mile beyond the intersection. He bent a little under the weight of the backpack and he wore the straw hat tilted so that his face was in shadow. He seemed old as he shuffled along the verge, perhaps in need, and the few passers-by avoided eye contact. Ninety minutes brought him to the coral-shower tree in the cut dividing the coffee plantation.

He continued a further half mile up the straight before surrendering to an old man's exhaustion. A flat rock beneath a calabash tree served as a seat and he sat slumped against the tree trunk, hat well down yet able to watch the road. Sheep had stripped every blade of grass beneath the tree and had pulverised the earth from which the breeze stirred the odour of dry dung.

The sky was clear and the moon and stars gave sufficient light for Trent to watch the road. Fireflies, bright as the stars, flicked on and off. Scraps of conversation drifted from a hut beyond the next rise. Trucks roared by every five minutes or so, drivers speeding to their dinner at Fronteras. And a few cars passed: Mazda, Nissan, a Ford Bronco with rust eating the wings. Their lights appeared first as a single beam rounding the curve two miles back towards the intersection. Trent sheltered his eyes as the lights parted close by the rendezvous point. The engine sound grew. Then came the blast of air as the truck or car sped by leaving the stink of its exhaust. None of the vehicles slowed on the long straight and no pedestrians passed in the hour Trent waited beneath the tree.

Satisfied that he was alone, he retreated into the scrub on the opposite side of the road to the coral-shower tree. Within the coffee plantation the protective shade of the trumpet trees kept the earth soft and damp and the air was cooler and freshened by the faint perfume of new growth. Trent snaked between the coffee bushes on his belly and he paused every few metres, head cocked as he searched the night scents for a trace of sweat or tobacco and listened through the sharp insect whine and stir of the breeze through the upper branches of the trees. An owl called softly from the edge of the coffee and an animal heavier than a rat scuttled through a patch of dry leaves – possibly an iguana or even a cat.

He found an angle of the slope some fifty metres beyond the coral-shower tree from which he could watch the road. Then he waited as he had waited on the track into San Cristóbal de los Baños. From a tall tree he could have seen the mountains, though not the town which nestled in the far flank above the river that flowed into the lake. He had small faith in coincidence and he could feel the extremities of a pattern form and reform. He even sensed, at moments, a familiarity. However, the pattern dissolved before he could track the roots of his feelings – as if it had a fluid centre – or multiple centres.

Estoban was a pawn and either could or would tell him nothing other than the name of his contact, Fabio.

Fabio was the sole *guerrillero* to remain active.

Fabio had destroyed the NAFAC finca after the ceasefire had been signed.

Then came Miguelito's employment with the ballet and the kidnapping.

The appointment to the ballet and Miguelito's exit permit were sourced in Cuba. Yet the Cubans had no control over the Guatemalan special forces.

The Americans controlled Guatemala's special forces.

Miguelito was kidnapped as bait for Estoban. The Americans would be delighted to have Estoban in their hands – or better yet, in the hands of their allies so that they could protest that their own hands were clean.

The American, Trautman, helped Estoban escape from Cuba.

However, it was possible that the Cubans allowed Estoban to escape.

Or intended him to escape.

What would the Cubans have told Fabio? That Estoban was now an enemy?

Then why had Estoban supplied Fabio's contact number?

What did Estoban expect from Fabio?

And what should Trent fear from Fabio?

The questions formed and reformed until a faint lightening of the sky to the east warned of dawn. Trent had exercised through the night by tensing and slackening his muscles and wriggling his toes and fingers. Now he drank from his water bottle silently through a straw and cut a pear into small pieces so that chewing was unnecessary.

Estoban Tur

Trent and the black American had departed in their inflatables and Estoban had crawled out of the sail locker. With Trent ashore, Estoban was unable to use the lights or the galley. Nor could he risk going on deck. Fumbling his way to the saloon, he sat at the table. He poured an inch of rum into a glass. Jamaican rum was too perfumed for his taste and he grimaced at the first sip. He had overheard the conversation between Trent and the American and he cursed Trent for having abandoned him for the whorehouses of Puerto Barrios. He concentrated all his rage and bitterness against the Englishman – hoped that he got Aids, syphilis, gonorrhoea, herpes. Whatever entered his mind, he always returned to the Englishman, blaming him. At the same time that he blamed the Englishman, Estoban knew that he was lying to himself. He had been lying to himself for months.

He understood much of what had happened. The attack on Finca Patricia was a warning to which he had shut his eyes. Guatemala was part of his fief. He had trained Fabio and financed and armed his guerrilla group. Authority to bypass Estoban could only come from Fidel's private office.

Nor had he investigated Miguelito's appointment to the ballet.

There was worse for Estoban to contemplate as he sat there at the saloon table: that in refusing to confront his suspicions he had been exacting vengeance on Maria and Miguelito for their lack of respect.

This suspicion of his motives had grown in Estoban during the voyage. To save his brother would have demanded that he confront and share his suspicions with both Miguelito and Maria and thus admit the quality of the master he served. Then, without faith, he would have become one more of those whom he had judged contemptible, time servers thieving from their departments, demanding bribes and making deals of self-interest with their fellow officials that promoted a similar discrepancy of privilege to that which existed between winners and losers in the capitalist society against which he had directed the struggle. He imagined all those dead by his direction rising from their graves to condemn his hypocrisy. So many dead. The politics of fear had demanded savagery.

Savagery . . .

His glass was empty and he refilled it for a third or fourth time. He had always been abstemious and had never understood his Russian instructors' servitude to vodka. Perhaps they also had suffered from lack of faith. An entire nation – as did Cuba.

No wonder Maria and Miguelito had mocked him.

Miguelito was very close. Estoban could feel him. Feel his pain and his fear and his despair. Most of all his despair.

He saw Miguelito race home from school, felt him in his arms, saw the trust and joy in the child's eyes as he offered to Estoban a child's fresh discovery, a drawing or something he had written and, later, victory on the track. All the memories were of childhood. Now, too late, Estoban accepted Miguelito as a man. He held himself very still at the table and watched Miguelito in the dancer's arms. And he faced Miguelito bent across the desk with the soldier in him and the other soldiers waiting in line. Their eyes met and Estoban didn't look away.

He felt the tears on his cheeks as he fumbled for the bottle. He whispered, 'Forgive me, I have sacrificed you to an unworthy god.'

Later, much later, he opened the trap in the saloon floor and lowered an empty bottle on a line into the water. He drank two tumblers of river water. Soon after dawn he inspected the medicine locker. He knew what he had to do. The Englishman would understand. Estoban had never believed in Trent's desire to sample the nightlife of Puerto Barrios. He had reported requesting Fabio for a meet in two days' time; he had avoided giving Fabio's reply. Now he had gone to meet Fabio.

Bergman

A fresh dawn and the woman, Manuela, crouched between Bergman's legs. He awoke to her lips. When he was finished, she knelt beside the bed, humble in her prayers to the Virgin. Later she would prepare herself for town. First she must work. The lavatory flushed and a tap ran; her sandals slapped the concrete stairs; in exercise of her authority, her tone was harsh. Soon the scent of coffee and freshly crushed garlic rose from the kitchen.

Such competence touched Bergman – his own mother had fluttered always on the edge of panic. More, he was touched that the woman should pay homage to the Virgin Mary for his presence.

Alone in the big bed he made his own prayers. *Thank you, Lord, for this time of peace you have vouchsafed your servant. Undeserving servant,* he corrected and listed the paucity of his worth: financial security and that he didn't beat her and perhaps most of all that he could be relied upon to be an infrequent and undemanding visitor.

Peace.

The woman had unpacked his bag. All his clothes had been

washed and ironed and were neatly folded within a white cloth on the dresser. Rubber thongs were arranged beside the bed. A fresh towel hung in the bathroom. He showered and, mindful of his role, shaved meticulously. Breakfast was ready laid at the table by the kitchen servery. Bergman's table, the table that offered maximum control of the environment.

The woman's husband had sat here convenient to the kitchen and with every table in the restaurant under his eye and the car wash in view immediately to the left down the slope.

The children watched Bergman from the shade of the trees where they crouched together, nervous as wild kittens. No response greeted Bergman's smile. He wondered whether he should go to them. Say something. Or leave them to develop this new relationship at their own pace.

The plumper of the two waitresses brought Bergman's freshly polished shoes and clean socks. For Bergman's convenience she had turned the feet of the socks inside out. The second waitress set a tortilla on the table. The woman brought coffee in a jug and stood beside him, her free hand resting on his shoulder as she filled his cup. A truck driver entered the restaurant and nodded respectfully to the new master.

Ironic, Bergman thought, that he had stopped here first because the track behind the car wash offered an escape back to the road. Now he was about to drive the children and their mother to an interview with the headmaster at the school in Morales financed by the banana corporations.

Trent

He swallowed the last of the pear. The first truck in more than an hour passed. Next came two laden pick-ups headed for the market in Puerto Barrios and the Pullman coach from Fronteras to Guatemala City. The sun struck long shadows angled across the tarmac and Trent watched a boy in shorts and shirt pedal down the road with a school satchel strapped to his bicycle. Then came an open truck from the Department of Public Works with a dozen men riding in the back. The truck halted at the far end of the straight to Trent's right and he watched, through his binoculars, half the men drop over the tailgate. The men carried shovels and machetes and one of them pushed a wheelbarrow. The truck reversed off the road, turned back towards Trent and dropped the remaining men with a second wheelbarrow half a mile to his left. Both parties sat for a while in the sun. Finally each party split into two groups, one each side of the highway and Trent watched the men chop the undergrowth back from the road edge. Every few minutes one or other of the men was forced by a weak bladder or by dysentery to seek privacy in the trees.

The party working from the right were first to reach the coffee plantation. The man pushing the wheelbarrow had collected fresh grass to feed a goat or a hutch of rabbits and he pushed the barrow into the shade of the coral-shower tree to keep the grass fresh. The men joked together, perhaps a little self-conscious as they squatted beside the barrow. One of the men, an Indian, scrambled up the bank below Trent. Much of the time he was out of sight as he sniffed and circled the edge of the plantation searching for signs in the dew. The dew had settled since Trent's arrival and Trent smiled to himself as the Indian returned to the road and repeated his search of the opposite slope.

Satisfied, the Indian rejoined his companions. The one with the wheelbarrow slid two Kalashnikovs and a double-barrelled shotgun from under the grass. The barrels of the shotgun had been cut short.

The Indian arranged the shotgun inside his right trouser leg so that it lay against his thigh. He sat with his back to the coral-shower tree and with his leg bent and his hand in his pocket so that he could blast anyone who approached. A thin, older mestizo took one of the Kalashnikovs and crawled halfway up the slope below Trent. A second mestizo found a vantage post amongst the coffee bushes on the opposite hill. The remaining three walked back along the highway with the wheelbarrow and halted four hundred yards away at the entry to the cut. Meanwhile the group to Trent's left had found shade beneath a broad-leafed *achote* at their end of the cut.

The meeting was at noon. A further half an hour passed before an old Ford bus on the Fronteras–Morales run panted through the defile and let a passenger out at the far end of the straight. The passenger waited for the bus to disappear round the next curve before turning and beginning the walk back. A small man, he walked slowly and limped on his left leg and he had a nervous habit of touching his left hand to his throat as if adjusting a tie or his Adam's apple. The sun glinted on his spectacles and he wore the cheap brown trousers and long-sleeved shirt of a clerk or minor employee in the telephone company or in a bank.

He plodded in silence past the men at the beginning of the cut. Nodding to the Indian, he climbed the slope to sit in the shade behind the coral-shower tree.

Fabio . . .

Trent studied his face through binoculars. The sunken eyes and deep lines were marks of ill health and tension and fear. To collect his men from their camp and make the move from the Central Highlands to the Province of Izabal would have required two to three days. So they had already made the move. They were here to kill Estoban before he could fall into the hands of the Guatemalan military and the CIA.

What had the Cubans offered? Normality? A new persona supported by some illusionary safety in which Fabio could believe? A house on a Cuban beach away from the tourist resorts so that he would have no fear of being recognised? Even a woman he could love?

The minutes passed slowly, a quarter of an hour, half an hour. The Indian beneath the coral-shower tree appeared to have fallen asleep. Finally Fabio rose and crossed the highway to hail a bus heading back to Fronteras. The truck from the Department of Public Works came twenty minutes later and the two groups of men each end of the cut loaded their wheelbarrows and clambered over the tailgate. The truck drove off the way it had come. The Indian awoke and limped on his stiff leg along the road. He was within Trent's sight when the truck returned to pick him up. Trent had to wait a further half an hour before the truck made a final visit to collect the two mestizos armed with Kalashnikovs.

Bergman

The headmaster was a small man with a tight paunch, thinning hair and sad eyes. He had been educated at an Adventist school funded from the US and was a man of letters deserving of greater recognition than the headship of the Corporation school. A rumpled linen suit, a shirt with the top button missing and a red bow tie thirty degrees off the horizontal gave him the appearance of a town drunk.

He had presumed the woman to be Bergman's whore. Nervous that she should think him judgmental, he was over-effusive.

Manuela thought him flirtatious and was insulted.

The children were bewildered.

The younger squeezed himself between Bergman's legs.

'La señora is a widow,' Bergman said. 'Her husband was a man of much courage. The war . . . '

'The war, yes, the war,' the headmaster murmured. Contrite, he nodded solemn acknowledgement of tragedy and chose carefully for the children two chemically coloured boiled sweets from a glass jar on the bookcase behind his desk.

So they progressed from sympathy to business.

'We wish to pay in advance for one year and there is a trust fund,' Bergman said. The 'We' was redolent of government.

Matters that were official yet not official were familiar to the headmaster – such was the way of Guatemala.

Bergman paid in cash and the headmaster summoned an elderly bookkeeper to prepare a receipt that included such extras as music and the midday meal. They shook hands with much formality, the headmaster patting the children on their heads and holding the war widow's hand between both of his as he murmured further condolence.

Bergman's duty was done. The woman frowned at him as he removed his tie out on the pavement. 'Yeah, I'm a slob. And don't spoil the kids,' he said in English and in Spanish, '*Vamonos*. Who can direct us to the ice-cream parlour.'

Trent

The Afro-American owner of the catamaran sat on the tube of his small red inflatable. His feet were in the water and he held a palette loaded with filler in one hand and a palette knife in the other; he was looking sideways along the side of the catamaran's hull in search of a shadow where he had repaired a gouge in the paintwork. He glanced up at hearing Trent's outboard and beckoned with the palette knife.

Trent cut the engine and the Zodiac drifted in alongside the cat.

The American waved the knife at the hull. 'How does it look?'

'Good,' Trent said.

The American nodded to himself. 'That's what I thought. Your crew went ashore. Black man?' he suggested in reply to the surprise Trent hadn't shown. 'Late thirties? Paler than me and more hair.'

'Right,' Trent said.

'Maybe half an hour. Got himself a lift to shore with the skipper of the French sailboat that just left. Skipper dropped him at the end of Market Street.'

'Shopping,' Trent said.

'Shopping,' the American agreed. He twisted round to lay the palette and the palette knife on the inflatable's floorboards. Then he scratched the back of his head and looked up at the apex of the bridge where Trent had spoken with the Guatemalan special forces team. 'There's been some activity the past few days. I noticed, that's all.'

'Thanks,' Trent said. He pressed the starter button and motored over to the dock at the yachtie hippie haven to the left of Market Street. Rock blared from twin speakers above the bar, a pair of unbathed long-hairs were discussing the meaning of life, the menu advertised fresh fish and the sewage emptied into the lake below the dock. Trent blew his nose as he hurried up through the grassed parking lot to Main Street where he turned right away from the bridge and slowed to a disinterested stroll. He spotted the Guatemalan heavies first, the threesome he had met the previous day. One of them leant against the counter at the cigarette kiosk on the lake side of the road. A second licked a chocolate ice cream further north while the sergeant and a new member of the team ambled towards Trent, one each side of the street, beaters at a bird shoot. The guns would be waiting at the foot of the bridge. Trent didn't bother looking.

Crossing the road, Trent greeted the heavy at the cigarette kiosk and bought a box of matches and a pack of Marlboro Light. Breaking open the wrapping, he offered the pack to the heavy. Estoban sat at a café table a hundred yards up the road. The distance was too great for Trent to read the Cuban's expression, however, his body language suggested boredom.

Trent watched the sergeant flag his companion to a halt a few yards short of the café. The sergeant crossed the road and used his foot to drag a chair back from the table to Estoban's rear.

Trent flicked a match to his companion's cigarette. The heavy inhaled and blew smoke through his nostrils. An optimist might have divined gratitude in the nod he gave Trent as he pushed himself upright off the tobacconist's counter. Trent watched him stroll down the street and take up position in the shadows of a clothing store half a block short of the café.

The officer came next. A current of unease on the street signalled his progress through the farmers and walnut-faced peasant women laden with shopping baskets. The officer walked bow-legged. Trent was reminded of a movie gunfighter

– the same pleasure at arousing fear was present – and the neatness: olive green Lacoste sports shirt, Ralph Lauren chinos, burnished leather boat shoes; for jewellery, a gold crucifix on a gold neck chain and the obligatory Rolex Oyster.

The officer sat opposite Estoban at the same table, no pretence. He said a couple of words. The Cuban's reply was equally brief. The officer raised a hand and a driver started an army truck on the down slope of the bridge. Trent crossed in front of the truck and sat at the same bar that he had frequented the previous day. The ducklings were pecking corn off the swept dirt.

The last of five dilapidated coaches parked at the kerb pulled out and blocked the army truck. The two drivers cursed each other while a horse pulled a cart out of an alley and blocked the coach driver's retreat. Two trucks and a pick-up backed up behind the cart while a tractor and trailer bounced down the bridge. Meanwhile a cement truck had begun unloading sacks at the Agricultural Co-operative beyond the café where Estoban sat. It was so obvious an ambush situation and the officer would have made a fine hostage against Estoban's half-brother. Trent found himself waiting for the first burst of automatic fire. Except that no one wanted Estoban rescued. They wanted him dead.

One of the policemen at the guard post at the foot of the bridge halted the tractor driver and enabled the army driver to reverse. The coach and the two trucks and the pick-up drove by and the army driver advanced again all the way to the café where Estoban and the officer waited at the kerb. Estoban buckled suddenly, forearms supporting his gut. The sun lit his face and showed his pain.

The sergeant gave Estoban a leg-up over the truck's tailgate and Trent saw a brown stain on the seat of the Cuban's pants. The sergeant and the three heavies followed Estoban in under the canvas top. The officer climbed into the front seat beside the driver. Two horsemen spurred their mounts away from the bank opposite the Agricultural Co-op and blocked Trent's view.

Trent scooped a duckling onto his lap and stroked its head. A motorcycle had halted to his right, a Yamaha 250 trail bike with a passenger seated on a folded towel on top of a chrome luggage rack. Both rider and pillion passenger wore crash helmets. The pillion passenger carried a parcel on his lap the size of a cigar box and wrapped in green and gold paper with a pink ribbon. A birthday gift, Trent thought. The driver revved as if waiting at a traffic light and the two-stroke motor barked. The passenger raised a hand to his throat and fingered his Adam's apple. Trent set the duckling down.

An Indian woman with a baby strapped to her back stepped off the kerb by the cigarette kiosk and the army driver eased round the cement truck. Two women screamed at each other on the corner of Market Street. The Yamaha barked again and Trent turned and called for a fresh beer. He thought that Estoban was sick and Trent was certainly sick. His stomach knotted. He wanted to be somewhere else or be someone else. Above all else he wanted once, just once, to be allowed to live his own life, make his own choices. And he was ashamed of himself. *It isn't fair* was a child's complaint. Fear was a child's illness. A girl, maybe eight years old, sprinted after the Indian woman carrying the baby. Arm in arm, two elderly yachtsmen lurched out of a bar and one of the horsemen shook his fist as the driver of the army truck blasted his horn.

The motorcycle driver let out the clutch and Trent fell sideways. He grabbed at the chair as he fell. The force of his fall swung the chair into the road. The chair legs caught in the spokes of the Yamaha. The driver tipped to his right and the pillion rider was flung into the path of the army truck. Trent dived for the parcel before grabbing the pillion rider under the shoulders. Heaving him to his feet, Trent whispered in English, 'Tough shit, Fabio. One word from me and the army will have you.'

30

Estoban Tur

Estoban had drunk two tumblers of river water and had swallowed ten laxative tablets and six anti-seasickness pills before coming ashore from the catamaran. The seasickness pills drifted him on soft waves and he smiled at his captors who sat on the truck tailgate. They were tough and wore the trainers and jeans, T-shirts and windbreakers admired by such men. Estoban disgusted them. He had soiled himself while waiting to be arrested in the café. Now he did so again as the truck driver slammed his foot on the brake.

The truck jerked forward and Estoban saw a rider heave his fallen motorcycle upright; Trent gripped the pillion passenger as if they were friends. Estoban chuckled with self-admiration. The game had a long way to run.

Trent

He saw Estoban in the army truck. The Cuban hung slackly from the pipes supporting the canopy. He looked drunk or ill. Their eyes met for a moment and the Cuban smiled. Then he let go of the frame and collapsed out of Trent's view. Trent recognised other soldiers in the street. The motorcyclist mounted the Yamaha. He was a minion and uncertainty held him as he looked towards Fabio.

Trent held the *guerrillero* close.

'I shout and the military have you,' Trent warned. 'Walk with me to the bar, there where you see the ducklings.'

They must have appeared friends to the motorcyclist who rode away and vanished beyond the cement truck.

The bar was thirty metres from the guard post at the foot of the bridge. Trent faced Fabio across a plastic-topped table. Fabio had taken off his helmet. The mists and rain of the mountains had left him pale and he was sweating, perhaps with a recurrent fever. He blinked every few seconds and he looked one moment down the road, then toward the bridge and at the bus stop. Nor were his hands still. He touched his throat, felt the edge of the table, picked at a scab on his arm, shifted a tin ashtray back and forth.

To calm him, Trent said, 'I am not a threat to you. We share common interests.' He placed Fabio's parcel on the table, beckoned the bar owner and ordered chilled Gallo lagers.

Fabio gulped thirstily and fumbled for a cigarette in a battered pack he took from the breast pocket of his shirt. His hand shook as he struck a match and the match head flew off.

Trent looked away as the Guatemalan made a second attempt. The Indian who had sat under the coral-shower tree squatted at the end of the block beside an old woman selling onions from an open basket. One of the mestizos paid for a cold drink at the tobacco kiosk and Trent recognised two more of Fabio's men propped against a hut wall by the bus stop. Others he was unable to recognise, men with knives who ambled aimlessly through the crowd, each change in direction bringing them closer to the table. The attack would be sudden – perhaps camouflaged by a street fight or a road accident or the chasing of a small boy seen stealing from a market stall. Already the motorcyclist would have received instructions from Fabio's second in command to whisk the leader to safety. Trent needed to urinate and he wanted to leave, now. He heard a fourth match strike and Fabio sigh with satisfaction. Smoke drifted across the table.

Trent returned his attention to the *guerrillero*. 'It was I who brought the Cuban here. Where will they take him?'

Fabio shrugged. 'This is not my area.'

'There are those who watch.'

'True, but they are not my eyes,' Fabio said. 'If you are of us . . .' he spoke of the profession of violence: '*If you are of us*, you will understand. This signing of the peace has destroyed what trust existed between *compañeros*.'

Trent divined neither sadness nor regret. Such were the facts; the conclusion. No matter the outcome, that it was finished was enough: the years of fear and pain and ill-health, of hunger, dirt and of permanent exhaustion.

Trent handed him the photograph of Miguelito. 'The brother. I wish to save him.'

Fabio had ordered and witnessed worse. Now he saw only the meaning of the photograph. He turned it between nervous fingers. His nails were bitten short and a cracked cuticle leaked pale yellow fluid. He watched two plain-clothes military from the bridge stroll by and duck into the shade of a café. A puff of breeze blew cigarette smoke in his eyes and he squinted at Trent through the smoke:

'There is a gringo who will know. The head of the CIA in Guatemala. He has been waiting here close to the Río for some days.'

'Bergman?'

'The same. He has a whore, the owner of a car wash and restaurant. He sleeps there now.' Fabio pretended boredom. 'Perhaps he wishes us to know. So it seems.'

'Bait.'

'Why else would he stay with a whore?' Head tilted, Fabio looked sideways at Trent, his smile almost sheepish as he touched his throat. 'You understand, to extract information from this man would give great pleasure, as would his death.' He spun the photograph, balancing it on a corner only to release it on the last turn so that it fell face down. 'Until now, he has been too careful.'

Such was the deal, the exchange: Bergman for Tur's brother.

'Tonight,' Fabio said. 'Meet me at the coral-shower tree.' He flicked the photograph face up and slid it back across the table as if he were a dealer at blackjack – a crooked dealer. 'He may have killed the brother.'

'The young one is necessary to make the elder talk.' Trent tapped the photograph 'Also there is sadism here. The man who commands will relish the brothers as witnesses to each other's degradation.'

Estoban Tur

Already dysentery had drained his strength. They had travelled by truck and in an open launch and by jeep. Now they were inside a building. Two soldiers supported Estoban – big men dressed in camouflage. They took their hands from him and he fell. The floor was old tile, cool in the deep shade. By the doorway the officer stood outlined against the sun. This was the officer who had sat next to Estoban in the café and had accepted his surrender. He was a small man, very clean and neat in his dress. Estoban knew that he had ordered the rape.

Soon the officer would command his men to fetch Miguelito. The officer would find pleasure in the brothers weeping at each other's pain. Perhaps the gringo would be present. Estoban was sure of the gringo as he was sure of the officer. There would be pleasure in witnessing the gringo's shame, perhaps Estoban's final pleasure. Only by remaining ill could he extend his life and keep Miguelito alive. He must be too ill to be aware of his surroundings and give pleasure to the officer. That was the key and he licked thirstily at the floor for fresh germs.

The officer snapped an order and one of the soldiers booted Estoban onto his back. The beams supporting the ceiling were of carved wood. A child whimpered in the doorway. Estoban groaned as a fresh convulsion within his stomach spurted gas and liquid down his legs.

Bergman

He had thought through every possible scenario, even that whatever boat the Cuban was on had sunk somewhere out in the Caribbean sea or had smashed on a reef. He had been waiting now for three days. That morning he had arranged schooling for the children; he had watched the midday custom at the car wash restaurant and had strolled up behind the car wash through the woods to scout the terrain. The children had followed at a distance as do stray dogs seeking a master. Now Bergman lay reading upstairs in the double bed.

Waiting had been a major occupation over the past years; waiting for reports of casualties or of the success of an attack or of an ambush; and, of course, waiting for faked results of Guatemala's presidential elections or news of the success of the latest coup d'état. Bergman was used to waiting and he was used to his own company. Mostly he read – by preference, history and biography and late nineteenth-century fiction. His present book was a fresh study of the Spanish conquest of Mexico written by Hugh Thomas.

He had left the shutters part open so that a shaft of sunlight slashed across the room and hit the pillow. His digital telephone shared the bedside table with his Beretta, *The Quiet American* and a leather-bound edition of *Don Quijote*. The *Don* was a high-school graduation award for Spanish studies and had been Bergman's travelling companion for thirty years.

Sandals slapped the concrete stairs and a knock came at the door and he called the woman to enter – Manuela. Bergman was embarrassed that she should knock on the door of her own bedroom.

Bergman watched her fidget about the room. She picked his shorts off the floor, straightened his shoes beside the bed, rubbed a finger over the furniture in search of dust.

'Tell me,' he said.

Nervous, she searched for the words. 'It is wrong of you to be here. Wrong *for you*,' she added quickly. 'For your safety. In the times before there was only once that you slept here for the entirety of a night.'

He remained silent, pretending to read.

She picked up *Don Quijote* and examined the rich binding before opening the cover. 'Jack Bergman,' she read. 'It is an award?'

'From school.'

'Perhaps the children will gain awards.' The dream held for a while. Then a truck drew into the car wash. She was waiting for a truck or a pick-up or a jeep – a vehicle with men in it come to destroy this temporary good fortune.

She stood sideways to the window, looking down through the part opened shutters. 'Why me?' she asked.

Bergman was unclear as to whether she asked why such things should happen to her or why he had selected her as a companion.

The truck and its occupants were innocent and she turned to face him. She dragged her dress over her head, stepped out of her briefs and dropped her brassiere. She stood within the slanting sunlight so that he was forced to see her.

'I am not so beautiful and I am not so young. Nor do you love me. I was convenient,' she said quietly. 'We are adult people, we can say such things. So tell me, why are you here when to be here is dangerous for you?'

He said, 'Forgive me.'

'For not loving?' She crossed to the bed and took his hand and held it to her belly. 'Feel,' she said and drew his fingers across the ladder of stretched muscles. 'You believe that you are evil in not loving me. For me love from a man has no importance. My children are important and that you help us and are kind to us. Kind to me.'

She spread a sheet on the dresser, opened the bottom drawer and laid her dead husband's clothes on the sheet. On the top of the clothes she curled a heavy leather belt. Then she folded the sheet and set the bundle outside the door on the top stair.

'Do you understand?'

'Yes,' he said.

'You should believe that you attempt to be a good man.' She sat on the bed with her back to him. Her weight thrust the extra fat in her buttocks outward to form a shelf on which he could have laid small offerings: a silver coin, a thimble filled with cane alcohol, the stub end of cigar – such were the traditional gifts to those amalgams of Spanish saints and African gods prayed to in Cuba and Hispaniola.

Bergman reached up to stroke her cheek.

She gripped his wrist, cupping her face against his hand.

A single tear swelled slowly on the tip of his index finger where it touched the corner of her eye.

'To attempt to be good,' she said, 'in this shit of a life that is the best that anyone of us can do.'

The telephone interrupted her and saved Bergman.

'We have him,' the major reported.

Bergman looked at the woman and she went through to the bathroom so that he would be alone with his secrets.

'How is he?' Bergman asked.

'Sick. Dysentery. He surrendered to us.'

'How does he look?'

'Like shit,' the major said and laughed. 'A doctor will be here shortly. I will call you.'

'Good,' Bergman said.

Good . . . he looked into the bar of sunlight and followed it to the window. He saw clearly in the sunlight. A part of him had hoped for circumstances that would obviate his need to confront Tur and face the Cuban's contempt, that Tur would somehow escape capture – even that Little Brother would escape . . . or die. Or for the Cubans or their henchmen to find Tur first, find and kill him. Such was the convenient end to the operation. Bergman could satisfy both Vorst and Washington with the limited success of the operation while expurgating his own conscience of direct responsibility.

The door to the bathroom was thin plywood and he listened to the woman humming in camouflage of her ablutions. She flushed the lavatory twice – Jack Bergman down the drain; Jack to his parents, Jackito to his Latino friends at grade school.

Bergman had been his own decision. Now finally he had turned himself into a lump of shit.

Manuela opened the bathroom door and stood watching him, waiting. . . to know his desires. The paymaster's desires.

He knew nothing of her family or friends.

He said, 'It is necessary that you close the restaurant and take the children.' He was about to give her his billfold; to do so would have been melodramatic and might have frightened her.

She sat on the bed with her hands in her lap while he counted the equivalent of one hundred dollars in Quetzals.

He wrapped her fingers round the bills.

'Is it bad?' she asked.

'Complicated,' he said.

He reached for the digital phone and dialled the major.

Trent

Sunset on the Río Dulce and snowy egrets back-paddled in to roost in the clump of tall mangrove cloaking the islet at the mouth of the creek. A launch had trailed its wake across the creek and the rippled surface of the river was emblazoned with serpent stripes of shadow and crimson gold. Trent brought his Zodiac alongside and boarded *Golden Girl*. The clatter of the town reached to him across the water yet the creek was at peace and he tiptoed across the cockpit. Estoban had left the saloon unlocked. The hatch in the saloon floor was open to the river. Estoban had spread a tea towel on the saloon table. A tumbler and a bottle with a cord tied round its neck were arranged on the tea cloth together with two bottles from the medicine cabinet: Stugeron for seasickness and Dulcolax for constipation. The bottle was a third full with river water. A quarter of a centimetre of sediment had settled and a half centimetre of scum floated on the surface. The water between was a yellowish green.

Trent thought that a teaspoon would have been enough for

Estoban's purpose. A tumbler was a frightening overdose. Add the pills and Trent was surprised that Estoban had reached the shore. The scenario was sound and imaginative; the Cuban must have been pleased with himself.

Trent replaced the pill bottles in the medicine cabinet beside the chart table. The chart remained open and he studied it awhile before drawing in a course for Honduras. Next he checked the monthly guide to wind and current patterns of the globe. New Zealand was missing from the terrorist map and ocean voyagers wrote of the beauty and perfect climate found in the Bay of Islands. December offered the least bad weather patterns for the Magellan Straits. Head north in the Pacific until he picked up the trades; first landfall at the Galápagos. He washed the jug and tumbler and his coffee cup in the galley and closed the hatch cover in the saloon floor.

Having taken a shower, he towelled himself in his cabin. The fear was thick as phlegm in his throat, the fear of not doing as much as the fear of doing. He had always been frightened.

He sat to pull on black socks and black sneakers and he wore loose black cotton trousers tied at the ankle. He carried a matching smock and a loose lightweight black raincoat up to the saloon.

The forward section of the settee slid free as did the forward panelling. The bulkhead was hollow. A section lifted and Trent withdrew a flat waterproof aluminium box. The box contained four packs of twelve-gauge shells and a pair of pump-action shotguns with pistol grip stocks and the barrels sawn off the same length as the magazines. He fetched a role of masking tape from the paint locker and strapped the guns down his back. He set his hair in spikes with gel, clipped a single diamond to his right earlobe and loaded a shoulder pouch with ammunition. The loose smock and raincoat disguised the guns and a black silk scarf part-covered his coral beads and hid the small pouch at the nape of his neck. Checking the mirror, he saw a man who believed that he looked good in black rather than a man who wore black so that he wouldn't be seen.

He tied the Zodiac at the Iguana Azul dock below the bridge

and collected the hire car from the parking lot. The guns were cold and the barrels dug into his shoulders. The drive to the coral-shower tree took twenty minutes: operating solo, he was unable to protect himself. He pulled into the verge midway to the rendezvous and vomited coffee into the long grass. Wiping his mouth on a leaf, he leant against the car, arms folded on the roof. Away to his left mountains rose above the lake and San Cristóbal de los Baños – Bergman – Bergman's barbecue. For a moment the stench of roasting meat filled his nostrils and he turned quickly away from the car and vomited the last dregs of the coffee. He hadn't eaten since the previous evening and there was nothing else in his stomach. Bullfighters fasted before a fight. Fasting lessened the risk of infection from a stomach wound.

He drove with the windows down to keep the air fresh. He slowed on the approach to the coffee plantation. Three men sat under the coral-shower tree. Fabio, a second Ladrino and a mestizo. The mestizo fetched an old sack from the scrub and sat up front beside Trent with the sack between his legs and Fabio and the Indian in the back.

Fabio said, '*Adelante, compañero.*'

'In your backside,' Trent said and the mestizo chuckled.

He slid Kalashnikovs from a binliner inside the sack and passed them back between the seats. Trent glanced in the rear-view mirror. Both Fabio and the Indian were out of sight on the floor or lying on the seat.

'You turn right at the highway,' the mestizo said. 'Then left on the road to Morales.'

A while later the mestizo pointed to a dirt turn-off into a field.

Trent switched off the headlights and coasted to a halt in the shelter of a thick hedge. One of Fabio's men shut the three bar gate to the field. Fabio spoke with him in whispers while the Indian and the mestizo led Trent aside and squatted at an angle that enabled them to shoot him without risk to each other.

Cows had grazed the field and had left the odour of fresh

dung. Fireflies flashed patterns; crickets called as did frogs from a nearby ditch. As much as five minutes passed before Fabio beckoned Trent over to the gate. The *guerrillero* commander pointed up the road to the darkness of a wooded hill. 'You will find a track through the wood that leads to the rear of the car wash. In normal circumstances the restaurant closes after midnight. One o'clock, two o'clock. The hour depends on the custom. Now it is already closed. We believe that the gringo is there, upstairs.'

'Bergman?'

'Yes, Bergman,' Fabio said.

'Alone upstairs?'

'Without protection.'

'So you are informed. Is it a report that you believe?' Trent asked. A single mosquito whined along the hedge and he turned to follow its flight.

'My informants have approached as close as they dare,' Fabio said.

Trent looked away from the hedge and up at the stars. The night was too clear for his liking. 'It is a trap.'

Fabio shifted uncomfortably and touched his throat. 'So one must suspect.'

'Into which you wish me to enter.'

'My men will cover you from the woods.'

Trent glanced at the Indian and the *mestizo*. 'There are more?'

'These three and three already watching,' Fabio said.

Trent had counted fourteen at the rendezvous: five in each of the fake work parties, the two mestizos with Kalashnikovs, the Indian under the coral-shower tree and the truck driver. Add Fabio for fifteen and the signs suggested a trap within a trap within a trap

'You?' Trent asked.

'Also.' Fabio rose and opened the gate. 'I will walk with you until we see the building.'

'Where you will give me the weapon.'

'Where I will give you the weapon.'

'And you will aid me in freeing the boy?'

'I have promised,' Fabio said.

They walked together across the road and up the track. The darkness within the wood was thick as was the foetid scent of wet moss, fungi and bromeliads. A bird heard them and cawed irritably from a high branch – or perhaps the bird was a soldier or *guerrillero*. The track crossed over the shoulder of the hill, then came a sharp dip from the top of which they looked down on the starlit tin roof of a two-storey house built of concrete block. The walls were whitewashed and a thatched roof protruded from the front of the building towards the road. At a lower level puddles glimmered palely in the open car wash.

Fabio handed Trent a .36 snub-barrelled revolver.

Trent broke it open. 'Three bullets.'

'One should be sufficient.'

'If there is no trap,' Trent said.

A rolling pebble thundered loudly as an avalanche and Trent walked carefully, feeling the ground with his heel at each step before rocking forward onto the ball of his foot. A small gravelled parking lot had been cut out of the side of the hill to the right of the building and of the *rancho*. An outdoor concrete stairway led up the side of the house. The stairway was open to the parking lot. Fifty men could have hidden in the trees overlooking the lot. Trent would be outlined against the whitewashed wall. He hated stairs. There was no cover from fire and no hiding place. Men gunned you down from above or below, it was all the same.

Here, with the moon directly overhead, there were no angled shadows on the wall to deceive a shooter.

Thirty strides across the car lot, eighteen stairs.

Trent took off his shoes. Belly cramps forced him to halt at the building.

It was not knowing if they were watching from the trees, watching and smiling at how stupid he looked taking such pains to be silent when he might as well beat time on a Salvation Army drum.

Charging the guns was easier. He had done it before. However, he had been frightened always and always guilty – both of his fear and of not doing the right thing. Of letting people down.

He had let his father down.

And he was still holding himself together.

Not climbing the stairs would be letting go.

Eighteen stairs.

He made it to the top. Two doors opened off a square landing. Bergman, the *poderoso*, must be in the front room, wider than the rear and with a view over the road and the car wash. A yellow slither of light showed under the door. The door was thin ply in a nailed frame and the lock wasn't serious.

Putting on his shoes would waste a second. Trent held his pistol in both hands and, standing sideways, slammed the door below the handle with the flat of his right foot. The lock tore out and the door smashed back against the wall.

31

Trent

Estoban's gringo lay on a double bed beneath a garish depiction of the Virgin Mary. The American's hands were open and empty above the white sheet. He lay on his back. His head and shoulders were raised against two pillows so that he could watch the doorway over the swell of his belly. What remained of his hair was crumpled with sweat. The look in his eyes was familiar – not the final look of despair worn by Trent's father in his office but a look his father had worn on and off in the lead up to his suicide – a look fatalistic in its acceptance that there was nothing to be done.

Trent crossed to the bed. He was certain that the American was unarmed and he didn't bother dragging back the sheet. With the fear gone he took shelter in anger. He knew how it would be, shooting Bergman; each recoil of the short-barrelled revolver would pump energy back up his arm.

'Screw you,' he said. 'You have a boy gang raped so you can get your hands on his brother. Next you're down on your knees – *confiteor Deo omnipotenti* and you die in peace.'

The Latin gave Bergman life. He said, 'My wife's the Catholic.'

'Screw you,' Trent repeated. He tossed his raincoat onto a chair and dragged the smock off. Seated on the bed with his back to Bergman, he drew his knife from the neck pouch and cut the shotguns loose.

'Mahoney – the Brit's rent-a-killer,' Bergman said. 'You were the bearded longhair with the rubber dinghy.'

'Yes,' Trent said.

Trent replaced his knife in its sheath and drew the smock into place. 'There's a *guerrillero* outside with a dozen men. Fabio? The deal is you tell me where you have Tur and his brother. I kill you and Fabio helps release the brother.'

'Fabio kills Tur? Tidy,' Bergman said. 'When do I get killed?'

'Once I have the information,' Trent said.

'San Cristóbal de los Baños.' Bergman dismissed the importance of the place with a small shrug. 'The major who did it has Tur.'

'*I* did it,' Trent said. 'Fired the first shot.'

Bergman managed a smile. 'In the Cold War? Or in the European conquest of Central America? Either one is kind of arrogant as a claim, Mahoney.'

'Trent,' Trent said.

'Bullshit. Kill me, do it in your own name.' Bergman combed his hair back with his finger and rubbed his nose on his forearm – preparing himself for a death neither man was prepared to execute.

A white cloth decorated with a border of embroidered flowers covered the top of the dresser against the wall facing the foot of the bed. Bergman's clothes were neatly folded on the cloth; a 9mm Beretta lay on the clothes – an altar to the two men's profession. Crossing to the dresser, Trent checked the safety catch and tossed the pistol onto the bed. 'You have to go in first. Set up the diversion. That's what we tell Fabio.'

'Why?'

'Why what?'

'Why do you give a shit?'

Trent crossed to the window. He was glad that San Cristóbal was the place. He said, 'It's something you have to do.'

'Or what?' Bergman asked.

Trent turned to face him.

Bergman sat on the edge of the bed. A sweat-wet strand of pale hair fell over his left eye; his breasts sagged; his white T-shirt had ridden up to expose a roll of white fat – plump thighs in crumpled boxer shorts, legs very white and without hair. Singularly sexless, Trent thought: the middle-aged lover.

'Or what?' Bergman repeated.

The abyss was close and Trent shivered and looked down at the road as a truck slowed briefly; the driver noticed the lack of lights in the restaurant and accelerated away.

'Why did you do it?' Trent asked.

'Trying to save my pension.' Bergman gave a dry sniff that pretended to be a laugh. 'What's your excuse?'

'I went to a Catholic school,' Trent said. 'Catholicism demands obedience.' He slipped the two shotguns under Bergman's clothes on the dresser, crossed to the shattered door and whistled softly. Then he walked halfway down the stairs and waited with the revolver dangling from its barrel tip between thumb and forefinger of his left hand.

One of Fabio's mestizos appeared from the shadows of the *rancho*. His Kalashnikov pointed at Trent's belly. Trent placed the revolver on the steps. The mestizo beckoned. Fabio sat at the table closest to the car wash. His hands rested on the tabletop, thumbtips tapping a Russian 9mm automatic with integral silencer.

Trent sat opposite him. Through the thin black cotton of his trousers, he felt a knot in the wooden seat. The mestizo stood behind him, lolling against the kitchen wall, and the shadow of a second man thickened a wooden pillar midway down the *rancho*. A car sped by, its lights bright enough to outline the second man's gun.

Fabio said, 'So, *maricon*, the gringo lives – or did you kiss him to death? Certainly there was no shot.'

The mestizo giggled.

'We have a new deal,' Trent said.

'Speak English,' Fabio interrupted and touched a hand to his throat. The darkness was too dense for Trent to see his eyes.

'The Cubans are at San Cristóbal,' Trent said. 'The *gringo* enters first. I take you up the lake in my Zodiac – you and your men. Once the *gringo* sees me, he will create a diversion.'

'What is my interest in these Cubans?'

'Duty?' Trent suggested. 'Honour? They've supported you for many years.' He smiled, waiting.

The silence was elastic, stretching and stretching, yet always at the point of fission. The silence intensified Trent's perception. He registered, in the strobe flash of a firefly, a change in angle of the man leaning against the pillar while a faint creak of leather came from his rear as the mestizo with the Kalashnikov shifted weight. A pig snuffled in a pen above the parking lot and the stink of dung blended with the odour of wet oil and of industrial cleaning fluid which rose from the car wash and Trent distinguished the separate kitchen scents of garlic, fried fish, fried chicken and black beans. Frogs called from the ditch surrounding the car wash and way in the distance a truck horn screeched an angry tattoo. An almost imperceptible scratching of metal on wood came from the tabletop as Fabio's thumbs prodded the Russian automatic. The muzzle shifted slowly until it pointed directly at Trent's chest.

'Bang,' Fabio said quietly. He touched his throat and seemed to smile. 'Even were I to have an interest, why would the gringo assist us?'

'Perhaps he is ashamed,' Trent suggested. He knew that he must appear very calm and in control. He shrugged and said, 'Should you wish to enquire you must climb the stairs. The gringo is armed only with two shotguns and a Beretta.'

'He didn't shoot you.'

'Perhaps he hoped that I would shoot him. Killed on duty secures his pension.'

'What use is a pension to one who is dead?'

'He has a wife, a Catholic.'

'A blonde whore,' Fabio corrected. 'The gringo threw her out, she and her daughters, years ago. All Guatemala knows.'

The pig snuffled again.

Fabio prodded his automatic. The muzzle shifted from Trent's chest only to return. 'You believe in his promises?'

'Yes,' Trent said.

Fabio nodded to himself. 'The shame I can believe in. Guilt is a gringo emotion and they exaggerate the importance of their sins – such is integral to their boast to own all that is biggest and of most value.' He slipped his pistol into his waistband. 'It must be dark when we go up the lake.'

'Tomorrow night,' Trent agreed. 'The fortress beyond the bridge, *El Castillo de San Felipe.*'

Bergman

Bergman listened for a shot or scuffle that would tell him who would come up the stairs: Mahoney or Fabio. Bergman had been on Fabio's trail for fifteen years. He had bribed fellow *guerrillero* leaders, attempted to infiltrate informers, set bait, hunted him with dogs and with helicopters, placed a price on his head. Now, as he stared at the floor, he recalled the attack on Finca Patricia. He recalled dropping from the helicopter and scrambling through the mud to join the men digging at the landslip. He recalled the urgency of their digging and the fear that was in them. They hit the edge of the armoured personnel carrier. Six of them shovelled. Finally they reached the rear door. Bergman opened the door – Bergman, the gringo. Doing so was his responsibility. The door opened to release the stench of a primitive abattoir. Rather than have his men smother slowly, the sergeant had shot them and shot himself. Some of the soldiers had tried to ward off the bullets and their fingers were missing.

The soldier nearest the door of the second APC clasped a medallion of the Sacred Heart; tears had washed pale rivulets through the streaks of mud on his cheeks; he was in his teens – perhaps a year older than the girl laid out on the bed in the spare bedroom at the manager's bungalow.

The helicopter had lifted Bergman to the finca. The dead lay in the rain at the foot of the broken barracks wall. Castro had orchestrated the attack on the finca to exclude NAFAC from Cuba – such was the way of governments. The killing of the soldiers was different. It was a deliberate act of viciousness perpetrated only for Fabio's personal satisfaction. Such clinically planned violence was Fabio's hallmark. Murder for kicks? Or perhaps murder to enhance Fabio's reputation, strengthen fear of him – or in revenge for the fear Fabio himself suffered each day and each night.

Feet scuffed the stairs and Bergman collected one of the shotguns and checked the breech before returning to his seat on the bed. The Brit's killer entered the room alone. He nodded to Bergman and crossed directly to the bathroom. The tap ran and Bergman imagined Mahoney – Trent – scooping cold water over his face and searching in the mirror for evidence of fear. Fear was always ugly.

The Brit returned and nodded again to Bergman. 'Maybe it's okay. We need to wait for daylight.'

He picked up the second shotgun and dragged a chair to the far corner. He sat with the gun supported on his thighs and aimed at the door. His finger rested on the trigger and the distance from the door gave him an extra one or two seconds in which to shoot an attacker.

Trent

Trent watched the doorway and listened for any slight alteration in the pattern of night sounds. Bergman dozed on the bed. The CIA agent had covered himself with a sheet. The scene was very Irish: the print of the Virgin Mary, the corpse soon to be dressed for the wake. Ireland had been hard, the viciousness too close, too real. In other lands distance had provided a protective barrier . . . as if Trent were playing an away match from school – Rugby football with the ground muddy and a biting wind – the game made bearable by the guarantee of a final whistle and that a hot shower waited followed by the comfort of the return coach ride. So it had been while waiting in the ditch outside San Cristóbal de los Baños. San Cristóbal had changed him. The stench of roasting meat was ineradicable and that he was the catalyst. He had studied the target's lifestyle. Perhaps Bergman had assembled the details . . .

Dawn and he and Bergman took turns to shower. Downstairs Bergman unlocked the kitchen and heated beans and fried eggs and made coffee. The two men ate at a table on the eastern side of the *rancho* touched by the sun; dust floated from the thatch roof and hazed the golden light. Birds called from the trees, the pig squealed for food, a truck pulled into the car wash and Bergman flagged the driver on.

'The general – Jiminez,' Trent began.

'Leave it alone,' Bergman said.

Bergman

Trent's need for absolution angered Bergman. 'Rat or saint doesn't change shit. You did your job. If you don't like what you did or what happened because of what you did, then the job was wrong, not who Jiminez was.'

The coffee pot was empty. Bergman carried it through to the kitchen and put the kettle on to boil while he washed out the stale grounds. Even in school he had been disgusted by the age-old litany:

I didn't know what I was doing.

I didn't understand what I was doing.

They did it first.

They did it too.

He told me to do it.

Original sin was the greatest cop-out:

Forgive me, I was born evil so it wasn't really my fault.

A decision preceded each evil act. Amritsar, Auschwitz, My Lai, San Cristóbal de los Baños: inhumanity was the mistaken label. Evil was very human.

'*Suffer the children to come unto me so that I may watch them rip the wings off butterflies,*' Bergman whispered as he poured boiling water over the fresh coffee grounds. He carried the pot out to the table and filled Trent's cup. Trent's thoughts had remained with Jiminez. It showed in his eyes and in the set of his shoulders.

'You want to know who you killed?' Bergman asked: 'A standard model Central American general who wanted his shot at president, which was a mistake because the State had their own general picked.'

Jiminez had raised funds to compete by playing with the Colombians – built an airstrip outside San Cristóbal they could use, sold them a few guns – the usual crap, except he shared his profits with his men and he got his boots dirty against the *guerrilleros*. The military liked him, the special forces. Out in the country the special forces controlled the ballot boxes. Jiminez might have won the election.

'So they brought you in,' Bergman said. 'I liked the man, so they kept me out of the loop.'

Trent

In the name of democracy, Trent thought. He strapped his shotguns to his back before walking down the road to the bottom of the hill and the field where he had parked the rental car. Three cows grazed the field under the care of a small mestizo boy dressed in blue dungarees and rubber boots many sizes too large. The left boot was ripped on the outside of the foot.

The boy watched blankly as Trent unlocked the car and reversed away from the hedge. Trent called to him to open the gate. Perhaps the boy was deaf. More probably he was frightened of being associated in any way with Trent and his car. Even to have seen a stranger could lead to questions. What did the stranger look like? How old was he? What make was the car? What colour? From which direction did he arrive? In which direction did he leave?

In countries like Guatemala such questions were routine and

children were routinely beaten by police, military, bandits or *guerrilleros* to confirm information.

Finally a ten-Quetzal bill worked its magic and Trent drove out onto the road and back to the Río Dulce. The black American watched him board *Golden Girl*, up-anchor and motor over to the Texaco dock. Trent filled the petrol and water tanks and bought canned supplies at the store. Returning to his anchorage, he wrote an authorisation for the care and use of *Golden Girl* and put the authorisation together with $1,000 in the plastic folder containing the yacht's papers. Transferring the Yamaha to the Zodiac, he motored over to the American's catamaran. The American had rigged an awning the length of the main boom to shade his saloon and cockpit and was laying a fresh coat of varnish on his tillers. Trent called up, asking whether he wanted fruit or vegetables from the market.

The American took his time answering. He wore Levis cut off below the knees and a sleeveless white undershirt scooped low enough across the chest to show a few puffs of grey. First he stretched the stiffness out of his shoulders, then he put the paint brush in a jar of thinners on the cockpit table and replaced the top on the varnish can. He looked over at *Golden Girl* and at the bridge and at the waterfront below Market Street and at the hippie yachties' haven and then back to inspect Trent for what seemed a minute or two. Finally he scratched the back of his head and said, 'Maybe we should have a beer first.'

He didn't wait for an answer – simply ducked down into his saloon.

Trent made the Zodiac fast and clambered into the cockpit.

'Cooler down here. You'd better come on in,' the American said. He poured Gallo lagers into a pair of vacuum tankards. He didn't look at the plastic folder Trent laid on the table. 'You find your crew?'

'The *Kaibiles* have him,' Trent said. He withdrew the photograph of Miguelito from the folder and placed it carefully on the table beside the American's tankard. 'His brother – half-brother.'

The American said, 'They'd have to be half.' He sipped abstemiously at his beer and wiped the sweat off the underside of his lower lip on the back of his hand. 'Mean sons of bitches – the *Kaibiles*.'

He levered the photograph up between the nails of his forefingers and dropped it on the folder. 'What are they?'

'Cubans,' Trent said. 'The older brother's Intelligence. The boy's with the ballet.'

'That's all?'

'The ballet? Yes, that's all,' Trent said. He grabbed his tankard as a tour launch raced by. The catamaran rose sluggishly to the wake.

'I've got a lot of junk on board, books and stuff,' the American said. 'She's overloaded by maybe half a ton.'

Trent nodded. 'It happens when you live on board.'

'Yeah. I used to keep stuff in an apartment,' the American said. 'Living on a pension . . . you know how it is. You keep the condo or you keep the boat. With me the boat won.'

'Good choice.'

'If I don't get too old.'

'Age can be a problem,' Trent agreed.

Then he said, 'I'd like is to leave the papers and the keys to *Golden Girl* with you. So you'd keep an eye on her. There's fax and telephone numbers of a Chief Superintendent of the Royal Bahamian Constabulary in the file. Skelley, they call him. He'll fly down.'

'Bahamian?'

'Yes,' Trent said.

The American rose and slid the folder in amongst the charts beneath the lid of the navigation table. He escorted Trent out into the cockpit and watched the Englishman board the Zodiac and start the outboard.

Bergman

Bergman wondered how the Brit's rent-a-killer prepared for a job – whether Trent had anyone to whom he could bequeath his possessions. Bergman's pension would go to his wife. The Toyota went to the woman as did Bergman's savings, though held in trust – free access and some local hoodlum would marry and beat her until she handed over the capital. That was the reality of the country in which Bergman had served fifteen years attempting to ameliorate the conditions of the poor. Looking back, he accepted that he had done little other than act as one of those gamekeepers rich Brits paid to keep poachers off their property and control the vermin. Even in this field Bergman had failed: Fabio remained at large – as did the major playing his games up at San Cristóbal.

He wrote a letter of instruction to his bank and enclosed a will. *Don Quijote* remained. Bergman opened the volume at the inscription of his award. *Jack Bergman*. Bergman was where it had gone wrong – letting himself become Bergman. He wrapped the book carefully. He thought for a while. Finally he addressed it to Estoban Tur's two boys. He knew the address.

Then he called the major and asked to be picked up at the bridge soon after dark.

Bergman had packed in a canvas satchel a cured ham, a bottle of Carlos I brandy and two bottles of whisky, Chivas Regal and Famous Grouse. He and the major ran up the lake in one of the big black-hulled inflatables issued to the special forces. The helmsman followed the south coast for nearly an hour before reaching a river that flowed from the jungle. Massive trees on each bank extended their branches over the water to form a tunnel so dense that Bergman was unable to see moon or stars. The bowman's spotlight hit a white sign on which red lettering announced that they were entering a prohibited area. A further fifty metres and a chain barred the river; notices on each bank warned: ZONA MILITAR: ENTRENAMIENTO CON BALAS.

A soldier appeared from the bushes and lowered the chain to

the river bottom. A further ten minutes and the trees thinned and gave way to grassland that rose steeply from the west bank. They drew alongside a wooden dock built at the intersection of the river with a small tributary that spilled down the hill from the hot springs at San Cristóbal de los Baños. A driver with a US army jeep waited. The distance up the rough track was less than a mile and the ride took only a few minutes.

San Cristóbal had never been much of a town. The Spaniards had built it early in their conquest and before they discovered the magic of the highlands. Bergman had expected that years would have transformed the ruins. He smelt wood smoke first and wet charcoal from the rain that had fallen earlier in the day. That the driver halted the jeep at the church was part of the major's game, as perhaps were the twin sets of floodlights erected on posts at the corners of the central *plaza* either side of the church. The church stood on a foundation of flagstones that rose some two metres above the level of the cobblestoned *plaza*.

Swinging down from the jeep, Bergman walked to the wall and ran his fingers over the holes in the stonework. Over the years, ants and flies and beetles had eaten away the dried blood. He turned and looked across the square to the *ayuntamiento* – mayoral offices. New beams supported a tin roof. Soldiers lounged at two trestle tables on the terrace; they stood to attention as the major strode up the steps. Two of the soldiers hurried into the building and re-emerged with a card table and two canvas chairs, which they set in the centre of the square beside an out-of-work fountain shaded by four palm trees that had survived the fire. The fountain consisted of a statue of San Cristóbal standing on a triangular base in the centre of a dry stone basin some four metres across.

The major beckoned Bergman to a seat. Eight streets entered the square, two at each corner. Prior to the fire, low houses painted with whitewash had faced the streets. Bergman retained memories of iron grilles and varnished shutters on the windows, wide double doors of wood, flower pots. Now smoke-stained the whitewash and the crumbling walls sagged and were pitted with bullet holes and cratered by mortar and grenade. Only the *ayuntamiento* had been repaired and sufficient of the church tower to provide a sentry post overlooking the streets and surrounding hills.

The major's gesture embraced the ruins. 'An excellent training ground for street fighting.'

'Clearly,' Bergman said.

'The first time you have returned?'

'Yes,' Bergman said. The insults of his schooldays had made him adept at hiding anger and he smiled as he surveyed the ruins. 'There is a certain charm. . . at least by moonlight. Though solar generation would be more peaceful,' he said of the diesel generator rumbling behind the *ayuntamiento*.

'A beer?'

'Cold?'

'Naturally.'

'*Con muchas gracias.*'

Bergman leaned back in the canvas chair and stretched his legs. The soldiers watched from the shadows. Many of them had been here at the burning of the town. They were on the major's team, while Bergman was *El americano* or *El gringo* – terms of disapprobation.

Little Brother brought the bottled Gallo lagers and two glasses on a tin tray. He walked with pain. Frightened of the major, he would have served the beers on Bergman's side of the table.

The major laughed; the snap of his fingers transformed Little Brother into a mongrel bitch, cringing and writhing as he approached his master. Little Brother kept his head bowed as he set the tray down and opened the bottles. Then he knelt at the major's feet and took a cloth from his pocket to wipe the major's shoes.

The major drank from the bottle and he toasted Bergman. '*Salud, americano.* Let us ask the Big Brother to join us.'

Two soldiers brought Tur. One of them carried a third chair and they supported the Cuban under the arms. He was semicomatose and remained dressed in the trousers he had worn when he surrendered to the major. The stench of dysentery was overpowering and the major ordered the soldiers to seat Tur downwind.

'Filthy pig of a Cuban,' the major said. While looking at Tur, he rammed a boot in Little Brother's chest. The young Cuban tumbled backwards and the major laughed again.

Bergman recalled the major's laughter on the day Trent had assassinated General Jiminez on the road into San Cristóbal. *Guerrilleros* were in the area and this major, who was a captain then in command of a troop of special forces, was on a search-and-destroy mission in the hills above the town. On news of the general's death, the major sealed the town and summoned the villagers to the square. His soldiers drove the adults at bayonet point into the *ayuntamiento* and herded the children into the church. The soldiers set the church alight and took the adults, men first, one by one, from the *ayuntamiento* and shot them against the church wall while the smoke and the flames rose through the roof and out of the windows and the children screamed inside. As each man or woman was shot, a soldier kicked the body down onto the cobbles.

On receiving a report of the assassination, Bergman had flown in by helicopter. Smoke was visible from miles away. The pilot landed on the outskirts and Bergman ran up the cobbled street into the *plaza*. Bergman remembered the dark scarlet wall of the church on the far side of the square and the bullet holes in the wall and that the blood spilled inches deep over the cobbles at the foot of the flagstone foundations. He recalled the heat on his face and the stench of roast meat and the buzzards and vultures circling above and the explosion of the wooden beams as they snapped in the flames and the roof collapsing inward and the strike of the bell as it crashed from the church tower.

Bergman had discovered the major sitting at a table in the shade of these same palm trees, perhaps this table. A bucket filled with bottles of beer and packed with ice stood beside him. He was drinking from the bottle and was a little drunk.

'*Hola! americano*, you are late,' he said and he smiled at Bergman, this same smile, and toasted him with the bottle . . . as he did now, deliberately, so that Bergman would remember. '*Salud!*'

The day of the assassination, he had pointed to the corpses piled below the church steps. 'Whores,' he called them. 'See, I have taught them not to give food to the *guerrilleros* who killed General Jiminez.'

The major, who was then a captain, had attended training courses at Fort Bragg and at the School of the Americas, as had two of his sergeants. The remaining soldiers had been trained by North American instructors in Guatemala. Scandal would have threatened funding of US military assistance. The war against the *guerrilleros* was at its height and what was done was done. Bergman brought in a bulldozer to bury the population and he ordered the soldiers to burn the town. Finally he requested the president (another general) to declare the ruins and the surrounding land a military training area.

In organising the cover-up, Bergman had made himself an accomplice. Sitting now in the square, he acknowledged that he had hated himself from that moment, even though he believed that he had made the correct decision. Now he must make a fresh decision.

Inspecting Tur, Bergman's disgust mirrored that of the major.

'Antibiotics?'

'Three more days,' the major said.

'Tomorrow maybe you should clean him up. Have one of your men take him down to the river on a leash.'

Perhaps he imagined a movement in the semi-shuttered eyes of the Cuban.

Estoban Tur

Estoban half lay in the canvas chair. He remained conscious by decision. He felt no surprise at Bergman's arrival. From the day of their meeting Estoban had known in his subconscious that his gringo was Bergman. Admitting his knowledge would have forced him to kill Bergman and he had needed him. Now they were familiar to each other. They had travelled together and suffered and shared each other's fear.

Bergman inspected Estoban as if he were dirt.

Bergman said. 'Yes, on a leash.'

Such words were out of character and Estoban allowed a stirring of intelligence to show for a moment in his eyes.

'Like a dog,' Bergman said.

The major laughed and raised his bottle to Bergman. 'Drink, *americano*. Tomorrow we will make the big dog watch while we drown the puppy.' Miguelito crouched at the major's feet and the major kicked him again and ordered him to the *ayuntamiento* for fresh beer.

Bergman

Bergman watched Little Brother scuttle across the square. Eight soldiers lounged at the trestle tables. They were victors in the war against the *guerrilleros* and the director of Cuba's G2 was in their hands. They were confident – as was the major, confident and already a little drunk. Two men stood sentry on a platform at the top of the church tower – access was by ladder from within the ruined walls. At least three men and a sergeant would stand guard through the night – men now sleeping inside the *ayuntamiento*.

'Your whore, how is she?' the major asked.

'The woman is well,' Bergman said.

'Whore,' corrected the major.

Miguelito returned with fresh bottles.

'Only a whore would sleep with a gringo,' the major said. 'I instruct you in how we think, Bergman, so that you may understand us better. Understanding is important for one in your profession.'

'True,' Bergman said. He raised his bottle. 'Victory.'

'*Victoria o muerte.*' Such was Castro's favourite slogan. The major chuckled at his own wit and toasted the unconscious Cuban. 'To us the victory, to you the tomb.'

Bergman withdrew the bottles and the ham from his satchel and placed them on the table. 'For us, major,' he said gripping the Chivas Regal by the neck. 'The rest is for your soldiers. In gratitude, major, and with your permission.'

32

Trent

He had attempted to sleep through the afternoon. Fear of familiar nightmares had kept him restless and he rose from his bunk dulled by depression. Naked, he faced himself in the full-length mirror screwed to the inside of the locker door. Scar tissue gave evidence of his erstwhile profession.

His preparations were methodical. First he showered and shaved and brushed his teeth. He dressed in the same dark green cotton sweatshirt and chinos he had worn for the approach to the rendezvous at the coral-shower tree. For walking he chose green canvas baseball boots and again he wore the pistol-grip shotguns strapped to his back. He polished the blade of his throwing knife before fastening the coral beads round his neck. Three boxes of twelve-gauge deer shot went loose into a white laundry bag which he packed into a small backpack together with a white smock and trousers, white trainers, half a dozen wound pads and a length of rubber to use as a tourniquet. He added both a Phillips and a straight blade screwdriver, electrician's wire-cutters and a roll of parcel tape. Finally he filled two bottles with cold water from the fridge and dropped the backpack into the Zodiac. Both fuel tanks were full.

Locking *Golden Girl*, he cast off and motored quietly over to the neighbouring catamaran. The owner leant across the cockpit rail to accept the keys. He didn't bother with the standard platitudes; a nod sufficed and he ducked back into his saloon.

As Trent sped upriver he felt already separated from the music beating from radios and tape decks. The purr of the Yamaha was reality, the slap and rustle of the flat bottom on the water and the long trail of foam tailing astern. Daggers of light lanced from the shore across the water. The upper curve of the rising moon showed above the trees. A truck driver changed gear at the apex of the bridge.

The old fortress stood within a grove of trees at the entrance to the lake. In the daytime women would have been beating laundry on the boulders at the water's edge. Now Fabio and his men waited in the shadows. Boarding in silence, the *guerrilleros* sat along the sidetubes, weapons across their knees, and shifted their weight forward to counter the thrust of the outboard which forced the bows up. The bows dropped and the Zodiac broke loose from the water, speeding flat across the moonlit surface.

Fabio crouched beside Trent. He had brought a guide, a boy, and knew of the chain across the Río San Cristóbal and the guard post. Fabio drew a sketch for Trent in water on the hull. The sentry might have a radio or use a boat to carry news of their attack to Fronteras; Trent sped a mile beyond the river entrance, then cut the engine and drifted back with the *guerrilleros* paddling. Easing into the lake edge, they set the Indian ashore with a second man.

'Wait until you hear the first shot,' Fabio warned.

They paddled beyond the next point before using the motor at low power. Their guide pointed to the coast two miles beyond the point. Hiding the Zodiac in reeds, they waded ashore and followed the boy through a strip of jungle to sloping grassland which led over a shoulder of mountain to a densely wooded ravine above the town. The water-table lay close to the surface within the wood and springs dripped over earthquake-shattered shelves of limestone. The scent of crushed ferns and of bromeliads was almost stifled within the compost odour of rotting leaves. Howler monkeys barked at them as they eased between the trees and one of Fabio's men

412

cursed as he tripped on a root. In all there were twelve *guerrilleros*, plus the two at the Río San Cristóbal – one fewer than at the rendezvous by the coral-shower tree. Perhaps the missing man had fled or been tempted by the government's amnesty. No matter – Fabio had waited until they were in the Zodiac to inform his men of the target.

The ravine narrowed below the wood and gave cover for the first half of the approach. The second half crossed open ground and the men were nervous. They squatted in a circle at the edge of the wood and peered down at the ruined buildings. Floodlights spread a pool of light in the centre of the town and illuminated a church tower and four palm trees; scraps of salsa music rose above the beat of a diesel engine and sparks spurted from the engine's upright exhaust.

Trent squatted beside Fabio a little apart from the other men. He had memorised plans of the town prior to his mission against General Jiminez and the layout remained as clear now in his mind as on the day of the kill. The moon was almost directly overhead and the pale ribbon of road that had led to the highway was clearly visible as was its dark border, which was the ditch in which Trent had waited for the general.

The ditch offered entrance to the town; so did a fold in the ground over to their left and the stream which carried the thermal water down to the river below. Trent cleared leaves from the soil and sketched the approaches with the point of a stick.

'The lights tell us that the soldiers are in the *plaza*.'

Fabio nodded.

'The gringo must see my signal before he makes his diversion. I will enter directly ahead,' Trent said and pointed down the hill at the open ground. 'Your men can enter from three directions. You will hear firing first,' he told the men. He had assumed command and expected discussion, even argument. Instead he felt the tension ease as the men contemplated their lesser risk.

Only Fabio moved, half turning so that his back was to Trent, and Trent heard the metallic slide and snick of a bullet

413

plucked out of a magazine and fed into the breech of Fabio's revolver.

'I will accompany you,' Fabio said.

'If such is your pleasure.'

Trent scraped the sketch clean and drew the *plaza* and the streets leading to it and the position of the church and of the *ayuntamiento*. 'Each patrol must follow the street to the *plaza* which is to their right hand as they face the town. This is important to remember, *compañeros*, so that each patrol is familiar with the position of the other patrols. Otherwise the risk exists that we will shoot each other. Shoot only those soldiers whom it is necessary to shoot and remember that we wish the two Cubans and the *gringo* to remain alive.'

'I want the officer alive. He has much to pay for,' Fabio said. 'Kill the others.'

'The Cubans and the gringo are our hostages,' Trent contradicted. 'Insurance for our escape. There will be a radio and perhaps cellular telephones that we must destroy.'

The *guerrilleros* nodded their understanding. They were thin men, made slighter by the weight of their weapons. 'We will give you forty minutes to reach your positions,' Trent told them.

He and Fabio watched the men fade into the darkness.

Fabio

He looked down at the town and at the open ground they must cross. Fear welled sour in his throat and loosened his bowels and he walked a distance into the wood so that the stranger and the boy who had guided them wouldn't hear. He squatted, defenceless, and mosquitoes rose out of the wet moss.

Hope had grown in him throughout the day, hope of a gateway finally opening back into what, after all these years, he continued to think of as reality – the world of his parents, of the family bank, the town house safe within its wooded compound, the holiday homes on the Pacific coast and on the shore at Lake Atitlán: the familiar reality of his youth, of servants and chauffeurs and the silent comfort and security of the Mercedes limousine.

Never before had the time been right and never before had he possessed the currency with which to negotiate his return. Now he had a gringo playing traitor – a gringo of that organisation hated throughout Latin America, the CIA. The government could use the threat of scandal to pressure the Americans for fresh aid and for trade concessions. And Fabio had this stranger to offer, an associate of the director of Cuba's G2, Estoban Tur – certainly someone of reputation – a man whom the Americans and his own government would consider an international terrorist.

A solitary officer commanded down in San Cristóbal: white-skinned, as was Fabio, product of the same school and of the same society; an officer who would understand the importance of the gringo's betrayal and of the stranger and would recognise his and Fabio's shared blood and their shared class and who could be bought if only he was presented with a reason that excused his being bought. As to the price, Fabio was his father's only son. $100,000 was reasonable.

First they must reach the town and this foreigner must give the signal. With the signal given, Fabio could kill his companion. There must be no witness to the killing. Fabio had brought paper and he wiped himself before raising his trousers. Then he walked back to the edge of the wood, drew his knife and whistled softly to the boy who was their guide. The boy had served his purpose and he died quickly and almost without sound.

Trent

He watched the town, cataloguing his recollections of the streets. The courtyard gardens must be overgrown and interconnected and open to the street through gaps in the ruined walls. His senses were acute in this time of waiting and he heard the wet cough choked off behind him in the wood. Fabio returned and squatted beside him.

Actors portrayed fear in their faces and with whimpers or panicked shouting. In truth, fear was silent and often invisible. However, the smell was unmistakable and Trent smelt it now in the sourness of Fabio's sweat and the wet voiding of his bowels.

Trent's own fear would come as he crossed the open ground and he knew that it would leave him once the action began. 'It would be better for us to wait at the entrance to the town,' he said.

'Lead,' Fabio told him.

'The boy?'

'Back to the boat – he was too young to fight,' Fabio said and touched his throat in that now familiar betrayal of nerves.

Floods had washed the ravine and the footing was loose limestone. The ravine opened where the ground flattened. A bush, bent at an angle by a fallen boulder, offered the last shelter. The white edge of the town was visible in the night – at most four hundred metres.

Trent paused a moment, collecting himself before easing into the open. Abrupt movement attracted the eye, so he walked slowly, his pace smooth. He divided the distance by any mark that rose in the moonlight: a stone, a cut in the earth, a curl of rusted wire, broken fence post, a discarded shoe.

He counted the steps as he always counted and his heart beat in time to the heavy thud of the diesel engine. The music grew louder; a woman sang. Trent promised himself that he would crawl from the point where he distinguished the first word of the song. The power of his concentration was such that he was left frozen when the music stopped. One foot raised, he would have overbalanced but for the start of the next set, a man this time, merengue from the Dominican Republic.

He was close to the first buildings. A man coughed and Trent froze, both hands to the ground, steadying himself. Tilting forward, he slid his feet back and sank to his belly. Face close to the ground, he inhaled the scent of both rain and sun imprisoned in the earth and the dry dung odour of animals that had foraged here before the destruction of the town and which he remembered from his previous visit: goats, sheep, cows.

The music and the diesel engine were now a barrier through which he strained to discern movement. A ruined cow shed lay directly ahead. And one man . . . doing what? Patrolling the circumference of the ruins? Liquid splattered against a wall and the soldier broke wind; next came a grunt of satisfaction as the man eased himself. Steel clattered against stone as the soldier retrieved his gun. Then came the pad of his boots in the dirt. The soldier's confidence was obvious. There was no expectation of attack.

Trent beckoned Fabio, then advanced slowly on toes and elbows.

Fabio

His companion reminded Fabio of a crocodile stalking prey; here was the same twisting advance across open ground. Yes, he was very expert – certainly a man of reputation. Fabio had crawled from the ravine in his companion's wake. Sweat had collected in the valley of his spine and his shirt stuck to his skin. He carried his pistol in a leg holster and a sling held his Kalashnikov across his back. A few metres more and they would gain the protection of the buildings. He was so close now to the end of fear yet fear was in him harder and more sour than ever in the past. Fear that he would fail, that the officer would be unreasonable or that a soldier should see him first and shoot before Fabio could reach the officer. He must follow until his companion signalled the gringo. Then he could kill him. Perhaps he would do it with his knife as he had killed the boy. Yes, with the knife, he thought and eased one leg forward and one arm forward, then the other arm and the

417

other leg, an animal crawling in the dirt. Most of all he longed to kill the gringo. The gringo who had hunted him for so many years . . . Bergman.

Bergman

Bergman and the major had eaten rice and beans accompanied by thick slices carved from Bergman's ham. They had washed their supper down with Gallo lager. Miguelito set fresh glasses on the table and Bergman watched the major pour Chivas Regal with great care. Recorking the bottle, the Guatemalan wiped a single drop of whisky from his fingertip with a clean white cotton handkerchief; he unfolded the handkerchief and refolded it so that the tiny mark of the whisky was on the inside.

Whisky in hand, the major lolled back in his chair, legs thrust forward as if he were wearing riding boots rather than polished loafers. Though a little drunk, he was in total command of himself and of his surroundings. Miguelito hovered in attendance. Estoban Tur had fallen from his chair and lay curled on his side, head pillowed against the stone basin that enclosed the fountain and sheltered from the moon by the shadow thrown by the statue of San Cristóbal. Four of the eight soldiers now seated at the table outside the *ayunta-miento* were fresh from sentry duty: two from the church tower, two returned from patrolling the circumference of the ruined town. Three or four more were probably asleep within the building. The soldiers at the table were drinking Bergman's whisky and his Spanish brandy. Though merry, they remained wary of their commander and sang softly to the radio. Only Bergman was beyond the major's control. Bergman, the gringo.

Bergman was familiar with the major's thoughts. He knew that the major hated him. The major believed that Bergman had prevented his promotion – that he would have been a full colonel or even a general but for Bergman.

'You gringos believe that your wealth makes you superior to us, yet we feel only contempt for you,' the major began. His smile was silky. 'I speak in the abstract, Bergman, impersonally and only to instruct you.'

'As always – and I thank you,' Bergman replied – fifteen years in Latin America had accustomed him to insults.

'You, in your guilt for the slaughter of your own Indians, call us Spanish of Latin America the savages,' the major continued. 'In so doing you show your lack of culture, Bergman. You understand? To believe that savages could build Antigua Guatemala, Cartagena de Colombia, Havana; cathedrals, churches, palaces . . .' He numbered the achievements on his fingers, fingernails manicured. 'Yes, all built by us, Bergman, while you built houses of wood plank such as those in which our *campesinos* exist. Houses suitable only for servants, Bergman, peasants, gringos.'

Such houses had seemed palaces to Bergman when he was a child: houses protected by white picket fences, white painted walls shaded by giant trees perpetually in blossom, windows sparkling with Windolene, fitted carpets of lawn, the spit of garden sprinklers – at rest in the drive, a long, low, sleek chrome monster shiny as the Hispanic gardener sweating amidst the flower beds.

'*Los moros*,' Bergman said. The Moors. . .

Estoban Tur

The major had repeatedly boasted of the purity of his Spanish blood.

Bergman's reference to the Moors was the deepest insult.

The major spoke very quietly and Estoban strained to catch his words.

'You call me a Moor?'

'Never,' the gringo protested. 'You misunderstand me, Major. I suggest only that your masons were educated in the Moorish tradition. You, Major, are the true *conquistador*.' Again it was an insult, though one which the major failed to recognise.

Estoban watched Bergman raise his glass to the major, 'Salud.'

The major returned the toast.

As for the gringo, having drunk, he lowered the glass to his lap and Estoban watched a dribble of whisky spatter the dust. The gringo appeared to be searching the shadows – waiting for an arrival. Setting the emptied glass on the table, he reached for the bottle. The beans had produced gas in his stomach and he shifted in his seat.

Estoban had become accustomed to his own stench. He appeared to be unconscious and the two men seated at the table were oblivious of his presence. He lay facing them, curled on his side, and could see, beneath the table, his brother cringe at the major's feet. The major was the image against which Estoban had fought each day of his working life – the major and Bergman. Estoban's hatred for them served to partially anaesthetise his pain at witnessing his brother's degradation.

Miguelito

Those who had seen the photograph had presumed that he was begging to be rescued. He was begging for forgiveness. He knew that he was at fault and that he should suffer punishment for what he had done with the dancer, Andres. Now pain had anaesthetised him. Pain existed and was bearable because he existed within it and because there was nothing else. There was no beginning nor end to it – pain and waiting for pain and being released from pain.

Trent

He reached the cowshed. Fabio remained twenty metres to his rear and Trent moved quickly, slipping within the shadows and through a gap in a stone wall into what had once been a vegetable plot. Weeds grew shoulder-high in the rich earth and a creeper bearing tresses of pale flowers tumbled over a doorway. At first the darkness appeared total within the building. Trent knelt against the inner wall opposite to the doorway. He shed his sweatshirt and sliced the shotguns loose. Next he dropped his pants and felt for the change of clothes in his pack. Dressed in white, he drew the laces tight on the white trainers and slung the white laundry bag of ammunition round his neck. His eyes had adjusted to the dark and he could discern the paleness through which he had entered and an even deeper wedge of darkness that was a second doorway leading further into the building.

Fabio hissed for his attention.

Trent stepped through the second doorway and saw sky through a gap in the next wall. His foot struck a fallen beam. He felt for the burnt break in the wood and patted the charcoal on his forehead and on one cheek, then in streaks on his clothes and on the laundry bag so that he would be camouflaged against the whitewashed walls of the burnt town. He hissed back for Fabio and heard the Guatemalan's foot strike a plank and the scrape of a pebble beneath his shoe against the tiles.

Trent stood against the wall, waiting and listening.

He was safe here within the darkness and the silence. Deeper into the town the small noises of a man's approach would be muffled within the throb of the generator and by the music played on the radio.

Fabio was visible as a movement against the white wall – sufficient to shoot.

Trent hissed again and the movement changed direction.

He reached out and found Fabio's arm, drawing him close. 'Keep your distance out on the street,' he whispered into the *guerrillero*'s ear.

He ducked out of the doorway and flinched at his own image drawn black by moonlight across the pavement. The far side of the street was in shadow and he crossed quickly and stood flattened against the wall while his retinas readjusted. Spitting on his hand, he rubbed whitewash from the wall and streaked the gun barrels and he held the guns at different angles. Fabio stood in the doorway opposite and searched for him – proof of the camouflage.

Trent shifted along the wall to the next corner. His shadow would reappear briefly as he crossed to the next block. These were the moments of greatest danger – six blocks in all. He squatted at the corner and peered round the angle of the wall. He waited to the count of sixty seconds for signs of movement before advancing to the shadows on the next block where he waited for Fabio. The Guatemalan seemed as visible as an ice-cream van.

Fabio joined him and Trent said, 'Rub yourself with white-wash or you will get us both shot.'

He headed up the street without waiting.

The generator was to his left. Operating alone, he would have destroyed it first and trusted to his expertise as a night fighter. The *guerrilleros* had survived in the jungle; here amongst the ruins they were amateur. And he was unsure of their commitment. His own kills had been designated by his Control. The *guerrilleros* had exercised free choice and had concentrated on soft targets: Indian villages, plantations, buses out on country roads. Even the attack on Finca Patricia had been subsequent to the ceasefire and therefore reasonably safe. Trent wanted to see them and know whether they were fighting or had taken to the hills. And he hoped that they would delay their advance until they were sure that he and their commander had reached the *plaza*.

He beckoned Fabio forward.

Fabio

Fabio hated him for his lack of fear. He felt the weight of the knife in his trouser pocket. The knife would be silent.

Trent

Fabio touched his throat in that same nervous gesture which had unmasked him in Fronteras. Trent heard again the wet choked-off cough in the woods and he saw the boy who had guided them up the lake – thirteen or fourteen years old. Something in Trent's eyes warned the Guatemalan and he was already leaping back as Trent grabbed at him.

They faced each other hidden in the shadows. 'Animal,' Trent called him in a harsh whisper, 'You murdered the boy.'

A pout of his lower lip displayed Fabio's lack of interest.

Trent looked up the street. Two blocks more. The spotlights had been sited to light the streets at the entrance to the *plaza*.

'Come close to me again and I will kill you,' Trent warned. He crossed the street and advanced towards the next corner. His shoulder brushed the wall and flakes of old whitewash pattered to the pavement. His shadow grew and darkened as he approached the corner and he was forced to his belly to hide himself. The beat of the generator was very close and soldiers sang to the radio. He glanced back across the street. Fabio was also on his belly. He had unslung his Kalashnikov. He saw Trent watching him and he aimed across the street so that Trent could see into the bore of the weapon. The *guerrillero*'s desire was thick as a lava flow. Trent thought for a moment that he could smell its heat flow across the cobbles. It would be easy to turn and crawl back down the street and slip through the ruins and over the mountain to the Zodiac. He would have boarded *Golden Girl* by dawn and be sailing downriver towards Lívingston and the open sea.

Boots struck and slithered on the cobbles ahead.

Trent froze, waiting. His weight rested on his elbows and he held the shotguns extended so as not to strike stone. Two soldiers crossed the street at the intersection. They were urbanites and glanced down the street from habit, checking for traffic. They even paused before crossing the road as if waiting for the lights to change. They crossed together and they saw nothing of the two men lying on the pavement each side of the street.

Trent breathed out carefully. He had no fear of Fabio. The soldiers would have reminded Fabio of his situation. If he were to make a move it would be after the firing commenced.

Trent crossed the intersection and crawled to the corner of the *plaza*. The church was directly ahead to his right. Bergman sat at a table beneath the palm trees. The officer who had arrested Estoban sat opposite him and with his back to Trent. He wore civilian clothes and held a glass in his right hand. Estoban's brother crouched at the officer's feet and a second man, perhaps Estoban, lay on the flagstones by the fountain. The angle of the spotlights blinded Trent as he looked up at the tower and he was unable to see into the church. The radio and the singing came from round the corner to his left – probably from the *ayuntamiento*.

Fabio had reached the opposite corner. He raised eight fingers for the number of soldiers and Trent nodded and held his guns to form a cross against the wall.

Bergman

Bergman had been unable to avoid drinking the beers. However, he had spilt most of the whisky and judged himself sober. The wall appeared to move low down at the corner of the *plaza* opposite the church. A cross formed against the wall. Bergman was almost certain of the cross. It was indistinct but, yes, he was almost certain. The arms were some two feet long and the cross moved left and right and up and down.

'What do you know of our land?' the major asked. 'You come in your aeroplanes to admire the ruins where in one day the Indians sacrificed ten thousand people. Priests gouged their hearts out with a stone knife.' The major grabbed Miguelito by the hair, aping the act. The theatre completed, he shoved the young man away so that he fell to the ground facing his elder brother – his half-brother.

'Mulatto,' the major said, as contemptuous of African genes as he was of Indians. 'We Spanish know who we are, Bergman. We possess a sense of history. We have learnt that the army alone stands against chaos.

'Look,' he commanded and spread his arms to encompass the buildings he had destroyed. 'I acted here so that the army, my people, are assured that I will avenge one death with the slaughter of an entire town.'

The major rocked forward in his chair and carefully refilled their glasses with Chivas.

He sipped and patted his narrow moustache dry on his handkerchief.

'Excellent, Bergman. I congratulate you on your taste.'

The major turned his drink in his hands and found a smudge on the tumbler.

Bergman watched him polish the glass on his handkerchief – cleanliness next to Godliness, Bergman thought and glanced again across the *plaza*.

The cross moved left then right, up then down. Bergman was positive. He was as positive of the cross as he was of the major.

Satisfied with the cleanliness of his glass, the major pocketed his handkerchief. '*Salud*, gringo. You remember? I sat at this same table.'

'I remember,' Bergman said. A whimper from Miguelito attracted his attention and he saw that Tur was watching him. Waiting. Wondering to what depth Bergman, in his silence, could debase himself.

'After the first ten or fifteen or twenty deaths I discovered that I was enjoying myself,' the major said. 'I sat here with my cold beer and watched the exercise of power. My power, Bergman.'

Fourteen men in all – plus the major. No, Bergman could discount the major.

'My congratulations,' Bergman said. Perhaps he meant to toast the major. However, he appeared to be a little drunk and he lost control of his glass and spilt whisky in his lap. Cursing,

425

he brushed at the drops with the back of his right hand and his fingertips touched the butt of the Beretta stuck in his pants.

'Yes, certainly. My congratulations, major,' he said.

33

Trent

Trent saw the table leap and the major's chair tip back. Then he heard the shot and he saw the major's head strike the ground. He saw the splodge on the major's shirt and the major hold himself as if attempting to keep his belly in. He saw Bergman seated in the green canvas director's chair and he saw the pistol in Bergman's hand. He thought that shooting the major created a very definite diversion. He dived round the corner into the *plaza* to protect himself from Fabio.

Fabio

That one shot obliterated Fabio's hopes of escape. The meaning of the shot punched up through his belly and into his throat and on up into his brain. Fear was back in him so that he trembled. He waited for his men to charge the *plaza*. He counted the seconds. As so often in times of fear, he thought of Che Guevara – Che who had allowed himself to be captured and had suffered the final indignity of a paltry execution in a Bolivian schoolroom. Those who were captured were amateurs and dreamers revelling in their own glamour – believing in their glamour, deluded in believing that their glamour would protect them. So it had been with Che, driven to his death by Fidel. Now Fidel wore Che's martyrdom as a romantic decoration for his revolution.

Sixty seconds and the fear built with Fabio's certainty that his men had deserted, escaping as he had planned to escape, melting back into the landscape from which he had drawn them all those years back. He was alone and he was incapable of supporting the fear. He had to terminate the fear, now, for ever. He registered a movement to his left – a soldier running back towards the *plaza*.

The soldier burst out of the street to Fabio's right. Fabio's vision was clear as the water in a *cenote*. He shouted his own name. *'Fabio!'*

The soldier spun to face him.

'Patria!' Fabio shouted. He fired from the hip, a single burst scything the soldier to the cobbles.

'Victoria o muerte!' Fabio screamed as he swung to face the *ayuntamiento*.

The table was overturned and had crashed down the steps. The soldiers were on their feet. They had grabbed their weapons. Fabio charged and fired as he ran and saw a soldier spin and drop. He saw with absolute clarity the bullets reach out to him and connect him with the soldiers. The stars streamed down at him. He was the centre of the universe. Fabio! not the word, the thought. That was all. Nothing else remained in which he could believe and the fear had ended.

Trent

The back of Fabio's head exploded. The *guerrillero* seemed to hesitate, as if wondering whether his wound was important. Trent rolled to his feet and sprinted across the corner of the *plaza* to the steps leading to the church. He dived for the steps and slid along the flags and into the corner formed by the steps and the raised foundations. The shadows were deep and the foundations protected him from anyone up in the church or in the church tower. Two soldiers charged out of the *ayuntamiento* and across the *plaza*.

Estoban Tur

Estoban saw Fabio charge into the bullets from the *ayuntamiento* and saw the back of his head burst. The shooting ended.
The gringo sat in his chair as if in shock. The major lay on the
ground. A sergeant had taken command of the soldiers. The
sergeant presumed that the major had been shot by Fabio. Two
of his men raced for the fountain to succour their commander
and secure the prisoners. Estoban grabbed the pistol from the
major's ankle holster. He waited until the soldiers were close
then dropped them both with bullets in the gut.

Deliberately in the gut.

For Miguelito . . .

Miguelito

The violence of noise opened Miguelito and the pain entered
and expanded as it had each time he had been possessed. He
whimpered as he had whimpered each time. He heard,
through his own whimpering, someone call his name. He had
learnt to obey and he fought to the surface so as to be able to
understand who had summoned him.

He saw his brother. He lay in his brother's arms and his
brother rolled with him to the fountain and forced him up
over the stone parapet and into the protection of the dry basin
and of San Cristóbal.

Bergman

Bergman had shot the major as a signal. He had expected a
dozen or more *guerrilleros* to charge the *plaza* – men who
recognised in him their enemy and he had expected to be
dead. Only one *guerrillero* had appeared, a man determined on
his own death. Bergman thought that he ought to be afraid.
Instead he felt foolish – a clown seated beside a fountain –

unimportant even to the two soldiers leaking their lives into the cobbles. Seeing him seated in his chair, the soldiers in the *ayuntamiento* must suppose that he was held at gunpoint by Estoban Tur. The soldiers were the major's men while Bergman was the gringo. As a hostage he had little value. Without looking round, he said, 'You could attempt walking me out as your hostage. They would probably shoot me.'

A burst of fire from the church tower confirmed his thoughts. The bullets spattered the fountain and the palm trees. A shotgun fired and the spotlight closest to the church steps shattered. That would be Mahoney, the Brit.

Estoban Tur fired twice at the other light and missed.

His brother whimpered.

Bergman dropped from his chair. He remained unsure of what side he was on. The fountain protected him from a second burst fired from the church tower. The men in the *ayuntamiento* joined the attack. They were firing high to avoid hitting their wounded companions. Bergman lay flat between the two soldiers and heard the bullets spit overhead and strike the stone statue of San Cristóbal. The soldier on his right wept softly, child's tears. He was young. Bergman remembered him from the car wash the day the major had fetched the dying student in the back of the truck. Bergman had killed the student to halt the boy's fear and pain. He felt for the soldier's hand and held it in both of his, smoothing the back beneath the ball of his thumb. 'Do you desire that I should pray with you?'

The soldier answered '*Sí, por favor, Don Bergman.*' *Don* in hope that a Don's prayers would be more efficacious than those of a mere *señor*.

'Hail Mary,' began the Protestant Bergman from memories of his daughters kneeling beside their beds at night; their short night-dresses had displayed the backs of their legs, always a little pink from the sun, and they wore their hair pulled back in pigtails. 'Hail Mary, full of Grace. The Lord is with thee . . . '

'Blessed is the fruit of thy womb, Jesus,' the soldier murmured.

'I require your gun.'

'Sí, Don Bergman.' The soldier grunted with the extra pain as he tried to lift his M16. Bergman reached across and took it.

Miguelito was weeping in the basin and Tur was repeating to him again and again, 'Miguelito, listen to me. Miguelito, I love you. I love you.' The profundity of the despair in his protestations frightened Bergman.

'Go with God,' Bergman said to the soldier.

'Gracias, Don Bergman.'

Trent

Trent thought in terms of targets. Fighting was easier that way, simple and less personal. Estoban Tur's half-brother was the target and Trent's task was to get the target out alive. Right now the target was in the fountain. The soldiers manning the church tower were static while the men in the *ayuntamiento* could escape through the back of the building and drive back into the *plaza* from opposite sides. The distance from the church to the *ayuntamiento* was approximately one hundred metres. A quality sprinter on the track could have run the distance in eleven seconds. Trent was slower than a sprinter and a bullet was a great deal faster. He ran across from the church into the side street. From the street corner to the next street corner was the width of the *plaza* minus the width of two pavements and two roads. Doing the mathematics kept him calm as he raced along the side of the square with his shoulder close to the wall so as to leave the minimum of shadow. Finished with the maths, he counted the steps: two steps to a metre.

He had destroyed the spotlight on his side of the square and was running in poor light. The soldiers hadn't seen him. They were firing at the target. Hitting the target would destroy any purpose to what Trent was doing. He fired twice from the hip at the *ayuntamiento* terrace. A soldier yelled as a pellet ripped his face. Two seconds for the shock, four seconds to change direction of fire and take aim. Six seconds in all, fourteen paces. Trent ran the fourteen paces in a low crouch before dropping flat directly against the wall. Bullets chopped chunks out of the wall all the way back to the end of the block. The soldiers weren't sure of Trent's position and they were aiming too high. Or perhaps they weren't aiming. They could be offering covering fire for a sally from the building or for their retreat through the back door and across the *ayuntamiento*'s rear garden.

Bergman

The Brit was trapped against the wall midway between the church and the *ayuntamiento*. The soldiers were firing at him and Bergman heard masonry fall. Tur was repeating his mantra of love for his half-brother.

Tur and Little Brother were on their bellies on the side of the basin closest to the church. They were safe as long as they didn't raise their heads. Tur's defences depended on the capacity of the magazine in the major's automatic – certainly insufficient to repulse an attack.

The soldiers up in the church tower concentrated on the fountain, firing a short burst every fifteen to twenty seconds. Bergman held the one M16 across his chest. He reached for the second rifle at the same moment that a burst came from the church tower. The fountain protected Bergman; however, the bullets frightened him – perhaps because he had decided. The dying didn't frighten him. Nor being wounded. He was frightened of being useless. He imagined bullets shattering his kneecaps and bent his legs only a few degrees as he wriggled backwards on his elbows, pushing with his heels. His head hit the stone wall of the basin. He waited for the next burst from the church tower, then rose sufficiently to slide the two M16s over the parapet. He eased back between the soldiers; both were dead. He lay between them and fired six shots from his pistol at the *ayuntamiento*.

Trent

Bergman's shots at the *ayuntamiento* distracted the soldiers. Trent had been immobile against the wall for the past three minutes. He darted fifteen paces towards the intersection before diving to the pavement as bullets hacked at the ruins.

An M16 fired from the fountain and shattered the second spotlight. Now the only light came from within the *ayuntamiento* and from two naked bulbs suspended from the ceiling out on the terrace.

Trent darted forward and slid skidding across the side street and into the ruins of the shop that had occupied the corner site. Two pavements and the intersecting roads separated him from the *ayuntamiento*. The intersection plus the pavements measured ten metres. He rolled round the shopfront and fired both shotguns into the terrace before ducking back into shelter. The spread of pellets was too wide to be effective and he didn't expect to hit any of the soldiers. He was giving a signal to the men in the fountain: Bergman, Estoban and the target.

At the beginning he had counted eight shooters on the terrace; two were immobilised at the fountain; two continued to shoot from the terrace; two had moved indoors and were firing through the open windows. The final two must have joined with however many had been inside the *ayuntamiento* at the beginning of the attack. Give them ten minutes to reach their new positions and all hell would break loose. The maths kept Trent calm as he peered across the square at the statue of San Cristóbal. The soldiers up in the tower must have been night blind in the first few minutes of darkness – a chance for Tur and his half-brother to escape from the stone basin. Energising the brother must have been difficult. Weeks of abuse had destroyed whoever he had been at the beginning of this thing.

Trent imagined Estoban's suffering at his brother's condition.

Estoban Tur

Estoban held his brother in his arms as he had when Miguelito was a child and hurt; rocking him as he crooned the same love that he felt for his two sons – a love that made him liquid inside. At the same time, he tried to concentrate on the battle. He had raised his head once over the parapet to destroy the spotlight. He suspected that Trent was preparing to attack the *ayuntamiento*. To do so was pointless unless the men in the tower were silenced. Estoban thought that he had a chance if he attacked the church at the same moment that Trent made his attack. Not a good chance – Estoban had never been much of a runner. Miguelito was the fast one.

Miguelito

Miguelito floated in his brother's arms. Even the pain was less. He registered the battle. At first it was only noise; then, for a while, it was part of a film the pictures of which he was unable to see, perhaps because Estoban judged the scenes too violent.

Miguelito remained a child within the protection of Estoban's arms. However, the surface was very near – a surface in which the adult Miguelito had found Estoban's protectiveness increasingly frustrating and even insulting to his manhood.

Aged eleven he had been inducted into the school cadet force. After graduating, he had completed his obligatory two years of military service in preparation for the American invasion threatened by Fidel.

Each time Miguelito touched the surface he understood more of the battle. He understood that they were under fire and he understood from where.

Estoban left him for a moment and Miguelito was alone with his pain and with his degradation. He saw the dancer, Andres, muscular and smooth skinned, in the bed beside him and he suffered the soldiers in their endless procession and he knew that he was to blame for all that had happened. The shame was

insupportable and he screamed aloud against it. His scream
brought him fully to the surface. Firing came from behind him
and he distinguished the deeper bark of a shotgun. Then came
a burst from ahead and from above and the bullets snapped
fragments from the stone plinth supporting the statue of San
Cristóbal.

Miguelito's brother rolled back from behind the statue. He
clutched two M16s in his arms. The moonlight displayed him
clearly. Miguelito saw neither the god who had protected his
childhood nor the frigid *poderoso* of later years. Instead he saw
his brother as his mother and stepfather had always seen him –
and as Andres would see him. Miguelito saw a middle-aged
mulatto who stank of wet shit and was overweight and
sweated with fever and was out of breath.

'I love you,' he whispered because there was too much pain
and he could no longer love. 'I am so very sorry.'

Perhaps there was something in his eyes that Estoban could
read.

'There is no blame,' Estoban said.

Miguelito took one of the rifles. The feel was familiar.

His brother said, 'There are two men in the tower. It is
necessary that I remove them.' He was about to raise himself
over the parapet.

Miguelito grabbed him.

'You were always slow,' Miguelito said. 'Remember?'

A dozen bullets smacked into the stone plinth and into the
statue behind them. Miguelito vaulted the parapet and
sprinted directly at the church.

Estoban Tur

Estoban had been impotent each of the many times that he
had watched Miguelito run on the track. He recalled those last
races, each more painful, the small white boy obliterated by
the massively muscled black students of the sports schools.
Estoban had stood always as close as possible to the finishing

line. He had watched Miguelito's legs and arms pump and seen the sweat glisten on his face and on his chest and he had longed to have the power of a vacuum cleaner to suck him forward.

Now, finally, he could be of use.

Trent

He knew the facade of the *ayuntamiento* with greater intimacy and detail than had the architect and masons who had built it. Eighteen arches faced the *plaza*; further arches at each end gave on to the north and south intersections. The arches were approximately three metres in width and three metres in height while the pillars were seventy or eighty centimetres square at the base. Two steps led up to the terrace and the terrace was some four metres in depth. The thick wooden doors that had once secured the interior had been burnt at the time of the massacre as had the shutters to the double windows facing through the arches to the *plaza*. The sill to the windows was less than a metre above the terrace flagstones. Two soldiers lay sheltered behind the pillars closest to the entrance doorway and fired short bursts at the fountain and at the ruined shopfront. The bursts were covering fire for whatever action the soldiers inside the *ayuntamiento* had plotted. The fire from inside the *ayuntamiento* was more sporadic and came from one window at a time, suggesting that only one soldier was responsible.

Trent crouched at the edge of the old shop window. He was unable to see the soldier closest to him; however, the M16 showed as a black line against the pillar each time the soldier fired at the shopfront. Trent thought that the soldier was shifting position as he shifted target, firing from the right of the pillar at Trent and from the left when firing at the fountain. Switching positions must take the soldier between one and two seconds and switching all the way from the fountain to the rear corner of the terrace could take as much as three or even four. The soldier was safe from attack from the front and had ample time to swing round and face a side attack in which the attacker must cross the street and pavements, jump the steps and still be some twenty metres away.

Trent waited for the next burst directed at the shopfront. Then he slid at ground level out through the ruins and along the pavement close in to the building. He was in dead ground as he crossed the street and lay below the *ayuntamiento*'s wall and slithered to the bottom of the steps at the rear corner.

He knew what he had to do. To maintain surprise it had to be done without pause. Violence was always 'It' and prisoners had no place in the equation. For fuel Trent saw Miguelito bent forward and he looked directly into the young Cuban's eyes and saw his own father at his desk.

Shots came suddenly from the direction of the fountain and the firing from the church tower was continuous.

Estoban Tur

Estoban stood against the statue of San Cristóbal. He was too occupied to be able to see Miguelito run. He held the M16 into his shoulder as if he were on the range and he fired directly at the balustrade of the platform up in the tower. He began at the left corner because he was a communist and swung the foresight slowly to the right, then all the way back to the left. The balustrade was made of stone and the sparks of his bullets sprinkled amongst the muzzle flashes. He leant into the muzzle flashes so as to keep himself upright against the statue and the bullets beat him back and down until he was sitting at the saint's feet. He thought that it was humorous that he, a communist, should die against a saint – even a stone saint. And he thought that there was nothing more that he could do for Miguelito or for Mario or for Tobanito. He opened his arms to hold them and his love was warm and wet where it spilled from his belly and from the holes in his chest. He thought that the firing had ceased from the tower though not from the *ayuntamiento*; he could hear the deep cough of Trent's shot-guns and he could smell his own blood through the cordite incense.

Trent

Trent leapt the steps, spun left and dived through the window into the interior of the *ayuntamiento*. He landed rolling, once, twice, three times. He was in a square room off the big *entrada*, clay tiles on the floor, white walls, one light bulb. The double doorway through to the *entrada* was open: two light bulbs showed a heavy table of dark wood against the far wall together with a pair of Spanish carvers with leather backs; four closed doors led to rooms each side of a wide corridor. Trent was on his feet as a soldier spun to confront him from the window at the far end of the *entrada*. Trent fired at the man's face. He ran straight at him and kept on firing. He had fired twice before the soldier fired. At Trent's third shot the soldier dropped his gun and clung to his own eyes. The soldier guarding the shopfront end of the terrace was on his knees facing the window and searching for his target. Trent shot him in the chest. The second soldier out on the terrace expected to be shot at from the interior and had crawled into the shelter of the wall. Trent rolled out through the main doors. He held both guns facing ahead and hit the soldier twice in the upper thighs.

Miguelito

Applause of gunfire encouraged Miguelito in his sprint across the square. The pain was in him as it had always been from midway through a race. His body opened and he ran out and ahead of himself as he had when a boy. In the past he had seen only the finishing tape. Now he saw the church. He reached the foundations and raced up the steps and into the nave. A ladder led to the platform at the top of the tower. The floor of the platform was built of rough wood and moonlight painted stripes in the gaps between the planks. The soldiers were on the side of the platform overlooking the *plaza*. Miguelito stood at the foot of the ladder and fired directly upwards. He fired with the discipline preached by his stepfather, the architect. His target was an imaginary line running fifty centimetres in from the wall. Splinters fell from the platform and the stripes of moonlight grew cankers along their edges. He was finished once the magazine was empty and he sat folded in on himself at the foot of the ladder as if he were a robot that had been switched off.

Bergman

Fire from the tower ceased, then from inside the church and from the *ayuntamiento*. Tur sat at the feet of San Cristóbal. He sat the way a doll sits, body bent a little forward and legs straight out in front. Bergman squatted beside him. The thick cloying odour of fresh blood mixed with the stench of the Cuban's dysentery and with the scent of the spent rounds. Bergman held his hand.

'Your brother is all right,' he said. The statement was grotesque and he said, 'I mean safe. Your brother is safe.'

Tur's fingers tightened slightly on his and the Cuban's lips moved.

Bergman lowered his head to listen and Tur said: 'Gringo, go fuck yourself.' It was the message Fidel had been broadcasting for forty years.

'Right,' Bergman said.

He turned to look at Tur.

The Cuban managed a small smile and his grip eased.

439

Trent

All gunfire had ceased. At least two of the three soldiers he had shot remained alive. Trent was careful not to see them; however, he was unable to avoid the sounds that accompanied their pain. He expected a counterattack from the side streets or from the rear of the *ayuntamiento*. He rolled back into the building and sat with his back against the wall and with his chest heaving. He sat facing directly into the corridor and saw that a human hand had been slammed in the bottom of the door at the far end. Trent's fingers trembled and he was clumsy in reloading his shotguns. He walked down the corridor and kicked the door open. The plain-clothes cop with whom he had talked on the bridge sprawled face-down on the tiles – the one Trent had judged to be the sergeant. He had been shot in the back.

Trent turned and walked across the terrace and down the steps and out to the centre of the *plaza*. Bergman squatted beside Estoban at the feet of San Cristóbal. The Cuban had been hit half a dozen times. He had reached the end.

'Where's the target?' Trent demanded.

Bergman understood that he was referring to Little Brother and said, 'In the church. How did it go in there?'

'Dead or dying. They shot their own sergeant.' Trent looked over at the church. 'I'll fetch him. We need to get out of here.'

'They've gone,' Bergman said.

'Gone?' Trent didn't understand.

'Home,' Bergman said. 'Soldiers and *guerrilleros* – the commanders are dead and the conscripts never did give a shit.'

Bergman

Shotguns cause dirty wounds and massive bleeding. Both soldiers on the terrace had bled to death. A third soldier lay below a window in the *entrada*. His face, including his eyes, had been shredded. Bergman held his hand and assured him that his wounds were minor and that a doctor was on the way. Then he shot him through the top of the skull. He found a spade in the rear garden and went back out to the fountain. Trent had found Little Brother.

Bergman handed the spade to Trent and hoisted Tur onto his shoulders. 'I'd like to bury him up there on the hill,' he said. 'He wouldn't have liked a graveyard.'

34

Bergman

They buried Estoban Tur at the foot of a rock on the mountain close below the tree line. Bergman determined to have a plate engraved and bolted to the rock: the Cuban's dates and name, nothing else; Bergman had planned such a stone for himself on the farm he had intended to buy and retire to in the highlands above Lake Atitlán.

The sky was pale and seemed transparent to the east. Traces of gold and orange heralded the sunrise and a colony of howler monkeys had awakened within the wood. Bergman sat with Trent beside the grave. Miguelito sat away from them. He sat with his back to them and with his knees drawn up to support his elbows and with his hands cupped as blinkers for his eyes. Bergman's attempt at comforting him had frightened the young man into a fit of shivering.

Below they could see clearly the ruined walls of San Cristóbal de los Baños.

'We made a real mess,' Bergman said.

Trent shrugged, 'You were a volunteer. Estoban and I were drafted.'

'For eighteen years? Crap,' Bergman said. 'That's how long you served. Tur had more excuse. The only way he could resign was with a bullet in his head.'

A shred of ham had caught between Bergman's lower plate and one of his sound teeth; he found a grass stem and picked it loose. Flicking the ham at the grave, he said, 'Tur and me, we were born the same – dirt poor *campesinos*. We had the same aims. We differed in how to carry them out.'

Trent

Trent said, 'I was further down the scale.' The curve of Miguelito's shoulders recalled a young Chinese woman Trent had rescued from kidnappers. She too had been abused and raped as a strategy rather than for pleasure.

Bergman snapped the grass stem he had been using as a toothpick. 'The mechanic.'

'Right,' Trent said. 'Fix the immediate problem. Keep it simple. You get lost if you start digging deeper.'

The lion roar of a howler monkey startled a colony of macaws.

'That's what happened?' Bergman asked.

'To me?' Trent nodded. 'I let things get complicated.'

The upper lip of the sun drew a pale orange bridge over the bottom end of the lake. Trent wanted to be back on board and heading downriver. 'I dive a lot,' he said. 'Diving is easy – there are fixed rules. And I don't socialise much.'

'Why are you telling me this?'

'The boy – he's the outsider in this thing. He needs a situation that rebuilds his self-respect.'

Daylight brought the vultures and the two men watched them wheel high above the ruins.

'I'd like to know who planned this thing,' Trent said. He didn't expect an answer.

The first vulture circled down into the *plaza*. Trent had seen them scavenge the dead often enough. At first nervous, the birds would land at a distance and hop across the cobbles, tear at a dead man, leap away.

'These things show in the tidying up,' Trent said.

Vorst

Vorst was content as he brought his board members up to date with the Cuban investment.

'There was some speculation that I had overestimated my influence over there,' he said. 'We had a confrontation between the old men and the new technocrats which the old men won. This was always on the cards. However, the technocrats gave total support to our proposals. They sacrificed the long-time head of their insurgency campaign in Latin America as a gesture of good faith. The minister involved in the negotiations laid his own life on the line.

'The old men won't live for ever. When the technocrats take over, we have an established history of support for their side. The agreement we have on the table will get us off the starting blocks ahead of the competition.'

Cuba

In Cuba, popularity is the jealously guarded preserve of *El Comandante en Jefe*, Fidel Castro Ruz. Jorge Mendez had trespassed on this preserve following his appointment as Minister of Finance. He was shot against the wall in the prison yard where the immensely popular Tony Ochoa and his brother had been executed in 1994. Jorge Mendez was charged with plotting to betray the revolution. Argument was pointless. He Who Decides had decided.

A lieutenant of security was executed on the same day. A counterrevolutionary, he had assisted the fugitive, Estoban Tur, in evading a road block. Those Cubans familiar with the lieutenant believed rumours that he had obeyed orders in permitting the fugitive's escape. However, Cubans are notoriously suspect in their beliefs. A majority believe that Fidel Castro ordered the murder of his rival for the leadership of the revolution, the people's hero, Camilo Cienfuegos – and most young Cubans believe that Fidel Castro drove the sainted Che to his death. A substantial number believe that Fidel betrayed Che to the CIA.

Glen

The president's special adviser on terrorism beat time on his steering wheel to a Country and Western radio station on his drive down to the Zoo. He had read Bergman's report of an attack on a military training area by *guerrilleros*. The leader of the *guerrilleros* had been killed as had a Guatemalan major and eight soldiers. The report made no mention of Tur and his brother nor was there any mention of them in the files at Langley. Bergman's pension depended on his silence. The same was true of his two superiors. Colonel Smith was the danger. Glen had always admired the colonel's capacity for manipulation.

Glen switched the radio to a classic station before entering the Zoo. Country and Western fitted his image in the White House. Outside he expected to be treated with greater respect. Parking his Cherokee, he carried his golf bag into the colonel's bungalow.

Colonel Smith

Estoban Tur and his confession should have been front-page news. The colonel finally discovered a three-line report of a *guerrillero* skirmish at San Cristóbal featured on page three of the *Post*. A further four days passed before Glen called to invite himself for a golf game. The colonel suffered twinges of rheumatism in his shoulders and was soaking in a hot bath when he took the call. He accepted that failure of the operation had made him a liability. Glen would be tidying up. The colonel had never liked North Americans. Leaving a mess would be fun. He possessed exactly the right weapon in his medicine cupboard.

The colonel dressed carefully in an ancient tweed suit, a check shirt and the most faded of his Eton ties. He found a black ballpoint in the kitchen. Seated at his desk, he wrote a new will. He left $10,000 to his Filipino houseman – the rest to Glen. Next he unscrewed the top of his Ronson fountain pen and wrote a note to his neighbour, suggesting dinner the following evening. He covered the bottom of the will with the invitation and traced his signature with the ballpoint, pressing hard. Then he carefully traced the indented signature in ballpoint at the bottom of his will. Wiping his prints off the invitation, he tore it in small pieces and dropped the pieces in the wastepaper basket beneath the desk. Next he used his fountain pen to write a second will in which he left all his possessions to John Patrick Mahoney. He sealed the two wills in separate envelopes addressed to his bank manager and strolled up the road to the Zoo's post-box. The box would be cleared in mid-afternoon. He had behaved as a good field agent and his thoughts went to Trent. As a youth, he had been beautiful. The colonel had never touched him. Perhaps there lay the hate, punishment for the tempter.

The colonel was at his desk when Glen arrived. The colonel was trying to open the top left-hand drawer. A book had stuck inside the drawer and the old man's hands were shaking with irritation. 'Don't just stand there,' he snapped at the American. 'Make yourself useful. Push the damn thing down. Use the ballpoint.'

The drawer open, he selected an old pocket watch as a present for the American. The watch was gunmetal and without value except to the colonel. His father had given it to him at the railway station the day the colonel first left home for boarding school. Seven years old, he had tried not to cry.

The gift restored the two men to that camaraderie special to those who have shared a long working relationship. The colonel had been about to take mid-morning China tea.

'Old habits die hard,' he said with a soft chuckle at his own wit. He poured from a fragile porcelain teapot.

Strolling to the first tee, the colonel hesitated, then asked

Glen to be kind enough to jog back to the house and tell the houseman he could leave. 'A mere bagatelle to a fit young fellow like you.'

They set the stake at ten dollars a stroke. The seventh hole ran alongside the lake and was furthest from the small clubhouse and row of bungalows. An oak tree shaded the tee and a wooden bench.

Glen was two strokes down. He dug a stainless steel vacuum flask from his golf bag, sat in the shade and unscrewed the cap and the inner cap.

'Mint julep,' he said. He poured carefully and the colonel accepted the smaller cup.

'Cheers,' Glen said. His smile was a miracle of youth and enthusiasm. 'Not a bad life.'

'Very pleasant,' the colonel said. 'The Tur thing went wrong?'

'Yes,' Glen said.

'Pity.' The colonel sipped abstemiously and wrinkled his nose in well-bred distaste. 'Never did much like these things. Not a man's drink, Glen. Too sweet.'

Glen's discomfort was obvious. He crossed his legs, uncrossed them, crossed them again; looked away across the fairway, through the wood, out over the lake – anywhere but at the colonel.

'Sit still, man,' the colonel snapped. 'You're wriggling around like a bitch in heat.'

Glen clamped his hands between his knees. His smile was one with the mint julep.

'A fool would know why you're here – and I'm not a fool,' the colonel snapped. 'If you have something to say, say it. And have the grace to look me in the eye.'

Glen met his gaze for at most a second before looking away. 'Now that it's failed, there's an idea this thing could cause damage if it got out,' he said. 'You understand how it is?'

'Absolutely.' The colonel was enjoying himself. 'I'm a risk to your employer and he wants me put down.'

'Not exactly him,' Glen said. 'It's more a feeling that's around that this needs tidying up.'

The colonel accepted the small white pill Glen proffered. 'Heart attack – to suit my proven health record? No trace?'

'None.'

'And no pain?'

Glen wriggled his enthusiasm. 'Right, absolutely right.'

'Alternatives?'

Glen's smile flashed in genuine pleasure at the colonel's decision to co-operate. He scratched the back of his scalp. 'There's always the bathtub – an electrical fault.'

The colonel returned his smile and shook his head. 'No, Glen, I don't think that's me. Imagine, will you. Discovered naked and one's hair frizzed.'

The colonel held the pill between thumb and forefinger of his left hand and pointed with his right up the fairway. 'Never seen so many magpies. Look over there. Three of the damn birds.'

Glen looked where the colonel indicated and the colonel reached into his pocket for the three pills he had taken from his medicine cupboard that morning. He dropped them into his drink. The signs would be as obvious to a doctor as the tracks of an elephant crossing a wet putting green.

'Cheers,' he said, and drained the cup. 'You're two strokes down – twenty dollars. Leave it for my houseman, there's a good chap.' He began counting as he swallowed Glen's pill – a method of combating tension which he had taught to all his agents. Paddy's son had said it was useful. Paddy Mahoney. The colonel saw him poised in his swimsuit on the bank of the River Trent on the day of a sunny summer picnic. Not the son, the father – his Paddy – his own dearly beloved Paddy.

35

Bergman

August early morning and the sun spread breakfast gold across a sea as smooth and featureless as steel plate. The duty officer in the tower on the point by Havana's Marina Hemingway watched through binoculars a yellow dagger speed out of the gold.

The *Yellow Submarine* possessed the low, sleek, almost vicious lines of a racing powerboat and such was her heritage. Built in the town of Poole on the south coast of England, she was a forty-eight-foot Sunseeker Superhawk. Three Mercruiser 900hp diesels drove her through Arneson surface drives rather than propellers. Lightly laden and in smooth water she could exceed sixty knots. Bergman had held her down to a comfortable cruising speed for the four-hour crossing he had made singlehanded to Havana from Nassau in the Bahamas. The seas had been easy and he had kept watch on the Decca radar while leaving the helm and navigation to the interlinked GPS and automatic pilot. Now, both hands on the wheel, he sat coddled in the outboard of twin racing seats. Each engine had its own throttle and gear levers convenient to his right hand. The compass and triple ranks of instruments paraded in a gleaming walnut dashboard. The seats and the big U sofa directly aft were upholstered in white. Further aft a sunbed extended over the diesels with, to starboard, two teak steps down to the teak boarding platform. The Japanese owner of this ultimate in big boy's toys, Tanaka Kazuko, was the founder of the Abbey Road Investigative Unit and both Trent's employer and his friend.

Pylons marked the passage through the reef into a lagoon. The customs and immigration dock lay to port on the corner of a grove of palm trees that shaded small 1950s bungalows and a swimming pool. Familiar with the value of face, Tanaka Kazuko had requested the Japanese Embassy to reserve Bergman's berth at the Marina Hemingway. Half a dozen Cuban port officials awaited his arrival. All wore leather shoes and Bergman laid a white rubber mat and a row of white rubber overshoes on the boarding platform.

Trent

He flew Iberia in preference to Cubana and travelled on an Australian passport issued in the name of John Richardson. He was clean-shaven, his hair cut short and greyed at the temples and he wore blue contact lenses. Letters and documents in a slim Asprey briefcase supported his cover as a lawyer with an international tax practice based in Liechtenstein. He looked the part in a dark blue tropic-weight suit, button-down cotton Oxford shirt in a paler blue and a dull silver on silver tie of raw silk. The toecaps of his black shoes gleamed, the laces were tied in a precise double bow and he carried a viciously expensive Yardby Gladstone bag in antique blue tapestry. Immigration and customs were polite.

A travel agent in Liechtenstein had arranged Trent's three-day visit and Trent had prepaid for a room with a sea view on the executive floor of the Hotel Nacional and for a rental Nissan. The manager at Havanautos' airport kiosk naturally denied any knowledge of the car. Patience, politeness and fifty dollars finally unearthed the relevant documents while a further twenty dollars bought Trent a free upgrade to a Peugeot.

His reservation on the executive floor saved him from an ill-tempered multilingual scrum in the lobby at the hotel. A pretty and polite receptionist confirmed Trent's booking and issued him a plastic door key to a room with a view into the angle of the west wing and the damp smell of a mushroom farm. Running a bath, he discovered that the hot water tap protruded too short a distance from the wall so that water hit the lip of the bath and spilled over the floor and on under the bedroom carpet. Twenty dollars was sufficient to change his room for one with a view over the hotel gardens and the Malecón and the Caribbean.

A secretary at the business service office made a morning appointment for him with the official at the Finance Ministry concerned with labour law affecting foreign investors. Trent plugged his IBM laptop into the telephone and sent a fax to Liechtenstein confirming his arrival and his departure date. He further confirmed his cover by working for an hour on his papers and laptop down by the pool.

Changed into khaki chinos and a sports shirt and loafers, he drove west along 5th Avenue in the early evening and parked at the dollar supermarket the seaward side of the Russian Embassy. One of the public phone boxes at the supermarket functioned. Dialling a sixth-floor apartment in Estoban Tur's building, he reserved a love room – Bergman had given him the number.

He bought a dozen packets of spaghetti, ten kilos of black beans, ten bottles of corn oil and five kilos of export-grade Cuban coffee. Locking the provisions in the boot of the car, he drove west to the Marina Hemingway. A parasol of white-flecked scarlet blossom floated above the foliage of the flame trees shading 5th Avenue. More of the palm trees that marched down the centre of the avenue had died since his last visit, none of them replaced; the *jineteras* on roller-blades were new and there were more cars on the road, many of them the resprayed Ladas and Moscovich of medallioned black-marketeers.

Concrete ridges across the road forced him to a crawl at the entrance to the Marina Hemingway. A security guard checked his passport while two black *jineteras* in white off-the-breast blouses, micro-minis and higher-than-high heels gave him the eye from the shade of a laurel tree.

Canals led off to his left. The first was empty, the second bordered by rent-a-villas. A pizzeria, advertised as Italian, nestled into a grove of sea grape trees. The Club Nautico in sick blue concrete stood at the head of the third canal with sailing dinghies hauled out on the lawn. Next came a shopping arcade and two more canals separated by a hundred yards of dusty grass. Yachts lay alongside all the way out to the marina office. Beyond the office a big neon portrait of Hemingway marked a disco and restaurant; diving boards projected from amongst the palm fronds.

Trent parked next to a pair of black Honda Rebels faking they were Hogs and crossed to the shopping arcade where two male Texan retirees were pawing the backsides of a pair of mid-teen mulattas at the perfume counter. The men were uniform never-got-starteds: bald crowns and ponytails, grey yachting stubble and an inch of fat white buttock on display between Dallas Cowboys T-shirts and patched Levis. Even the details were perfect: brass bottle-opener buckles and Buck knives on their belts, Nike trainers with different colour laces, beer cans.

The men rode off on the Hondas, arses on the seat, belly on the gas tank, teeny-bopper *jineteras* perched above the rear wheel. Trent bought toothpaste and toothbrushes, shampoo, soap and skin moistener. Typical tourist, he strolled up past a second security barrier to inspect the yachts. The first to draw his admiration was an aft-cabin teak ketch named *Serengeti* flying a Cayman Island ensign. A handsome brown man wearing a gold Cartier watch and a six-month-old baby sat under the awning humming a very English lullaby. A champagne flute and a bottle of Mumm in an ice bucket shared pride of place with the baby's bottle.

'McGrewer,' Trent suggested of the yacht's architect and builder.

'Close,' the man said. 'Bute Shipyard.'

The ketch was pure class and out of context in a marina

where the majority of yachts were downmarket fibreglass live-on-boards, both ageing and short on maintenance – as were their owners. The ports of register were mostly US. The crew were invariably young, female and Cuban – foot soldiers of the Cuban economy.

The *Yellow Submarine* was a second jewel amongst this flotsam. Bergman sat at the cockpit table beneath the Bimini top. Perhaps the American's right eyebrow rose a millimetre on seeing Trent.

Trent walked to the end of the dock before crossing over to the other canal and returning to his car. A pale mulatta and a natural blonde, both in their early twenties, flagged him from the bus stop opposite the entrance to the marina. The mulatta asked his nationality. He said Australian. The natural blonde tried a few words of German scavenged from past encounters.

The mulatta spoke Spanish interspersed with a smattering of English and was ahead of her companion in separating Australia from Austria. Accepting Trent's invitation to dinner, she suggested a private restaurant on 15th Street in Vedado with a reputation for imaginative cuisine at a reasonable price by non-Cuban standards. They ate in a jungle patio: cold fillets of red snapper marinaded in orange juice and accompanied by a watercress and avocado salad followed by duck in a sauce chasseur. The mulatta ate as if she hadn't eaten in a month and didn't expect to eat in the coming weeks. Between courses she related that both her parents were doctors in general practice as was her elder brother. Parents and children lived in a one-bedroom apartment in Old Havana on a total monthly family income of fifty-four dollars. Getting laid by a tourist once a week kept her family in clothes and had paid for a refrigerator, a second-hand TV and two pedestal fans.

Trent played with a cup of coffee while the mulatta devoured a vase of chocolate ice cream cloaked in whipped cream sprinkled with nuggets of black chocolate. She ate quickly and kept checking Trent's watch and urged him to pay the bill. Back in the rental car, she pleaded with him to hurry.

At Tur's apartment building, she instructed Trent to wait in the car while she fetched the love room's owner to open the garage. Ten minutes and the garage doors opened. The owner of the apartment directed Trent to the rear of a pillar that shaded the rental car from the solitary light bulb. The owner introduced himself as Doctor Enriquez, the doctorate in civil engineering. An elderly janitor wheezed purposefully by the elevator and Trent tipped him a five.

Doctor Enriquez led the way to the sixth floor apartment and introduced Trent to his wife and two high-school daughters, none of whom shifted their attention from the colour television. The mulatta was ensconced on a sofa. She patted the seat beside her and put her arm round Trent and snuggled against his side without once taking her eyes off the screen – Sunday church service replaced by Thursday's Brazilian TV soap opera.

The mulatta joined in the critical analysis which followed the soap. Only Trent was an outsider. Finally Doctor Enriquez's wife prevailed upon the elder daughter to prepare coffee and show Trent and the mulatta to what had been the apartment's principal bedroom. Thursday was a no water day on this block. The mulatta turned on the tap on a converted oil drum set on a high frame in one corner of the en suite bathroom and they showered in a weak dribble.

Two in the morning and his bed companion snored gently. Trent removed his blue contact lenses before taking the elevator down to the garage. He fetched the shopping from the trunk of the Nissan and rode up to the eighth floor and scratched on Estoban's door; the electric bell might have been overheard in other apartments. Five minutes brought the sound of keys in the lock. The door opened on Estoban's wife rubbing sleep from her eyes. Her hair was bushed and she was dressed in an outsize black T-shirt.

She took the photograph of Miguelito bent over the desk. Then she looked at Trent, memories awakened of the end to Roddy de Sanchez's father. Trent and Estoban had spent the night hunted by de Sanchez's men and were fortunate to have survived. Maria had cooked them breakfast. Now anger was her first reaction. Her eyes were almost black and flat of any expression. Stone eyes, Trent thought: stones ready to be cast . . . waiting only for the moment.

'Guatemala. Estoban saved him.' He proffered the packages.

She kept her hands by her side so that he had nowhere to put the gifts.

'Estoban lives?' came the first stone, whispered to avoid awakening the children or her neighbours.

Trent didn't answer.

'Dead?'

Trent wanted to tell her the circumstances of Estoban's death – how bravely he had died and that he had saved his brother.

She remained frozen within her black marble carapace.

He was unable to see beyond her into the apartment. Two months since Estoban's flight, did a new lover lie in her bed?

Had Maria shed a tear for Estoban or for Miguelito, he could have offered sympathy. He said, 'Please,' again. His out-stretched hands grasped the thin plastic shopping bags: bribes, he thought.

'Please, Maria. Miguelito is so hurt. He needs those who love him.'

She was incapable of hearing him through the barriers.

'The secrets,' he said, knowing that the secrets were the destroyers. 'Please . . . it's not what Estoban meant to happen. He thought he was doing the right thing. Serving?' he said, wanting her to understand. He found it easier to plead for Estoban than for himself.

'*Chantaje*,' she accused – blackmail.

'I'm sorry.'

That much she believed. 'Yes.'

'Can I come in?'

'No.'

Trent placed the shopping on the floor. One of the bags fell open and two packets of black beans slipped out. He crouched to recover the beans and, looking up at her, said, 'Estoban loved you. And the children.'

Yes, she knew. 'He destroyed them.'

He said, 'He did his best.'

'Best? *Madre de Dios*! What obscenity. You people!' One of the shopping bags fell over and a can of tomato paste rolled against her foot. 'You destroy everything,' she whispered harshly. Trent thought that she might throw the can at him. Instead she appeared to shrink within the black cotton shirt. A crack had appeared in the flat black of her eyes and Trent saw her pain surface.

She said, 'I don't care about the people you kill out there.'

A slight movement of her right hand encompassed Trent's world, Estoban's world, the world of betrayals and subterfuge; of knives in the dark and bombs hidden in refuse bins and cars packed with explosives; of mother's bone stripped of flesh, babies tattered, broken toys scattered amongst the wreckage of an airliner, Miguelito raped.

'I am ashamed that I don't care. Can you understand?'

'Yes,' Trent said.

'I want to be left alone. Nothing more. The children and me.' Cuba was familiar to her. She knew how to navigate the difficulties.

'And Miguelito?' he said. 'He is in Florida. Papers were arranged for him. For the moment he is in hospital and sees a psychologist each day – a specialist in trauma. An apartment is available once there is someone to care for him and he will receive a small pension. A government pension,' he added to give the picture substance. In Cuba everything came from the government. 'The local high school needs teachers with Spanish.'

Trent tried to sound matter-of-fact and without prejudice or interest in her decision. 'You can teach what you want, choose the books. Your choice. Noon tomorrow. Bring the boys to the Hotel El Comodoro. I'll wait by the entrance gates.'

'No,' she said. 'I will never leave Cuba.'

She picked up the shopping bags, then appeared surprised at their being in her hands. 'Thank you,' she said and she spoke his name for the first time: 'Trent. The other visit – you brought bacon and cheese.'

'From my boat,' Trent said. 'Noon tomorrow.'

The mass of springy hair shuddered as she shook her head and she retreated into her apartment and closed the door.

Trent returned to Doctor Enriquez's love room. Rings missing, the thin cotton curtain hung slackly on a peeling brass rod. A shallow bowl of moonlight shone above the curtain. The mulatta lay on her right side with her back to the window. The sheet had slipped to her waist. The moon lit her cheek and her shoulder and her left breast and drew the darker shadow of her breast on the sheet. Trent wanted to wake her and hold her. He watched a curl above her left ear fight the fan's breeze. The breeze was cold on his cheeks and he went through to the bathroom and washed his face in a trickle of cold water from the oil drum.

Easing into the bed, he wriggled his back against her until she stirred and, still asleep, slipped her arm over his shoulders, holding him close. Her breath was warm on his neck and he lay awake and watched the reflection of the shallow dish of moonlight creep up the wall.

Bergman

Bergman washed his breakfast cereal bowl and tea cup while listening to the weather report on short wave from the coast guard station on the South Florida Keys. He emptied the vases on the saloon and cockpit tables, dumped the flowers in the refuse bin midway along the dock and paid his harbour dues at the marina office. Ten o'clock and he arranged the white rubber overshoes on the mat on the boarding platform before casting off his mooring lines and motoring slowly round to the customs and immigration dock. The customs inspection was cursory, immigration officials both friendly and polite. Bergman rewarded them with a cold beer while they completed the documentation in the cockpit.

He took his time below, first filling a stainless-steel vacuum flask with tea and checking the stowage in each locker prior to securing the locker doors. On deck, he readied a marlin rod with a Pen reel in the chrome rod holder on the port side of the boarding platform. He ran the line back to the cockpit and tied the end to the handle of a plastic jug. Finally he loaded his flare gun with a green cartridge before returning it to the holster outboard of the helmsman's seat.

Trent

The bar terrace and restaurant at the Hotel El Comodoro face a small private beach protected by a hideous breakwater. Cubans are forbidden entry to tourist hotels unless accompanied by a foreigner and high fences barricade each end of the beach. Trent bought two cans of cold Heineken at the bar and threaded his way between the ranks of tourists dozing on sunbeds. An agency of the Ministry of Tourism rented pedalos and half a dozen Kawasaki jet-skis at the water's edge. Trent presented the Heinekens to the attendant and raced one of the Kawasakis out past the breakwater. The motor was in reasonable condition and he paid a reservation fee for the next two hours.

Returning to the entrance gates to the hotel grounds, Trent told the security guard that he was expecting a guest for lunch. The guard expected the guest to be a woman and accepted a neatly folded twenty-dollar bill.

Trent listened to the radio in his rental car in the shade of a palm tree in the parking lot to the right of the gates. He doubted whether Maria would come.

An overweight businessman parked a Mercedes 240E beside the Peugeot and eased his bulk out from behind the wheel. Trent's watch showed 12:16. He looked back up the street leading from 5th Avenue and spotted Maria walking hurriedly down the shaded pavement. Oleanders hid the children until they reached the main road parallel to the hotel. Maria led them by the hand and rushed them across the road behind a bus. The children were excited and laughing while Maria looked anxious and very frail and small in a short cotton dress.

Trent hurried to meet her at the gates.

She introduced him to the children as a visiting teacher.

Trent enquired whether they had ridden a jet-ski.

Never, they answered, though they had watched them speed past the rocky shore below the Russian Embassy.

'We'll have a go in a little while,' Trent said. And to their mother, 'Relax, Maria. There are life jackets and it's only a short run.'

They found a free table on the terrace and Trent ordered fresh orange juice for the boys and a mojito for their mother. He took the older boy first on the Kawasaki, tying a red life vest round his chest and sitting him between his thighs. The breeze had dropped and out beyond the breakwater the sea was smooth and sparkling beneath the harsh sun. Feeling the child nervous, Trent murmured encouragement as he would have to a nervous horse; and he kept the speed down, the turns long and gentle.

Next he took the younger boy, Tobanito. The child was more confident than his brother and shouted for Trent to go faster. Speeding out from the breakwater, Trent spotted the *Yellow Submarine* a mile to the west.

Bergman

He eased the Sunseeker Superhawk away from the customs and immigration dock and out through the narrow channel. Clear of the reef, he slipped the engines into neutral and clambered aft down the steps to the boarding platform where he paid out a long loop of line from the marlin rod and he fetched the fishing harness stowed in a cockpit locker.

Two game fishing boats on half-day charter followed each other towards the marina and further out to sea a forty-foot sloop flying the US ensign headed in from Key West. Bergman turned east and trolled at a comfortable six knots a quarter of a mile off shore. Locals in skimpy swimsuits crowded the rocks east of the Russian Embassy and he counted half a dozen jet-skis hurling spray. Four of them were from the marina and he left them astern; the remaining two came from the El Comodoro Hotel.

Trent

Trent left Tur's two sons playing in the shallows and bought a fresh beer at the bar for the beach attendant and a second mojito. He set it in front of Maria. She seemed to him to have shrunk while sitting at the table, a small dark island marooned within the naked Caucasian flesh and thoughtless polyglot chatter of the tourists.

He said, 'You're sure?' and she nodded.

He asked a security man to keep an eye on their possessions while they went out on the jet-ski.

He sat the bigger boy, Mario between his thighs with Tobanito sandwiched on Maria's knees. He turned the starter key and the Kawasaki coughed and spluttered.

'Less throttle or you'll flood the engine,' the attendant warned.

Trent tried again. The motor fired, caught for a moment, then died.

'What's wrong,' Tobanito asked and his mother shushed him. Her nervousness was almost a physical force against Trent's back.

Trent said, 'Here's hoping,' and laughed as he turned the key.

The engine fired, caught, almost died, then caught again.

'Shit petrol,' the attendant said.

Trent opened the throttle gently and motored slowly out from the beach and round the end of the breakwater. The *Yellow Submarine* lay half a mile away to the north west.

Bergman

A jet-ski nosed out from behind the breakwater: an adult and three children or two children and a small mother. The canopy sheltered Bergman and shadow hid him from the shore as he raised his binoculars. Trent.

Bergman left the helm and scurried to the aft end of the cockpit to check the fishing line. At the same time he toed the plastic jug clear. The drag of the looped fishing line yanked the jug down onto the boarding platform and into the sea. The line straightened, the marlin rod bowed, the reel screamed. Bergman leapt back to the controls and snicked the engines into neutral. Then he clambered down to the boarding platform and grabbed the rod out of the holder. Setting the butt in the bucket on his fishing harness, he tightened the brake on the reel and struck hard against the supposed bite of a fish.

The jet-ski had risen to the plane and curved smoothly away up the coast toward the Russian Embassy. In the distance beyond Havana's harbour the chimneys of an oil refinery belched black smoke. Out to sea the crew of the US-registered sloop dropped their sails and an airliner drew a trail above a thin puff of white cloud.

Bergman pumped the rod and reeled line in pantomime of a fisherman. The performance would pass given that this was the natural hour of siesta and even those on watch would be inattentive.

The jet-ski had doubled back and raced abreast of the hotel close to the shore. The children waved at Bergman and he waved back one handed before dipping and lifting the rod tip to gain slack.

Trent

He ran the jet-ski on towards the marina before circling out to sea and back toward the El Comodoro on a course that would take him close to the Sunseeker Superhawk. The harsh note of the Kawasaki's exhaust echoed off the houses lining the shore. Maria had her mouth to his ear.

'That is the boat?'

He nodded and heard her say to Tobanito, 'We are going on that boat to be with Tío Miguelito.'

Trent brought the jet-ski fast in alongside the boarding platform. Bergman hurled the rod clear and grabbed Mario off the seat.

'Up the steps, quick,' Trent told the boys. Already on the platform, he grabbed Maria by the hand and swept Tobanito off Maria's knees.

Bergman was ahead of him up the steps, Mario in one arm.

'Go below,' Trent called to the boy and released Tobanito into the cockpit. Bergman was already at the controls as Trent turned to heave Maria onto the boarding platform.

'Keep the children below,' he told her.

Bergman hit the triple throttles with the heel of his right hand. The throttle rammed nearly three thousand horsepower through the Arneson drives and the Sunseeker shuddered and threatened to rise like a dolphin on its tail. She steadied, the bows dropped and Bergman headed straight out to sea.

Trent shouted down to Maria to hold the children on the carpet and dragged the safety belt over Bergman's shoulders, clamping the buckle and fastening his own harness. The radar screen above the walnut dashboard showed their position in regard to the coast. The supercharged engines howled as they hurled the *Yellow Submarine* skimming over the surface.

Twelve miles of territorial water separated them from safety. Three military airfields lay within a dozen miles. Five minutes to scramble a MiG. How many minutes before the pilot was authorised to fire? That was the gamble. And the threat was real. Only the previous year Castro had authorised the shooting-down of two small single-engine civil aircraft from Florida.

Flight Lieutenant Francisco Muñoz

Turf camouflaged the blast shelters at the far end of the runway. The shelters housed three MiG25 interceptors. The flight leader, Francisco Muñoz, eased his shoulders and checked the clock on the right of the instrument panel. He had completed one hour, seven minutes and thirty-eight seconds of a two hour tour of duty. Once the duty was over he would ride his 1950s Triumph motorcycle down to his parents' two room apartment in Vedado, change into beach clothes and head out to the Playas del Este where he hoped to pick up a tourist girl; preferably a young one and pretty, who would pay for dinner and drinks at a front-room restaurant run by Francisco's cousin. With luck the tourist would invite Francisco to the hotel disco and smuggle him up to her room, perhaps buy him a new pair of trainers in the morning or a T-shirt.

The scream of the siren ruptured his fantasy.

Ten seconds for the single Tumansky turbofan engine to power. Seven seconds to the runway apron. Twelve seconds and airborne. Wheels up. Climbing. Missiles armed. Wingman in position. Target, one speedboat Yellow hull, speed fifty to sixty knots. Destroy.

Trent

Two black dots climbed vertically beyond the shore. 'MiGs,' Trent said and checked the radar to see how far short they were from international waters. 'Two and a half miles.'

Maria thrust the children up into the cockpit. She ignored Trent's protest that they were safer below. Instead, she hustled the children to the after end of the cockpit and confronted the planes.

Trent stood behind her.

Francisco Muñoz

The yacht was a yellow blob in his sights. His thumbs rested on the red firing buttons. He spotted the family group in the cockpit. To be a hero in Miami or in Castro's Cuba? He had seconds to make up his mind. Mortality rather than morality governed the decision. Old age must soon end Castro's dictatorship. Power would shift to the returning exiles. Francisco was less than sixty feet above the ocean as he thundered over the speeding Sunseeker.

The controller was screaming at Francisco's wingman to sink the boat with cannon fire and use his missiles on Francisco.

'Sink the boat and shoot the son of a bitch down.'

'Wilco.' The wingman stabbed the afterburner switch. The extra power rammed him back in his seat and he dipped the nose of the MiG.

The explosion seemed to shake the *Yellow Submarine* as the MiG pierced the sound barrier. Cannon fire blasted a curtain of spray two hundred metres ahead of the *Yellow Submarine*.

The pilot waggled his wings and eased the stick over to follow Francisco toward the Florida coast. *Florida!* He knew exactly what he was going to eat that night. He could see the steak on his plate, the pat of garlic butter, French fries, a Caesar salad and, for dessert, chocolate chocolate chip ice cream topped with natural whipped cream and fresh strawberries.

Bergman

Bergman eased back on the throttles. The bellow of the triple exhausts faded and they could speak in normal voices.

'We're safe,' Trent said.

Maria faced him.

He saw her tears and he read the anger and the contempt in her eyes. She crouched to comfort her children.

Bergman turned in his chair. She appeared small to him and very hurt. He wanted her to recognise that he wasn't a child; that he was a man and that he accepted responsibility for what he was and for what he had done. He said, 'It was my fault. I was wrong.'

Maria gave a small nod of understanding. 'All of you were wrong. It is something that happens.' And to her children she said, 'Let us go down into the cabin. Perhaps we will find something good to eat.'